Tri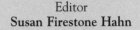Quarterly 101 — Winter 1997/98

Editor
Susan Firestone Hahn

Managing Editor
Gwenan Wilbur

TriQuarterly Fellow
Karen Leick

Assistant Editors
**Francine Arenson, Christopher Carr,
Ian Morris, Rachel Webster**

Editorial Assistants
**Russell Geary, Jacob Harrell
Dylan Rice, Karen Sheets**

Contributing Editors
**John Barth, Rita Dove, Richard Ford, Sandra M. Gilbert, Robert Hass,
Lee Huebner, Li-Young Lee, Lorrie Moore, Alicia Ostriker, Carl Phillips,
Robert Pinsky, Fred Shafer, Alan Shapiro, Mark Strand, Alan Williamson**

TRIQUARTERLY IS AN INTERNATIONAL JOURNAL OF WRITING, ART AND CULTURAL INQUIRY PUBLISHED AT **NORTHWESTERN UNIVERSITY.**

Subscription rates (three issues a year) — Individuals: one year $24; two years $44; life $600. Institutions: one year $36; two years $68. Foreign subscriptions $5 per year additional. Price of back issues varies. Sample copies $5. Correspondence and subscriptions should be addressed to *TriQuarterly*, **Northwestern University**, 2020 Ridge Avenue, Evanston, IL 60208-4302. Phone: (847) 491-7614.

The editors invite submissions of fiction, poetry and literary essays, which must be postmarked between October 1 and March 31; manuscripts postmarked between April 1 and September 30 will not be read. No manuscripts will be returned unless accompanied by a stamped, self-addressed envelope. All manuscripts accepted for publication become the property of *TriQuarterly*, unless otherwise indicated.

National distributors to retail trade: Ingram Periodicals (La Vergne, TN); B. DeBoer (Nutley, NJ); Ubiquity (Brooklyn, NY); Armadillo (Los Angeles, CA).

Reprints of issues #1-15 of *TriQuarterly* are available in full format from Kraus Reprint Company, Route 100, Millwood, NY 10546, and all issues in microfilm from University Microfilms International, 300 North Zeeb Road, Ann Arbor, MI 48106. *TriQuarterly* is indexed in the *Humanities Index* (H.W. Wilson Co.), the *American Humanities Index* (Whitson Publishing Co.), Historical Abstracts, MLA, EBSCO Publishing (Peabody, MA) and Information Access Co. (Foster City, CA).

A Short Note from the New Editor
Who Has Been Here a Long Time

This issue marks the end of the transition of *TriQuarterly* into its new home at Northwestern University Press and the beginning of a new era for the magazine. We are now well-protected within the university and, as you can see from what you are holding in your hands, we're looking and feeling terrific. We *are* fortunate, we know it and we are grateful.

I'd like to thank President Henry Bienen for making all of this possible, and Associate Provost Eugene Lowe; Nicholas Weir-Williams, director of the press; and Kimberly Maselli, *TriQuarterly*'s new publisher; for their enormous help with the transition. I have to say that during the many months while I was in my world of reading manuscripts, dealing with writers and filling issues, these people were working on the practical and delicate intricacies that made #101 (and all issues to follow) a reality.

I intend this comment to be short (better to publish an additional poem). However, I do want to name *TriQuarterly*'s contributing editors—all but three of whom are new. So far, I'm batting 1.000—everyone I've asked to be a contributing editor has responded with a resounding *Yes,* and I think that speaks wonderfully well of what *TriQuarterly* has been and what these dazzling writers feel about its future. *Thank You* and *Welcome* to John Barth, Rita Dove, Richard Ford, Sandra M. Gilbert, Robert Hass, Lee Huebner, Li-Young Lee, Lorrie Moore, Alicia Ostriker, Carl Phillips, Robert Pinsky, Fred Shafer, Alan Shapiro, Mark Strand and Alan Williamson from the staff at *TriQuarterly*, the press, and I know also, from all readers of this, now and forever, amazing "little" magazine.

Susan Firestone Hahn
January, 1998

Contents

Cover painting, *Island Collage*, by Mark Strand

Cover design by Gini Kondziolka

This issue of *TriQuarterly* magazine
is dedicated to

Jessie Firestone

my first reader
when I was a child,
the first reader
of my own creative work
and, for sixteen years,
a reader of every issue of
TriQuarterly
from cover to cover.

This issue is also dedicated
to *all* first readers—
for the purity of their passion
for the written word,
for their time and their patience,
for their love.

Four Poems

Sandra M. Gilbert

At Cleopatra Bay,

where the great yachts pause, and the smaller craft,
the Turkish boatmen say
She stopped here once,

and I struggle to see the fire of her barge
standing among the outboard motors,
the parasailors, the daytrippers,

as if she and her straining mariners
might drift from the Mediterranean sky
englobed in gold, or better still

explode from the cold
where the sunken cities loll,
her handsome imperious face,

with its lithe cruel brows, tipped eyes,
lips that taste of bitter leaves,
unmoved by our futuristic engine-grind.

Three thousand years—a splash of centuries!—
and the bay is still the same,
the rocky coves where dabs of fish

stitch little seams of light and dark,
the feathery southern pines
that stoop above the streams they shadow

as if searching for new images
through mirrors of themselves,
the spit of sunstruck island where perhaps

she might have walked an hour among
trivial grasses, armguards flashing
as she took the measure of her men—

Then Ahmet breaks the spell:
Everywhere you turn around here
there's another place they swear she stopped:

every other inlet brags
it's Cleopatra Bay!
Ubi sunt:

she was everywhere, is nowhere.
There are no footfalls
on the vanished stair,

the drowned landing.

Catedral at Tlacolula

No space left empty, not a scroll
or curlicue unused, even the frames of scribbles
are scribbled on, as if the builders
had to keep busy every second,
as if to cease from motion
would mean lapsing into the glare
that threatens color, sickens shape. . . .

Explosions of artifice! Rocket
bursts of plane geometry! The whole
vault of wall and ceiling
vaunts a history of squiggles,
conquering the dust of the *alta plana!*
And cargoes of martyrs incomprehensibly
unloaded at every port!

Locked in glass boxes, the lounging saints
brood on torment, insouciant
as *gringos* contemplating lunch,
or now and then an eager one
leans into the wall of pain, mouth agape,
the way a specimen bird, flouncing in its cage,
might yearn toward its next feeding.

But the tiny virgin in her black brocade,
mailed with mirrors reflecting
everything and nothing,
stares beyond saints and squiggles
into the glittering toy heaven
her doll baby promises
with his flat black Zapotec eyes.

Shelling Beans Outside Pollenca

Dying to be devoured, the beans
plunge from the pod to the pot,
whole generations linked
in every long slim creamy-yellow
scarlet-splotched canoe.

God made them to be eaten—
built their hulls to dangle, crash,
split, smash, deliver each one
naked and clutching its starch
into the maw of dirt or rock.

Two fields away the animals
choir their utter oblivion:
sheep-groan, rooster-scream, dog-howl
swell above the giant insect-
buzz of the ground.

And how imperious the mountains are,
vaunting their indigestible granite!
How stately the fandango of pines
whose needles haven't been shredded yet!
And the silvery olives, picturesque, antique—

how indifferent to the doom of brine, of mulch,
how alert and feathery
their tiptoe toward a roaring sun
you'll never feel or love
or see again.

Death

When the great sea-turtle came,
dragging its *casita*
of black and white geometry,

and staggered onto the beach
at Puerto Pollenca, its almost phantom
flippers, fin-thin, flailing

faintly as if to ward off
just the old green
buffetings under whose sway

it had swelled from egg
to lizard length, archaic eye
and carapace,

and humped its pain
up the hill of glare and scratch
toward children digging the coarseness up

and the oiled breasts
of mothers and smoking
fathers telling jokes,

and quivered a minute
in its far place,
resting its sorrow a minute,

though the bathers gaped
it had come to die,
nothing inside the hardness

wanted to move, nothing
wanted another drop
of Mediterranean soup,

of flesh or brine
or the pulsing that flickers
among weed and rock,

but the swimmers flung it back
and back into the long deep
life it hated now,

until it drifted, staggered, clambered
onto a hot blank foreign
solid again,

forlorn in its distance,
and the beach boys scooped it
into an iron shovel

and wound it in a trash bag
and bore it off
on a bier of stacked sunbeds,

marching one at the head,
one at the foot,
in the ancient way,

with a trickle of children following,
some shaken and sad, like mourners,
some grinning, even jeering,

as if they were skeptics
(though skeptics about what?)
or scoffers

(but why?).

The Trope Teacher

Chaim Potok

ONE

That melancholy April, two weeks after Benjamin Walter's wife fell ill, a woman moved into the Tudor on the other side of the rhododendron hedge. The postman, the gardener, and the owner of the local bookstore made it a point to inform him that the woman was the noted writer, I. D. Chandal. Benjamin Walter, preoccupied with scholarship and struggling for months with his memoirs, had little time for fiction. But he knew the name I. D. Chandal.

He was sixty-eight, and ailing. A tall, lean, stately man, with thick gray hair, a square pallid face split by a prominent nose, and large webbed eyes dark with brooding behind old-fashioned, gold-rimmed spectacles. His long large-knuckled fingers swollen at the joints, the dry papery hands flecked with age spots; his lips thin and turned down at the corners; his body fragile, bones prone to breaking.

At times, in the company of intimate friends, he referred to the memoirs as his deathwork.

Much to his wonder and disquiet, when he'd begun the task of remembering his early years he discovered that his zone of deep memory was, as he put it to himself, well-fortified and resistant to frontal assault. Only reluctantly did it begin to yield to determined probing, surrendering now and then a tiny territory of uncertain value: a narrow city street deep in snow; a parental voice quivering with anger; a man's pale eggplant features spectrally detached from name and frame; a wisp of odd melody curling and fleeting as a morning mist. He barely recognized those fragments from his past, was unable to locate what he single-mindedly sought and uncovered in his scholarly tunnelings: the linking trails of cause and effect; the cords of connection, as he labeled them, that invariably led him to a unified chronicle.

He would sit in his oak-and-leather desk chair or lie back on his worn recliner, brooding, searching, writing, discarding. He had for fifty years not reflected much about his very early past, believing always that he could retrieve it with ease. How very disconcerting, the obsidian face that it now presented to him.

Especially as memory was what he was best known for; most notably, his remembering of war. War was his subject: war in general; the two world wars in particular. He was foremost among the sociologists of war, celebrated, esteemed. His monographs were studied in universities throughout the world, at West Point, in the Pentagon. Put to him an inquiry about the rise of the knightly class in Europe and he would trace it to nomadic incursions from the steppes and to Viking raids; about the causes of the fall of Constantinople to Mohammed II in 1453 and he would connect it to the horrors of the Fourth Crusade 250 years earlier; about the rise of the cannon and firearm and he would begin a discourse on the crossbow, its stock and recoil; about the connection in the First World War between tranquil English town, hamlet, club, and pub to the ghastly stench and slaughter near Ypres, Wytshaete and Messine and he would respond with a lecture on the speed of the British postal service. Query him on these and similar matters of war, and you received unambiguous replies delivered in the rhythms and accents of exquisite Oxford English, with not the vaguest trope to indicate his New York beginnings.

His current reputation was vast; his embryonic years clouded. Information found in the usual brief biographies of notables yielded only bare bones: born in New York City in the 1920s; a void about his early years; then, in the Second World War, to England, France and Germany with the American army; a decision to remain in England after the war; a bachelor's, master's, and doctorate from Oxford; marriage to an English woman of the aristocracy; scholarly articles and reviews for estimable American and international journals of sociology and military studies; a member of various august scholarly societies; abrasive essays in the *New Republic* and the *New York Review of Books*; the first major work, published when he was thirty-five, *Clausewitz and War: The Birth of the Battle of Annihilation*; and seven more books, among them the much-honored *Triumph of Thanatos: War in the Twentieth Century*, and the disputatious *Why So Late: America's Entry into the Second World War*. And his return to the United States.

Now, in near-old age, perpetually in the limelight, regularly approached, noted, quoted. In *Time*, *Newsweek* and *Vanity Fair*, he was the Professor of War. The reason no doubt behind the *New York Times* report, in its Friday Book Notes column, of the impressive six-figure advance for his memoirs, and the widespread anticipation awaiting its appearance.

In the third week of that unhappy April, he sat laboring at his desk one morning, his wife ill in the adjoining room, the nurse at her side, and after a futile inroad into early memory, he raised his weary eyes and gazed out the window at the rhododendron hedge that was part of the border between his home and the Tudor, and saw I. D. Chandal, the new owner of the neighboring house. From a distance of about forty feet his weary eyes let him see narrow hips garbed in tight dark-blue jeans, and breasts covered by a light-blue, short-sleeved jersey. She stood gazing at the hedge, looking surprisingly young and trim for a woman said to be in her middle years.

He put down his pen and closed his eyes. Nothing was happening with the work that morning. Barren wells, puerile words. Might as well meet the new neighbor, clear the head of the long night's frequent wakings.

He informed the nurse that he was stepping outside for a while. Fresh air, a walk in the woods. His wife lay asleep, breathing shallowly. White hair uncombed on the white pillow; beads of sweat on her pale forehead and cheeks; bluish half-moons under her eyes. She lay diminished, her chest nearly flat. Once robust, moist and wondrous with love in bed. His heart throbbed with grief. How recapture the past when the present exhausted him so?

But no, he told himself as he left the house and started along the flagstone path to the lawn and the hedge, it was not the accursed illness that had drawn up the blockade to memory; it was something—and here the warm air of the sunny morning fell upon his eyes and face—no, someone, some being from the past itself, a creature elusive as waning shadows and morning mist.

Well, he thought, approaching the figure by the hedge and feeling the heat of the late morning sun rising from the young spring grass on the lawn, she is a good-looking woman, indeed. Change of neighbor, change of luck?

The hedge was about thirty feet in length, extending from the tall spiked wrought-iron front fence to nearly halfway up the lawn. Beyond the hedge the lawn ran smooth and straight, vanishing into the shadowy dead-leaf interior of dense woods. Three or four feet deep, the rhododendron hedge was situated on a section of the borderline between the two properties, and I. D. Chandal stood on the Walter side, peering intently into its leafy interior, her back to Benjamin Walter. Close up, a woman small and dainty in stature, jeans tight, without the revealing curve of panties, he could not help but notice; sandals and thin ankles and bare toes; he felt the beat and drum of his blood.

She must have sensed his approach, for she straightened and turned. He noticed immediately the bony shoulders and small firm breasts and the nipples beneath the blue jersey. She was not wearing a brassiere. Pretty face, oval-shaped, high cheekbones, dark inviting eyes. How old is she? Forties? Fifties? Face astonishingly unlined. How long has Evelyn been teaching her work? Five years, maybe longer.

A singular fragrance, richly sweet and warm, rose from the hedge. Strange. These rhododendrons have never before given off a scent. More likely blowing in from the woods behind the house. Trees and wild flowers stirring and the two water oaks budding and the grass in the cemetery rising after the storms of the winter.

"Good morning, Ms. Chandal," he said. "I hope I'm not disturbing you."

"No, no. Not at all."

"I saw you through my study window and decided to come down and welcome you to the neighborhood."

"Why, thank you," she said; and added, "Professor Walter."

A demure smile. Lovely cupid's-bow lips. And the smooth face so white, set off by raven hair in a pageboy cut. And a long slender neck, white, alabaster white.

"Ah," he said, with a slight bow.

"Those who informed you about me informed me about you." A throaty voice, musical.

"We are a close-knit community."

"And gossipy."

"Gossip is a way communities protect their values."

"I remember reading that in one of your books. Was there gossip on the street when the Tudor fell vacant?"

"It was expected to be a difficult house to sell. Indeed, it stood empty for more than a year."

"It's vast. I love it."

"You live in it alone."

"Entirely alone. And relish it."

"Never married?"

"Once married. A recent mutual parting. Two children, grown, long gone from the nest. And you?"

"Married, three children. My wife is home ill."

"I'm sorry to hear that. About your wife, I mean."

"Otherwise she would have brought you some of her English things by way of welcome. Cakes she likes to bake, and teas. She is from England. Does literature. Formerly at Oxford, now at Princeton. She teaches your books. Big fan, as they say."

"I'm flattered." A faint crimson tide rising to the white cheeks, a diffident smile, averted eyes.

"I regret I read no fiction these days, experiencing a bit of a bottleneck with my own work, my memoirs, difficulty locating certain memories tucked away, you might say, tucked away somewhere quite deep. Do you encounter similar problems on occasion?"

She turned her eyes fully upon him. Almond-shaped, with a dark gaze. "On occasion? No."

"Ah."

"Always."

"Always?"

"Incessantly."

"And how does one manage under the circumstances?"

"One sits and ponders."

"Ah, my dear Ms. Chandal. If I could tell you of the hours I have spent sitting and pondering—"

"Relentlessly, pitilessly."

"Yes, indeed."

"Pondering, probing, prying."

"Ms. Chandal—"

"Please. We're neighbors. We've been engaged in conversation now for more than, what, five minutes. Call me Davita."

"Well. Indeed. Davita. And you must call me Benjamin."

"Benjamin."

"The hours I have spent at my desk—"

"Try talking. You know, the way you learn a language. Out loud. Tell it to the air. See how it begins to unravel."

"It is more like attacking a fortress."

"Memory is like a ball of woolen thread, Benjamin. If the pen cannot unravel it, the voice can. All my books are unravelings of voice and pen. Would drive my poor husband to distraction, not to mention the children. They thought I had multiple personalities. A loony wife and mother. He's a very uncomplicated man, my Donald. Childhood sweethearts, enormous mistake. I would've left him sooner but for the kids. He owns a headstone business. For graveyards. Very fancy carving, and very expensive. Benjamin, I think you're standing too long in the sunlight. It's nice to have met you. May I shake your hand?" She rubbed her right palm

19

on her jeans. "A bit grubby with earth, I'm afraid. Sizing up a flower bed."

Fingers short, slender, dry. Tendons ridged along the underside of the thin wrist. Smooth.

"You write by hand, I see," she said, gently turning his hand as it lay against hers and rubbing the tip of a finger over the small hillock of callus on the first joint of his middle finger. He felt her finger through the dry mound of dead skin. "Same thing with me." She showed him a callused finger.

"Everything, monographs, letters, books."

"Your *Why So Late* I read in college and wrote a term paper on it. Memorable. The book, I mean."

"Thank you."

"Your account of the final German offensive. Frightful."

"Indeed."

"Were you there?"

"Oh yes, I was certainly there."

"Benjamin, you're perspiring, you should go inside. First really hot day, beware too much noonday sun. I will invite you and your wife over one day soon."

He looked toward the woods behind the house and at the cemetery visible through the trees. The air thrumming with birdsong.

"I doubt my wife will be able to join us."

"I'm genuinely sorry."

In another month the trees would shield the cemetery from view. The sun on the Revolutionary War gravestones, white, sparkling.

"I believe that there is always a ram in the bush," he heard her say.

He turned to face her. Small white expectant features, jet-black hair. Wide unblinking dark eyes overlaid with a transparent yellowish film flecked with pinpoints of golden light, probably from the sun. A serpent's eyes, they almost seem. The eyes of a story writer?

"A ram in the bush, you say."

"I believe that."

"How very nice to think so."

* * *

The following day he flew to Chicago. A graduate seminar on Clausewitz; an interview with the Op-Ed page editor of the *Tribune*; a private lunch with two deans and the provost; an afternoon colloquium on the Persian Gulf War.

High piercing noises emanated from the speakers and rendered the large audience restive. He stood helpless behind the podium. Why am I here? Why am I doing this? A sudden vision of his house, his study, and the rhododendron hedge in the sunlight. The nurse waiting patiently until he returned. Once again he spoke into the microphone, but it hurled back his words in fierce electronic resistance. He leaned heavily against the podium, his legs aching, a twinge in his right arm below the elbow. Bones beginning to hurt. When did I take the medication? A scruffy ponytailed young man in slovenly jeans hurried down the aisle and onto the stage, and checked plugs, wires, outlets. Proper sound and order restored, the audience again focused on him. Benjamin Walter spoke for an hour, detailing his position on the war, his voice a rich baritone, his tone properly ironic and dry, his Oxford English echoing faintly off the high walls of the crowded auditorium. He invoked Weber, Durkheim, Freud; he cited Churchill, Fussell, Janowitz. He analyzed roots and causes and drew tight the cords of connection. Nevertheless, during the question-and-answer period, contentious voices were raised: Was this not antiquated gunboat diplomacy? Regressive, imperialist, colonialist, favoring oil interests and decadent regimes? How could he be so certain of the causal lines he had drawn up when one might easily see it this or that other way? Why did there have to be cogent causal lines at all, why could it not all simply have, well, happened? Someone cited Kuhn; another, Rorty. He felt himself growing weary. This young generation, nothing sacred to them, reduce everything to a postdiluvian shambles. He held his own, he thought, gave far better than he received, he was certain, and afterward one of the younger faculty, a bright assistant professor of English, who knew Evelyn's work on Virginia Woolf and I. D. Chandal, accompanied him to the university bookstore and then drove him to the airport.

Seated in the airliner, the huge jet airborne, he removed from his briefcase the collection of stories he had purchased in the bookstore, the most recent book by I. D. Chandal. Its title, *Calling upon Hell*, and the photograph on the back of the dust jacket displaying an I. D. Chandal quite different from the one he had met near the hedge: gray-haired, plump, wearing a man's shirt and tie, a tweed sports jacket, dark slacks, and with a strange fierce look in her eyes. Round-faced, heavy-bosomed, the early traces of a second chin, tiny lines biting at her lips. The jacket unable to conceal the hefty endowment of hip and thigh. Apparently, between the book and the hedge she had dyed her hair and lost a lot of weight.

He turned to the epigraph in the front of the book.

There was nobody left who had not experienced more misfortunes in four or five years than could be depicted in a century by literature's most famous novelists: it was necessary to call upon hell to arouse interest.

The words were by the Marquis de Sade.

He sat reading.

Strange stories. Many situated in the Upper West Side of Manhattan. Old-world men with threadbare dreams entering the fearful midnight of their lives. Elegant pre–World War I apartments, tall ceilings, paneled rooms, dark wood tables, upholstered couches, tasseled lamps. In the first story, "A Rainbow Costs 50 Cents Extra," an elderly man orders a birthday cake from a bakery for his dying wife, and is infuriated by an unexpected fifty-cent-extra charge for the decorative rainbow he requested to be added to the icing as a symbol of love and peace. He recalls rainbows he and his wife have seen in skies churned by storms, returns to the bakery with a .22 revolver, and shoots the storekeeper dead.

In the story "Spring Gardens Only," an aging artist who is also a gardener lives in a brownstone in the midst of the city, and in a patch of ground behind the house he plants the gardens he then paints. His watercolors are exquisite, famous. He starts his gardens in April, abandons them in July. One spring a visitor from his past appears, a male lover from a distant hungry winter before the time of fame. They renew their affair; they quarrel bitterly; the lover leaves. The artist, overwhelmed by memories of the original affair, installs a fountain in the garden wall. The water attracts songbirds, one of which on a lightning impulse he kills with a stone. He sketches it, paints it, a male cardinal, gorgeously feathered, and buries it in the garden.

Some of the stories were about women. "Fresh-Cut Color" was a monologue by a once-famous lesbian film actress about to find out if her adopted daughter has been accepted into the first grade of a highly prestigious private school. The child is rejected. Memories flood the actress: her early rejections, her successes, her current fading career. The vengeance she wreaks upon the school. . .

A renowned architect returns to Krakow on a search for Holocaust memories; a former colonel of the KGB recalls his years as an interrogator and torturer; a professor of Western intellectual history faces a plagiarism scandal; an aging homosexual goes on a Russian roulette of cruising in the wake of his young lover's death from AIDS—all nearing the end of their active lives, all tangled in memories of the past, which come to them too late and return nothing, not an echo, not a whisper, not a hope. Relentless, the cold tone of the tales; exquisitely baroque, the lush, alliterative language, the exuberant figures of speech. A grandeur of style painting lives sown with salt.

Enough. Slightly unhinged by the language and dismayed by the lives, he closed the book and proceeded to pick at the food placed before him by the airline attendant. But the book, which he had inserted into the seat pocket before him, seemed to be sending forth tendrils that were sliding toward him. The stories were a *presence*. Quite understandable that Evelyn was teaching her work.

He fell into a troubled sleep and was awakened by the bump of the landing gear on the tarmac. That late at night Newark terminal was nearly deserted. He retrieved his car and drove along a foggy parkway and country roads to the town; the roads littered with branches, here and there dark puddles in the headlights of the Saab. Tired, very tired. Legs and arms aching, and now the back of his neck and his eyes.

It was shortly after ten o'clock when he turned into his driveway, and saw the asphalt wet and strewn with branches. Lights burned in the living room and master bedroom. Oddly, the Tudor stood dark: no interior lights, no outside lights. The previous owners—elderly people, he an investment broker and she an interior decorator, who had gone to live with their only daughter in Phoenix—would set the house ablaze at night. "Tudors are built to be dark," the man had once remarked to Benjamin Walter. "Spooky place without lights." Advise her to put the exteriors on automatic. Not good to leave the house dark at night. The exterior floods had switched on each evening and off early each morning all through the year the Tudor had stood unsold and uninhabited.

He parked the car in the garage behind his house and climbed out from the front seat, pain flashing in his legs, then went to the trunk for his travel bag and briefcase. The storm had done nothing to cool the air, which smelled of mist and sodden earth. The night was sultry, waterlogged, stirred by moist winds.

A voice startled him. "Welcome back, Benjamin."

His heart skipped, raced. He looked around, saw no one.

"Over here."

He spotted her then, about thirty feet away, near the rhododendrons.

"Hello," he called. What was she doing there outside in the dark? And wasn't the lawn sopping wet?

"We had a very bad storm, Benjamin. Lost two trees over on the next street. No damage to your trees, though."

No damage to his trees? Had she walked through the woods, inspecting? The previous owners had never entered his section of the woods, not to his knowledge.

Carrying his bag and briefcase in one arm, he stepped out of the garage, pushing the button that lowered the door.

"A long trip?" he heard her ask.

"Chicago." She stood just beyond the rim of his exterior house lights, her face seeming to hover like a dimly lit globe beside the hedge. "I read some of the stories in your current collection on the flight back."

"Did you?"

"An eagle's language, a scorpion's bite, if I may say so. You depict a unique hell."

"We live in a strange time. A different hell is called for, most definitely, wouldn't you say?"

"Aren't you standing in a very muddy lawn?"

"Oh, I don't mind the mud. Actually, I'm watching the fireflies."

The lawn was ablaze with the tiny low-flying creatures, lending the dark air the appearance of a star-sprinkled sky.

"Light without heat," he heard her say. "Since early childhood, fascinated by fireflies. Did you deliver a talk in Chicago?"

"On the Persian Gulf War."

"Ah, of course, the Professor of War discoursing on war. You must tell me what you said. Did you use anecdotes in your talk?"

"Davita, it's quite late."

"Like all writers, I am eager for good stories."

"I teach tomorrow."

"I didn't mean right now. Over coffee, one day soon?"

"It will be my pleasure."

"Goodnight, Benjamin."

He went along the side of the house and the flagstone front walk to the porch. Climbing the three steps, he looked briefly to his left and saw across the lawn the vague globe of her head still suspended in the darkness near the hedge.

Inside, the nurse sat waiting. They talked briefly about the day—Evelyn's progress, her response to the medications, her frame of mind—and the nurse then slipped quietly out of the house with a murmured goodnight. He turned off the lamps, leaving only the night light burning, a faint greenish glow near the foot of the stairs. The house, once resonating with the buoyant mayhem of children, now sepulchral with silence. Slowly, he climbed the well of carpeted stairs.

A wedge of yellow light from their room spilled onto the dim second-floor hallway. He entered the room, set down the bags. She opened her eyes.

"Benjamin." An effort, her whisper.

"My dear," he said softly.

The pneumonia was deep this time, exhausting, but still treatable at home. Large shadow-rimmed gray eyes in a thin long face drawn pale and tight across the temples and cheek bones. The warm acrid odor of her sweat.

"Is there anything I can get you?"

She replied tonelessly, "Dear Benjamin, how about a dill and yogurt soup?"

He lowered his head.

"Don't forget to add a generous grinding of pepper." Her voice matter-of-fact, a near whisper. "And veal alla marsala. Again, don't forget the pepper."

"My dear—"

"Rice creole, once again the pepper. And ratatouille."

"Dear—"

"Shall I have a salad? Perhaps a string bean salad with vinaigrette?"

"Dear, dear Evelyn," he murmured.

"It is all still very astonishing," she said, and closed her eyes and turned her face to the wall.

She lay very still, breathing with difficulty. He turned off the light and stood gazing into the deep blues and purples of the darkened room. The partly open windows faced the rear of the house and he distinctly heard the trees: the oaks and pines, the cedars and elms.

Arms and legs throbbing, he undressed and slipped into pajamas. Skeletal underpinning slowly but irreversibly splintering and fracturing; Humpty Dumpty in slow motion. In the bathroom he washed and took his medications and gazed at himself in the medicine-cabinet mirror. Not yet the ravaged midnight features of W. H. Auden. He thought of the face of I. D. Chandal. The two faces, the one on the lawn and the other in the book. It occurred to him that his wife's library must have old hardback copies of works by I. D. Chandal, and he went quietly through the bedroom and crossed the hall into her study. Undisturbed the past two weeks, the air inside musty. Six novels by I. D. Chandal, and two short-story collections. He found her photograph on the back of only one of the books, a novel four years old. The same photograph as the one on the book he had purchased in Chicago—and which, he now realized with dismay, he had forgotten on the airplane! Annoyed over that. He put back on the shelf the novel with the photograph and, as he turned to leave, glanced out the study window, which faced the side of the Tudor, and noticed a ground-floor room, the kitchen, earlier dark, now lit. At a table sat a woman, her face concealed by her hand. The rhododendron hedge did not extend that far down the length of the lawn, and he was able to see clearly her pale blue nightdress and portly form and graying hair.

Fatigued now beyond easy measure, and the sleeping pill he had earlier swallowed beginning to take hold, he returned to the bedroom. Cool sheets, moonlight on the windows, the trees murmurous. Evelyn breathing steadily. She'll wake at least once. From the woods the hooting of an owl and before his aching eyes the sudden image of the picked-clean skeleton of a squirrel on the front walk one morning. The children gaping at it, shrinking back, fascinated, horrified. Tiny, delicate, glistening bones: spinal column, feet, all neatly splayed, as if pinned for dissection. Owls do that, he said, pick you clean to the core. Evelyn said, No, dear, that was not an owl, owls eat everything, even the bones, and if it's eating a bird it will leave only the feathers. More likely the work of our neighbor's cat, she added in that wondrously amiable way she had of imparting knowledge without the least display of conceit; the Tudor people'd had a white tabby in those days. He scooped up the skeleton of the squirrel with a shovel and tossed it into the garbage bin near the garage, the children watching, shocked, unnerved. Were they thinking: Will this happen to us too, one day reduced this way to bone? Should've talked to them about it afterward but they went off to school and the incident was never brought up and why was he remembering it now, oh yes, the owl. He thought, woozy from the medication: How tedious and commonplace, this business of mortality. Infrequently considered, and when considered too quickly put aside. What returns it to remembrance is irony. A war trench repeatedly shelled is soon lost to recollection. But bomb a sleepy town—the irony will nail it solidly to memory. There, the owl again, from the woods or the cemetery. Oh yes, an explosive device ravaging an innocent airliner is the very guarantor of memory. Is that the reason we remember forever the biblical Amalekites who attacked Israelites during the exodus from Egypt? The assault upon helpless, fleeing people a bitter irony. What would that strange man, the trope teacher, have said to that? The trope teacher! Why have I suddenly recalled the trope teacher? A quickening beat of the heart in the swiftly gathering clouds of sleep.

His wife woke him later that night, and he went to her. Feverish again and soaked with sweat. Gently, he raised her, dried her with a towel, helped her into a fresh nightgown. He murmured to her reassuringly: she would come out of this as she had before. She coughed and belched. He helped her to the bathroom and supported her so she would not tumble from the toilet. She lay on his bed as he changed her sheets.

"Actually, dear, I would prefer lunch in Davy Byrne's with Leopold Bloom," she said.

He laughed softly.

She murmured, as he helped her into her bed, "One can hardly believe that one's own body could become such an awful enemy."

She fell asleep.

He remained starkly awake and after a while went to the bathroom for another sleeping pill. But he decided not to take it, the after-effect would smother him in a woolly blanket of exhaustion that would linger into the morning and he had a full day awaiting him in the university. Spend an hour or so now working on the memoirs, fall asleep over that.

He entered his study and, looking out the window at the Tudor, saw I. D. Chandal in her kitchen, yellow-lit, framed by the window, obese. All the rest of the Tudor had melted into the darkness. She sat hunched over a pad, writing. He watched until he grew sleepy and then returned to his bed.

The nurse arrived punctually, as always, in the early morning. A hot cloudy day, more storms predicted. His wife was still asleep when he left the house. The oaks behind the house, silent. And hushed, too, the woods.

He went along the driveway toward the garage and saw I. D. Chandal, shovel in hand, bent over a wide length of raw earth she had dug from the end of the hedge to the border of the woods. Her black hair was covered with a bright yellow bandana. Firm breasts, shapely hips. A dizziness came over him.

She said, straightening, "Good morning, Benjamin. It will storm again today."

He was fighting off the sensation of being slightly unhinged.

"Benjamin?"

A pause. Two or three deep breaths. Then, "Good morning. You're up early."

"A wonderful day to plant. Earth soft from yesterday's rain, and put the flowers in before the next rain."

He climbed into the Saab.

She said, "How is your wife?"

He closed the car door, rolled down the window, and started the engine. "My wife had a bad night."

She raised toward him slightly the hand that grasped the earth-encrusted shovel: a gesture of sympathy.

"Davita," he said through the open window of the car. "Your ram in the bush?"

"Yes?"

"Where is it?"

She gazed at him without expression.

He moved the car along and glanced at her in his rear view mirror. She stood, shovel in hand, watching him turn onto the street. Even from that distance he could see clearly the look of ferocity on her face.

* * *

He drove cautiously along the winding country roads and the curving corrugated parkway, sticking always to the right lane, watching out for the potholes, aware of the cars in the center and left lanes racing past him. On both sides of the parkway tall trees with infant leaves silhouetted against the cloudy sky. Broken patches of road jarring the steering wheel and his fingers and hands. The upper deck of the bridge nearly lost in a yellow fog and the wide river dull gray and running into mist and the city endlessly bleak beneath a blockade of low dense clouds. Tiresome this drive. Still, the Max Weber Chair in Sociology sufficient reason to have moved here. But to live in the city—unthinkable. Yet the travel time. And Evelyn's commute to Princeton. And the costly private schools for the children. Poor choice in the end? Maybe. Hindsight always the winner in the war of wits. Hardly the streets of Oxford and the bike rides to Balliol. Destitute England like a wheezing invalid then, my mother secretly sending the food packages, my father utterly mute. That old bike with the basket in front and the dead metallic sound of its warning bell. Riding down the road and turning left and passing the playing fields of Magdalene. Cool sweet-scented air and flowers spilling over onto the sidewalks, houses pink in the early light and the gravel path to the residential street and on into the park with the broad fields and the cricket matches on Saturdays. And just inside the entrance to the park the tall thick-trunked tree with the haven of greenish shadows beneath its branches. How I loved that tree. And flowers lining the gravel path and the river running narrow and slow to my left along the water walks until it opened out into the wide water where Evelyn taught me to punt. Trees green and dense along the banks and the shadows of leaves on the dark-mirror surface of the water. Putting the pole in, feeling it slide into the muddy bottom, pushing, punting. And Evelyn reading aloud from Auden about seas of pity lying locked and frozen. Why am I suddenly remembering that? Seas of pity locked and frozen. She taught me a great deal, my Evelyn: how to truly read and write, how to blissfully forget. And the gravel path led to the road that ran past the museum and the Bodleian and the pub and into Broad Street and Balliol, the quadrangle, the stone archway, the dining hall, the dorm rooms, the open green with the garden outside the chapel, and trees, lovely trees. Evelyn on her bike; long russet hair trailing in the wind. Color on her high-boned flushed cheeks and sweat on her face even in winter and the musky smell of the sweat between her breasts and under her arms. And the perpetual look of surprise in her eyes; surprise that she and her parents and her two brothers had survived the war; surprise that she had gone from nursing soldiers to reading literature; surprise that she had fallen in love with a Yank, an ailing Yank, a Jewish Yank, she being vintage Church of England stock and a descendant of William of Waynflete, who had been Bishop of Manchester, a loyal minister of Henry VI, and founder of Magdalene College. True, I wore a different face then: lank and pallid from the illness and not a little apprehensive, but handsome, and eyes glittering with a hunger to take in the world. And the infinite wonder each time the seeming fragile thinness of her would turn fiery and tumescent during the turbulence of sex.

The car lurched and plunged and climbed through a dip in the cobblestone street. Europe cobbled with the bones of war dead. Where did I read that? So tired this morning. All that anger in Chicago, exhausting. Is that rain? No, street grit on the windshield. His eyes swollen with fatigue; his fingers tight on the wheel, aching.

He steered the Saab into the side-street garage and left it with an attendant. Umbrella in one hand and briefcase in the other, he had a gangly, flat-footed walk. Dark homburg and charcoal-gray suit; starched white shirt and icy yellow tie. Curious glances from the jeans-and-T-shirt crowd. Evelyn tells me that I bring to mind T. S. Eliot walking to his bank. Big fuss in academe now over Eliot's wretched anti-Semitism. Suddenly discovered America, as my father would say.

He took one of the pedestrian paths into College Walk.

The paved center lane was crowded with cars. Water splashing in the fountains of the plaza. Steps thronged with students. The sunless air strangely still; the flags drooping on their tall poles. Security guards: alert for the rites and tumults of spring? Posters announcing meetings, films, plays, demonstrations. Gays. Lesbians. Afro-Americans. Asians. Women's rights. Pro-Lifers. America Balkanized. *E pluribus plura.* What is this? A colloquium on Heidegger. Repellent philosophy from a damnable man. And another on Derrida. That too shall pass. All this academic cacophony, with the city as backdrop. Beginning to rain.

He rode the elevator up to his office and some while later sat before a microphone lecturing to nearly one hundred students in a large, stuffy hall whose open windows seemed to suck in the noises of the cars, buses, trucks and pedestrians on the four-lane street. A steady background of sound during the fifty minutes of the class. Some of the students slept. One kept rolling his head: probably on drugs.

Before lunch a dissertation conference with a graduate student: a nervous, balding young man from India, too anxious to please. Then a lengthy telephone conversation with Stuart Fox, the head of the history department, about a candidate for a recently vacated professorship. Replacing the telephone, he turned to his mail. Invitations to conferences in Washington, D.C., Berlin, Tel Aviv, Amsterdam. Keynote a State Department think-tank in Aspen. A request from a prestigious journal of American history for a piece on his army experience in Europe during the war. A catalogue from a rare-book dealer in London. Behind him a sudden rumble of thunder. Turning, he saw through the tall window a whitish green sky and, after a moment, a flash of lightning. Again, thunder. A light rain falling.

He ate lunch alone in the faculty club—a bowl of soup, a green salad, coffee. Many called out greetings as they moved past his table; none offered handshakes; nearly all knew of his fragile hands. It was raining steadily when he left the club.

He detoured to the library, entered the stacks, and in a cool silent corridor lined with books discovered half a shelf of critical works on I. D. Chandal: one by an Oxford scholar, another published by Harvard, yet another by Chicago; a volume in the Twayne's United States Author Series; a number of UMI-printed dissertations; and a Modern Critical Views volume, with essays by Alfred Kazin, Harold Bloom, Robert Alter, Elizabeth Hardwick, Susan Sontag, and Cynthia Ozick. He took with him the work by the Oxford scholar and the collection of essays.

Leaving the library, he ran into Robert Helman, who was standing in the doorway, looking forlorn and waiting for the rain to let up.

"Robert, share my umbrella."

Robert Helman murmured his thanks and ducked under the protective cover.

Together they walked in the rain, Benjamin Walter tall and mannerly, Robert Helman slight, in his mid-sixties, graying beard and hair, red bow tie, rumpled dark suit.

The rain was suddenly wind-driven, heavy, drumming upon the umbrella. Students rushed by. On the paths were miniature dark seas made turbulent by the wind and rain.

"Your wife?" asked Helman under the umbrella.

"Not well, I'm afraid."

"So sorry. A difficult time for you." His small voice, with its middle-European accent, sounding breathless, barely audible.

Benjamin Walter thought: Theresienstadt, sixteen months. Twelve months in Auschwitz. Helman an expert on difficult times.

"Your trip to Chicago?"

"Be careful of that puddle. Stormy opposition to the war. Saddam Hussein sitting on our oil flow an insufficient reason for interference in a regional quarrel."

"They favored appeasement?"

He knows about appeasement, too. Prague his provenance. "Inclined toward waiting."

"Evil feeds on waiting."

The wind gusted, the rain slanted, the umbrella jerked and pulled.

They entered their building. Benjamin Walter shook the rain from the umbrella. Puddles formed on the floor.

Helman delicately raised the bottoms of his trousers, tapped the rain from his shoes. He said, clearing his throat and adjusting his bow tie, "The candidate for the position in history, did you hear?"

"Oh yes, the news reached me."

"And did you hear that she does not have the necessary language?"

"That I heard too, yes."

"Don't you think it strange, Benjamin, for the university to hire someone to teach the history of a people who doesn't know that people's language?"

"Fox told me this morning that he is taking the position that she was deprived of a proper language education because she's a woman."

"Oh, really? Well, I was deprived of a proper education in physics because of my genealogy. Am I therefore now able to teach physics?"

"Fox claims that her dissertation is outstanding."

"Benjamin, permit me to tell you a little story about dissertations and doctorates. In my current research on the Wansee Conference I have discovered that, of the fifteen men who sat around the table establishing the bureaucracy for the murder of European Jewry, eight held doctorates."

"Fox wants this woman and will turn it into a war."

"How sad if he does that."

"You'll lose even if you win."

"And what is your position on this?"

"I've written on war in Japan, and I don't know Japanese. Good translators are more than adequate."

"I don't know about the Japanese. I know about Jewish history. No language, no historian. This will be a war worth waging."

"Fox won't forget, Robert. He'll make you pay in a thousand ways, and war will be the winner. War always wins."

Robert Helman shook his head and sighed. Pale forehead creased, eyes deeply furrowed at the corners; premature aging and permanent sadness, wearing visibly his years in the German factories of murder. A great historian, hard-nosed, public and private opponent to Benjamin Walter's notion of underlying cords of connection, a proponent of what he called the three laws of the chaos theory of history: chance, chance, and chance. The haphazard, the accidental, the arbitrary, the contingent; discrete events banging randomly against one another, with humans creating the fiction of connection. "Historians record, clerics connect"— an oft-quoted remark of his, uttered in exasperation one day at a conference. His wife taught art history in the university, they lived in a nearby apartment building with an exquisite view of the river, and there were four grown and lovely children.

Robert Helman thanked Benjamin Walter for the sanctuary of his umbrella, asked to be remembered to Evelyn, and went off to meet with Stuart Fox.

Some minutes later, Benjamin Walter stood at the tall window between the floor-to-ceiling bookcases in his office, watching the rain. The quadrangle, dripping and depleted of hues, lay deserted. A diagonal streak of lightning ripped across the sky, followed almost immediately by drumbeats of thunder that rattled the windows. In the ensuing silence he thought he heard someone at the door.

"Come."

The door opened and a young man entered and closed the door. He wore rain-stained blue jeans and a soaked white T-shirt and sandals with no socks. Muscular arms and chest, veins and tendons clearly showing. Blond hair tied back in a ponytail, wet strands on his forehead and ruddy cheeks. A small gold earring.

The young man said in a matter-of-fact tone, "Professor, I can't take the exam, I've got to go home right away."

Benjamin Walter recognized him. A senior, infrequently present in class, with a show of indifference to the subject, but very bright those few times he'd spoken up. His parents of western Pennsylvania aristocracy.

"I do not give makeup examinations."

"Professor, I was just on the phone with my mother. My best friend, the friend I went to school with from third grade on, is very sick."

"That's of no—"

"I mean, it's pretty serious. He's in some kind of a depression or something, and he's asking for me."

Benjamin Walter said, "In such matters, the department requires corroboration."

"I can get that."

"Where does he live?"

"He's at Yale." Blue eyes chilly even in this distress. Features blank. Flat, glacial voice. Bred for self-control. "So can I take a makeup exam?"

Benjamin Walter nodded.

The young man left the office without another word.

Outside, the rain had come to an end. Water dripped from the branches of the scrawny street trees. Patches of blue sky shone above soaring gold-rimmed clouds.

He sat for some while, working on his memoirs, filling the margins of the manuscript with notes in his minuscule handwriting. Two hours went by, the phone did not ring, no one knocked on his door. But it was futile; he had already set down most of the middle and more recent years, but nothing of the beginning, nothing to which he could connect his later life—and how does one write a life without a seed, a source, a commencement? His mother and father and sister and brother—he remembered. But there was someone else he could recall only in dim outline, a teacher, yes, a teacher of trope, but, more important, also of, of—elusive, a phantom of some kind. Why am I not able to resurrect him?

He put down his pen and sat back, exhausted, his fingers aching. No more work on the memoirs today. Thus far, the memoirs a book without a beginning.

Umbrella in one hand, briefcase containing the manuscript in the other, he walked to the garage and retrieved his Saab. The air smelled of dank streets. Late-afternoon sunlight cast a pale pink wash across the walls of tall buildings. Traffic inched along the streets to the parkway. He drove with his windows open, staring fixedly at the road, ignoring the horns directed at him.

The sky was barely lit when he entered the town. Street lights shone upon the debris-strewn wet roads. When he turned into his driveway he was momentarily startled, certain he had erred: this was not his home.

Jagged fragments of raw wood lay everywhere, on the lawn and the driveway and near the garage, some small, others the height of a man and thrust deep into the earth. Blocking the end of the driveway just beyond the entrance to the garage, was a huge tree limb. Beyond the rhododendron hedge stood the Tudor, all its windows ablaze. And emerging from the line of trees and hurrying toward him was I. D. Chandal.

TWO

The two oaks at the edge of the woods were nearly as old as the core of the house, and the cemetery beyond the woods was older still, with some gravestones from colonial times. And the woods between the cemetery and the house—the wild, cool growth of trees and underbrush with their greenish whisperings and murmurings—the woods predated all.

From the first moment he'd set eyes on the house more than thirty years ago he'd silently accepted it as an echoing link with a moment in his past from which he no longer felt a need to flee; the woods and cemetery seemed to possess a kind of welcome enchantment. The history of the house—recounted by the realtor—contained a beguiling mystery.

Built originally as a farmhouse during the Revolutionary War, said the realtor. Whoever owned it around the time of the War of 1812 knocked down an outside wall and added a room that doubled the size of the ground floor. The one who owned it during the Civil War built a new staircase: dark oak steps and a carved banister smooth and warm to the touch. Near the end of the First World War, before the winter froze the earth and the influenza epidemic began its murderous rampage, the then-owner put down a patio of brick and flagstone outside the kitchen. And during the Second World War the people who owned it had a den built in the space between the rear wall of the parlor and the back lawn.

When Benjamin Walter had stood in the driveway gazing at the house that first time, an odd shiver had coursed through him, a pull of memory, and he asked the realtor if he could take a walk alone through the woods. He went about some while in the cool green interior, the earth soft and moist beneath his shoes. Insects buzzed in the lacy patterns of sunlight that shone like shimmering water upon the leaves. A rhythmic hum of cicadas and the sweetly piercing sounds of birdsong and the rustle of animal life in the underbrush. Trees tall and old, thick-trunked, bark like the hide of elephants, bulging roots deep and gnarled. Beyond the woods lay a gently rising sward, a cemetery, gravestones ancient and recent. The trees were still that day. The trees were merely trees that day.

Evelyn had wondered if the Tudor next door might be for sale. Closer to her heart, that sort of house. Keen memories of her family's country home before the war, before she'd met and fallen in love with her Yank, before the years at Oxford, before the wrenching move to the United States.

The realtor had made inquiries. No, the Tudor was not for sale. Its owners were quite content and had no intention of selling, thank you very much.

So they made an offer on the old farmhouse and accepted the counteroffer and signed the settlement papers in November 1963, four days before the assassination of John Kennedy.

Five years later, they had completed major books: he on war, she on Virginia Woolf. The children young and active: the house untidy, crowded, and clamorous with their friends.

Evelyn loved to give dinner parties. People came from New York and Princeton. Scholars, poets, writers, artists.

He and Evelyn decided to expand the kitchen. The country was then at war in Vietnam. He was at a sociology conference organized by Philip Rieff at the University of Pennsylvania the day workers broke through the outside wall of the kitchen and found the old newspapers. Six-year-old Kevin mentioned it the next day during dinner.

"Which newspapers?"

"Old newspapers, Daddy."

"What are we talking about here?"

"Stinky old," said Kevin.

"You are a stupid little fellow," said Laura, twelve, the older daughter. "Newspapers from the First World War, Daddy."

"Where are they?"

"Mother threw them into the trash," said Beth, nine, the younger daughter.

He looked across the table at Evelyn.

"Ben, they were falling to pieces."

After dinner he went outside and brought the trash can into the kitchen and hauled out crumpled brownish newspapers, which he set down on the floor and opened carefully. Pages dry and brittle. A local newspaper, the *Nyack Eagle*, no longer in existence. Its masthead an American flag draped around an eagle; headlines black and bold. Probably stuffed into the wall for insulation. Evelyn and the children stood around watching quietly as he spread the newspapers on the floor in proper sequence. The headlines read:

AUSTRIA DECLARES WAR, RUSHES VAST ARMY INTO SERBIA

BRITAIN ON VERGE OF WAR WITH GERMANY

LUSITANIA SUNK BY A SUBMARINE, PROBABLY 1,260 DEAD

WILSON BREAKS WITH GERMANY; WAR IMMINENT

WAR IS DECLARED BY U.S.

GERMANS TAKE MOST OF MESSINES RIDGE

GERMANS GET CHEMIN DES DAMES IN NEW DRIVE

OVER 1,000,000 U.S. SOLDIERS SENT ABROAD

AMERICANS DRIVE GERMANS BACK OVER MARNE

GERMANS AGREE TO SIGN; NO CONDITIONS

GERMANY GIVES UP; WAR ENDS AT 2 P.M.

One of the pages disintegrated as he unfolded it. He set out its bits and pieces on the kitchen table:

M RI NS TACK B TWE SE D AR ONNE OREST

"'Americans attack between Meuse and Argonne Forest,'" he said to his wife and children, feeling a sudden drumming in his chest. Argonne. Ardennes. Memories of his own war.

The kitchen had begun to reek of rot and mold. He scooped up the newspapers and carried them to his study.

In the days that followed, he'd cut out the headlines, had them mounted and framed—four frames in all—and hung them on the wall in his study that carried memorabilia of his life: degrees, awards, accolades, photographs with distinguished colleagues, university presidents, senators, and Presidents John Kennedy, Lyndon Johnson, Richard Nixon, Ronald Reagan. He had a skilled craftsman glue the headline fragments to a heavy gray matte cardboard and enclose it all beneath nonglare glass in a black frame, which he hung on the wall over his desk. The framed headlines cast an odd imbalance over the room, as if dwarfing everything else on the walls and even the glass-enclosed floor-to-ceiling bookcases with their rare and precious volumes and folios on war.

"They are quite overpowering," Evelyn said.

"Part of the history of this house."

"But that wasn't our war, darling."

"Oh yes, it was. One long war with a brief respite to facilitate recovery from the influenza epidemic and rearming. It was certainly my parents' war."

"You never talk about them, but you'll put their war on your walls."

"Nothing to talk about, my dear. They lived, they died. Unremarkable people."

"But they were your mother and father."

"Recollection very vague now. Retrieve it all if I must one day."

"How can you be so sure of that, Benjamin?"

All this—returned to memory by a felled tree limb. In their years on this property the woods had been struck by lightning five times, though this sixth time was the closest it had ever come to the house. Astonishing to have so much come hurtling back into memory, as if an electric switch had been turned on: the blasted oak, the awful war, the shattered woods; the history of the house, the resurrected headlines, the Argonne and the Ardennes, his parents, and—yes!—the trope teacher. A long cord of connection.

He sat behind the steering wheel of his car, staring in shock at the huge tree limb that lay across the driveway and in the same moment seeing I. D. Chandal, coat and hat stained dark with rain, emerge from the woods and go hurrying toward him along the wet rear lawn.

* * *

She said, "One of your trees took a direct hit."

"Which?"

"One of the oaks. It probably saved your house."

"One of the oaks?" He felt dazed.

"You'll need a tree person."

"A what?" What was she saying? She seemed so calm amid this devastation: a shattered tree, splinters everywhere.

"A specialist. To assess the damage."

"One of the oaks," he said, looking toward the trees.

"Benjamin, I'd love to stand here and talk to you, but I have to go to the bathroom. Listen, come over later for a cup of coffee, if you're so inclined."

He watched her move off behind the rhododendron hedge and head toward the Tudor. He parked the car and walked over to the oak nearest the house.

The tree was nearly one hundred years old. It stood illumined by the sodium floods. There was a faint smell of freshly splintered, charred wood. The limb had been hurled onto the driveway. And all those shards. Some like spears and swords with their points buried six inches in the earth. He shuddered at the image of a shard embedding itself in human flesh. Deep darkness lay upon the branches facing the woods.

Very still, the woods.

The silence chilled him. He entered the house through the back door.

The nurse sat waiting for him in the kitchen.

"Oh, the storm was something fierce. Mrs. Walter, the Lord bless her, is so brave. The lightning frightened her. Scared me too. Like the Last Judgment, it was. The hand of God. We thought the house was hit, but it was only a tree. I gave her a pill, and she'll sleep four, maybe five hours."

"Thank you."

"You should get a night nurse not only for when you're away."

"I can tend to her."

"For the next time, I mean."

"I'll worry about it then."

"I can recommend someone."

"If it becomes necessary."

"I'll let myself out."

He ate cold chicken, reading and half-listening to the news on NPR. Merciless bombardment of Sarajevo. Centuries of hatred surfacing. Tenacity of memory. An image came to him and he looked up from the book: I. D. Chandal hurrying across the rear lawn in her raincoat and hat. She'd worn sandals and no socks. An odd woman.

Upstairs, his wife lay sleeping. In his study, he removed from his briefcase books and papers and the manuscript of his memoirs. He sat down at the desk and opened the manuscript and stared at his writing. Lackluster words lay heaped on the pages: dead leaves. Amid the words he saw a man dressed out of fashion, giving off the stench of morgue and carnage; spittled lips and a diabolic grin; a blizzard of ashes and vile coiling hair. He trembled, his heart thundering. A sound from the wall on which hung the framed headlines: the house did that at times: moaned and creaked and sighed. Through the window he saw the Tudor, all its windows lit.

A moment later—it seemed a mere instant—he was standing at the door of the Tudor, ringing the bell.

* * *

The door opened. She stood there, small, face white and eyes dark, hair shoulder-length and black, and smiled openly and warmly.

"Why, Benjamin. How nice."

"That cup of coffee you so kindly offered." His voice with a slight quiver in it; hesitant, vulnerable.

"Your wife?"

"She is in a deep sleep."

"You're sure?"

"The nurse gave her something."

"All right, then." She stepped back, opened the door wide, motioning him in. He stepped inside and heard the door close behind him.

"The kitchen is this way."

He followed her through an empty center hall with a curving carpeted stairway into a large octagon-shaped room. Walls bare; floors bare; not a chair or table anywhere. Dull lights from naked oval-shaped bulbs in antique brazen wall sconces. Their feet on creaky oak planks.

"There's furniture on the way. But I can really make do without much furniture."

He thought of Evelyn's exquisite aristocratic taste in furniture; and remembered the apartment of his childhood: heavy mahogany tables and chairs; horizontal hanging mirrors nearly as long as a wall; floor lamps with tasseled shades; upholstered sofa and easy chairs; blue oilcloth on the floors, white shades on the windows; the chicken, fish, potato, and vegetable-soup smells in the kitchen. Of all things, why was he remembering the apartment? The dismal light. His father's penchant for low-wattage bulbs. Save money on electricity and spend it on more important things. Give an extra dollar or two to the teacher. The trope teacher.

They went through a dim hallway lined on one side with floor-to-ceiling dark wood cabinets and entered the kitchen.

It was a drab space with old cherry-wood cabinets, a sink and refrigerator and stove that seemed of 1950s vintage, and an overhead light fixture that emitted a cheerless yellowish luminescence. A rectangular brown wood table and four wooden chairs near a window. On the table two stacks of newspapers. In the sink a heap of dirty dishes. Reddish tiles covered the floor; faded light-green paint on the walls. And the walls bare—not even a calendar.

He noticed immediately the large open writing pad and the black fountain pen on the table near the newspapers and stood watching as she quickly flipped the pad shut, smoothly scooped it up together with the pen, opened a cabinet drawer, slipped the pad and pen inside, and pushed the drawer shut.

"I've interrupted your writing."

"No, no, I hadn't begun."

"I'm so sorry. I should have called."

"No, really, it's all right. Please excuse the mess. I'm not the tidiest person. One of the things my husband always complained about. The lack of tidiness, I mean. His funeral business he kept very tidy. Well, now, coffee. I have, let's see, hazelnut, Irish cream, espresso, Swiss mocha. Regular and decaf."

"Espresso regular, please."

She busied herself at the sink. "Sit down, Benjamin. Relax. Push the newspapers to one side."

He sat at the table near a window that offered a view of the oaks and the woods. Looking to the right, he saw the gray fieldstone side of his house and the window of his study. He had left the lights on.

"You want a doughnut, Benjamin? I love doughnuts."

"Thank you." What am I doing here? Evelyn so sick and me in this woman's house. Keeps herself neat and trim. No doubt dyes her hair. Good-looking woman. Seems a different person when she writes. Puts on weight somehow: window-glass distortion? But the gray hair. Didn't she just say something?

"Please excuse me, my mind was elsewhere."

"I asked, Benjamin, if you wanted a single or a double espresso. I'm having a double."

"A double for me too, please."

"Here we are. Two double espressos and two doughnuts."

She set down the tray and sat across from him, gliding lightly onto the chair. Her sudden close presence. Smooth cream-white face; long neck; the clear outline of her breasts beneath the jersey. Hungry, glittering eyes. Moist lips. He felt a momentary dizziness; heart pounding, palms sweating.

The coffee hot, black, bitter; the doughnut stickysweet.

"Are you all right, Benjamin?"

"A little faint."

"Can I do anything?"

"A slight vertigo. Comes and goes."

"You should see a doctor about that."

"Davita, I see many doctors. I have an illness of the bones, which medications deftly control."

"And the dizziness?"

"As I said, it comes and goes. Tell me something, Davita. During supper I read an essay on your work by a noted critic who marveled at your memory, which he called, if I remember correctly, 'the memory of a sealed well, filled with water and leaking nothing.' A quaint metaphor. How do you do that?"

"I can't presume to know what he means."

"I am encountering a great deal of difficulty remembering certain matters."

"For your scholarly writing?"

"For my memoirs."

She bit into a doughnut.

He sipped espresso. His fingers trembling slightly, the beginning of a headache. How strange! Inside the kitchen of I. D. Chandal, drinking espresso, eating doughnuts. The downed limb of a lightning-struck oak across his driveway. Huge and deadly pieces of wood strewn about his property. His wife in a drugged sleep. Newspapers on the table.

SARAJEVO CLASHES IMPERIL RELIEF EFFORT, DRAW U.S. WARNING
LEADERS IN MUNICH WARN RIVAL FORCES IN BOSNIAN STRIFE

The vertigo again. What year was this? He read:

PLAN TO TIGHTEN EMBARGO ON IRAQ SUGGESTED BY U.S.
NUCLEAR ACCORDS BRING NEW FEARS ON ARMS DISPOSAL

"You see, I have no idea how to continue. I have a book without a beginning."

She put down her cup, patted her lips with a napkin. She gazed at him guardedly, seeming to be calculating, measuring.

"Well, Benjamin, I start from the zero point of memory."

"The zero point?"

"From the very least bit of memory."

"I'm not sure—"

"From the involuntary memory that comes like a bolt out of the blue. From the memory that is your aura."

"My what? My aura?"

"Listen to me, Benjamin. When I say the word 'war,' what comes immediately into your mind?"

"I don't—"

"The word 'war,' Benjamin. *Immediately!*"

"'Why?'"

"Why what?"

"The word 'why' comes to mind."

"And who speaks that word?"

He hesitated.

"*Who*, Benjamin?"

A wildly careening search. "An old teacher."

"What is he doing and saying, your old teacher?"

"I can't—"

"*What*, Benjamin?

Still he hesitated.

"You'll excuse me, Benjamin, but I see in your face that you have a story to tell. So tell me the story, get down to your zero point of memory. Or call it a night, go back to your wife, and I'll get on with my work."

A desperate effort. "Let me try."

"Good. Another espresso? Another doughnut?"

* * *

Why, I'd hear my classmates ask, did Mr. Isaac Zapiski wear those dark clothes? Fall, winter, spring and summer: dark double-breasted suit, dark wide-brimmed hat, dark wool coat in cold weather, dark high shoes, dark tie. He wasn't a rabbi; he wasn't even a teacher in our school. Their somber garb accorded well with their sober calling: the handing on of an ancient tradition. But, as far as we knew, Mr. Zapiski eked out a living solely from the teaching of trope. Why, then, the dark clothes?

And the same dark clothes at that. Weekdays, holy days, sabbaths,

festivals—the same seedy suit, the same shabby coat, the same shabby
hat. We were all poor—those were the ghastly years of the Great
Depression—but each of our fathers owned at least two suits, two pairs of
trousers, two shirts, two ties. And the same pair of high black shoes,
scruffed, misshapen, bulging out at the toes and down at the heels—why
did Mr. Zapiski own only one set of clothes and shoes?

And why did he walk moving his left foot forward in a shuffle and his
right foot trailing? Shuffle and scrape, shuffle and scrape, an awkward
drag-footed gait. A small, bumbling, stooped man who wore his hat low
over his eyes and his jacket or coat collar up, his neck squeezed into his
shoulders, looking for all intents and purposes like a turtle in the act of
withdrawing into its shell. He had a habit of shaking his head in a sort of
nervous twitch, jerking it from side to side, as if trying to disentangle
himself from some web in which he had been caught. He didn't do that
often, but when you saw it, it was frightening, because the pupils in his
eyes would slide up to the top and all you saw was the white, and his lips
would become flecked with spittle, and you were sure he was going to
faint. But he never did, it only lasted some seconds and it was over, and
he seemed never to remember what had happened.

In the corner store on our street, where he bought his newspaper, I'd
see him sometimes counting out his money with shaking hands from the
small black pocket purse he carried, the sort with the little metal knobs
that snapped shut. I'd have come in on an errand for my parents and he'd
acknowledge my presence with a nod and a cough—he had a nervous
little cough, a kind of perpetual need to clear his throat—and he'd be
standing there with his cane under one arm, slowly counting out his
money. He smoked endlessly, with enormous intensity, holding the
cigarettes between his thumb and forefinger and sucking in the smoke as
if his life depended on it. He went about beneath a weight of darkness
save for his short white beard and frayed white shirt.

I remember asking my mother, "How old is Mr. Zapiski?"

"Mr. Zapiski and your father were born two days apart."

"Why does he look so old?"

"He went through a great deal in the war."

In the winter my heart would go out to him whenever I saw him
picking his way through the snow on our streets, stopping before a patch
of ice or at a corner heaped with snow as if to muster strength to venture
forward, while the wind lashed at his hat and coat. Once in a storm I
offered to help him and he took my hand. I felt his weight as we made
our way across the street in the snow and, climbing to the opposite

sidewalk, he slipped and we both went down, and his cry when he fell haunted my dreams.

Some of my classmates would mockingly imitate his hobbled walk, his rasping voice, the way his face would twitch as if it had a life of its own. Most were indifferent. We all knew that he would inevitably enter our lives at a certain time and become a sort of teacher to us for a period of months.

It was inevitable that someone like Mr. Zapiski would give rise to tales and rumors. All the talk about him seemed connected to the Great War. Some claimed he had once been a Bolshevik general. Others insisted that he had served as an officer in the army of Emperor Franz Josef of Austria. Still others swore that he'd been a secret agent of Kaiser Wilhelm; a machine gunner in a Polish regiment of the Austrian army; a courier in Switzerland for Lenin.

To me he was the least likely person to have qualified as a great warrior. He seemed to have been born broken.

He was, as far as I could then tell, my father's closest friend. Friday evenings and Saturday afternoons he'd eat at our table. Though he rarely spoke more than a few words to me or to my younger brother and sister, he seemed unquestionably a member of our family. I learned early on that he was the only one in his family who had left Europe. All the others— parents, brothers, sisters, uncles, aunts, cousins—had chosen to remain behind, and for reasons I could not fathom were now unable to come to America. During our meals, there were often long periods of silence; when he and my father talked, nearly always in Yiddish—we talked Yiddish among ourselves, English on the streets—their conversation invariably turned to politics: labor strikes, socialism, communism, Roosevelt, Hitler, Stalin, Franco, Trotsky. In my presence they never spoke about the Great War. My mother served and sat in silence, listening, sighing from time to time as memories of her life in Europe returned to her.

None of the talk interested me. I'd play word games with my brother and finger-rope games with my sister. When I was young I often sat on Mr. Zapiski's lap; but, growing older, I found him discomfiting, and I came to dislike intensely the cigarette stench in his clothes and the yellow stains in the beard around his moist lips. His mouth emitted fetid vapors.

The years went by. Eventually the time came when I was to be given over to Mr. Zapiski.

"Listen to me," my father said after supper one evening when he and I were alone in the kitchen. "I am going to tell you something, and I don't ever want to hear from you that you didn't hear me say it. Mr. Zapiski and your father grew up in the same town in Europe. We served in the same regiment in the Great War. For months we lived in the same trenches. We ate together, slept together, fought together, and suffered together. No one can ever be closer to you than the soldiers with whom you shared a trench during a war. Mr. Zapiski is my closest and dearest friend. Do not let me hear from him that you are not learning everything that he is teaching you."

My father leaned forward across the kitchen table and put his fleshy features and dark eyes close to my face—and I had a clear image of him hunched over his worktable in the window of the shoe-repair shop where he now labored as a repairer of clocks and watches, his sweaty balding head gleaming in the yellow light of his work lamp. How abruptly he had fallen from a successful dealer in antiques to an indigent fixer of timepieces.

And so I began, twice a week in the evenings, to walk from our apartment to Mr. Zapiski: a gauntlet of gritty Bronx streets. Old red-brick apartment houses; scrawny cats and emaciated dogs around the garbage cans in foul alleyways. Trucks and automobiles rattling past on the cobblestones. Rectangles of yellow light behind drawn shades and sometimes a partly dressed man or woman in a window, smoking a cigarette and looking down at me as I went by, a bony, too-tall kid, walking very quickly even though this was my neighborhood and I need not have been frightened; but my mother's fears had somehow attached themselves to me, her real terrors were often my imagined ones. And under the elevated train and up the street past an enormous red-brick brewery, whose hot, pungent stench was the plague of our neighborhood.

Mr. Zapiski lived in an apartment house on top of a steep narrow cobblestone street. The heavy metal-and-glass front door creaked as I pushed against it. I'd walk up four flights of badly lit marble stairs, voices and cooking smells—beef, cabbage, potatoes, bacon—drifting through the closed doors, and I'd cross the hall to a wooden door, one of six on that floor, and twirl the knob on the old doorbell, which made the lifeless noise of a clapper striking lead.

Through the door I'd hear his shuffling gait as he came along his hallway. "Who is there?" he'd say, and I'd respond, "Benjie Walter," and hear him pull back the bolt and unlock the door. His face would appear in the narrow space between the door and the jamb. "Go into the parlor," he'd say, and I'd pass through the dimly lit narrow apartment hallway, while behind me he'd busy himself locking and bolting the door. I'd go past his kitchen—invariably, dirty dishes in the sink, a teakettle on the stove, Yiddish newspapers on the table, and often roaches on the walls—and into the parlor. There I'd sit in an easy chair: upholstery worn and grimy to the touch, springs hard against my rump and spine, an odor of dust rising from the fabric.

The first time I went to him was a bitter cold evening in late November. I was uneasy; my father's words still echoed in my head. We sat in silence for some while in the dimly lit kitchen, drinking the tea he set before us. On the table lay Yiddish and German newspapers. I had the sense I was going to be put through some sort of initiation rite.

"Tell me, Benjamin, these days what do you really like?"

I told him I liked baseball and movies.

He wore a tall black skullcap. His head was balding. I knew that under the skullcap a four-inch vertical scar and a two-inch horizontal scar ran across his head and intersected above the right temporal lobe. There were tiny pockmarks on the parts of his face not covered by the beard. His face was pale and gaunt, almost bloodless.

"You still like to read, Benjamin?"

"I like adventure stories, sea stories, war stories."

"Yes? Well, there are plenty of war stories in the Torah. And a big war story in the section you will learn to read."

That was all he said, though he kept glancing at me over the rim of his glass. He had pale gray pupils and his eyes bulged somewhat in their sockets and were encircled by bluish shadows and webbed skin. Though I had known him for years I understood that we were now entering upon a distinctly new relationship: I was no longer merely the son of his closest friend. He was about to become my teacher, I his student. A wall of unspoken expectations was rising between us; it would be my obligation to surmount it.

He slurped tea from his glass, coughed, and wiped his lips with a not-very-clean handkerchief. I counted four roaches on his kitchen walls before we were done with our tea. He put the glasses into the sink and told me to follow him.

In the doorway to Mr. Zapiski's parlor hung worn purple portieres. On the windows were run-down curtains and shades. Cracked brown linoleum in the hallway; faded carpeting in the parlor; peeling light-green paint on the walls and ceilings. Books lay on end tables and chairs, some face down and open. The walls were entirely bare, without even the traditional velvet picture of Jerusalem. He seemed to fit perfectly the tatterdemalion apartment: his dark clothes threadbare, his beard unkempt, his shoes cracked, with his right foot resting on the floor at an odd angle to the other.

He motioned to an easy chair and I removed two books and took the chair, feeling myself sink deep into the seat. The chair seemed to seize me like one of those flowers that snaps shut upon unwary insects. He dropped down into the sofa, from which rose little tendrils of dust. He stretched his left leg out in front of him, leaned forward with a low grunt, placed both hands on the trousers of his right leg below the knee, and swung the leg and lowered it so that it lay limp across the left leg.

"Now you will begin to learn the trope," he said in his hoarse voice, and coughed. He lit a cigarette and tossed the match into an ashtray that was close to overflowing. "First, I will teach you the notes and the grammar of the notes. Then I will teach you the meaning behind the grammar. And if I see that you have truly mastered that, I will teach you the magic of this music, things few people know."

At that point, because I'd always been inclined to pry into matters that aroused my curiosity, I said, "Excuse me, is it permissible to ask a question?"

"Without questions there is no learning."

"Why do you have in your apartment so many books about war?"

In my world we sized up people by the books they read and by the libraries in their homes. Walking through the hallway to the parlor, I'd noticed bookcases filled with volumes, in Yiddish and English, about the Great War.

His face twitched with annoyance. He'd no doubt expected an inquiry about grammar and trope.

"Because I was in the war, and I am trying to understand it."

"What did you do in the war?"

"I was a soldier like your father."

I have no recollection why I put to Mr. Zapiski the next question. Remember, I was not yet thirteen years of age; why would anything about that awful war have remotely interested me? Overheard private conversations between Mr. Zapiski and my father, perhaps; or that curiosity of mine boiling over. The answer is lodged in deep memory to which I have at present no direct access. In any event, abruptly, for no clear reason, I heard myself ask Mr. Zapiski, "Whose side were you on?"

My query startled him. His pale features turned crimson. He did not answer for a moment. Then he asked, in a tremulous tone, "Why do you ask me that question?"

The word he used for "why" was "*warum*," which is both German and Yiddish. He pronounced it "varoom."

I told him I was only curious.

He said, after another silence, "Your father and I fought in the army of Emperor Franz Josef of Austria, on the side of Germany, against England, France, Russia, Italy, and America."

On the side of Germany! They had fought on the side of the enemy! Was that something to worry about? It had never occurred to me that my father had fought against the United States. How had he and Mr. Zapiski managed to get into America if they had once fought against it? Perhaps they had been asked and had lied. What if the American government should ever find out? Would Mr. Zapiski and my father be sent back to Europe?

Mr. Zapiski stirred and coughed. His head shook briefly from side to side and the skullcap slid from it, revealing the two intersecting scars and the curls of thinning white hair on the nearly bald scalp. How could he and my father be the same age? They looked thirty years apart. The skullcap tumbled to his lap and he put it back on his head.

"Enough about that cursed war. That is not why you came here. Open the book and we will study what your father sent you to learn."

He began to chant the notes in his hoarse and rasping voice, and I followed along in the adolescent quavering that would after some years change into the baritone you now hear.

He taught, and I learned. The weeks passed. Regularly, my father would test me and nod, satisfied by my progress.

All that winter I trudged through snowstorms and frozen streets, and studied trope with a man who had fought against my country in the Great War.

He drilled me in the complicated grammar of the sacred writings: long and short vowels; open and closed syllables; soft and hard dots of emphasis; the reasons for the placement of primary and secondary accents; the meticulous rhythms and trills of the musical notations. To grind the grammar and the music into memory, I'd walk home from Mr. Zapiski singing into the icy winds of the winter, and in the darkness of my small room I'd repeat to myself rules of grammar and take apart and put together lengthy verses of sacred text. He taught me the music of the book written by the Creator God. I am not now a believer, but I was then, and felt certain that I was learning the music chanted by God Himself whenever He opened the pages of the sacred narrative. And the angels, too, used that melody each time they told that story to one another. So Mr. Zapiski informed me one evening. Sweetly the celestial choir sang the sacred trope, and the music ascended through all the heavens and reached to the seventh heaven wherein was the Throne of Glory on which sat the Creator God, and the Creator God would hear the chanting and be transported with joy, and the joy would overflow and drift downward from the Divine Presence, down like an invisible benevolent rain through all the lower heavens and the fiery stars to our troubled Earth, and brush humankind with its radiance, and for a time there would be peace in the world and an abundance of happiness.

Often, about halfway through our hour, he'd drop off into sleep. It was a strange and fearful thing to see: one moment he'd be wide awake, the next his head rolled forward onto his chest. He seemed then a helpless rag doll of a man. Wrinkled dark pants and jacket; stained white shirt, disheveled white beard; pale pockmarked features; the bad leg lying on top of the good one as if it needed more than the floor for support. Perhaps he slipped into a trance of some sort, the way his eyes were open to slits with only the whites showing; the occasional twitching of his face as he slept; and sometimes a low deep snoring. None of my classmates ever saw him like that; they studied with him only in the school, during recess or after classes, where he would never fall asleep. I was the only one he taught in his apartment, because of his friendship with my father.

The first time it happened I sat frightened until he woke. Then I realized he'd sleep about fifteen minutes each time. I began to use those minutes to browse through his books about the Great War.

Most were too difficult for me to understand. Some were in languages other than English and Yiddish and had horrendous pictures of blasted trees and fragments of human bodies and torn-up trenches and ravaged countrysides in which nothing remained except the sky. As a result, I began to have dreams of Mr. Zapiski and waves of faceless men climbing from their trenches and attacking over duckboards laid across knee-deep mud and machine guns rattling and cutting them down like scythes leveling fields of wheat and rye.

One day in January I asked my mother, "What happened to Mr. Zapiski during the war?"

She said, not looking up from the kitchen sink where she was peeling potatoes, "About such matters, you speak to your father."

"Can it happen to me if I fight in a war?"

"Pooh pooh pooh! Don't say such things. Go talk to your father."

I asked my father.

His angry response startled me. "You little snotnose, why do you keep poking into matters that are not your concern? Turn your curiosity to more important matters. Your business is to learn Torah."

Standing before Mr. Zapiski's door one night in early February, I set down the bag of food my mother had told me to take to him and wondered how he climbed all those stairs. He must exhaust himself. No wonder he slept during the trope lessons.

And indeed he fell asleep that night and I turned to his books and opened a volume of photographs on the war between Austria and Russia and was leafing through it when he woke suddenly from his trancelike state and without preliminaries proceeded to speak to a point in the air behind me. He said, speaking rapidly in Yiddish, "Hear me out on this, Victor. I want you to hear me out. Not everything that sounds like music is truly music." There was a wildness in his eyes, a hollowness to his voice, as if some unbridled creature were speaking from inside him. "The tyrant Phalaris roasted his prisoners in a huge bronze bull, in whose nostrils he had his servants place reeds in such a way that the prisoners' shrieks were transformed into music. The sounds came out as music, but were they indeed music?"

There was a pause, a resonating silence.

"What do you think of that, Victor?"

I sat stupefied.

"Victor, what do you think?" he asked again, staring into the air behind my head and speaking now in a reasonable tone that was somehow more frightening than the previous wildness.

I didn't know what to do or say and thought to get up and run from there, but just then his head dropped forward onto his chest, and after two or three deep snorting breaths he was again asleep.

Frightened and bewildered, I went quickly on tiptoe from the apartment, my ears reverberating with the imagined screams of those burning captives. I asked myself: Should I tell my father what had happened? I didn't want to embarrass Mr. Zapiski. Besides, it would make no difference, certainly the lessons would not come to an end merely because Mr. Zapiski had experienced a bad dream in my presence. Also, in truth, I rather liked the lessons, I savored being with Mr. Zapiski, I was as intrigued by his strange behavior as I was by his books on the Great War. Indeed, as I hurried past the brewery and under the trestle of the elevated train, massive and monstrous in the night, I realized that much of my revulsion about Mr. Zapiski had left me, and in its place had come an irresistible curiosity. Who was he? How could I find out more about him? And at that moment I sensed someone walking behind me, and I looked quickly around but saw no one.

At home that night I asked my father, "Was Mr. Zapiski a teacher in Europe?"

"In Europe Mr. Zapiski was both a teacher and a student."

"Where did he go to school?"

"In a university in Vienna."

"What did he study?"

"He studied history. Then history caught up with him. What did he teach you tonight?"

I told him.

"That was all he taught you?"

"He was tired and not feeling well."

My father, his face stiff, turned away.

Some days later I brought Mr. Zapiski a copy of my talk, which I had carefully researched and written over a period of three weeks. This, my first public address, I was to deliver before the assembled throng of celebrating relatives, friends, teachers, and classmates as an example of my maturity in years and proficiency in learning.

"I want us all to be proud of you," my mother had said, watching me labor over the talk. "That's all I ask."

I read the talk to Mr. Zapiski.

* * *

"Well, my dear Davita, I do hope I am not boring you. I must tell you that many of the details of this story have been entirely forgotten by me until now, hence the story may lack the refinement of narrative and no doubt has about it thus far some dull and trying moments. But please accept my assurance that you will be recompensed, if memory serves, by what is soon to follow. In the meantime, I must use your toilet. I shall be only a moment."

* * *

"Where was I? Ah, yes. The talk I had written and was now reading to Mr. Zapiski. Indeed, a refill on the coffee will be appreciated.

"First, three or four sentences by way of introduction.

"My *rite de passage* was to fall on the Saturday morning when the biblical portion that is read aloud from the sacred Scroll of the Law deals with the war waged by Amalek against the fleeing Israelite slaves. Joshua organized the Israelite troops and fought off the Amalekites, aided by

Moses, whose arms, raised heavenward, brought about the help of the Lord and spurred the Israelites on to victory.

"My little talk was about loyalty in war."

* * *

I sat sunk deep in the tattered easy chair and read in a shaking voice a brief essay, which—how astonishing!—I think I will now be able to recall in detail. I began by asking: Why do people wage war? Would people kill and let themselves be killed unless there was a very convincing reason for doing so? If conquest is the only reason for a war, conquest from which only the ruler stands to gain, then people should refuse to fight. If, however, a war is to be fought for the defense of one's family and property, then men should fight with all their heart and might. The war against the Amalekites was a war of defense. In such a war, *all* must participate; no one has the right to refrain from taking part. And the cowards and deserters, all who would benefit from the courage of the brave, they have no right to share in the victory, and should be punished. Deserters most especially should be punished, because they run away in the face of danger, they leave it to others to fight and perhaps die in their place, they are the lowest of men, they—

My little talk, I must tell you, contained a splendid array of proof texts from sources both sacred and secular, over which I had labored long and hard. But that was far as I got with it. For a sound had begun to emanate from Mr. Zapiski, a noise that sounded like *"What? What? What?"* in Yiddish, and I looked up and saw his normally pallid features had turned crimson, and a blood vessel had risen and lay like a vertical ridge along the center of his forehead.

"What are you saying?" he shouted.

I stared at him, mute and quivering.

"Who told you this? Surely not your father or mother!"

I hadn't the vaguest idea what he was talking about.

He leaned stiffly toward me and winced with pain as his hand inadvertently struck the knee of his right leg. The pain seemed to make him angrier still. I thought he might suffer a stroke and die of rage; I had heard about such things. He rubbed the knee, grasped the trouser with both hands, raised the leg so that it hung a moment suspended, lowered it onto the left leg, adjusted it. He took a deep tremulous breath.

"Why did you choose this subject, eh? Is this what you intend to tell the people who will come together to celebrate your entering into adulthood?

This? What do you know about it? Go fight in a war, God forbid, and then see what speeches you make. It isn't enough that your father suffered the way he did? Why must you now add to it with your cruel words?"

He fell silent, breathing heavily, glaring at me out of swollen eyes. He coughed and wiped his sweating face with a ragged handkerchief. The chair, the air, the room, the rage—I felt myself becoming entombed.

In a trembling voice I told him I did not understand what I had done wrong.

That seemed to infuriate him even more. "Don't play the ignorant innocent with me, you smart aleck! I know you. I see right through you. Nothing escapes you. You want to wage war against your father, do it another way. Erase those sentences from your talk!"

"Which sentences?"

"I told you not to play the dummy with me! You should know that I was once a candidate for a doctoral degree in a great European university."

"But I don't know which—"

"Read it quietly to yourself and then read it to me again!"

I stared at my notebook, swiftly searching through the talk. Which words was I to omit?

And here, Davita, we come to a moment of memory that is still unclear to me. Hastily scanning my words, I decided to drop all mention of desertion, and I cannot remember why I did that—perhaps because it was the only part of the talk that had come from my own being, everything else I'd borrowed from other sources.

In a quivering voice, I read the talk once again to Mr. Zapiski. It seemed a shadow of its former version, the heart gone from it. Mr. Zapiski listened intently. He took deep breaths, he grew calm, he wiped his face and lips, he nodded approval. Then he lit another cigarette with trembling fingers and ordered me to repeat by heart some matters of grammar—and promptly fell asleep.

I removed the cigarette from his fingers and stubbed it out in the ashtray on the end table where I left it. I had no stomach that night for books about war. Silently, I slipped from the apartment and started home in the winter night, and, as I hurried past the brewery, suddenly sensed alongside me a terrifying presence that set my knees shaking and prickled my skin, but, turning, saw only the vacant street and patches of snow, yellow-lit from the street lamps.

A night of dread and sleeplessness followed. I tossed, I turned. I stared wide-eyed into the darkness and heard Mr. Zapiski saying, "*What? What? What?*" I gazed out my window at the concrete backyard and saw Mr. Zapiski in its deepest shadows. Why had he become so incensed?

Had someone close to him deserted during the Great War? I'd read in one of his books that deserters, when apprehended, were executed. Perhaps *he* had deserted? Suppose—my agitated heart churned out the fearful possibilities—suppose he had bolted from his guard post in the trenches one night and my father had furtively gone after him and brought him back? Or maybe, just maybe, *it was my father who had deserted*, and Mr. Zapiski had forced *him* back—and on returning been badly wounded by an exploding shell? Would that account for his lost leg, the marks on his face, the scars on his head, his wretched health, his grown-old look?

And then a horrifying thought occurred to me. What if my father had indeed been a deserter? And what if the American government ever discovered that he'd fought on the enemy side and determined to send him back to his old country? Would he then be executed for desertion?

Fear-ridden days and nights followed. I grew irritable, couldn't eat, lost weight. My mother became concerned, kept glancing at me with worry in her eyes. I began to wonder if one day a newspaper headline might announce the presence in America of soldiers who had fought on the German side in the Great War. ENEMIES DISCOVERED IN OUR MIDST. Would the entire family be sent back? I found myself cringing at the sight of the newspapers on our kitchen table, dreaded looking at the headlines. I would not go into our kitchen or living room when I saw my father there reading his newspaper. Once I spotted a crumpled newspaper in our garbage can and thought I saw the words "Great War" in a headline and removed it with trembling hands and straightened it out on the table and saw with relief that it had nothing to do with the enemies of America but was about a statesman who was predicting another great war, one much more terrible than the Great War itself.

One evening during that awful time, I climbed the stairs to Mr. Zapiski's apartment, carrying the usual shopping bag of food, and found a note on the doorbell that read, "Benjamin, I am sick. The door is open. Please put the food in the icebox and return in two days."

Yielding to my diffident push, the door opened wide and I stepped inside.

How stifling the apartment was—a steamy inferno of radiator heat. The wooden floor of the hallway groaned; the linoleum wobbled and buckled. In the kitchen, food-encrusted pots and dishes cluttered the counter and filled the sink, and old newspapers lay on the table and chairs. Roaches careened crazily across the floor and walls and vanished into drawers and appliances. I imagined rats moving stealthily in the spaces between the walls.

I put the food into the icebox—a nearly vacant and malodorous white cavern—and turned to leave, when I heard a cry from beyond the portieres that separated the hallway from the rest of the apartment. Someone had called my name in a high-pitched voice I could not recognize.

I stood terrified.

The voice called to me again. "Benjamin, is that you?"

It was Mr. Zapiski.

"Yes."

"Come here and help me!"

I rushed through the hallway into the parlor. There, with windows sealed and shades drawn, the air was even more stifling than in the kitchen.

"Where are you?"

"I am in the bedroom."

I hurried across the parlor, bumping my knee painfully against an end table, and cautiously entered the bedroom.

It was a small room, with pale green walls. A yellowing shade covered the single window. The stagnant air carried scents of medicine and camphor. I saw an old wooden chair, a narrow bed, a worn carpet, an old bureau with a mirror that stood tilted to the right. The room in the mirror looked oddly distended, a grotesque fun-house reflection, walls bare of pictures. Mr. Zapiski lay in the bed beneath a shabby gray blanket, his tall skullcap on his head. On the night table next to the bed were some books and bottles of medication. He lay on a crumpled white pillow, looking forlorn and gasping for breath.

"Benjamin, be so good as to go to the medicine cabinet in the bathroom and bring me the bottle with the red label."

That I did quickly. With a shaking hand, he poured the liquid into a teaspoon, swallowed it down, and lay back on the pillow. I stood staring at him and found that I couldn't take my eyes from the space in the bed where his right leg should have been but which lay flat beneath the blanket alongside the rise of the left leg.

Some minutes passed and his breathing eased. I had in the meantime looked about the room and noticed at the side of the bed his wooden right leg and stared in fascination at the length of wood and the misshapen dark shoe attached to it.

"Benjamin."

I took my eyes from the leg on the floor.

"Tell your father that I fell in the snow and am hurt."

I nodded.

"Benjamin."

He was propping himself up with his arms. The empty space where his right leg should have been gave him the look of half a man.

"Be so good as to give me my leg."

I hesitated, trembling.

"It's on the floor next to the bed."

I bent and picked up the leg. An assemblage of wood, straps, grooves. Strangely cold to the touch despite the overheated room. And heavy, awkward. Holding it made my skin crawl.

He took the leg. Straps dangled awfully in the air.

"Now go home, Benjamin, and return in two days knowing backward and forward the rules I asked you to memorize."

I started for the bedroom door.

"Benjamin."

I stopped and turned. He was still sitting up, clutching the wooden leg with both hands.

"If there are any books you want to read, you may take them with you."

My face turned hot. I hurried through the apartment without taking any of his books and left the building. The night was bitter cold. As I passed under the trestle a train roared by overhead, its lights flickering and flashing through the darkness, and I thought I heard over the rhythmic click and clatter of its wheels a high-pitched wail like that of a child crying. But there was no one else in the street.

When I told my father that Mr. Zapiski was ill, he put on his overcoat and hat and rushed from the apartment.

And now for the conclusion. A grand success it turned out to be, my *rite de passage*. My mother, proud. My father, accepting as his due the congratulations of our clan. My siblings, jealous. My classmates, envious of my ease with text and talk. My teachers, all lavish with praise. Myself, a lightheaded turmoil of emotions: pride, joy, smugness, and exultation, as if victorious in—in what? Is this what it's like to be triumphant in war, I asked myself at one point that day, this climbing soaring surging explosion of emotion? Then what is it like to lose, to be among the permanently wounded, the hopelessly defeated?

As for Mr. Zapiski, he congratulated me, and that pleased me more than the praise of all the others. My anxiety about whose side he and my father had fought on during the Great War soon faded. My mother sent me to him regularly with packages of food, and sometimes my father handed me envelopes with money to give him; but we rarely talked. On occasion he'd offer me a book from his library, which I'd return unread. I had discovered other interests: sports, girls. My winter with Mr. Zapiski became an increasingly remote interlude. I had mastered a melody and a grammar that I now put to regular use, for my father insisted that I read periodically from the Scroll of Law during services in our little synagogue. I turned into an accomplished reader. People who babbled regularly during prayer would fall silent as I chanted. I became quite adept at dramatizing events like the Creation, the Flood, the binding of Isaac, the Exodus from Egypt. I developed a distinctive panache when it came to reading aloud the various wars fought by the Israelites during their desert wandering, and in particular the Song of the Sea, which celebrates the drowning of Pharaoh and his army as they pursued the Israelites across a body of water. Mr. Zapiski came over to me one day and thanked me for the way I had read the section on the war against the Amalekites. He looked pale, shaky. His eyes were moist. He seemed shabbier than ever.

And then one evening my father announced at our supper table that Mr. Zapiski was returning to Europe.

I was stunned.

Day after day, from the radio and the newspapers, all we heard from Europe was the lunacy of approaching war.

"Why?" I asked.

"He wishes to return to the history he left behind," said my father, with anger in his voice.

I stared at him in bewilderment.

My mother nodded sadly, as if she understood.

The next day I went to see Mr. Zapiski in his apartment.

About two years had passed since my last lesson. Nothing had changed inside those dim and airless rooms. The creaking linoleum, the worn furniture, the shabby rug, the shelves upon shelves of books about war. He welcomed me in his hoarse voice and brought me into the parlor and ordered me into the chair with the encompassing seat and protruding springs that I once again felt upon my rump and spine.

"Your mother did not give you anything for me?"

"My mother doesn't know I'm here."

He coughed. "Does your father know you are here?"

"No."

"What is the reason for the secrecy?"

"Is it true that you are going back to Europe?"

He shifted his right leg slightly. "And what business is that of yours?"

I said I was curious.

"Your father has already told you that I am going back. Why do you ask me if I am going back if you already know that I am going back?"

"I wanted to be sure."

"You wanted to be sure. Why is it important for you to be sure that I am returning to Europe? What do you care what happens to Isaac Zapiski?"

I mumbled a response I can no longer recall.

He was silent awhile. Then he coughed and said, "I see you in the synagogue and in your home, but we never talk. Tell me what you are doing."

"I go to school, I do sports."

"Your grades are good?"

"Pretty good."

"I'm sure they are. What sports do you like?"

"Swimming, running, basketball."

"What do you like to read?"

"Sherlock Holmes. Books about detectives and stuff."

"You no longer read my books about war."

"I don't like war and I don't like history."

He sighed. "This America of yours is not a country that values history. Where I was raised, history was the heart and marrow of a person. I am returning to the inside of myself the war forced me to leave behind."

I've cited precisely what he said: "I am returning to the inside of myself."

Then, abruptly, he asked me to leave. He was tired, his leg hurt, he had things to do the following day.

The night before his departure he huddled with my parents in their bedroom, and I heard their voices raised in anger. My mother said repeatedly, "Isaac, Isaac," and my father seemed beside himself, but they were speaking Polish and I understood nothing.

When they emerged from the bedroom, Mr. Zapiski patted my cheek with a trembling hand, mumbled some words of farewell, coughed, and hurried out, accompanied by my father, who was in the blackest of moods. My mother choked back tears.

The next day he sailed for Europe.

Weeks went by.

A letter arrived. Mr. Zapiski was in Vienna.

I asked my father, "Why is Mr. Zapiski in Vienna?"

"He is trying to get into the university."

"Will they accept him?"

"Of course not. Austria hates Jews more than Germany does, if such a thing is conceivable."

"Did you save Mr. Zapiski's life during the war?"

"Whatever gave you that idea?"

"Did he save yours?"

"He gave me his mask during a surprise gas attack and went to find one for himself but was a minute or two late."

"How did he lose his leg?"

"When I was carrying him to the aid station a shell landed near us."

"Was he deserting?"

"What?"

"Was he planning to desert?"

"Where do you get these crazy ideas?" But why the sudden nervous glance at the door and window? And the lowered voice like a reflex, and the abrupt, "Enough curiosity, go do your homework." He was silent for a moment, looking at me through narrowed eyes. "Listen, I'll tell you what I told you already. You can't begin to understand how war binds soldiers together. Only soldiers grasp that. May you never know from it."

"But why did he go back? Won't there be another war?"

"He would rather be there in war than here in peace. He went back to catch up to himself."

I didn't understand that but felt it might be best to stop asking questions about Mr. Zapiski. A few weeks later, my father announced during supper that the new store he had recently opened was doing well, and we would soon be moving to a larger apartment a few blocks away, in a house across from a park. In our language, "a few blocks away" often meant another world.

We would make good use of the added wall space in the new apartment, my father added.

"For what?" I asked.

"For the books."

"Which books?"

"Mr. Zapiski's books."

Mr. Zapiski, it turned out, had left his entire library in my father's care.

A month after we moved, Germany invaded Poland and the war broke out. We stopped receiving mail from Mr. Zapiski. As time went by and it became clear we might never hear from him again, he literally began to haunt me. Oh yes, in the old-fashioned way, like a ghost of sorts. I would think of him, see him quite clearly in a waking vision or a dream, wonder if he was still alive, ask myself if he would have appreciated the way I had read trope that morning in the synagogue. With the entire world now at war, I began to read some of the books he had given my father. How orderly they stood on the new shelves in the hallway and eastern wall of the living room in our sunlit apartment. My mother had dusted them; indeed, had insisted on doing the task herself, turning away the help offered by me and my sister. "Go, you do your homework, and I'll do this." She labored with light shining from her eyes and memories softening the lines on her face. And so, as I read the books, there was no dust in the bindings and the mustiness was gone. I read books in English and Yiddish, books about the causes, tactics, military operations and statistics of the Great War; books by and about generals, politicians, ordinary soldiers; books of memoirs and diaries. Why was I so captivated by those books? A youngster beguiled by the gallantry of war? A sudden necessary tethering to the trope teacher? Why? Crucial connections fail me here. There were two English books that I read absorbedly, though not with full understanding, during my last year in a Jewish parochial high school: *Anti-Semitism Yesterday and Tomorrow*, by Rabbi Lee J. Levinger, and *Anti-Semitism Throughout the Ages*, by Count Heinrich Coudenhove-Kalergi. In all my years with my parents, my teachers, my friends and the trope teacher, no one had ever really taught me about anti-Semitism, no one had sat me down and said: Listen, the world hates us because they say we killed their god; they say we are in league with the devil to destroy the Christian religion; they say we poisoned wells, we murdered Christian babies and used their blood to bake matzos, we loaned money to poor people at very high interest, we've been punished by God and made to wander eternally across the face of the earth.

In the book by the rabbi I read:

The German Jews considered themselves good Germans; they wanted nothing else; they volunteered for service in the World War, were deeply grateful and proud of their recently given civil rights. Of all the discriminations of the Nazi regime the one they resent most deeply is the exemption from the military draft, which converts them into second-class citizens.

In the book by the count I read:
For nearly twenty centuries the Jews have been disarmed and ever since they have not been the subjects of war but its objects. They can no longer

conquer through war, but suffer through it.

And I read:

For the sake of its faith the Jews have waged a world war against the whole of Europe for twenty centuries, and they have acquired the right to consider themselves as an heroic nation of the first rank. All just men are bound to admit this, for war and fight are two very different things. Besides, wars are not the only touchstones of bravery. To most men it will appear easier to go out to war than to cling to their convictions in front of the stake.

And I saw illustrations of Jews in the fifteenth century wearing Jew badges; a medieval ghetto set on fire by a mob; Jews before the tribunal of the Inquisition; a synagogue in Palestine looted by Arabs; a middle-aged, balding Jew forced to walk the streets of a Nazi city, wearing a sign that said *Ich bin Jude*; he looked a little like Mr. Zapiski. Was that the world to which Mr. Zapiski had returned? What a confusion rose in me upon reading those two books! And immediately upon graduating from high school, I enlisted in the army. Oh yes, I could have applied to a rabbinical school and received a draft deferment; or, failing that, waited to be drafted; it might have given me added months with my family. But I was a little berserk by then, decidedly out of control, in flaring rebellion against my parochial-school world, which I felt stifling me, and bloated with manly visions of fighting the armies of Hitler. And also, somewhere along the margin of my thoughts and feelings, was the insane notion that in Europe I might meet Mr. Zapiski! My decision to enlist in the army was met with grim and silent resignation from my father and a cry of dread from my mother. And from then on Mr. Zapiski became a sort of talisman to me—a creature of magic and enchantment. But that, Davita, is another story. Thank you for the coffee and doughnuts. I must now bid you goodnight and look in upon my wife.

* * *

Benjamin Walter returned home, climbed the stairs, and found his wife asleep. She awakened some time later, sweating and shivering, and he tended to her.

When the coughing subsided, she could speak again. "Is it very difficult for you, Benjamin?"

"I do love you, Evelyn."

"If things become very bad—"

"My darling—"

"—you should get a night nurse."

"Things need not become bad for quite a while. You'll come round this time as you did before."

"But if things do, Benjamin."

"You are going on about it a bit much, my dear."

"Am I? All right. My mind keeps jumping back and forth. Earlier, I was remembering our week in Prague."

"Isn't it strenuous for you to talk?"

"Yes. But I'll talk anyway. How remarkable."

"What?"

"I remember those Peruvian street musicians in front of our hotel on the square."

"Oh yes, those musicians."

"Their red headbands and red and black ponchos and their guitars and little drums and odd wind instruments and the Indian music they played."

"They kept us awake until three in the morning."

"And remember those booths selling Russian military caps and medals? Such an inglorious end to that awful empire."

"Perhaps you shouldn't talk, my dear."

"Wasn't it in that lovely restaurant, not far from the little house where Kafka once lived, that I was terribly ill for the first time?"

"You're tiring yourself."

"Was I coughing then?"

"The coughing began in Amsterdam."

"Those Prague doctors hadn't a clue as to what was the matter, did they? The thrush on my tongue, the seborrhea in my eyebrows. Imagine, all of them leaving the hospital at one o'clock in the afternoon and going home for the day, and locking the patients in their rooms. A quite inefficient system, don't you think? One wonders what they saw in it for so many years."

"Countries get sidetracked, just as people do."

"I suppose. Do you think you might wipe my face?"

"Of course."

She said, after a brief while, "I find that I miss the children."

"Shall I ask them to come? They'll come immediately."

"Do you want them to?"

"I think not."

"You are in no mood for sentimentality. Am I right, Benjamin?"

"I don't want to share you with anyone else now."

"In some ways, you are more English than I am. Or at least you play at it well."

He was quiet.

She said, "How my mind jumps about. Do you know what I'm remembering? The song I made up and sang to you the second or third night you asked me out."

She sang weakly to a familiar tune:

"Oh, when you Yanks came marching in,
You mucked our language, drank our gin;
You wooed our girls, and all the while
You gave your lives for the English isle."

He listened and was quiet. And then said, "You were the best thing that happened to me in the army. You were my very dearest friend."

She murmured, "I would so very much like to complete my book on Virginia Woolf. Do you think I might live long enough to accomplish that? Do leave me alone now, Benjamin. I am so bloody, bloody tired."

And she closed her eyes.

Now he sat gazing out his study window at I. D. Chandal, who was at a window of her kitchen, wearing a pale blue housecoat and half-moon eyeglasses. She sat at a table, writing absorbedly and looking preposterously bloated, the yellow light falling cruelly upon her pudgy features and gray hair. A trick of the light? Fatigue? The medication affecting my vision?

After a long moment he felt himself a voyeur and looked away.

The next morning he emerged from the house and walked to the edge of the woods where he gazed up into the branches and leaves of the huge oak: green and blue shadows and the golden wash of early sunlight and the stunned faltering aftermath of a serious wounding. Lightning, he remembered, traveled at one-third the speed of light; its force at the point of impact quite unimaginable. The lightning bolt had struck the oak, seared the crown, spiraled downward along the contour of the trunk, and cut deeply into the bark, sending chips and huge slabs of wood flying in all directions. He shivered, having suddenly remembered a battlefield bombardment. But the smell was different here.

He turned away.

I. D. Chandal stood near her newly turned patch of soil, at a small bed of fire thorns, trowel in hand, watching him. She wore her tight jeans and jersey. Small, trim, clear-eyed, cheerful.

"Quite a night in my kitchen, Benjamin."

"The coffee and doughnuts were splendid."

"You'll finish telling me your story?"

"Oh yes."

"Then I'll get us some more doughnuts for tonight."

Her lips shaped a buoyant smile. She looked at the oak. "You'll need a tree surgeon. I know someone."

"Please ask him to clear away the debris but do nothing to the tree until I talk to him. Oh yes, and ask him to check the woods for a ram."

She stood watching as he went to the garage and slid his lean frame into the old Saab, started the engine, and backed slowly down the driveway. Just before his rear tires reached the street he caught a glimpse of her through his front window, standing on the lawn and staring up at the stricken tree, and was chilled by the look of rage he saw on her face. A fury so palpable he thought he heard her shouting. Angry at whom? At what? A very strange woman. Standing there at the edge of the woods with a trowel in her hand, and apparently screaming. Perhaps calling for the ram?

THREE

That night his wife woke and he calmed her and brought her a fresh nightgown and changed her pillowcase and sheets. Later he sat working on his memoirs and from time to time turned to gaze at I. D. Chandal in a second-floor window of the Tudor. An odd-looking creature when she sits writing. Some kind of biological anomaly? An alteration in her body chemistry? Absurd! More likely a poorly manufactured windowpane.

In the morning he left the house and, striding past the stricken oak, entered the woods. Two or three times a week he took a walk through the woods to the cemetery. Cool bluish pools of shade that morning; a cloying moisture in the air; the crowns kindled to golden light by the sun. East of the woods lay the cemetery, stately acres of green meadow rising gracefully to a mound at the far end, on which had been built the mausoleum of a noted local family, one of whose sons, William Henry Bullock, had perished at Winfrey Field in the Battle of Chickamauga during the Civil War, and another, Robert William Bullock, in the Ardennes Forest during the last German offensive of the Second World War; the garrulous real-estate agent had delivered the somber details in response to Benjamin Walter's probing. Near the edge of the cemetery, he stopped and stood gazing at the length of sunlit meadow. Insect life in the air and the rich scent of warming grass. Rows of stones: many old, weathered, leaning; others polished, straight, names and dates still clear. Generations of life, casualties of battles fought as far back as the Revolutionary War, and many children; but most appeared to have lived the conventional span of years. He returned after a while, walking slowly through sun-spangled shade along the leafy, unexhausted earth and the tangled roots. How calming, these woods; trees living and dying as nature intended.

Later that morning in the university he sat in his office reading the manuscript of the memoirs. After a while he rang for his secretary. She stood before him, a dark-haired woman in her early forties. He handed her the manuscript, wishing to be rid of it for a time.

"It's an early draft of the first chapter. You may run into some blurry patches here and there."

"Professor Walter, have I ever had any trouble reading your handwriting?"

After she left he sat gazing out the window at the trees. There was a knock on the door.

A young man stood uneasily in the doorway, dressed in a dark suit, a white shirt, a dark tie. Handsome and muscular; long blond hair gathered in a ponytail, the lobe of one ear ornamented with a gold ring. He remained in the doorway, awkward and hesitant, then stepped into the office and closed the door.

"I just got back," he said in a low voice.

"I beg your pardon?"

"The funeral was yesterday."

Benjamin Walter suddenly remembered: Yale. Someone sick. "My sympathies."

The young man jammed his hands into the pockets of his trousers, hunched his shoulders. "I can't believe he's dead."

"I'm very sorry."

"He used to get depressed. They'd give him pills so he could stay level, but it made him sleepy and he couldn't do his work. Whenever he went off the pills he just, like, well, folded up into himself. He was a really great guy, good family, never did drugs, worried about AIDS, wouldn't screw around, just me and him, O.K.? And two days ago he flew back home, walked over to the bridge near his house, and stepped off. Two women saw him. He climbed up on the rail and just stepped off."

A suicide, thought Benjamin Walter, and suddenly recalled his years at Oxford, where one student jumped out of a fourth-floor window and another took cyanide crystals. He'd read Dante one spring and remembered now the passage on the Seventh Circle of Hell. The Woods of the Suicides. Their souls encased in the thorny trees; the leaves being devoured by the frightful Harpies. As the Harpies ate, blood poured out of the suicides' wounds, which enabled the souls in the trees to speak. The souls within the trees speaking only as the blood of the suicides gushed forth! Like Mr. Zapiski's shrill tale of the treatment of prisoners by the tyrant Phalaris: roasting them alive inside that huge bronze bull. The screams of the prisoners turning to music; the blood of the suicides turning to speech. Connections?

Listen to him, he seems unable to stop talking, this sad young man.

"Once I found him in his room with a loaded gun between his legs. His father's gun. I talked him into putting it away and didn't tell anyone about it. I'd go up to Yale some weekends and we'd hang out, and he'd ask me to watch out for him if he ever had too much to drink. The signal that he was drunk was when he started to sing, 'Whiskey after beer, have no fear. Beer after whiskey, mighty risky.' Sometimes when he'd come out of one of his depressions, he'd think he could dodge bullets or fly. I had to watch him real close then. I loved him, and he just walked off the bridge, like he thought he could fly."

Benjamin Walter felt pain in his fingers and saw himself tumbling head over heels toward a forest very far below. Tall trees waiting.

"You know, this is the third person I've gone to high school with who's committed suicide. Something out there is killing my friends."

"There are people here who can help you."

He shuffled his feet, blinked. "I'm ready for the exam."

"I beg your pardon?"

"You said you'd give me a makeup exam."

"Perhaps you should wait a day or two."

The young man removed his hands from his pockets and fixed his eyes upon a point behind the head of Benjamin Walter. "Allan, you son of a bitch!" he suddenly roared. "You were my best friend! Why'd you do that? You said you'd never do that!" His shouted words reverberated inside the office. He choked back a cry. "Sorry, sorry, it's making me a little crazy."

He turned and strode from the room, closing the door.

Benjamin Walter stood staring at the door. He thrust his hands under his armpits to still their trembling. Assaulted by a rush of images: Evelyn in her bed and I. D. Chandal at the window and the newly turned earth of the garden and the scarred oak and the eerie sounds of voices from afar and a uniformed man lunging at him with a bayonet. A shadow fell across the window. When he looked he saw only the cool blue sky and sunlight on the spring trees.

* * *

He lunched with Robert Helman in a small second-floor restaurant near the university, staring without appetite at the feta cheese in his Greek salad. Robert Helman, in a gray tweed jacket, red bow tie, and dark rumpled slacks, sat over his vegetable soup, eating absorbedly, looking fretful and displeased.

"You seem tired, Benjamin. Is it Evelyn?"

"Actually, I expect Evelyn will be on her feet again soon. Tell me, have you ever read anything by the fiction writer I. D. Chandal?"

"I don't read fiction. I have no patience with plots and narratives."

"I'm intrigued by the clever ways she connects things."

"No doubt a nineteenth-century pen working on twentieth-century horrors."

"Why are you so testy today, Robert?"

"I have a nineteenth-century story for you, Benjamin."

"Not especially interested."

"It was told to me by a boy in Theresienstadt."

"Theresienstadt?"

"I was teaching him the section in the Torah about the binding of Isaac, so he could read it in celebration of his bar mitzvah."

"Excuse me, you taught trope in Theresienstadt?"

"Why are you surprised?"

"I didn't know."

"I never told you, so you didn't know. I was sixteen at the time. In Theresienstadt there were all kinds of classes during the day, and concerts, operas, lectures, and cabarets at night. Hunger, dysentery, disease, and culture. And in the early mornings—transports to Auschwitz. That's how we lived. Anyway, I was teaching this boy, I didn't even know his name at first, he came to me one day and said he'd heard I knew trope, would I teach him—I can see him clearly, pale, thin like a stick, big dark eyes—he wanted to learn the section about the binding of

Isaac so he could read it to his family on his bar mitzvah, and I said I would be happy to teach him, so we found a corner somewhere under a staircase and I was teaching him the section sentence by sentence, he had a sweet tenor voice, not loud, with a beautiful vibrato. One day he broke into tears. We were crouched under the stairs, I remember there was a children's art class nearby, and four people were sitting on the stairs discussing Mann's *The Magic Mountain*, and the boy was crying uncontrollably. I asked him why he was crying, and he said he remembered a story his Uncle Jakob had once told him about the ram."

"The what?"

"The animal sacrificed in place of Isaac. The ram."

Walter Benjamin had the distinct sensation that someone had placed heavy hands upon his shoulders and was propelling him this way and that.

"I asked him what his uncle had told him that could make him cry so, and he said, 'The ram was from the heavenly Garden of Eden, a beautiful animal, golden skin, magnificent head. Uncle Jakob said that just as there was a Garden of Eden in this world, so is there one in heaven, where angels and animals live in peace, and that day all in the Garden were watching Abraham binding Isaac to the killing place on earth, it was as if the future depended on the events of the next moment—surely all creation would be transformed with the death of Isaac and the end of the Jewish people—and suddenly the ram pleaded to take Isaac's place. But the ram was beloved by the angels, who refused to let it go, and the ram cried out, "The future must be saved!" and in a single leap it bounded from the Garden and vaulted off a bridge of stars and hurtled through space to the mountaintop near Abraham, and called to him in a human voice not to slaughter his son. Three angels flew after the ram to bring it back, but the ram deliberately entangled its horns in a thicket and they couldn't release it, and it called again to Abraham, who unbound Isaac and managed to free the horns and sacrificed the ram in his stead.'"

"The boy was crying for the ram?"

"And because he thought that *he* was the ram."

"He?"

"He, we, all of us were the ram."

"Where did he get such an idea?"

"He was a very clever boy."

"If all of you were the ram, who was Isaac?"

"I asked him that."

"And he said?"

"The civilized people of the world."

"He said that?"

"I told you, he was a very clever boy."

"And who was Abraham?"

"I asked him that, too."

"And?"

"For a long time he wouldn't answer. When I asked him again, he said, 'Maybe the ones who are holding the knife.'"

After a moment, Benjamin Walter said, "What happened to the boy?"

"He read splendidly for his bar mitzvah and gave a talk describing the ram, its beauty and wisdom, its self-sacrifice to save the future of creation. A crowded room, a clandestine gathering. Everyone cried. Four days later, he was shipped to Auschwitz, where they killed him right away. There you have it, Benjamin. The sacrifice of the ram. A nineteenth-century story. Connections, yes?"

"It explains nothing."

"Every story is some kind of explanation, which explains why I dislike stories and do not read I. D. Chandal. I became a historian so I would not have to explain anything, only recount the evidence, the facts." He looked around. "Where is our waiter? I'm going to have to leave you, Benjamin, unless you've finished eating."

"I'll take care of the check."

"No, let me."

"Why are you so angry today, Robert?"

"I have a meeting with the provost about the historian whom Fox wants to bring in."

"Oh yes, the language-deprived woman."

"I will tell the provost that if he and Fox intend to make her an offer, I intend to make a telephone call."

"To whom?"

"To the one who funded the chair and has in mind the funding of another."

"You know him?"

"We were in the war together."

"What do you mean? I thought—"

"In the same barracks in Auschwitz. I saved his life when they herded us through the woods ahead of the Russian army."

Distinctly, someone held Benjamin Walter by the shoulders and was pushing him steadily backward into a landscape thickly befouled with death. How his arms and legs ached.

"Life connects us, Benjamin, not artifice. Ah, here's our waiter."

* * *

The driveway had been cleared: no trace of the splinters and the fallen limb. He parked the Saab and walked on painful legs to the oak. The spiraling scar seemed inconsequential in the late-afternoon sunlight. Surely the lightning-wounded wood would soon dry, scab, heal.

How still the street was, the air calm, the woods serene. I. D. Chandal was nowhere to be seen. The length of soil she had cleared from the lawn lay planted with infant mistflower, goldenrod, coleus, impatiens. At the end of the garden, where it approached the woods, she had rooted a bush with strikingly twisted branches. What a day's work she had put in!

Inside the kitchen the nurse was preparing a clear broth for Evelyn. His wife was so much better today, thank the Lord, the nurse said. Her color was greatly improved, her strength returning. The tree man had been there earlier, and would the professor believe what he'd told her? The oak tree had taken the lightning bolt meant for the house. Yes, that's what he'd said, those very words. The mysterious ways of the Lord. Now she would bring the broth to his wife and then give her the sleeping medication, it was good for her to sleep long and deep. Did the professor need anything? Benjamin Walter said he would take the broth to his wife and spend a bit of time with her. He went upstairs and found Evelyn awake and sitting up in bed.

"It appears you'll be able to finish your Virginia Woolf after all."

She began to cry and he comforted her and fed her the broth and waited until she was asleep and the nurse had gone. He ate some chicken in the kitchen and went back upstairs. From the window of his study he looked out at the Tudor and saw it was dark. He had forgotten to take his medication and his arms ached painfully. Downing the pills in the bathroom, he gazed upon himself in the medicine-chest mirror and saw eyes that brimmed with memory.

Back in his study he sat at his desk, apprehensively reading the pages typed by his secretary. How very sad, the story of Mr. Zapiski, she'd commented upon returning the manuscript. She'd no idea Professor Walter came from such a background.

Cool dry night air blew through the open window. The Tudor was strangely dark. Where had she gone? The clock on the wall above the framed fragments of headline read close to eight. He stared at the headline.

M RI NS TACK B TWE SE D AR ONNE OREST

A different time, a different war. His father's and Mr. Zapiski's war. Each generation and its own conflagration. But why, really, had he framed and hung those headlines? A connection between his war and theirs?

He would need to write the chapter about his war. But as much as the first chapter had resisted being written by him, he himself now resisted writing the second. The obstacle was not a paucity of memory, but a surfeit. Memory, once begun, swelling to a detonation, a blazing eruption. Do I need to do this? Weary, weary. Fingers in pain. Drop it. An act of hubris, these memoirs. Give yourself some well-earned years of rest. Attend to Evelyn. Put the deathwork aside.

The light came on in the kitchen of the Tudor. He closed the window and in the very next instant, it seemed to him, was standing at her door, she in tight jeans and jersey. He gazed at her openly and without shame as she swung the door wide and stepped back.

"I saw your light."

"Please come in."

"I'm not interrupting?"

"No, no."

"I noticed you were busy with your garden today."

"Isn't it pretty? Especially the mulberry bush. Watch how quickly it grows. Its leaves turn a marvelous golden color in the fall."

They entered the kitchen. For some reason, he expected it to be different this time. But nothing had changed. He saw the same bleak yellow light; cherry-wood cabinets; 1950s stove, sink, and refrigerator; reddish floor tiles; wooden table and chairs; light-green paint and bare walls; and piles of newspapers on the table.

"Coffee? Doughnuts?"

"Thank you."

"How is your wife?"

"Much improved."

"That's wonderful news, Benjamin. And how are you?"

"Tired, achy, struggling with the memoirs."

"Too many memories or too few?"

"Far too many, tumbling over each other, difficult to sort out."

"How fortunate for you! The floodgates have been opened. Let it all pour through."

"Not so easy to do, I'm afraid. I've begun to doubt the entire effort."

"Doubt? What do you mean, doubt?"

"I'm not sure of its worth."

"What are you saying, Benjamin? You want *sure?* Go to your tax collector, get hit by lightning, that's sure."

"I didn't bargain on it being so—disquieting."

"You want memory *and* comfort?"

"Having frequent nightmares. Bits and pieces of memory skittering about like the squirrels on my roof even when I'm driving. Cannot talk to Evelyn, of course."

"Why don't you talk to *me*, Benjamin? Who can better appreciate a story?"

Her presence across the table—intoxicating. Dark eyes, oval-shaped features, high cheekbones. No makeup. Her face without a wrinkle. How does she manage that? And alluring breasts. An image of his hands cupping her breasts, fingers caressing the nipples.

She sipped coffee, studied him over the rim of her cup. "Well, Benjamin, are you going to tell me your story?"

* * *

Do you know about the final offensive of the German army against the Allies in the Ardennes Forest? It began in early December 1944. At first, thousands of our men deserted, and by the time it ended eighty thousand were dead. In January, of the thirty-six men originally in my platoon, four were left.

We all did odd things to stay sane and alive. We talked to photographs of our fathers and mothers and sweethearts and wives and children. We kissed crucifixes and Stars of David. We made vows. The second day of the Ardennes offensive Mr. Zapiski suddenly appeared beside me. Dark suit and hat and tie. Not an image in my head but actually there. I heard his raspy voice and smelled his cigarette breath. How I welcomed him! I was overjoyed. He walked with me and slept with me. He would chant the trope of passages from the Scroll of the Law, and I would quietly chant along with him. In fire fights he would tell me clearly when to zig to the right and when to zag to the left, when to lie prone, when to jump up. Whenever we were being shelled, he would show me which tree to get behind and where to dig my hole. He would run alongside me, holding on to his dark hat. Strangely, his wooden leg seemed not to encumber him. He kept me alive through that terrible time. The Germans hacked us to pieces in the forests, but finally we pushed them back and straightened the line. By the end of that winter, we were moving forward again.

One morning we were reconnoitering through some woods with five or six tanks, all that remained of a battalion. A chill morning and a gray-white dawn, with ground mist covering the roots and curling up around the tree trunks. Suddenly the Germans started to pound us with artillery and tank fire. The proximity shells were exploding on contact with the treetops, and the coniferous trees and hardwoods were falling all over us, showering us with jagged splinters, and one of the guys near me caught a piece of wood in his neck, like an old-fashioned arrow. I distinctly heard Mr. Zapiski tell me to crouch behind a tree and fire into the underbrush up ahead, which I immediately proceeded to do, though I saw no enemy. Suddenly a soldier in a green uniform and helmet emerged from the underbrush, bleeding from a wound and lunging at me with his rifle and bayonet. I shot him in the face and stood near him, vomiting. Our tanks were returning fire. It went on for a few more minutes. And then it grew very quiet. I looked around and trembled. Mr. Zapiski was gone.

The infantry was ordered to advance ahead of the tanks. We moved forward through the woods, our squad in two fire teams, advancing and covering. The ground mist was absorbing the smells of the tank exhausts, which intensified the other smells: cordite and moist earth and leaking sap and newly shattered trees. My squad had just leapfrogged forward and I thought I saw something moving up ahead, but it was only the mist eddying around the shredded fragments of a tree trunk.

Then we were out of the woods and in a meadow. The mist was thinner and a breeze had risen and suddenly there was a different smell in the air, and we stopped.

The smell was like nothing I had ever experienced before—not like the charred-wood and broken-stone odors of bombed-out towns and villages, or the blood-and-gunpowder stink of a field after a fire fight, or the sweaty stench of combat soldiers. It was a pungent, acrid, throat-tightening odor, and it was up ahead and moving toward us.

Then the whole forward line stopped, and we could hear the tanks behind us stopping, too.

Up front, the lieutenant was in a crouching position with his binoculars to his eyes, and behind us the tank commanders were searching through the mist with their periscopes.

And then the order came down to hold our fire. I thought I saw something moving through the mist.

The lieutenant put down his binoculars and stood up. Something moved past him. Perhaps "moved" is not quite the proper word. Something shuffled and scraped past him, a shadow of some sort. Then another shadow. A host of shadows came through the mist, some crawling on their hands and knees. They were about twenty-five yards away, and they kept coming.

The first thing we noticed was their ghastly emaciation. Then we saw their wide and dark eyes. And then we saw that they had no teeth, only rotting stumps.

Two of them were advancing directly toward my squad. I heard voices, but couldn't make out what they were saying. They kept on moving toward us and one of them stopped about three feet from me—a grotesque figure of a man; the stench that rose from him!—and he reached out and grabbed hold of my arm, and croaked at me, "*Warum?*"—and my blood ran cold. He said again in Yiddish, "*Warum?*"; and added in Yiddish, "Why did you take so long?"; and again, "Why? Why?"—and I gaped at him in horror and pulled my arm away, and he went shuffling and stumbling off toward the woods. There must have been about thirty or forty of them; they all disappeared into the woods. Later I found out that most of them had traveled laterally and died in the woods; only about a half-dozen made it to the other side.

We were ordered to move on. Whoever those apparitions had been, they were not our problem. We were merely infantry, ground-pounders; as far as we were concerned, those people were only a piece of information: there was something up ahead we had to watch out for.

The ground mist soon lifted. We advanced toward a slight rise. Behind us came our tanks. There was not an enemy soldier in sight. Then we spotted smoke beyond the rise.

When we got to the rise we saw some sort of encampment about a mile away: tall fences and low buildings and guard towers with machineguns. We advanced toward it slowly and could smell it, and most of us gagged and some vomited as we went along.

From a distance we could see that the gates were open. We leapfrogged, doing reconnaissance by fire, toward the guard towers. It turned out they were deserted. Bodies lay on the perimeter fence. We charged through the gates.

Half-human, ghoulish creatures stood near the buildings, staring at us as we entered. They seemed not to know what to do or say. It had rained recently; the ground was a quagmire. There were hard narrow paths through the mud, and duckboards had been laid down, and we deployed rapidly.

The stench was horrendous: the foulest of pigsties; an open cesspool of reeking excrement. Hot, thick, pungent. A putrid, cloying, acidic smell that seemed to coat our palates and throats. The camp was about a half-mile long by a half-mile wide. We went past squalid buildings that looked to be barracks, and then a broad open space, and an inner encampment of well-kept buildings, and a brick building with a chimney that turned out to be a crematorium, and beyond that we came upon the most heart-numbing sight I have ever witnessed: a vast graveyard: trenches upon trenches of putrefying whitish bodies stacked one on top of the other like wood.

And there I found Mr. Zapiski.

He lay half-covered with earth and quicklime in a trench in the mass cemetery; and facedown on the ground, reeking and begrimed, alongside a duckboard; and rotting into the mud near the fence, decaying in his urine and excrement; and among the murmuring phantoms we found in the barracks who gaped at us when we entered and began a low keening when we told them we were Americans, one of them crying out in a broken voice, "Why did you take so long to get here?"

"*Warum?*" I heard him say. And again, "*Warum?*"

The lieutenant asked them, "Where are the guards?"

They did not understand him.

I translated his question into Yiddish.

They stared at me, stunned. A soldier with a weapon, in an American uniform, speaking Yiddish!

"Most ran away," one answered. "A few are still in those houses." He pointed toward the rear of the camp.

The lieutenant sent our squad over to secure the houses.

Two of the houses were empty. We found six guards inside the third, all drunk, their holsters empty, but still wearing their helmets.

The sergeant asked them, "Where are the others?"

They stared at him, muttering in German.

"You fucking bastards," the sergeant said. "Where are the others?"

"Where are the others?" I said to them in Yiddish.

One of them, a corporal, stiffened and looked at me.

"Where are the others?" I asked again.

He said, drunk and sullen, "They took the vehicles and ran off. There wasn't enough transport for all of us."

"He says they took off and left them behind," I said to the sergeant.

"Tell him if he's lying I'll have his ass," the sergeant said.

"If you are lying we will kill you," I said.

The corporal trembled. "It is the truth."

"He says it's the truth."

One of the guards, a tall heavy-shouldered man with a jutting lower jaw and a pockmarked face, suddenly said, "What kind of German do you speak?"

"New York German."

"That's not German."

"*Warum?* Is that O.K. German?"

"You are not speaking German."

"What's going on?" the sergeant said.

"Go fuck yourself, you piece of shit," I said to the guard. "Is that good enough German for you?"

He muttered something, his fingers twitching.

"I am one of those you were killing!" I suddenly shouted.

He stiffened. His face grew red. A Jew shouting at him! He reached for his empty holster.

Absently, as if in a dream, I heard scurrying sounds and shouts.

An M1 Garand rifle is a semiautomatic weapon, with eight bullets in a clip. The rounds have a muzzle velocity of 2800 feet per second, and an impact velocity of one and one-half foot-tons per square inch. That amounts to ten to fifteen tons of pressure at the point of impact.

I did not have to raise my weapon but simply pointed it at him.

I fired twice. Both bullets hit him in the chest. The second must have struck bone; he was lifted about six inches off his feet and thrown against the wall behind him and fell dead. On the wall were blood and bone from the exit wounds.

There had been only two rounds left in my clip. It had ejected with its characteristic clink. I shoved another clip in.

"Was that good German?"

The other guards shrank back.

Faintly, through the pounding in my head, I heard the sergeant say, "Cease fire!"

I turned the weapon upon the cringing guards.

The sergeant said, "As you were, soldier!"

I pointed the weapon downward.

The sergeant said, "What the fuck was that all about?"

"He reached for his pistol."

"What pistol?"

"His holster. And he was wearing his helmet." I turned to the guards and asked in Yiddish, "Are there more camps like this?"

They glanced at each another.

"I asked them if there were more camps like this," I said to the sergeant.

"Jesus, Mary, and Joseph," the sergeant murmured.

He ordered me outside.

I walked around the camp. Everywhere I went I saw Mr. Zapiski, dead and dead and dead in the vile exhausted earth.

The sergeant, reporting the incident to the lieutenant, made a point of the German's threatening gesture and the fact that they hadn't fully surrendered because they were still wearing their helmets, and the lieutenant determined that my reaction was justified, and the matter was dropped.

Ten days later, I came down with a bad case of diarrhea. Within twenty-four hours I was burning with fever. Terrible hallucinations accompanied the fever: lights kept flashing on inside my head, illuminating frightful scenes: I was shooting the German guard over and over again; then I was killing the other guards; then I was running through the camp chanting at the top of my lungs the trope to the Biblical account about the attack of the Amalekites, and the melody drifted through the meadows along which we had advanced; it penetrated the ruined woods, and there the human shadow who had grabbed my arm heard it and threw back his head as he walked shuffling and staggering and began to chant it too in his croaky voice, sounding precisely like Mr. Zapiski, and he stumbled against a shell-blasted tree and the tree opened itself to him and he vanished inside.

It turned out that I had contracted typhus.

From the field hospital I was evacuated to an American hospital in England, where I lay ill a long time. Then I was sent for convalescence to a place in the English countryside. I remember sleeping a great deal and being fed and waking once after a bad dream about Mr. Zapiski and seeing a lovely face gazing down at me with profoundly earnest concern. The face of Mr. Zapiski slowly dissolved and the face of a young English nurse took its place, creamy white skin, pink islands on her cheeks, no makeup, straight nose, full lips, and sad gray eyes. In time I discovered the reason for her sadness: she had lost her fiancé during the Ardennes offensive. She was of the English aristocracy, her family going back centuries. I had lost my trope teacher and fell in love with her; she had lost her fiancé and fell in love with me. Both of us were sick to death of the worlds from which we had come, where disgrace seemed to stare at us from nearly every human face, and so we made our own new creation. I crossed the threshold of my young life; the man deserted the boy. I did not return home, and no doubt broke my parents' hearts. I married in England, took my degrees in England. Quite trying at times, those postwar years, everything scarce and no true acceptance of me by her family—but how happy we were! I did not return to America for the funerals of my parents, who had disowned me, had actually sat in

77

mourning over me and recited the Mourner's Kaddish, because Evelyn would not think of converting out of the Church of England. Finally, I returned to America to teach, and discovered, during a telephone conversation with my sister, that my father had given Mr. Zapiski's library to a local high school. I have no idea what the school did with the many Yiddish, German, and French books. My brother has in his possession Mr. Zapiski's Bible, the one from which he taught me the trope. He intends to use it, he says, when he teaches his two sons the trope.

There you have it, Davita. My narrative.

* * *

A silence followed. Benjamin Walter nibbled at a doughnut, sipped coffee.

"No comments?"

"I'm a little breathless, Benjamin. That's a knockout story."

"May I use your bathroom? Among the many things ailing me these days is a swollen prostate."

He returned to the kitchen some minutes later to find her at the window looking out at the woods.

"Your story will keep me awake tonight, Benjamin."

"My apologies."

"No, no. Stories that keep me awake are my life's blood."

"I should go back."

"Did you really forget about your Mr. Zapiski?"

"Oh yes. Entirely."

"And now you'll be able to sail right through to the end."

"I believe I know the end. It was the beginning I couldn't write."

"The story you just told me is part of your beginning?"

"It is the myself that predates what I am now. And having recalled Mr. Zapiski for my memoirs, it is my intention to put him out of mind again as quickly as possible."

She was still looking out the window. "A pity."

"Mr. Zapiski? An antique, a disgrace. He should never have gone back to Europe."

She pointed out the window. "I meant the tree."

"The oak?"

"It will have to be taken down."

"The oak will have to be taken down?"

"It will be dead in two or three years. The tree surgeon said the lightning seared through it, crown, core, and root."

Frightful images of broken trees, shattered woods. "How very sad."

"Benjamin, did you leave the lights on in your study?"

"I don't recall."

"There's no one in your house?"

"Except my wife."

"I thought I saw someone in your study."

"Not likely."

"I look forward to meeting your wife after her recovery."

"I'll tell her. But there's no chance of full recovery."

"I'm sorry to hear that, Benjamin. Is it cancer?"

"No, it is, I regret to say, Auto Immune Deficiency Syndrome, from tainted blood she received some years ago during a surgical procedure. We take it a crisis at a time."

"I'm truly sorry to hear that."

"Yes, well, we rarely get to choose our own destiny, though this borders a bit on the absurd. I should go."

"Come back any time for coffee and doughnuts, Benjamin. An open invitation. You needn't bring more stories."

"It occurs to me, Davita, that our ram has not appeared."

"But you say your wife is better."

"The future, as I told you, is bleak."

"A ram comes always as an astonishment. Do you know what a ram is, Benjamin? R-A-M. A random act of *menshlichkeit*."

"You know about rams."

She turned to look at him. "My stories are about what the world is like when there are no rams. Benjamin, as a person whose specialty is war, doesn't the ram interest you?"

* * *

Evelyn stirred as he entered the bedroom; she opened her eyes, raised her arms to him. He went to her bedside and held her. Frail, thin almost to emaciation, but the fever gone. She would regain much of her strength and weight; for how long, no one knew. They had been told about the hazard of a third pregnancy. The surgery and the transfusions, everyone had then thought, saved her life. Now, as it turned out—a life for a life. Roar with rage against the void. The very day of the diagnosis she'd said, "We've given each other the entire middle of our lives. I've no regrets, I've had a truly wonderful life with you, but one's end, you know, belongs with one's beginnings. We've little control over our beginnings and endings; we're in the hands of others. So I ask you to promise me that you'll send my body back to my family for burial in England."

He had given his word. They had trusted each other with their lives; she would trust him with her death.

He waited until she was asleep and went into his study. The halogen lamp on the desk was on; it sent a focused light onto the area where the manuscript lay and left the rest of the room dim. He stared at the framed headlines on the walls, barely able to make out the words, and remembered, with a lucidity that forced upon him a sharp intake of breath, Mr. Zapiski's stumbling walk and rasping voice and dusty war library. He noticed the kitchen in the Tudor was dark, the house itself, exterior lights off, seeming to fade into the night. He leaned across his desk to open the window. A light came on in a third-floor window of the Tudor and he saw I. D. Chandal at a table, writing. He glanced at the clock on the wall over his desk—a few minutes after eleven.

He found himself at the ornate wooden front door of her house. The old-fashioned doorbell echoed dully inside.

There was no answer.

Above the doorbell was an antique knocker. He used it a number of times and stood listening.

No one came to the door.

He walked to the side of his house and looked up. There she was, visible through the closed third-floor window. How attract her attention? A shout might be overheard and bring the police.

He walked to the rear door that led to the kitchen and tried the knob. The door swung open.

Inside he stood still until his eyes grew accustomed to the darkness. He moved through the dining room and living room. At the foot of the stairway, in the entrance hall, he called, "Davita," and listened as her name rose, echoing.

How could she not have heard? Possibly the door to the third floor was closed. He could go to his own house and telephone her from there. But he didn't know her number. Certainly the operator would give it to him. But he craved to see her as she sat at her desk. A craving beyond lust. A view of the act of creation, the forging of connections.

He climbed the curving stairway. The carpeted steps creaked and groaned.

All five doors on the second floor were open. He peered into each room. Four were empty. In the fifth, an old chair and dresser, an unmade bed. Towels and toiletries in a small bathroom with a white porcelain sink and an antique claw-foot tub.

At the end of the hallway, a narrow uncarpeted wooden stairway led upward into darkness. Slowly, he climbed the stairs and came to a closed wooden door. He pushed the door open and found himself inside a vast dimly lit ballroom, with stained-glass windows, a wide-planked oak floor, a vaulted ceiling lacy with lights and shadows. Antique furniture stood about as in a storeroom: floral-patterned stuffed chairs, eagles and dragons carved from their arms and legs; long tables, their tops cut with zodiacal markings; lacquered Oriental dressers; desks of Victorian design; canopied beds. On the floor lay three piles of carpets adorned with mythic bestiaries, richly plumed birds, enchanted gardens, densely treed woods. The possessions of the previous owners. Why had it all been moved to this floor?

Against the far wall, before a window, I. D. Chandal sat at a rolltop desk, clutching a pen with three fingertips of her right hand, writing. She sat about forty feet away, bathed in yellow light from the lamp on her desk, and he made out plainly her rotund features and thick lips and double chin and uncombed gray hair and face glistening with sweat. The pale blue housecoat she wore could not conceal the buttocks and thighs that spilled over the edge of her chair and the immense breasts pushing against the desk. She paid no attention to him as he came alongside the desk. He heard her breathing, the wheezy breathing of an asthmatic, and inhaled her sweat. She was writing on one side of a large spring binder. He wrote that way too, leaving the other to be added to, if needed, at a later time. The heat that rose from her! He saw her lift her eyes and look out the window directly at his house and return to her writing. She moved her lips, mouthed words in silence, cocked her head this way and that. "*Warum*," he heard her say, and stood cold and trembling, listening to his heart. She gazed again out the window and, following her line of vision, he saw the dark portals of his house. At the rear above the roof stood the oaks, reflecting darkly the outside lights.

A sudden bright rectangle appeared in the wall of the house. Someone had turned on the light in his study! He was able to see directly into the room: the framed headlines on the wall; his old chair and recliner; the top of his desk with books, magazines, journals, and the manuscript of the memoirs. Was Evelyn walking about?

A shadow fell across the desk. Benjamin Walter, the skin on his scalp rising, saw a form slide slowly into his chair. It sat still a moment, then lifted its eyes and stared at him directly through the window.

Dark clothes, white shirt, dark tie, tall black skullcap, graying beard, in the moist lips a cigarette with a long gray ash arched like a melting candle.

I. D. Chandal took a wheezing breath. "Hello, Benjamin. You have a nice home."

He was unable to respond. The pain in his arms and legs; the hammering of his heart.

"A place full of connections."

The light in the window winked out.

Benjamin Walter stood frozen with horror.

I. D. Chandal murmured, "Causes, connections, and rams. All over the place."

He stared at her and then at the house.

"Please go home and let me finish my work." Her tone was sharp.

"But—"

"Go home." Her voice had risen.

"My dear Davita—"

"I'm sorry, but now you're interfering, Benjamin."

"But I feel—"

"Benjamin, leave!" The lashing fury in her voice. What had he done to deserve that?

Inside his house another window abruptly ignited. His wife's study. Everything in it—books, papers, journals, wall pictures—arranged with an English sense of order. And on her desk, the manuscript of her book on Virginia Woolf.

A shadowy form glided into view, stood over the desk.

Benjamin Walter, roaring with rage and dread, rushed from the third-floor ballroom and down the stairway and out of the Tudor. Breathing with great difficulty, a reddish luminescence flashing before his eyes, he paused at the foot of the stairs in his living room and saw only the dim night-light. Evelyn stirred when he entered the bedroom, but did not wake.

He hurried into her study. It was dark; nothing appeared to have been disturbed. In his study, he switched on the ceiling light. The manuscript of the memoirs lay on the desk where he had left it. Glancing outside, he saw I. D. Chandal still writing at the third-floor window of the Tudor. What was that? He threw open the window and saw a shadowy figure limping along the driveway toward the woods at the back of the house. A burglar! Call the police. But then he heard the whispered word "*Warum*" and the trope chant began from the woods. Slowly rising and curling like early morning mist, drifting. From splintered trees and barbarous graveyards; and entering through the open window and also coming from the wall of headlines behind him and the piercingly recalled apartment of Mr. Zapiski. A long moment passed before he recognized that the word and the chant had risen from him, from his own lips. And it was then that he broke through the ramparts into the illumined entry of himself and saw as he had never seen before the exposed roots and tangles of long-buried connections, and was overcome with an infinite sorrow.

* * *

In the cavernous third-floor of the Tudor, I. D. Chandal put down her pen, rubbed both hands over her breasts, shivered with delight, and smiled.

Three Poems

Carl Phillips

Autumn. A Mixed Music.

Believe me, I would sooner
speak true—
And not of the leaves as the once-green

accomplices that, failing,
I shall most miss now,
October,

and how they sang to me
like water, singing
what was often enough

loss, eventually,
into choruses of *Something*
is lost, Something is still

gainable: You who call yourself
hunter, never lay
your bow down.

When was it all dreaming became
the one dream: myself
on the pier safe again, waving and

still waving, the body
at last separate—a vessel
steerable, but no longer

my hand steering—
and impossibly shackled
to it,

that god whose best trick
is to proffer madness as a balm
so sweet, who wouldn't

pick it up,
who wouldn't slather, in it,
his own body—Hypnotic—Ah,

well. . . . October. And all the leaves
not failing—merely filling out entire
that space marked "Being Leaves."

And all the lives they covered, laid
bare now, finding elsewhere
to hide, to continue

variously toward an end that
comes always, however much a small
other thing beneath, standing

for Yes, *inevitably, but
not yet, there is still a distance*
continues . . . Whatever edges, at

this lean hour, into view,
it is not the god;
is not, by other messenger, the desired

release granted; it isn't
the soul,
as too long imagined,

stepping into the visible world—

Listen: that doesn't happen in this world.

A Kind of Meadow

—shored
by trees at its far ending,
as is the way in moral tales:

whether trees as trees actually,
for their shadow and what
inside of it

hides, threatens, calls to;
or as ever-wavering conscience,
cloaked now, and called Chorus;

or, between these, whatever
falls upon the rippling and measurable,
but none to measure it, thin

fabric of *this stands for*.
A kind of meadow, and then
trees—many, assembled, a wood

therefore. Through the wood
the worn
path, emblematic of Much

Trespass: *Halt. Who goes there?*
A kind of meadow, where it ends
begin trees, from whose twinning

of late light and the already underway
darkness you were expecting perhaps
the stag to step forward, to make

of its twelve-pointed antlers
the branching foreground to a backdrop
all branches;

or you wanted the usual
bird to break cover at that angle
at which wings catch entirely

what light's left,
so that for once the bird isn't miracle
at all, but the simplicity of patience

and a good hand assembling: first
the thin bones, now in careful
rows the feathers, like fretwork,

now the brush, for the laying-on
of sheen. . . As is *always the way*,
you tell yourself, *in poems*. Yes.

Yes, always,
until you have gone there,
and gone there, "into the

field," vowing *Only until*
there's nothing more
I want—thinking it, wrongly,

a thing attainable, any real end
to wanting, and that it is close, and that
it is likely, how will you not

this time catch hold of it: flashing,
flesh at once

lit and lightless, a way
out, the one dappled way, back—

To Get There

Thus would I have a large wound coming
unstitched
come unstitched, goes the grace
by which they
mark, there, the morning,
and the fog with it
—leaving mountains, for other mountains—

There, all the time, it's like
the moment in betrayal, just before it,
when the body insists *There are no drivers,*
it's as the driven, now, we do
what we're about to, until
even conscience—thin
sheet in a wind—says so.

Am I saved?
Am I ruined?
These are questions
they never ask—however: always,
they mean to. You can see it
in certain customs
like the one of, from the hummingbirds that

bloom there in abundance,
each year netting two of, say,
especially fair wing,
of throat more stunningly than usual
bejeweled—
and then releasing them,
into the blast of the town forge,

there
to die breathless,
to remind that, less
than to be beautiful

and chosen, what will matter
is what it is we're chosen for.
                              To get there,

you'll want direction.
Stop the first face beneath which
already
you will have dreamed yourself—January
branch beneath its casing of ice—
bending.
Follow me,

                    —I'll take you there, he'll promise.

The Big Shrink

John Barth

The party was over, really, but a few of us lingered out on Fred and Marsha Mackall's pool deck to enjoy the subtropical air, the planetarium sky and a last sip before heading homeward. Half a dozen or more at first we lingerers were, then just our hosts and Roberta and I, sitting in deep patio chairs or on the low wall before the Mackalls' great sloping lawn.

"The other thing I wanted to get said," Fred Mackall went on presently, "—that Marsha's story and those stars up there reminded me of?—is that the universe isn't expanding anymore, the way it used to."

We let that proposition hang for a couple of beats in the cricket-rich tidewater night. Then my Bertie, with just the right mix of this and that, set down her decaf, kicked off her sandals, said brightly "Oh?" and propped her feet on a low deck table.

"If you're starting that . . ." Marsha Mackall warned her husband— *amiably but not unseriously,* I guess I'd say.

Fred twiddled his brandy glass in the patio-torchlight. The catering crew, assisted by the Mackalls' caretaker couple, were unobtrusively cleaning up. In a tone calibrated to match his wife's, "It's what's on my mind to say," Fred said.

"*I'm* ready," Bert volunteered, who generally was. "Hey: There went a meteorite."

I corrected her. Mildly. Good-humoredly.

Sleek Marsha Mackall pushed up out of her Adirondack chair. "Tell you what," to her husband: "I'll go help the help while you do the universe."

From his wall-seat, "You do that," Fred seconded—*levelly but not disagreeably,* I guess I'd say. And she did.

"Did you see it?" my wife asked me.

"Didn't need to, actually. Meteorite's what hits the earth. Right, Fred?"

"You didn't *need* to?" *Quizzical but with an edge,* Bert's tone, and I thought Uh-oh. "How do we know it *didn't* hit the earth?" she asked me further, or perhaps asked both of us.

"For a while there," Fred said on, "the universe expanded, all right, just as we were taught in school: your Big Bang and all? The whole show expanded in space up there for quite a little while, actually, everything getting bigger and bigger."

"Well . . ." I could tell what my wife was thinking: not expansion *in* space, Fred-O, but expansion *of* space; space itself expanding, et cetera. Bert might get meteors and meteorites ass-backward, but she knew more stuff than I did, and we shared all our interests, she and I; discussed everything under the sun with each other. What she said, however, was "Try eight to twelve billion years, O.K.?"

Fred Mackall turned his perfectly grayed, aging-preppie head her way, then shook it slowly and spoke as if to the flickering highlights in his glass: "Fifty, fifty-five, I'd say. Sixty tops. Then things sort of stalled for the next five or so, and after that the *volume* of space held more or less steady, but your galaxies and stars and such actually began to *shrink*, at an ever-increasing clip, and they're shrinking still."

In the Amused Nondirective mode, one of us responded, "Mm *hm*."

Down-glancing my way, "The effect," Fred said, "is that your astronomers still get pretty much the same measurements—your Red Shift and such?—but they haven't yet appreciated that it's for the opposite reason: because everything's *contracting*, themselves included: everything but the overall universe itself. Not condensing, mind: *shrinking*."

We didn't laugh, as we would've just between ourselves. *The rich man's joke is always funny*, goes the proverb, and the rich host's anecdote is always respectfully attended. By an order of magnitude, the Mackalls were the wealthiest people we knew: light-years out of our class, but hospitable to us academic peasants. They were Old Money (Marsha's, mainly, we understood), with the Old-Money liberal's sense of noblesse oblige. Fred had once upon a time been briefly our ambassador to someplace—a Kennedy appointee, I believe, or maybe Lyndon Johnson's. Latterly, he and Marsha had taken a benevolent interest in our little college, not far from their Camelot Farm: stables, kennels, black Angus cattle, pool and tennis court, gorgeous cruising sailboat in their private cove, the requisite eighteenth-century manor house tastefully restored, overlooking the bay, and more acreage by half than our entire campus.

Cockamamie, I could almost hear Bert saying to herself. But apart from her professional interest in the Mackalls, which I'll get to presently, she took what she called an anthropological interest in them—ambassadors indeed, to the likes of us, from another world—and with Fred especially she had established a kind of teasing/challenging conversational relation that she imagined he enjoyed. I myself couldn't tell sometimes whether the fellow was being serious or ironic; but then, I had that trouble occasionally with Bertie, too, even fifteen years into our marriage. In any case, although they made a diplomatic show of interest (perhaps often genuine) in their guests, both Mackalls had the philanthropist's expectation of being paid deferential attention.

My turn. "So your theory's different from the Big Crunch, right? The idea that after the universe has expanded to a certain point, it'll all collapse back to Square One?" No polymath even compared to Bert, I was an academic cobbler who stuck to his trade (remedial English and freshman composition), but I did try to stay reasonably abreast of things.

"Oh, definitely different," Fred said. He perched his brandy glass beside him on the walltop and tapped his half-splayed fingertips together . . . *as if in impatient prayer*, I guess I'd say. "In the Big Shrink, everything stays put but gets smaller and smaller, and so your space between things appears to increase. *Does* increase, actually."

"Now hold on just a cotton-picking minute," my Roberta teasingly challenged, ". . . ."

"There's no holding on," Fred said. Smoothly. "And no stopping it or even slowing it down. In fact, the shrink rate increases with proximity to the observer—just the reverse of your Big Bang?—but since the measurements come out about the same, it's not generally noticed." He smiled upon his fingertip-tapping hands, his say said.

Neither of us knew quite how to reply to that; *I* didn't, anyhow, and Bert seemed to do a five-count before she cleared her throat *mock-ostentatiously* and asked, "So where d'you get your fifty billion years, Fred, when your cosmologists all say eight to twelve billion?"

She was teasing him with those *yours*, I was pretty sure; Bertie'd do that, feed your little idiosyncrasies back at you, and not everybody took to it kindly. Now instead of tapping his fingertips five on five, Fred Mackall kept them touching while he expanded and contracted the fingers themselves—not *splayed and unsplayed* them, but *pulsed* them, I guess I'd say; pulsed them leisurely—leisurelily?

I give up.

No I don't. Fred Mackall pulsed his spread-fingered, fingertip-touching hands leisurely like . . . some sort of sea creature, say, and said, "I didn't say billion." *Smiling, though not necessarily with amusement.*

There.

"Did I say billion?"

Without at all meaning to, I presume, the Mackalls had gotten Bert and me in trouble once before in one of these post-party nightcap situations. Just a year or so prior to the scene above, it was: first time they and we had met socially. Bertie had recently landed her new position in the college's development office, where part of her job description was to "coordinate" the friendly interest of potential benefactors like the Mackalls. In her opinion and her boss's, she turned out to be a natural at it; in mine, too, although I was less convinced than Bert that her jokey-challenging manner was universally appreciated. In any case, now that our kids weren't babies anymore and we had to start thinking Tuition down the road, I was pleased that she had this new job to throw herself into with her usual industry. The Mackalls, we agreed, were doing at least as much of the "coordinating" as Bert's office was; the April buffet dinner at Camelot Farm that year was their idea—for our young new president and his wife along with several trustees of the college and their spouses (development was hoping that Fred would agree to join the board); also Roberta's boss, Bill Hartman, and his missus, who happened to be a friend and part-time colleague of mine, and—bottom of the totem pole—Bert and me: Assistant to the Director of Development ("Not *Assistant Director* yet," Bert liked to tease her boss when she gave her full title) and the lowercase director of the college's freshman English program, although I suspect that I was there less as Faculty Input than as my wife's Significant Other. The evening went easily enough: We were a small college in a small town with a clutch of well-to-do retirees from neighboring cities and a few super-gentry like the Mackalls; the prevailing local tone was relaxed-democratic. Toward the close of festivities, as most of the guests were making to leave, Marsha Mackall said "Anybody for another brandy and decaf out under the stars?" and although President and Ms. Harris begged off along with the trustees, Roberta said right away, "Count us in." Bill Hartman—whether pleased at his protégé's quick uptake or concerned to monitor the conversation—glanced at his wife and said, "Sounds good," and so we were six: same venue as this later one, but a fresher, brighter night.

Don't ask me how our conversation turned to Inherent Psychological Differences Between Women and Men, a minefield at any time of day but surely even more so at the end of a well-wined evening. Marsha Mackall— as tanned in April as the rest of us might be by August—was the one pursuing it, apropos of whatever. The form it soon took was her disagreeing with Becky Hartman and my Roberta (good liberal feminists both) that there were no "hard-wired" psychological differences between the sexes; that all such "stereotypical gender-based tendencies" as male aggressiveness versus female conciliatoriness, male logical-analytical thinking versus female intuition and feeling, the male hankering for multiple sex partners versus the female inclination to exclusive commitment—that all of these were the effect of cultural conditioning (and therefore malleable, in their optimistic opinion) rather than programmed by evolution into our respective chromosomes and therefore more resistant to amelioration, if amelioration is what one believed was called for.

"Some of them are like that, maybe," elegant Marsha had allowed—meaning that some of the above-mentioned "tendencies" were perhaps a matter more of Nurture than of Nature. "But when it comes to polygamy versus monogamy, or promiscuity versus fidelity—"

"Objection," put in Fred Mackall, raising a forefinger.

"Sustained," Bill Hartman ruled, *mock-judicially*: "Counsel is using judgmental language."

"Counsel stands corrected," Marsha conceded. "I don't mean it judgmentally—yet. And we're talking happy marriages here, okay? Happy, faithful, monogamous marriages like all of ours, right?"

"Hear hear," Bill Hartman said at once.

"All of *mine* have been like that," Fred Mackall teased, and lifted his glass as if in toast.

I followed suit.

"All I'm saying," Marsha Mackall said, "is that sexual fidelity comes less naturally to you poor fellows than it does to us, and that while some of that might be a matter of cultural reinforcement and such, what's being reinforced is a plain old biological difference between men and women. O.K.?"

"Vive la différence," Fred said—not very appositely, in my judgment.

"Men are just naturally designed to broadcast their seed to the four winds," Marsha concluded. "But pregnancy and maternity make women more vulnerable, so we tend to be choosier and then more 'faithful,' quote unquote—and we evolved this way for zillions of years before things like marriage and romantic love and conjugal fidelity were ever invented."

"Before they were *valorized*," handsome Becky Hartman said, "is how the jargon goes now," and Marsha Mackall nodded: "Valorized."

"Amen," Fred said.

I hated conversations like this, whether sportive or serious. In my view, which I wasn't interested enough even to offer, women and men are at least as importantly different from other members of their own sex as they are from each other categorically; I myself felt more of a kind in more different ways with Roberta than with either Bill Hartman or Fred Mackall, for example—and, truth to tell, maybe more of a piece *temperamentally* with Becky Hartman (we had successfully team-taught a course or two in past semesters) than with my wife, even. What's more, it didn't seem nearly as obvious to me as it evidently did to them that a culturally acquired trait is ipso facto more manageable than a genetically transmitted one, where the two can even be distinguished. Et cetera. But intelligent people do seem drawn to such subjects—women, in my experience, more than men. This much I made the mistake of volunteering, by way of a Bertie-like Teasing Challenge to the three ladies—and then, of course, I was in for it. Becky Hartman now took the (Female Conciliatory) tack of agreeing with our hostess that, whatever the cause, men were indeed categorically more inclined than women to sexual infidelity—"seriality, polygamy, promiscuity, call it what you will—though mind you," patting her husband's knee, "I'm not saying they *pursue* the inclination, necessarily . . ."

"Heaven forfend," Bill Hartman said, *mock-solemnly*.

"—only that the inclination is definitely there, more often and more strongly than it is with women."

"Now we're talking," Marsha Mackall said, satisfied.

"I deny it," firmly declared my Roberta. "I don't believe Sam's anymore sexually interested in other women than I am in other men."

"Uh-oh," Fred Mackall warned, or anyhow uttered in some vague sort of warning spirit.

"We're not saying that he goes around panting after the coeds," Marsha made clear.

"Much less that he *drops his pantings*, huh?" Fred said, and ducked his handsome head. Bill Hartman politely groaned; Bertie hissed. "Sorry there," Fred said.

"Right," said Becky Hartman, agreeing with Marsha. Directly to her, then—I mean to Becky, as I had only just met the Mackalls—I said, "What *do* you mean, then, Beck?" and, in a way that I remembered with pleasure from our team-taught classes, she pursed her lips and narrowed her bright brown eyes in a show of pensiveness before replying, in this instance with a hypothetical scenario: "Suppose there were absolutely no guilt or other negative consequences attached to adultery. No element of betrayal, no hurt feelings—let's even drop the word *adultery*, since it has those associations . . ."

"Right." Marsha Mackall took over: "Suppose society were such that it was considered perfectly O.K. for a married man to go to bed with another woman anytime they both felt like it . . ."

"Neither admirable nor blameworthy," Becky Hartman specified, in my direction; "just perfectly O.K. with all parties, absolutely without repercussions, anytime they felt like doing it . . ."

"Then would you?" Marsha asked me—with a smile, but not jokingly. "Or not?"

Lifting his right hand as if on oath, "I plead the Fifth Amendment on that one," Fred Mackall said at once, although it wasn't him they were asking, yet.

"Like-*wise*," Bill Hartman agreed, with a locker-room sort of chuckle. But it was me the two women happened to be pressing, and I had the habit, even in social situations, of taking seriously-put questions seriously and replying as honestly as I could. Occupational hazard, maybe, of teaching college freshmen in the liberal arts.

So, "Blessed as I am in my marriage and happy as a clam with monogamous fidelity, I guess I might," I acknowledged; "in some sort of *experimental spirit*, I imagine, if there were no such fallout as guilt or social disapproval or hurt feelings or anything of that sort, so that it wouldn't even be thought of as 'adultery' or 'infidelity.'" I used my fingers for quotation marks. "Which is unimaginable, of course, so forget it."

"But if things *were* that way," Marsha Mackall triumphantly bore in, "then you would. Right?"

I reconsidered. Shrugged. "I guess I have to admit I might."

Bert said to me then "I'm astonished," and although her tone was amusedly *mock*-astonished, I saw her face drain. "I'm totally astonished."

"Uh-oh," Bill Hartman said, quite as Fred Mackall had earlier.

"No, no," my wife made clear to all: "No blame or anger or anything like that—"

"*No hurt feelings,*" Fred teased, "*no guilt, no repercussions . . .*"

"I just couldn't be more surprised if you'd said you're bisexual," Bert said, to me, "or had a thing for sheep."

"Sheep," Fred said, "bah," and most of us duly chuckled.

"It's an impossible hypothetical scenario," I protested to Bert, and without blaming Marsha Mackall directly (we had just met the couple, after all, and they were our hosts, and Development was courting them), I declared to all hands, "I feel like I've been suckered!"

"My friend," Fred Mackall said, "you *have* been suckered."

"No, I swear," Bert tried to make clear: "I'm not upset. I'm just totally, totally surprised."

Becky Hartman did her lips-and-eyes thing but said nothing. Notching up his characteristic joviality, "Time to pack it in, I think," her husband declared. Perfect-hostess Marsha made a few let's-change-the-subject pleasantries, perhaps with Roberta in particular, and we did then presently bid our several good nights.

In the car, I apologized. "No need to," Bertie insisted, and as we drove homeward down the dark country roads under the brilliant stars, she reaffirmed that she didn't *blame* me in any way; that she felt as did I that all this essentially-male/essentially-female business was so much baloney—that had been precisely her and Becky Hartman's *point,* remember?—but that for all those years she had thought our connection to be something really really special . . .

"It *is* special!" I rebegan, more calmly: "That was a dumb-ass hypothetical scenario, hon, and I made the dumb-ass mistake of taking it seriously instead of doing a *faux-galant* cop-out like Fred Mackall and Bill Hartman."

"Maybe they weren't being fake-gallant," Bertie said from her side of the car. Her voice was distant; I could tell that her head was turned away. "Maybe what they said was *true*-gallant, but expressed ironically under the social circumstances."

My face tingled: She had me there, as not infrequently she did. "So," I said—mock-bitterly but also true-bitterly, et cetera, and in fact with some dismay: "The honeymoon is over."

"No, no, no," my wife insisted. "I was just surprised, is all."

"And disappointed." I felt miserable: annoyed at Marsha Mackall, at Becky and Bert, at myself. Bum-rapped. But mainly miserable.

"Yes, well."

Sixteen months later—smiling, though not necessarily with amusement, and pulsing his spread-fingered, fingertips-touching hands leisurely like some sort of sea creature—Fred Mackall said, "I didn't say fifty *billion.* Everything's shrinking, see, but since it's us who're shrinking fastest of all, other things seem larger and farther away." He picked up his empty glass; set it down again. "That's why Marsh and I don't get to Europe much anymore, you know? We used to pop over to London and Paris as if they were Washington and Philadelphia, but even though the planes fly faster and faster, everything's too far away these days. And this *house* . . ." He turned his perfectly grayed head toward where the caterers were finishing up. "We rattle around in it now, where before we were forever adding on and buying up acreage left and right. There're parts of this property that I don't set foot on anymore from one season to the next."

"I get it," Bertie said: *cheerily*, as if a joke had been on us. "So even though the farm and the house are shrinking too . . . " She let him take it from there.

"They're all farther and farther apart from each other, not to mention from town. D'you know how long it's been since I trekked down to our dock to check the boat? And look how far away the house is now, compared to when we-all came out for a nightcap!"

"You know what, Fred Mackall?" Bertie said, *mock-confidentially*. "You're right. Sam and I will never get home."

"Oh, well, now," Fred said, chuckling my way as if across a great divide: "You two are still in the Expanding mode, I'd guess, or at most in the capital-P Pause . . ."

One patio torch guttered out; several others were burning their last. Fred Mackall spoke on—about "your stars and such" again, I believe, although I could scarcely hear his words now, and about how his Big Shrink theory applied to time as well as to space, so that what astronomers took to be billions of years was actually no more than fifty or sixty. "My" Bertie's tone was still the cheery straight man's, mildly teasing/challenging to draw him out, but essentially in respectful accord.

I say "tone" because *her* words, too, were barely audible to me now across the expanse of pool deck, theoretically smaller than it had been when Fred Mackall began his spiel, but in effect so vast now that I didn't even try to call across it to my wife. I'd have needed hand signals, so it seemed to me: semaphores such as beach lifeguards use to communicate from perch to perch. We still had what you'd call a good marriage, Bert and I: We were still each other's closest friend and confidant, still unanimous with the children, or almost so. But it wasn't what it had been. We made love less often, for example; less passionately, too, lately, by and large. Par for the course, some might say, as time shrinks and the years zip by; but our connection truly *had* been special, just as Bert maintained. The queen-size bed on which she and I had slept and such for fifteen satisfying years had come to seem king-size; although per Fred Mackall's theory it was doubtless down to a double by now and on its way toward single, its occupants were even further reduced, and thus farther apart.

I happened to recall from some freshman textbook a journal entry of Franz Kafka's, I believe it was, about his grandfather: how the old fellow came to marvel that anyone had the temerity to set out even for the neighboring village and expect ever to arrive there, not to mention returning. I remembered how my own mother, in her last age, found going upstairs in her own house too formidable an undertaking, like a polar expedition. Once upon a time I might have contributed those anecdotes to this nightcap conversation: a bit of Faculty Input. By now, however, I couldn't even hear Fred Mackall's and Roberta's voices, much less have called across to them. Even if I could have—by bullhorn, cellular flip-phone, whatever—I doubt I'd have found the right words: They, too, were retreating from me, would soon be out of my diminishing reach altogether, as would even my self itself.

The star-jammed sky was terrifying: moment by moment emptier-seeming as all its contents reciprocally shrank. We would never imaginably pull ourselves out of the Mackalls' Adirondack chairs, Bert and I, and make our way off their pool deck, enormous now as an Asian steppe; far less off their interminable estate, through the light-years-long drive home, the ever-widening, in effect now all but infinite space between us.

Two Poems

Michael McFee

Nothing

Once he was back home, driving around doing nothing
with a woman he'd loved decades ago, he'd asked her
to be his girlfriend in tenth grade but she wrote back
saying, No thank you, I've already got a boyfriend:

they were both long-married now, happily, with kids,
they were satisfied in their separate lives, nothing
was going to happen tonight or ever, they were headed
back to her house where their families were waiting

when they passed a convenience mart whose gas pumps
were on fire, colossal pillars of flame blistering
the canopy, not a soul in sight, not a car, nothing:
he pulled to the curb and they sat watching them blaze

waiting for the big explosion, for somebody to come
put the fire out, for something to stop this burning
that might last all night long—but after a minute
he put the car in gear and drove away, saying nothing.

Woman in a Second-Story Corner Room

From the sidewalk, I couldn't tell
if she was dressed, or using a mirror, or alone,

all I could see was her silhouette
combing long black hair, up and over and far down,

her head rolling slightly backwards
with every deliberate pull of hand across scalp,

a dozen strokes, two dozen, three,
like she was considering something, again and again,

she was not my mother in heaven
remembering me, she was not my wife before we met

imagining me or somebody better,
she was simply a backlit shape whose steady motion

was brushing the stubborn tangles
out of night, its long damp strands of darkness

slowly drying in the morning sun
as I kept walking by, my head up and back, tingling.

from Scattered Psalms

Jacqueline Osherow

II. (Pure Silver / Seven Times)

> The words of the Lord are pure words, refined silver (clear to the
> earth)/ (in a furnace in the earth), purified seven times.
> Psalms 12:7
>
> . . . the degraded man says in his heart there is no God . . . .
> Psalms 14:1

Let's pretend, for an instant, we're not degraded,
That we'd know, if we heard it, the sound of pure silver
Fired in a furnace seven times.
Could it possibly be transcribed?
And if it's *clear to the earth*, who needs transcription?
And if it's *furnace of the earth*, why are we listening?
An earthly furnace for the words of God?

Unless David means his own earthly body,
How he crossed words out, rewrote them, seven times
Or tried chanting them, his mouth not his,
Mumbling beneath his breath, there is no God
Unless He's here beside me, writing psalms,
Offering a kingdom for some molten words
Perfected in an oven seven times . . . .

Only David didn't say that about God;
That's an innovation of my own
Which is why God never trusts me with His store of silver.
Imagine. All that untranslated vision,

The earthly furnace a courtesy to us,
To let us know how very lost we are.
God's refinements always come in sevens:

Here too, the first brought light and, therefore, darkness,
The second worked to disentangle chaos,
The third divided fluid—meaning—from solid,
The fourth made a hierarchy of brilliancies,
The fifth made portions float while others soared,
The sixth refashioned it as human speech
And the seventh gave it poetry, its Sabbath.

Unless it wasn't all that complicated—
God spoke to David from His holy mountain
And David was reminded of, say, Bathsheba's bracelets
As she took them off to come to bed.
It could be a matter of wishful thinking,
My friend who swears she saw her daughter, in a coma,
Move, when she asked her to, her arm.

But who's to say she didn't move her arm?
That when David lured Him with his purest words
God didn't answer from a holy mountain?
And even if *pure words* are an invention of desire
In the face of everything that's horrible
(Is that the earthly furnace seven times?)
Surely they are, nonetheless, still pure . . . .

Perhaps *clear to the earth* means transparent
And all the words are written on the air,
A hundred thousand verses in the open space
Between me and these pages of the Psalms,
Each revised entirely by any passing breeze
As clouds and moon and stars plunder their silver
And sift it through the heavens seven times.

III. (Thrones and Psalms)

You are holy, enthroned upon the psalms of Israel.
Psalms 22:4

God sat enthroned on the flood . . . .
Psalms 29:10

This is the way I like to think of Him:
Not on Ezekiel's throne of sapphires,
Which was only, after all, a likeness.
But held aloft by the religious ladies
(To whom I still owe eighteen dollars)
Who, every day, recite every psalm.
It's how they heal the sick (they saved my niece;
Her own doctors said it was miraculous)
Though surely it can't be just as afterthought
That they arrange the place where God will sit . . .

And what would it look like, this throne of psalms?
All those hallelujahs must be pillows—
Each one filled with cures for every malady
And hand-embroidered with a joyful noise—
The massive frame, the echo of God's own voice
Shattering Lebanon's unlucky cedars.
For decoration, there would be the letters:
The exotic *shin* with crowns, the ornate *tzadi*
Arranged as leaping mountains, harps on willows,
Floods clapping their hands, upright palms . . . .

Unless it *is* those floods that are His throne.
I was never wild about that line,
But you can't really argue with destruction
And anyone can argue with a psalm.
A flood will diminish, on the other hand.
And who's to say what happens to a psalm?
If Noah had written one before the flood
(Instead of getting so involved with gopher wood)

God might have decided to change his mind
Or the music might have served as a distraction,

Which means, it seems to me, we'd better start singing
Or I'd better send those ladies my donation.
You know, the other day, that massive hurricane?
God just needed somewhere to sit down.
Or maybe—who knows?—He started thinking
And tears began to fall. It's not unusual.
He didn't even notice as they fell.
And then—He had no choice—He blew His nose.
He never meant the dying and destruction.
All He wanted was a little praise.

IV. (Darkness/Wings)

> He mounted a cherub and flew, He swooped on the wings of the
> wind. He made darkness His concealment, round Him His
> shelter—the darkness of water, the clouds of heaven.
> Psalms 18:11–12

> You will light my lamp, God, my God, illuminate my darkness.
> Psalms 18:29

I'll tell my daughter
Don't be afraid
It's only God
Hiding Himself
No need to worry yourself
About the dark
Imagine He's a rider
In a deep black cloth
What would lurk
In such a path?

And if she asks why God
Needs a hiding place?
Whom He's hiding from?
Who would know His face?
Do I tell the truth
Or keep it simple?
I could quote the psalm
For example
Fiery wrath
Wings outspread

But why the wings?
Why the cherub?
Why does God
Need a ride?
And what's it like
Mounting a cherub?

Does he buck
And flail his wings
Or nod
And glide?

And where
Will he alight?
Does he go far?
Maybe at the center
Of a dark ex-star
Whose energy
Gravity?
Is so compact
It's far too strict
To let out light

A lamp unto my feet
Concealed in darkness
A light
To illuminate
The dark
A whirl of black
Its mass
So dense
That it was once
Pure light

Maybe each black hole
Is God concealed?
What do I tell
My daughter?
If the light's let out
What exactly is revealed?
Darkness of water
Darkness of cloud
Don't be afraid
It's only God

The Facts

David Baker

How far on one wing
        the night whistle flew

to our lives, long note
        from the railway cross-

road over highways
        and fields every night:

midnight's freight on time.
        The neighborhood shut

down to its black doors
        and blue lights. Years passed

in a mower's rev,
        in our cookout smoke.

We hammered short pla-
        cards into our front

yards each fall. Who knew
        what haunted the field

across our street, scuffed
        its small hooves through the

drying black weeds, and
        decided to fly.

It must have been great
        speed swept one deer past

a fence in the dark,
        clamor of asphalt

onto our trim yards.
        It must have seen that

scrubbed window as grass,
        a spread of meadow

or starlight, sweet sky.
        What we don't know soars

with us, without cause.
        We heard the sudden

explosion of glass
        and wild skin punctured,

and gathered in time
        to find the brown leg

pumping, a piston
        of want, muscle, bone,

feel the hot billow
        of breath drawn badly

where she lay down in
        tremors, the picture

window, furniture
        splintered, our neighbors'

house so like our own.
        Then the medic came,

a man with blue lights
        dotting his pickup.

Where we live the whole
        sky can take on the

calm swirl of a dance,
        the wind and its star

figures and those wild
        ancient myths spun with

meaning. But what can
        explain one deer, slick

with flight, where we stood
        with our facts and lives,

our late sorrows—there
        where we lived, live still.

There was one moment
        of complete silence.

We were what we would
        always be. That's when

we heard the train pull
        away in the night

and the animal
        blood spread. Who knows why.

Frieze

Claire Malroux

Translated from the French by Marilyn Hacker

I

in connected
sentences set in a stable climate
cocoons laid out of the waves' way
is how we'd like life to unroll itself
a flat horizon-line
pristine

forgetting the sheer plunge of periods
the weariness of commas
the blank spaces
and those swift breath-shifts blowing behind the waves
which becalm in indentations
with no likely transition

stranded on
one of those mounds of chilling words
with the black hole of the sea
for sole perspective

there's no way out but descent
in a whirlwind of molecules
to claim back some shapeliness from death
the way an ant
dazed in an avalanche of sand
its survival kit
secured to its back
climbs blindly back upwards

II

don't say black
black is a visionary color
intense and desiring substance
a diamond facet
attracting toward the density
of its depth

cite blind transparency instead
the snare of emptiness

the hole would be a white-walled cube
a mirrored sphere
where a shadow twists
in search of a drop of blood
on clouds' reflections

III

where to watch for an exploding sun
instead of and in place of love
this absent hand

hand
with gentlest fingers
which know how to sew
close eyelids
unfold a leaf
with its secret lifelines

wash out the sheets of the wounded
caress the ciphers of the shroud

IV

its eyes barely closed in the night
a plant drinks light
which our eyes can't see

thought, for it, is its patience
and the air, water and sunlight are patient
in their lightning-flash touches
for the plant, love is unperceived time
vein melted into the block of shadow

not distinguished
from the other elements
of life's chemistry

as for me, man or woman
I require
that blue emerge from gray
that lead be transformed to gold
awkward alchemist
I have to brew my own love

V

night embellishes
the aquarium-city
neon signs flash past
like bright fish
sand starred with golden leaves
surges up under footsteps

in festive ballrooms
the city can finally breathe
celebrations are promised
on electrified pediments
feel the darkness grow weightless
the street levitates
someone has lifted a lid from the sky

pedestrians brush past each other
impatient to be back
beneath the skylight
with the contents
of their illuminated boxes

the hidden word enthuses
listen my heart O listen
to the gentle night which . . .
the Hotel Baudelaire
bursts forth incredibly

and the recollection
that Andersen's mermaid
wrenched from oceanic night
exchanged her voice
for legs, human and
doomed

VI

on the glassed-in porch
sun brings the alembic to white-heat
in a mythic noon
of somnolence and boredom

the laundry done
games around the washtub
become ceremonies

decant the escaping water
from vessel to vessel
hold the instant suspended
opaque and transparent
as a pearl

containers shatter
but this thirst remains

once more to be a sorcerer's apprentice
apprentice diviner
to stanch time's long wound
with a child's lips

the scar breaks open again at daybreak

VII

priestesses climb the hill
a book on each one's hip
a book on each one's breast

within sight of the temple portico
they become confused
the cicadas' song
drills into their skulls
crammed with scribblings of silence

clumsy apprentice sibyls
they'll be thrown at feeding-time
to the portly tigers of Adonis
into the briars
of an unimproved
elephants' graveyard

no city will spring up from their teeth

VIII

Penelope's tapestry
petrified as she waits
empty-hearted while her fingers
glide as on lute-strings
over slack fibers

nothing but backstitching
toward the wedding tunic

the baby's romper
to reverse the point of no return
unreturned love
strayed in sorceresses' arms
and the even more inconstant
arms of the sea

only the warp and woof
of untextured days
when the sun
hardly disturbs the night
when sleep seizes your body
to fling in the oven of shadows
into a survivors' mass grave

life splits in two
like a bad fingernail

IX

the tree's sails flap
rip themselves
on the wharf always ready to get on board
it's the seasons that travel

it's the sun the breezes
raising bright pennant-colors
on flagpoles

the tree is just a mannequin
dressed and undressed at will
a prototype-human
with changeable or exchangeable
nerves and organs
a future robot

and the storm is a game
to achieve that swift shuddering
the route of a billion wheels

trampling the childish lines
of her palm, black woman
Earth

              X

my children whom I never knew
one passing a chamois-cloth over a long steel flank
the other clasping and wrenching apart two hands
like wing-stumps

both of them fallen into the glacier

the face that waited for you
which you couldn't wait for
only accessible
at the instant everything freezes

until then troubled
and trembling like water
with no form other than the always other

              XI

in dialogue with daybreak
perennially deferring evening's answer
I put my hope
in the irresistible ascent of light

even when masked with snow or hail
light advances
night's bivouacs and
insomniac phantoms surrender

lighthouses brighten on their islands
to guide dawn to the wharf
and exchange fraternal
signals

one by one, light whisks off the slipcovers
in abandoned houses
raises the flag again on the roof-peak
and in the liberated windows

poises on the highest portal
a triumphal arch

Two Poems

Karl Kirchwey

Skin Cards

Pliny tells how a man once fell in love
     with Praxiteles' Cnidean Venus.
      He visited her at night, and his embrace
left stains on the marble where the thighs cleave.

O perfumed brink, sweet pelt, world's predicate,
     forgetful verb, to your one agile place
      the dark tends, sunset-edged, regret's deep fosse
through myth and all the centuries of heat.

Roman Spring

The wow of zinc hoardings in the *tramontana*
       with naked bodies on them (a cellulite pill)
(Hope they don't catch cold in this lapidary weather);
       artichokes and underwear in each market stall;

rain-soaked brickwork, and a stained mattress
       abandoned in a field of trampled crim-
son poppies; jasmine and excrement; flowering capers;
       the salt sea smell behind the smell of petroleum;

the first strawberries, in from Terracina,
       where the Romans built Jove Anxur a temple
on arcades which seem to retreat forever
       into the middle distance of pure will;

the warble of a police walkie-talkie
       outside the home of the Vatican ambassador (who
is an ex-mayor of Boston), incongruously
       reminiscent of a thrush in the Massachusetts woods long ago;

that moment, early on a foggy morning,
       when the domes of all the city's churches press
upward like the bubble of aspiration in a running
       prayer from the plain that once kept Romulus;

and a travertine curb polished like something priceless
       by the bus's slow turn as it grinds uphill;
the strong grip of those packed and swaying riders
       as they are carried through the Papal Wall.

Three Poems

Linda Gregg

The Calves Not Chosen

The mind goes *caw, caw, caw, caw,*
dark and fast. The orphan heart
cries out, "Save me. Purchase me
as the sun makes the fruit ripe.
I am one with them and cannot feed
on winter dawns." The black birds
are wrangling in the fields
and have no kindness, all sinew
and stick bones. Both male and female.
Their eyes are careless of cold and rain,
of both day and night. They love nothing
and are murderous with each other.
All things of the world are bowing
or being taken away. Only a few calves
will be chosen, the rest sold for meat.
The sound of the wind grows bigger
than the tree it's in, lessens only
to increase. *Haw, haw* the crows call,
awake or asleep, in white, in black.

Fish Tea Rice

It is on the earth that all things transpire,
and only on the earth. On it, up out of it,
down into it. Wading and stepping, pulling
and lifting. The heft in the seasons.
Knowledge in the bare ankle under water,
amid the rows of rice seedlings. The dialogue
of the silent back and forth, the people moving
together in flat fields of water with the patina
of sky upon it, the green shoots rising up
from the mud, sticking up seamlessly above the water.
The water buffalo stepping through as they work,
carrying the weight of their bodies along the rows.
The wrists of the people wet under the water,
planting or pulling up. It is this earth that all
meaning is. If love unfolds, it unfolds here.
Here that Heaven shows its face. If Christ's agony
transpires into grace, spikes through the hands
holding the body in place, arms reaching wide,
it breaks our heart on earth. Ignorance mixed
with longing, intelligence mixed with hunger.
The genius of night and sleep, being awake
and at work. The sacred in the planting, the wading
in mud. Eating what is here. Fish, bread, tea, rice.
Actual shade under the trees made by the sun.
The babies sleeping on their working mothers' backs.

The Precision

There is a modesty in nature. In the small
of it and in the strongest. The leaf moves
just the amount the breeze indicates
and nothing more. In the power of lust, too,
there can be a quiet and clarity, a fusion
of exact moments. There is a silence of it
inside the thundering. And when the body swoons,
it is because the heart knows its truth.
There is directness and equipoise in the fervor,
just as the greatest turmoil has precision.
Like the discretion a tornado has when it tears
down building after building, house by house.
It is enough, Kafka said, that the arrow fit
exactly into the wound that it makes. I think
about my body in love as I look down on these
lavish apple trees and the workers moving
with skill from one to the next, singing.

The Grand Prize

Daniela Crăsnaru

Translated from the Romanian by Adam J. Sorkin with the author

He didn't recognize Beetle at first. And how could he have recognized him, so very plump, with his mustache flowing downward over the corners of his mouth, with his Buffalo plaid jacket ready to split at the seams, with the beginnings of baldness unsuccessfully hidden by the hair combed upward from the sides of head. Who would have said twenty years ago at the graduation banquet at the university that the tall, slender, handsome boy, whom half of the girls in philology were chasing after, would someday resemble this pudgy, double-chinned, already half-bald individual. And that he would not just resemble this person but that he would be him. These things happen, after twenty years. Some turn fat and others lean and hollow-cheeked, and still others die. Whoever decides to come to such a meeting must be prepared for everything. And concerning the girls, better not say anything. About them there was a real sadness, not to say a tragedy.

All of them were kissing one another in a natural effusiveness (some of them hadn't seen each other since then, when they were assigned their jobs upon graduation), without fully knowing who was kissing whom.

"Hey, I'm Doina, man. Don't you recognize me? I can't believe it! Give me a compliment, tell me that I haven't changed a bit, so I can slap your face like I used to slap you in the second year of comparative grammar when I failed the midyear exam because of you. It's me, Doina, man, and she's Luci. My dear, don't tell me that you didn't recognize her from the first look, because I'm already losing all my confidence in men."

Yes, she was Luci indeed, the skinny girl (girl?) with thick, curved lenses over her eyes with blue shadow on her eyelids (oh, her eyes, yes, of course, there's no way Cristian could have forgotten those eyes which made him lovesick for an entire summer during practice teaching in Cobadin).

"As if, dear," Doina went on, "you think you look the same? And don't stare at us all befuddled, because you'll give us complexes, and if we kiss each other, peck peck, in a friendly way, let's first of all know who we are. So come here, mister, I can introduce everybody, because I have a very good memory. If you want, I can tell you by heart the first three lectures in Old Slavonic, and in dialectology, and in whatever other courses you didn't use to take notes in because you borrowed mine, already written by this little hand which, look at it, how it's swelled up now from washing diapers and men's underwear and all sorts of other not particularly philological or aesthetic matters, which over the span of twenty years must be untangled by an intellectual woman with her pretty little hands, yes sir. Because, Mr. Editor-in-Chief, sir—that's the way they must address you when they come to you with their play scripts for you to tell them yes or no, and what about this problem with the positive characters and the not very positive, and with the plot, the conflict which must be, but, at the same time, must not be . . . and with . . . well, let's drop it, the problems with dramaturgy in general—because I myself read your articles in the Romanian press, I don't have access to any other. Well, that's how it is in a small provincial town. Well, do they know, those who come to you, do they know what a slacker you were at the university, what a bramble thicket was inside your curly little head, because you couldn't distinguish this from that, and that from anything else? Do they know what a scared conformist, what a sweet little mouse Mr. Editor used to be, who today has such courageous literary opinions, and not only literary? Because, well, as you see, some of us still keep on reading, what else can we do? We still keep on reading, I mean we who are swallowed up alive by the provinces."

Yes, that was surely Doina. Bracing. The same as twenty years ago. Sarcastic, and feisty, and sincere, always helpful, and funny and conscientious. And what else? Yes, one hell of a sweet girl.

When they came upon Beetle, Doina stopped for a moment, pursed her lips, narrowed her eyes (exactly the way when, in the university, she was ready to make a crucial point but first she studied you for a few seconds to judge how to be more effective). "Cristian, I think you recognize your good friend Andreescu, called the director, called Beetle. It would be more than likely that you recognize him though disguised in this fashion by his mustache and his pleasing hint of baldness. Because surely he recognizes you. What do you say?"

Beetle at once embraced Cristian in his arms, kissed him with a smacking sound on both cheeks (he smelled of pipe tobacco and Chess aftershave), stepped back to take a better look at him from top to bottom, circled him, and again stood in front of him with his feet apart and hands behind his back like Napoleon.

"Bravo, old man," Beetle exploded at last, "you've accomplished all that you've accomplished, but you didn't get older, not even a second. That's some achievement. Look at us (excluding the girls, of course, because it's very normal that they must never get older) and then look at you. No belly, no baldness."

"Ah yes, but his importance has grown," Doina (who else?) interrupted. "I think you realize, dear Beetle, that this distinguished gentleman, our dear colleague, is some kind of a big shot. And it would have been a great pity for him not to be this after he worked so hard at becoming one of the bosses. Why shouldn't we have someone to be proud of? From the common and amorphous mass of professors, and librarians, and pedagogues whom we have become, there has emerged our strongest shoot, our representative, the first of our class, the distinguished Cristian Grecu, who today grants us the honor of appearing among us in blue jeans and without a tie, free, casual, cool, not like you in dark suits and white shirts, you provincial people, awkward and emotive. Can you, Beetle, tell me, can you detect a crumb of sentiment in this honorable man? No, you don't see a hint of one. You don't, because he has none. Our distinguished editor is trained like a cosmonaut. And not merely since yesterday or the day before."

Doina rattled on with huge enjoyment, and her words had a kind of wistful aggressiveness of which, probably, she wasn't quite aware—because what reason could she have now, here in this restaurant (category deluxe), rented for the evening, for this sort of comic-ironic assault, with no effect other than, eventually, the discomfort and embarrassment of everyone?

"Hey, come on, it's not really that way," said Beetle to repair the atmosphere, as if he would say, Doina, don't you see that he's a human being himself, I mean he seems to be one of us, since he came here? "How could he not have feelings? All men do after twenty years, in such a situation as this."

"Of course he does, too," added Doina. "It's just that he's afraid to be asked for something, because, you know, this is a big problem for the bigwigs. Their most unpleasant relationship is with their former colleagues and old friends (in the event that in their youth they could have been imprudent enough to make friends deficient in future importance). They're worried that these former friends will appeal to them for one thing or another. Didn't you see it on TV? There are some comic skits on this theme."

Doina burst into laughter. She had a contagious laugh like a waterfall, the tonic laughter of a healthy and self-confident person.

"I hope that you didn't lose your sense of humor forever, sir. That would be truly tragic, let me tell you, tragic for you, too, to be like the majority of those people who, upon being 'anointed,' in the same instant they're deprived of their humor and normal reactions. As if humor and normal reactions would be detrimental and nonconformist to standard development. But in relation to me, dear Cristi, don't be concerned. For, insofar as my turning instantly irresistible again and forever ingratiating, I must inform you that I haven't the least intention of ever asking you for anything, because I don't need anything. I have two children, I have a house, I have a bank loan, I have an advertised modern Alba Lux 2 washing machine, I have an asphalt road, running water, electricity, if I want to go to Iaşi I have an express train to the city once a day, I have a youth group, I even have some responsibilities, because I'm group leader for the Young Pioneers and I'm in charge of the Party bulletin board at work, I have plastic curtains with red poppies in that classroom where I'm the grade principal, I get to go every summer for free to the Navodari campground on the Black Sea, I have a freezer—do you have one? you see, you don't?—I have such nice prospects: I'll spend the New Year's holiday in Bulgaria, I'll earn an honorable mention with the Young Pioneers brigade at 'The Festival in Praise of Romania,' I'll buy a fine rabbit-fur jacket and newfangled door chimes that 'bing-bang-bong-bing,' I'll have a winning ticket in the state lottery. What more?! I'm a contented individual and I need nothing more because, if we add anything to this immense, vast happiness . . . So you see, my sweet Mr. Editor, you can rely on me, I'm the most comfortable friend in the world, the ideal friend, the one who never asks for anything. And now, are you hungry? Let's go eat. Because I feel that my energy is flagging, and if I lose my energy, I'll lose my charm, and without my charm . . . "

* * *

The table was arranged in the shape of a U, as for weddings and all festivities of the kind. Along the table's short (and official) middle leg the professors were seated, those who were still alive, those who resisted the flu, official restructurings, senate meetings, earthquakes, arteriosclerosis, heart attacks, changes of temperature and pressure, the winter wind from the steppes, the spring thaws. Twenty years during which the wind blew however it would blow, sometimes from there, sometimes from other places, said Cristian Grecu to himself. Twenty years, while some of them got older like the assistants, some others, oh ho! became lecturer and professor, and others went still farther, some of them very high up, everyone with his or her own particular destiny.

Who could guess that this shriveled little man, with parchmentlike skin, with red, congested eyelids, all the time beaming with equal warmth at his former students (whom, of course, he couldn't distinguish from other former students), at the waiters, at the tablecloth, at the festive fir-tree branches, is the very initiator and the leader of the celebrated campaign against "good morning," the same personage who more than twenty years ago filled all the Romanian newspapers with his argument against this most banal formula of greeting. The phrase "good morning"? . . . It implies mysticism, because wishing someone a good morning, on the one hand, means that you admit that a supernatural force makes it be a good morning, and, on the other hand, it means that you have doubts about that truth according to which our days cannot be otherwise than serene, happy and good. And therewith, dozens of articles from which other archaisms didn't escape either, "good luck" or "here's to your health" and similar formulas with roots in that obscurantist past with which our people have had to make a break forever in order to be able to advance freely on the way of progress. And Comrade Professor suggested the replacement of "good morning" with other more vigorous and forward-looking formulas, more revolutionary, clearer, which after so many years he himself has thoroughly forgotten and hopes that everyone else has done the same. Because people are used to forgetting stupidities easily. At first they wonder, then they resign themselves to things, and then they forget under the pressure of some new and bigger stupidity, in a perfect dialectical progression. Now R. H. is smiling benignly at the head of the table among those in the position of honor.

Beside him sits the deputy dean's portly wife, with her round face, screwed up in her impressive triple chin like an Elizabethan collar, a smooth wax mask, interrupted by the firm, thin line of her mouth—a straight line like in children's drawings. For her sake a young engineer had thrown himself from the second floor! For her!? (Let men likewise commit suicide out of love, Doina had remarked then, when all the university had roared—it's very good for them to become so sensitive, for them to cut their veins, to take poison, to throw themselves onto the train tracks. Long live Werther's nephews!) The engineer didn't die. He fell down, I don't know how, on something and then on something else, so he was left with a metal rod in one leg, definitively cured of the passion in his heart.

And Mr. Deputy Dean, what was he doing during that period? Indeed, what he did was to confront head-on the class character of language, that is to say, the incontrovertible fact that the language of the people was one thing and the language of the oppressors wholly another. And taking into consideration the truth that the exploiting classes lack character, one can say that their language likewise is of a piece with them. Is this clear? Of course, it was clear, and convincing, too, it had to be.

Less clear seemed to be the problem concerning great writers' language, because, unfortunately, not all of them came from the lower class, because there were some who derived from the landowners, princes, bishops, and the such. About this issue things seemed to be more muddled and contradictory. Ah, only *seemed* to be, because Comrade Deputy Dean never let himself be intimidated by rebel reality, and in the end he always succeeded in putting actuality into the organized and systematic frame of that theory which allows no deviation. A short time after that, the great specialty of the deputy dean became the ferreting out, the identification (a result of that action named by Doina "the quest by candlelight") of at least three impoverished relatives in the family of every great writer, from whom he extracted "the good sap of the true language," because it's impossible, isn't it, not to discover even for an aristocrat like the nineteenth-century playwright Alecsandri, somewhere on his huge genealogical tree, at least one stunted branch, a "downtrodden, oppressed, but healthy element," as Comrade Deputy Dean used to proclaim, to establish as its necessary heritage "the true and vital language of the masses."

All this blossomed again for him in Cristian Grecu's smile, oh yes, he had memories too, not only Doina Stăncescu (by the way, what was her family name now?). These, and others from the same period, "obsessive," some were calling it now—what a joke! Why was this period any more obsessive than others, than the whole century, the whole millennium? Cristian Grecu asked himself, absently chewing the meatballs and sausages. Each age with its unique obsessions, or rather, with its fun, if you know how to break with the past smiling, and this, the best solution—for preserving your nerves—didn't originate with him, but he'd adopted it rapidly and most usefully ever since he had stopped being a student . . .

> "Should auld acquaintance be forgot
> And never brought to min'? . . .
> We'll tak a cup o' kindness yet,
> For auld lang syne."

Everyone stood up, he stood, too, with his vodka in his hand, clinked glasses with the blond, beside him, Simu's wife, and with Simu, and with the engineer on his right (it seemed he'd said he was an engineer), Luci's husband, and with Tomescu, and with Picu:

"And let's live it up, my dear, and let's see each other more often, in five years, why wait to wear out completely? . . . Are they your children, Luci? So big? Enjoy them. But you must see mine. No, I have no photos with me, because I left in a hurry, directly from the auto service, because on Thursday someone hit my car. Yes, a lot of money. They still get away with it, no restraints, they went so far as to take my jack from the trunk. Oh, hell it's small! For what? Damned baksheesh! Is someone to pay me more than my salary? No, no, I'm not going to agree with you about this despicable Balkanic habit. You can't even buy a book without tipping . . . I have a cousin there, and since they are making freezers he doesn't answer my calls . . . Principles? What kind of principles, man? . . . First you could hear a noise, then it made a loud clunk, then it didn't go at all . . . 3200 *lei*, a fortune . . . Despite their three, they're good for nothing, because you have to go from one to another, they won't help, and my mother-in-law lives there too, so you can imagine . . . The supervisor said it's impossible for four of them to have to take a repeat examination in Romanian language, because this is our maternal language and it's impossible that it not be known to every Romanian by heart, and he punished me, he yelled at me, only in the worst grammar, and in the end he said that he would forgive me 'for the momentary,' but this was never to be repeated, never, and all I could do is go home crying and . . . Well, that's the way it is with the people, so let's march in the parade alongside them . . . Beer makes me feel sick. But vodka. That's the stuff . . . Impossible, man, you can't be knowledgeable about everything, not even during the Renaissance, not even Leonardo da Vinci who . . . And he, no, no, no, and no again until I got ticked off and I said, hey you, you're so clever, you'd better realize that rock 'n' roll wasn't invented by you, we, we're the Beatles generation, we who're now in our forties."

A moment of thrilling silence settled over them. Who was the one who spoke about the Beatles? Picu? Tomescu? Beetle? It doesn't matter who, since everyone there feels a kind of weariness, something like a wave coursing through the neck, and curling there it in a painful knot. Let's cure it with vodka, let's cure it with beer, let's cure it with something. It still can be cured. It will go away . . . "Yesterday."

"Adrian didn't come. Does anyone know anything about Adrian Lascu?" Luci's voice was small, tremulous, hesitant, as always. "None of you used to dance like him. Do you remember? He was extraordinary!"

"We used to be colleagues at the Institute for about three years," said Picu. "Then he left for a year abroad for advanced study. It's a long story about Adrian. I saw him a month ago. I visited him at the hospital."

"The hospital? What's up with him?" Tomescu asked.

"That's the point, because it's nothing definite they can put their finger on," Picu went on. "I spoke with him nearly an hour. He was absolutely coherent, but his wife indicated that the doctors wanted to keep him there a month, at the minimum. He has good moments and moments of depression. I was lucky. I caught him in a good phase. He was calm and somehow detached from that story because of which he had to stay in the hospital. For you to understand at least some of this, it would be necessary for me to tell you about the atmosphere in our Research Institute, but I don't have the energy for such a long story."

"Oh come on, man, what in fact happened?" Tomescu asked again. "What have you done to him?"

"That's the whole point, nobody did anything to him, or, to be more accurate, nothing I could discern at all. Anyhow, nothing concrete. Do you understand? I mean he was not kicked out, nobody took credit for his articles and signed them in place of him, nobody put roadblocks in his way when he had to go abroad, there was nothing at all. All was going well. Very well. Too well, maybe, those in his department used to say. He married a graphic artist, a talented and gorgeous woman whose father used to keep bees, they had a nice child, they bought a car, and then a house, he got a scholarship for one year in England, and after he returned home, he was made a principal researcher; by the time he was thirty-five, he already had two published books and was awarded the Academy prize. Then some rumor began to be heard throughout the Institute that Adrian had somebody backing him, because otherwise it's impossible, everyone knows, to rise so fast. I heard this rumor myself, but most of the time they kept things like this away from me, because they knew we used to be students together at the university. It's impossible, you know, that he does not have someone 'sponsoring' him, said Mrs. P. M. (the one who has the weekly TV talk show). There are other very capable researchers, others who work hard, and others, too, who are correct, congenial, good-looking, and still they haven't made it as far as this Adrian Lascu. His wife doesn't cheat on him, his child is winning honors in school, he's healthy, he has no professional disappointments, he never complains about money—something's not right here, she said. But she wasn't the only one who said so.

"After a while, and this was to be expected, the rumor came to Adrian's ear. At first, he had no reaction (he told me this himself at the hospital when he tried to explain to me what happened, and how). Then, some time later, he began to feel obsessed by this whole business, and next he began to question himself: do I have someone supporting me behind my back? Suddenly he began to understand that everything in his life was going exceptionally well, when he thought in fact that his life was just going normally. X was in court with his former wife to divide their possessions. Y couldn't succeed in writing a minimally acceptable Ph.D. thesis. Z's boy gave up the university for a ballerina who convinced him to become an auto mechanic. Well, everybody in fact had his trouble, temporary and commonplace human worries in the end, not tragedies, but, anyhow, enough to make them apprehensive, to make them bitter, to give them complexes. And during this time he, Adrian, began to feel himself (as he confessed to me at the hospital) an unreal character kept in an aseptic vessel by a novelist who wanted on purpose to introduce into a normal story, full of living and plausible characters, a hoax, a puppet, a false type, a positive hero from a to z with no defeats, no failures, no shadows or nuances, the symbol of a thesis about happiness in vitro.

"Everything in fact began from this point, because, you all know Adrian very well, he wasn't content only to note it. He began, you won't believe this, his 'investigations'—this is the exact word, and it's his. Not immediately. For a while he didn't do anything special. He still had intervals, he said, when he told himself that if there really was someone backing him, it's this someone's business as long as he himself feels fine and no one asks for anything in return from him. But if one day it turns out that he's going to be asked for anything, if one day a deadline passes and someone informs him, that's it, little boy, it's your turn now, and if he weren't ever able to pay (or wouldn't want to), because who knows in what kind of 'money' he'd be asked to pay . . . Anyhow, Adrian said there in his hospital room (where we were talking all the time, the nurse never once stepped out), a perfect, A-plus life, without family conflicts, without professional failures, without missteps and misfortunes, I don't think that could have been paid for (if it came to anything like a bill) with merely a smile and a sincere thank you from the bottom of my heart. Who knows what kind of smell, taste, and color that wad of bills would have they could have asked me to pay with?

"You have to realize that I didn't interrupt him and that I didn't try to tell him *then* that he needed a period of R and R, a vacation somewhere in the mountains, or that he should have talked to someone, a friend who might have comforted him or might have told him, in practical terms, look here, Adrian, if your life's an A-plus, it's because you're a top-grade A-plus man, because you're gifted and serious, and because it happened to be you who had this luck, oh yes, this opportunity and nothing more, this chance for everything to be all right for the time being. Don't drive nails into your own coffin, because you've no reason to. I said nothing like this because, anyhow, it was too late, nothing would have mattered. And he went on telling his tale in such a fever, he was so 'absorbed' in it, that any interruption of mine, even of approval, might have upset him, and that nurse, glued to her chair in the corner of the room, seemed to be waiting for such a thing to throw me out."

"Well, what did Adrian do? Did he immediately get put in the hospital? His nerves went bad, all of a sudden, because of a fanciful supposition?"

"Oh, no! In fact this isn't half the story. Because, as I already said, he didn't stop at this point, I mean noting all this and tormenting himself. He began his 'investigations.' I couldn't understand what exactly he meant by 'investigations' and what he actually did, but it's for certain that after some months of research with no result, I mean without coming any nearer to identifying 'the man in the shadows,' the secret someone who arranged for his success—and I think you realize what kind of expense of psychic energy such a quixotic undertaking implies—Adrian realized that his man purely and simply didn't exist. Well, a normal assumption, we ourselves would say now, in our tranquility and with clear minds. And still more normal it would have been, after such a determination, for him to calm down and mind his own business like before, since backing Adrian Lascu, was, it turned out, nobody other than Adrian Lascu. As for myself, such a conclusion would have strengthened me. But Adrian, instead, was crushed, destroyed. There began his fears, his hesitation, his downfall. Nothing worthwhile came from him anymore, he couldn't concentrate, he was always irascible and unfocused. His colleagues from his department said, 'What's with this Lascu fellow? Has he fallen in love? He doesn't know what world he's in any longer. He didn't finish his research paper by the deadline, for the first time in twenty years. And he's also lost files which can't be replaced'—well, lots of things like these, a whole chain of them. Then I stopped working there, so for a long period of time, I wasn't up-to-date. I heard about much of this at random from a mutual friend, the same one who by chance later let me know that Adrian was in the hospital. This is the way it was with Adrian Lascu. He was always a little bit, how can I say it?—'strange.' Do you remember that time when we were in our third year at the university, the story of the vote, with . . . "

And Picu broke off suddenly at the very moment that he realized that Cristian Grecu was right in front of him—hmm, he was about to commit a faux pas, if he hadn't already—so he finished all in a rush, "Well, he'll get better and then we'll have a big bash to celebrate, but before then, let's hoist a glass to his health and rattle our old bones a little. What about it, Luci, shall we dance? Baby, let's shake it. I don't dance like Adrian (because I couldn't do that twenty years ago, either), but if we give it a try and mash ourselves together a little bit . . . I hope that your husband won't get the wrong idea, it's Mr. Engineer, isn't it?"

"Go ahead, take her, man, take her, I let you have her open-heartedly," the engineer said, laughing, "because, as for myself, I've never danced in all my life, and this is a single one of five hundred weak points of mine that my wife already knows by heart. I'm the man with the production, with the plans, with the engines. Dance as long as you wish, and as for me, if I have a small glass in front of me, I feel all right, even here. Here someone like me can talk with people in the high society. I'm getting more cultivated myself, because we engineers don't have much time to read—not like you, who went to a college for reading novels—a pleasure, sir, to read novels and poems, and to get a university diploma for this, and to see your name in the papers. Right, Mr. Grecu? Excuse my question— you know, I've never been in contact much with people like you—do you also get paid some money for what you write in the newspaper, I mean, besides your salary? Because, you know, we work in the factory until our eyes pop out of our heads . . . Well, you know, you, since you're a former colleague of Luci, I can permit myself to ask you, is it true that writers are rolling in money? Or is this a mistaken opinion?"

"Wrong, mister, wrong." Cristian Grecu cut him short—the engineer had already begun to irritate him. How lucky that Luci wasn't there, because otherwise she would have felt embarrassed.

"And unless it shouldn't be this way, the way I've already told you I've heard about," the engineer persisted, "you know, I'd like to begin to write myself, I bet I could do well, by God, because this Romanian language couldn't be more complicated than mathematics! 'Cause this Romanian language, as it's said, we all know it, all of us—and in this respect I myself agree with that supervisor someone here was talking about previously. But I didn't want to enter the discussion, because it's not nice at a festivity like this one to contradict someone, it seems to me, so that's why I kept silent. What do you say?"

Cristian Grecu said nothing. He raised his glass of wine (Great Hill label, pretty good!) and began to drink it slowly in small sips. He felt that he was beginning to grow angry (and not only because of the engineer), and he didn't at all want his ulcer to start bothering him again. That ulcer which he could date to exactly that senate meeting when he and Doina and Adrian *had to* vote, that meeting which Picu has never forgotten, nor Doina, nor, probably, any of them.

"And let me tell you that I have good subjects for a novel," the engineer droned on. "Yes. A lot of them. From the maintenance department to the chief mechanic. I could even write a play. I haven't tried so far, but if I practice it a little . . . Because, as you know, I have no training in writing with letters, ha ha, because we, you know, we're much better with figures. That's the profession. But if you say so, that you don't make a lot, hmm," said the engineer, looking at him suspiciously in disbelief, and his eyes seemed to say, Don't try to trick me, I heard what I heard and there's no use telling me no if it's yes, because I don't intend to take your share, after all, we're both human beings. "Take, for example, yes, here's one, there's a guy, a Mr. Plum, the chief of the team. This man is a hell of a character! This guy always says that everything he's doing is perfect, and you can say as loudly as you want that he fucked up, because he, no, no, no, and this particular guy has, man, astonishing explanations that will stupefy anybody. All the rest are afraid when they deal with him. But it's not enough for him to know that the others are afraid, no, he wants them to love him, believe it or not. And he tortures them as if they were horse thieves. And they caught on to this weakness of his, and they keep on saying, Mr. Plum, there's no one in the whole factory braver and more efficient than you, God Himself chose you specially, because if we were by chance on Mr. Săndulescu's team or Mr. Ticǎ's team, we'd be nothing, like dust. And this Plum, what do you think he does then? He strikes his own people from the list of bonuses. And then this Plum, he comes to me satisfied, and I ask him, Why, Mr. Plum, why? They're your own men. Let them be, he says, so they'll know fear of me, let them know that here *I* am their father, because if you don't keep tight reins, they'll think they're loose in the field and won't work at all, and then the hell with the plan and bonuses. Let them be afraid of me and thank me from early morning to bedtime, because Plum's the one, I'm making real men out of them, and I know they love me, much more than for any bonus, they love me because I'm like the way I am, I'm their father, the one and only Plum. And I, I make the mistake of telling him it's quite the opposite. Mr. Plum, these men go around all day long cursing you behind your back, because if you cut someone's money, that someone will never forget you his whole life. And Plum turned red with fury—because it's impossible for anyone not to love him, and he'll show them, screw these villains' mothers! And from then on, he treated me no differently from them, and during the next party meeting he said that I was at the most rudimentary level of political education, and moreover I'd been married twice, and this and that, in addition—what can I say, he painted me so prettily that, when the conclusions came to be summarized and it was my turn to speak, I couldn't say anything except to tell them, all this is enough, comrades, as for me, I myself agree with everything, we're in total unanimity.

"Oh, and others, too, especially good for a novel, because this Plum, he's really something, a real piece of work. You know, no more than one month ago, the leader of the Union of Young Communists came to me, with his pale face white like fresh whitewash, and told me, almost speechless in amazement: 'Comrade Plum has taken ill. He has swollen glands.' That's to say, dear sir, what an infamy, illness doesn't have a solid criterion upon which to dare touch our Comrade Plum in the slightest. That's it, sir, why should we add anything else? They love him, they love him boundlessly."

Cristian Grecu felt that he was suffocating. He had to find some pretext, any excuse, to flee from being next to this future novelist or playwright or whatever he wanted to be, to dance with a girl, to go to the toilet, to escape anywhere else. He stood up firmly, cast his eyes all about the room, as if searching for someone, and then said politely, "I have to exchange some words with a former colleague who couldn't arrive earlier because he lives in the far north, near Sighet. I'll come back and we can go on with our discussion."

"But do you think that this Plum would be good for a character? If not, I have others, many more, who . . . "

"No, I'm sorry, I don't believe that he'd be very good," and he let issue forth that saving sentence heard at the last editorial meeting: "He's a peripheral character. In fact, without doubt, he's in no way typical of our society. He's an isolated case. Anyhow, any story that could have at its center such a, let's say, a caricature would have no message. And without a message . . . "

"Message? What kind of message should there be, man? What message?" the engineer repeated, with a totally confused face.

"Well, that's the very problem, that's it!" Cristian Grecu threw back to him enigmatically, going courageously to the men's room.

It was already nearly eleven. At one o'clock this tale had to come to its conclusion, Cristian Grecu said to himself, searching with his eyes for a place to sit for a few minutes—anywhere other than next to the engineer—to breathe for a while, to let the engineer calm down. He felt someone catch his arm. He turned his head. It was Beetle.

"Could we speak together quietly for two minutes?" said Beetle, smiling somehow embarrassed, as if he feared a denial or a delay.

They passed through the pairs of dancers and went out to the terrace. It was a clear June night, with an occasional breath of wind. Cristian Grecu tripped over an upside-down chair, and the violent pain in his knee added to his bad humor; whatever one might say, he didn't feel at ease.

"Damn it! They don't have any light here. You can crack your head open."

"As long as we have stars, and look how big they are, it's the best time to economize on electricity," Beetle laughed.

They sat themselves in the right corner of the terrace, as far as they could from the racket inside. They sat in silence. Grecu felt his heart constrict, he was overcome by a vague feeling of discomfiture. He waited for Beetle to begin. But Beetle said nothing. He slowly and methodically filled his pipe, staring hard to see it under the feeble natural light of the stars—a few of them big stars, like in the scenery of an operetta. Unreal. False.

"I'm going to get two glasses, so we won't sit here dry. I'll be back in a moment."

Beetle stood up and Grecu gazed after him as he went away, with a sense of release (yes, release—any delay is a release in such situations), until he watched him push aside the velvet curtain that hid the door to the terrace, and he registered, for a moment, the wriggling of the people inside, his fellow students from twenty years ago. Then the curtain fell back into place, like an eyelid over an ephemeral image, only this image—nearly a freeze frame—with flushed faces, with sweaty brows, with makeup streaked over their wrinkles—didn't vanish at once with the fall of the curtain, but continued rolling on his retina somewhere within in an endless corridor, and its painful movements he knew at this very moment would be repeated and repeated long after.

* * *

From the very beginning, reading the simple announcement in the cultural weekly *Free Romania*, he knew that he should remember it, that he would be obliged to remember it, everything about it, in full detail. To remember? What does it mean, to remember, since he had never forgotten it, not one bit, not for a moment? It's true that in time the event suffered some changes in his memory, took on other contours, other significances, but without ever losing clarity of outline, without ever blurring and fading. Quite the contrary.

That morning, in his editorial offices, when he read the announcement, he reconstructed, almost despite himself, the whole senate meeting, as he had never yet done in all those twenty years. Of course, once in a while, some event in his subsequent biography triggered the thought, *there* and *then* in that amphitheater, but he had never summoned up the strength to reconstruct everything. He tried to forget, he forced himself to modify the data of the problem in his mind, in such a manner that his guilt (was it his alone?) would lose its sharpness, would blur. Every time, however, there intruded brutally an element of the present that was linked in one way or another to that day, of course, sometimes obliquely and symbolically, but wasn't this sufficient to keep fresh and painful in his mind the memory of that day? The first years after graduating and being assigned to his job he endeavored to make himself useful, to say yes always, not to think too much, not to ask anything during the meetings, and above all not to ask himself anything. Those were the most peaceful years when everything went without a hitch: promotions, insignificant appointments to all kinds of committees and commissions, and so forth, until he became a man of importance. Everything was good and became better and better (in fact, he had pushed himself toward this from the time he was a student at the university, as Doina used to point out), up to that moment when the editor responsible for the current issue (Cristian worked at that time for the folklore department) told him, "Comrade Grecu, in two days you have to put together some Christmas carols for the second page, about three or four, but you know, very up-to-date, understand? You'll have to write them and to sign them as Ion Stancu, Gică Florea. Choose a typical name as you think best, but they have to sound wholesome, authentic. And put in some villages. Ion Stancu, make him from Cochârleni-Ilfov. Have you got it? Come on, everyone, back to work, all of you to work, we don't have time to waste," Georgescu added after calling for the layout editor. Cristian Grecu reentered his office, confused. He felt that something was wrong, but in order to clarify things for himself, he'd have to think, and he, Cristian Grecu, had decided since that senate meeting that it wasn't good to think too much, because thinking too much would lead him off a precipice, would disorient him, would get him lost. He picked up some sheets of paper and was tapping the table absently with his pen when he caught Ancă Ganea glancing at him a little bit amused and a little bit questioning. "And what are you doing? Christmas carols, too?" he asked then, seeing all of them with their noses to the paper. "No, little ducky," said Ancă, "only you. You're the only one. We're country children, and Georgescu doesn't dare to ask us to falsify folklore. We told him no, and it's remained no to the end. But Georgescu knows that he has a reliable person, someone he can count on. He knows that among us there's one comrade with great prospects who always says yes, and that means his excesses of zeal (because I don't think anybody could have asked him to produce such an idiotic thing) can be materialized, thanks to you, as in fact he expected. So, no surprise for us. On the contrary, if you had refused him, we would have wondered, so get on with the job, and 'in the winter's cold the three kings said, we bring you eggs, we bring you bread.'"

Then followed his awakening. A brutal awakening, like that of a boxer, after a few hard punches. Only after that did he begin to realize what in fact had happened years before in that meeting, which almost unwillingly he reconstructed upon reading the announcement in *Free Romania* . . .

The three of them in the front row of benches. Always the representatives of the students were placed in the first row of the amphitheater, under the eyes of those who presided. Only he knew what it was about, because during the first hour of classes that morning, the dean had summoned him to his office and told him how pleased he was to have a student like him and that he had a lot of confidence in him and that it should be better for him to speak and to say such and such, the positive things, for example, how the student Andreescu had integrated perfectly and moreover that he had an aptitude for philology and pedagogy, and that he would surely make a good teacher, et cetera, et cetera. Hmm, a good teacher, when Beetle would have been an exceptional film director . . . During the first days after Beetle joined them, he spoke to nobody. He had a bored air and seemed somehow detached. "An 'angry young man' abandoned among us," Doina used to say. Blond, slim, mysterious. Excellently suited for a class with eighty girls. Soon all of them somehow found out that Beetle had participated in a festival of students' films in Poland, that the Cinematographic Institute had chosen two films for the festival, but that Beetle had taken with him a third film without approval of any kind, another film made by him (like the other two). Something with some worms, insects, beetles, something symbolic, a parable in short, something "earthshaking." And there in Poland the film was awarded the grand prize. This was Beetle's misfortune—the grand prize. When he came back home, he said nothing. After a while, the dean received international congratulations for the prize-winning film. How could a film that had not been sent to the festival be awarded a prize? They wondered and wondered and then kicked him out. I mean, Beetle—

for his name remained Beetle—and they likewise kicked out the two others who happened to accompany him to the festival. That was more or less the story. The story? The legend? The truth?

Doina and Adrian knew nothing about the day's agenda. The meeting opened with the note of boredom common to all the other meetings which the three of them had attended for two years, since their election as representatives of their school year in the senate. At first, they used to participate, with curiosity, and then they became less and less impressed with the grandiloquent and enthusiastic language which no longer amused them at all.

"Comrades," said the dean, at point four on our agenda, "we have to discuss the situation of the student Radu Andreescu.

"The student Radu Andreescu was expelled from the Institute of Theatrical and Cinematographic Art in his fourth year of study, following a serious disciplinary violation, but being vouchsafed the right to reregister in another humanistic faculty, as a second-year student. We do not focus on the deviation from policy because of which he was expelled. That analysis was made two years ago in the faculty from which the comrade comes—so it's purposeless for us to waste our time. Student Andreescu reregistered in our university center in the faculty of philology, which he has regularly attended and with productive results in learning . . .

"Next," the dean continued, "with the force of the collective and, what's more, with the personal example of other students, Andreescu has been taken back into the fold beyond all expectations, he has even directed small performances here in the faculty, he does not seem to be a disruptive element anymore," et cetera, et cetera.

Cristian Grecu was no longer attentive, the words passed by him as by the others (some of them were nodding) when he was startled to hear his name: "Cristian Grecu! I grant you the floor in your role as colleague and friend of Andreescu and, of course, in your capacity as responsible representative of the student group in which he belongs."

Without the least sense that he was doing any harm (wasn't this true, or—?), Cristian proceeded to repeat all that the dean "suggested" to him earlier.

"As you've already heard," the dean then contributed, "the student Andreescu is perfectly integrated into the collective in which he belongs; moreover, he has an aptitude for philology. That's why I consider his request that he receive our favorable recommendation for readmittance into the faculty of directing now, after almost three years of studying philology, to be a childish gesture. Comrades, this is useless now. Why should he return there, if he has proved himself here a capable element? We went so far as to consult with our comrades from the Theatrical Institute and with the comrades from the Ministry, who communicated to us that the student Andreescu could even now reenroll in directing, but not, of course, without our concurrence. Why, however, should he reenroll there if he is completely integrated here? And more than this, if here he has the chance to continue to direct? I mean by this, direction of some programs of sketches, some student performances—he can be in charge of the students' performing brigade. And, likewise, of the artistic brigades belonging to other faculties, if his time permits."

And the dean again launched forth, he spoke with verve, he expatiated, he advanced new arguments, and from time to time, he quoted him, Cristian Grecu, the one—wasn't he?—who best saw how profoundly Andreescu was integrated.

"What have you done, old man?" whispered Adrian through his teeth. "You destroyed Beetle with the smile of your lips, praising him. Stand up, stand up now, and tell them that Beetle's vocation is to direct, that directing is his life, that he was born for this."

"I'll stand up myself, I'll tell them everything myself," said Doina.

"It's not you who must do this, but this conscienceless little mouse. He must say it, because if it's you, all of them will presume that you've been put up to it. He's the one who has to speak. Stand up, man, don't you hear? Don't take away his one chance! On what ground do you claim the right to alter his destiny? For the reward of those filthy fifty one-hundredths of a point which good young communists get added to their averages? So you'll have the highest average this year, ahead of Doina and me? For this, man, for this?"

Perhaps Cristian Grecu didn't remember the dean's exact words anymore, but Adrian's whispered words were precisely these.

Then the vote came. Everyone agreed that the student Andreescu must remain in philology (since he was so well integrated), not counting Doina, who abstained, and Adrian, who was against it.

Of course, the dean knew how to raise the issue: who is in favor of the student Andreescu? Everyone was in favor, being in fact against. Against Beetle's one last chance. Only Adrian Lascu, being against, was, in fact, in favor. Only Adrian had the courage to do what he thought better. Adrian, and, in her way, Doina, who abstained. That was the meeting. Cristian Grecu didn't come across Beetle right afterward. For about a week, Beetle drank continuously. After that he seemed pacified. He was somehow another man. He had been waiting for his chance for three years. And just like that, he lost it. Forever. Now he no longer waited for anything. He must enter into another character's skin. Enter it forever. That's it, finished with the symbols and parables, finished with the grand prize, finished with beetles. Indeed, finished. When Cristian Grecu looked for the first time into Andreescu's eyes after that senate meeting—about half a year later, before the exam period in the winter, in the final year— Cristian didn't see in them any reproach, any contempt. No disgust, no fury. His eyes seemed to say: you must give me a new birth, do what you want and how you want with me, let's see what we come out of this with, let's see, *I mean you*, because as for me, I myself won't ever be able to realize anything.

* * *

"Excuse me, old man, for keeping you waiting for me," said Beetle as soon as he entered the terrace.

In one hand he had a bottle of vodka, and in the other, two glasses. He put them on the table, and in the same instant a thick notebook with green vinyl covers dropped from under his arm.

"I made a quick trip up to my room, because I wanted to bring this for you." He pointed to the notebook with his hand. "Maybe you can find the time to flip through it and see what your friend Andreescu is up to these days."

No, there wasn't the slightest trace of irony in his voice. Maybe just a little emotion, the emotion and the embarrassment of an amateur who asks for the considered judgment of a professional who, by chance, was a fellow student. A colleague who became a professional while he, Andreescu, took an opposite path. From the grand prize at an international festival to the House of Culture in the little town of M——, where he was amateur stage director and secretary and lyricist for the theatrical sketches, and had a good chance to become a manager, and maybe eventually a deputy chief of cultural activities, because the artistic brigade won second place in the district phase, and the theater team honorable mention at the national level, and they always give unstinting support and, there you have it, all's well that ends well.

"Here's my work from the last several years," Andreescu said, pointing toward the notebook with green covers that now lay between them, like a dark sign on the white surface of the table, a boundary marker, a buoy, beyond which and before which were not even memories, only the present, the concrete and nostalgic present of a summer evening after twenty years.

It would have been polite for Cristian Grecu to reach out his hand and pick the notebook up from there and ruffle its pages for a moment, despite the impossibility of reading it under the natural and invisible light of the stars. But his hand remained clenched around the glass of vodka, incapable of any movement. Through the tips of his fingers he now felt how the chill of the glass penetrated him through and through; suddenly he felt cold (how can you feel cold in June at the simple touch of a glass?). And it seemed that he should say something, now, not later (Stand up, stand up now, and tell them, stand up, man, don't take away his chance!), but now his lips were clenched, too, and his teeth, so tight that the soul itself should not find room to issue forth.

"It's a notebook for directing; in fact, there are some character descriptions, notes on simple people from different workplaces in M——. I saw them, I interviewed them, I also interviewed their trade union comrades about them. Thus, I have serious and compelling documentation. On this documentary basis, I'll compose the texts for the brigade and . . ." Andreescu spoke by the book, the sentences were prefabricated, like all the sentences in all the meetings where, there was no doubt, he had said the same things, the same stereotypical thoughts said the same way, with the same for-a-meeting intonation. Yes, Andreescu was what he'd proposed he had to become then, twenty years ago, after waking up from his drunken stupor. He had succeeded perfectly, he didn't play, he didn't pretend; he was totally the character he doomed himself to be. "Frankly speaking, with this methodology, I do not see how I could miss second place at the national level with my brigade of amateurs. In fact, you'll surely see this when you read" (no, there was no longer the faintest trace of the initial shyness of the amateur in front of the professional, but instead of this, a kind of aplomb acquired over time, the aplomb of one who knows that everyone can produce art and that the professional has a solemn duty to support the amateur, not as a poor or second-rate relative, but as a fellow soldier in the cause, something like this could be understood, not from Andreescu's words, but from the resoluteness with which he articulated them) "and you'll probably be surprised by the form in which those sketches are arranged. Because they are not simple character sketches but more—in fact, they're small literary pieces, so to speak, you'll see, and then you'll tell me what you think about them. Comrade Ştet himself, from the Ministry of Culture, saw them, I also showed them to the deputy managing editor for our newspaper, and both of them congratulated me, so that I've already had two highly competent opinions. However, I'd like you to see them yourself. Yes, in the form they are, so as to let you, too, make your own judgment. What do you say?"

Cristian Grecu succeeded in nodding his head yes.

"Then, cheers? To good luck and glory!" said Andreescu, lifting his glass.

"Luck!" Cristian Grecu echoed, and their glasses met together above the notebook with green covers, on which a small drop of vodka lazily trickled—a shivering kiss of crystal, in the unreal light of the stars.

"Shall we go inside?"

"No, I'd rather stay out here awhile."

"O.K., I'm going in, to chat with some others of us. Who knows when we'll see each other again? Don't forget my notebook here, or you'll ruin me," said Beetle, pushing the notebook slowly but firmly toward Grecu.

"Don't worry. I'll look it over tonight. Tomorrow morning I'm going to depart at about ten. If I can't find you, I'll leave it at the reception desk. Would you like me to take the notebook with me to Bucharest, to read it more carefully, and to send it back after that?" Grecu heard himself speaking all in one breath, with polished alacrity. It seemed that his feeling of tension had disappeared, and now he used the same studied amiability he put on anytime when needed, or anytime when he had to deal with those who came knocking at the newspaper doors.

"No, old man, don't take it to Bucharest. Not for any reason other than if I don't feel it with me every day, I don't feel like I'm a man. Look over as much of it as you can tonight, and maybe I'll be coming to Bucharest in the autumn, because I already ordered some folk costumes from there for the team of dancers, and then we'll see each other and . . . Is that all right?"

"Fine."

As before, Grecu gazed after him as he walked away. Very soon Beetle had to push the curtain aside from the terrace doorway, and in the rectangle of light Grecu again observed, in a flash, the feverish agitation of the people inside, his fellow students from twenty years ago.

In fact, what did he think? What did he expect Andreescu to be now? A disoriented man? an alcoholic? a sarcastic misanthrope? a shy, withdrawn, disappointed person who cannot find his place? a defeated voice of perpetual lamentation? No. Andreescu was exactly what he decided to be, what he was forced to decide he would be. A perfectly adapted man. A cultural animator from the provinces, industrious, enterprising, well-rooted in reality, a reality accepted with no comments—he had left all the comments there in the images of that film from what was now twenty-three years ago. He is what he is, without complexes, without suffering, without irony. He has succeeded.

He lifted the notebook from the table. At the very touch of its covers, he felt, nobody knows why, a wave of bitterness drowning him from his toes up to his head. He had never until now had the concrete evidence, the material proof of the consequences of that senate meeting (of course, Cristian Grecu was overreacting, but on such occasions—which come to people, isn't it so, but once in twenty years?—you have the right to a different kind of sensitivity, if only for a night).

Inside, people were exhausted. Small laughs, the exchange of addresses, promises, empty bottles. The festive little fir-tree branches lay wilted on the tables with crumpled napkins and pieces of bread and apple cores. The engineer was staring fixedly at the empty bottle in front of him and seemed to be interested in nothing anymore. Not even the prospect of becoming a novelist or playwright. He had drunk quite a lot. And Simu too had drunk rather a lot. Simu's wife was pale and had teary eyes. At the official table the wife of the deputy dean remained at her seat, dignified and screwed up in her triple chin. All the others were probably scattered now among the former students where, anyhow, it was less boring:

"He paid, of course he paid the child support, but he never gave her his name . . . I think that he'll come back, that's what I think . . . And I said that they could never reach such a point, and look, they could . . . With epoxy, with epoxy or with wood glue . . . You put in three eggs and then add the beaten egg whites . . . The Ph.D.? All the cretins have one now. No, sir, better to train as a tailor . . . No, the wrong doesn't come from there, but it derives from the structure itself . . . Come on, it's not brick. It's Styrofoam blocks . . . Elastic? I saw it myself last summer in a fabric shop in Covasna . . . It isn't possible, they have no weapons, they took the weapons from all those and all these from the others . . . What sacrifice, sir? . . . Until when? Until seven o'clock when my mother-in-law goes to take her from the kindergarten . . . The ultimate purpose is the human being. We must sacrifice everything for the human being. But not the human being himself, because we'll fall into mysticism . . . Of course, there's a vaccine, but not for the Asian strain . . . Two-thirds from the salary, no more . . . Let sleeping dogs lie, because . . . "

> "For he's a jolly good fellow
> For he's a jolly good fellow,
> Which nobody can deny . . . "

They again raised up their glasses and clinked them, and kissed each other once more, and again promised to see each other more often, because it's such a pity not to.

Cristian Grecu had a room on the second floor, near Simu's. He climbed the stairs (there was no reason to wait for the elevator for two floors), and when he reached the landing between the first and second floor, he saw at the top of the stairs the silhouette of a woman leaning upon the balustrade. When he had climbed until he stood near her, he recognized her. She was Simu's wife. Her blond hair, which at the beginning of the evening had been carefully put up in an elaborate bun, now fell in disorder on her shoulders.

"Can I help you, madam?" asked Grecu. The woman turned her head toward him (until then she had stood looking over the balustrade) without answering him.

Her big gray eyes, bloodshot because of crying, had the gleam of a young, hungry animal. She stared at him a second, maybe two, after which she turned her face again and was leaning upon the balustrade.

The closer Cristian approached the door to his room, the more he felt a mad desire to turn back to take that woman with him for the night, of course she wanted to, at least her eyes said so . . . But he opened his door, switched on the light, and tossed the notebook on the table. If only there's *something* there! If Beetle were still Beetle? If . . . He had no more patience. He opened the notebook. On the first page there was the following motto:

> We ever must think, must work, must fight
> To shed on life a glorious light.

Under this motto was written:

> files for the texts for the arts brigade
>   or
> small, flawed photos on the page
> of a better than perfect age.

On the second page there were some verses followed by a short commentary. He turned some more pages. All had the same structure. He read one at random:

> A worker in our section, Stan,
> Should have been a model man.
> He's industrious, quick, correct.
> But oh, poor Stan has a grave defect.

He drinks in taverns and at home
Strong brandy, rum, and beer with foam.
We've said, out of consideration,
Don't come in such inebriation,
Our collective won't permit at all
A worker who's tippled alcohol.
We tried our best to help and rescue
The once good worker Stan Popescu.
So listen, comrades, don't follow Stan!
Alas, he's not a model man.

After that, there followed a commentary (in prose) connected to the attitudes and activities (real, concrete, and documented) of worker Stan Popescu—from the second section, the machine tool factory in M——. Opinions of fellow workers, of the leader of the trade union group, of his wife.

He read a few more (about deceivers, slack-offs, achievers, thieves) and closed the notebook. No, not now, he cannot think about anything now. Tomorrow, to think with a clear mind. Tomorrow in the light. He took a shower—amazing, in this hotel, there was hot water at so late an hour! When he came out of the bathroom, it seemed he could hear someone crying. He pressed his ear to the door. Yes, crying. She was crying. There, on the stairs, Simu's wife. To open the door now, to go up to her, to take her in his arms. Now . . .

In the morning, in the car on the way back to Bucharest, he surprised himself several times humming to the refrain in his mind:

> "For she's a jolly good fellow,
> For she's a jolly good fellow . . . "

Three Poems

Alan Michael Parker

The Vandals

In the poem about the vandals, the vandals
Back their Dodge 4 x 4 up to the door

Of the abandoned town hall and theater.
In untied boots, they carry in their canvas bags

And carry off the oak wainscoting.
Above the wings and pit and stage, the ghosts

Of two starved porcupines command
Twin mounds of scat, respectively,

The prickly hats of king and fool.
(The chairs don't care, bottoms up, attentive.)

As the vandals stomp inoutinoutinoutinout
All in one breath because poetry

Is an oral tradition, the ghosts of the porcupines
Fill the air with rhyme: Visigoths and *mishegas*,

Gherkin and curtain, howitzers and trousers.
The vandals stomp inoutinoutinoutinout:

In their arms the split and pocked wood,
In their wake the porcupines

Are unaware of God's universal love.
In the poem, no one is free:

The ghosts of the two porcupines
Got in but they can't get out,

Starving over and over. The vandals—
Who sometimes look like you

And sometimes me—will never
Go home to cozy vandal homes

To make of their deeds a poem.
In the poem about the vandals,

Because a poem is an abandoned theater,
The porcupines have eaten the scenery:

Padua, Venice, Alexandria, Verona, gone;
Love prostrate on its pyramid.

And the vandals stomp inoutinoutinoutinout,
And the vandals stomp inoutinoutinoutinout.

Before the Vandals

In the poem about the vandals
Who have yet to arrive, you and I

Are lovers, our caresses no less
Sad or urgent for what will be.

The vandals have been sighted
Near the city walls, as close

As they will get, because the words
Of a poem only represent the real.

The vandals sing their raucous songs
Around their cookfires smoking in the rain,

Vulgar songs heard far away:
You trace the line of my jaw with your

Wet finger, smile, grind
A bit against my groin, smear me

With your blowzy mouth, your tongue.
(My blowzy mouth. Yours.)

In the poem our room fills
With the acrid stink of rabbit stew,

The future ends with a declarative sentence,
But no one can hear the dead

Save the living. We know, you and I,
That somewhere beyond the walls

The vandals stir their vandal stews
And sing of currants and gingerbread men.

We know the vandals have their own ideas
About what they'll do with me, with you.

Cruelty, the Vandals Say

Is learned. In this poem they're right,
Cold and huddled 'round a trashfire

Underneath the trestle bridge,
Hunger chewing on self-pity.

Look. Here comes the boy
Who will be your father,

A glass jar in a paper bag,
Holes jammed through the metal lid

To let a doomed toad breathe.
(The boy has your hands, your smile.)

Watch him leap the ties, counting
One-oh, two-oh, three-oh, here we go.

Smell the smell: ash and creosote.
(Why must the toad die? you ask.

Because the rhyme has told us so.)
The vandals clench their frozen fingers

Into fists, sing their vandal songs
Of switching yards, railway dicks, the moon

In strips across a lover's back
(On you, on me, on the

Everlasting.) The boy unbends
A safety pin, says

Hey. C'mon. Wake up—
And skewers the toad. (Listen

For the whistle, the train
Is almost in the poem.)

And the vandals break into a howl
As the Limited roars o'er their heads

Like the very roar of Being;
And the boy hops off the tracks

—He shall not die—
Unscrews the lid, shakes out the mess

(The toad, its soul, whatever).
Oh, you say. Oh dear, oh me oh my.

Meeting the Barbarians

Ha Jin

> *Cherish those from a distant land.*
> —Confucius

The First European

Having waited for twenty years—
preaching the Gospel along the coast,
poring over our classics at night,
finally he was summoned to Peking.
He brought along a map, a clock,
a breviary of a gold binding,
a cross adorned with gemstones,
a purse containing relics of saints,
two prisms, an hourglass, a clavichord,
and within him an essential Europe.

The sight of the Imperial Palace
disheartened him, as he realized
his paltry presents might not ensure
an audience from Emperor Wan-Li.
He was right. His map was unacceptable.
How dare he put our Middle Kingdom
on the margin of the world
like a large island! He was made
to revise it, to restore our Empire
at the center of the universe.

Naturally the Emperor wasn't impressed
and ordered to send him back.
But before he mounted his camel
two eunuchs rushed in, asking him to
go to the court immediately
because the clock had stopped

and nobody knew how to make it run.
He chuckled, believing this
must have been God's intervention.

In the Forbidden City he took apart the clock,
showing the eunuchs how to repair it
and how to wind and oil it.
He invented a word for every part.
Still none of the eunuchs could make
head or tail of the springs,
the gears, the perpetual pendulum.
They wondered why the clock,
unlike a peacock or a monkey,
didn't need feeding or grooming.

Then he was invited to teach them
how to play the clavichord.
Then he helped improve our calendar.
At a dinner he impressed the chancellors
by reciting poems backward after
reading them only twice.
He could do that even with a list
of forty names written in disorder.
All the young scholars present felt lucky
that this man was a foreign monk, or
he would surely have come out first
in the Royal Examination on classics.

The Emperor's messengers came every day
and asked him about the West's soil,
farming, birds, paintings, words,
hunting, architecture, cities,
astronomy, population, fishery.
So he stayed, provided with a stipend
and grain, though never allowed
to see the Emperor's pale face.
He built his church,
whose steeple like a needle
punctured the sky of our capital.

On his deathbed he said to his fellow Europeans,
"I'm leaving you a door opened that leads
to great reward, but only after
dangers encountered and labor endured."

Etiquette

As only one sun rules heaven
there should be only one Emperor on earth.
How ignorant are those barbarians
who dare to claim to be our equals.
In King George's letter, he calls our Emperor
"My Dear Brother," demanding an embassy
in our capital and five trade ports.
More outrageous was his man named Macartney,
who refused to kowtow to the Son of Heaven,
claiming England, unlike Korea or Burma,
was the first monarch of the West,
so its envoy should be treated specially.
He refused to kneel on both knees before
our Emperor, declaring he would do that
only in front of God or women.
He proposed to kiss our Emperor's
hand while kneeling on one knee only.
This was absolutely impossible
—no one should break the rite
or touch the body of the Holy Dragon.

Because he didn't behave like those from
other states who knelt down three times
on both knees and knocked
their heads on the ground,
Macartney sailed back with nothing
except for a letter from our Emperor
addressed to King George, saying,
"We are mindful of your tribute envoy's
ignorance and rude manners,
but we forgive him, you, and England,
considering that yours is a tiny state
in a waste corner of the world."

(Actually the letter had been drafted
before Macartney came.)

Trade

The Sea Barbarians live by trade,
wanting in any high purpose.
For us, who have been self-sufficient
since heaven separated from earth,
trade is unnecessary.
They buy our tea, silk, porcelain, rhubarb
(with which they cleanse their bodies
and restore their spirits because
they eat too much milk and meat),
whereas we have no need for
their gadgets, calico, locomotives.

Many times they have complained
that the trade is unbalanced
and that we are unfair not to
allow them to do business inland.

This is our land
and we don't go to theirs.
Why do we have to let them in?
Is it our fault that their silver
has flowed out of their hands?
Why do they need to set up
consulates in four provinces?
Who ever heard the term "International Law" or "trade port"?

We know they want to carve up our land
and suck out its marrow and grease.
That's why they came with warships
loaded with opium and troops.
They mean to drug and butcher
our Empire, which for them
is no more than a crippled dinosaur.

An Opium Smoker

After the eleventh pipe,
the idiot-smile blooming on his face,
again he becomes a vegetable.
The naked stone slab beneath him
feels softer than eiderdown
while he's mounting the clouds.

He sees radiant palaces over rainbows,
a thousand ships carrying his soldiers,
under his orders columns of horses
charging forward, his generals
in the forms of lions and tigers.

For such glory, all he does is remain
tranquil in this filthy den,
oblivious of the other "skeletons"
around him and of those kept
in the morgue behind the house.

Wrapped in his heaven, for the moment
he has no ear for the sobbing
of his teenage daughter pawned
at a brothel for forty dollars,
but in a few hours he will again
twist like a possessed worm.

A Parade

Having caned his ass and tied his hands
we fixed a chain around his neck
and took him to the street
An official beat a gong ahead of us
while two men were thrashing
the criminal's back with rattans

Hundreds of pedestrians gathered
to watch the pair of tiny flags
planted through his ears
which announced his crime:
Traitor—a Dog of Foreign Devils

He claimed his master was an American
from the other side of the world
not from the island called Britain
We knew he lied, because
that devil babbled the same sounds
as those redcoats

A Condemned Viceroy's Talk

After we lost the war I recommended
to His Majesty a book
about England's history.
He said to me a few days ago,
"I can see that it's a country
good at warfare and depends on trade.
They always go to war."

Look at those warships anchored
at the mouth of the bay.
Some of them, powered by steam,
can run three hundred miles a day
without wind or tide,
even against the current.
That's faster than any horse.

How could we fight them?
Their eight-inch guns
can turn in any direction
and sweep our fleet away,
smashing our junks like coffins.

Now the whole country curses me
for signing the shameful treaty.
But what else could I have done?
Without modern ships and guns
there was no diplomacy—
no way to save our battered face.

An Edict from the Empress Dowager

Last summer the Sea Barbarians
attempted to enter the Peiho River,
but in the twinkling of an eye
their ships were sunk
and thousands of bodies floating
in the water became food for fish.
I thought this lesson would teach them
to be more circumspect,
but they returned this year
more numerous and more insolent.

Taking the advantage of the low tide
they disembarked at Pehtang
and then attacked Taku Forts.
Like true barbarians, they approached
the forts only from the rear.
Our soldiers, always meeting
their enemies face to face,
did not expect such perfidy.

Emboldened by the success that
should have shamed them,
they turned to seize Tientsin.
My anger is soaring to the clouds
and I want to have them exterminated.

Now, I command all my subjects,
Manchu, Chinese, Mongols,
to hunt them down like savage beasts.
Let your villages be abandoned
as these wretches come near.
Let your wells be poisoned
from which they draw water.
Let your crops be burned

before they can use them.
Let all provisions be destroyed
which they are eager to secure.

Thus they will perish
like shrimps in a frying pan.

Breach

The big-nosed barbarians claimed
they came for peace, but they brought
twenty thousand troops from the sea.
They meant to despoil our land,
so we fought them with every means.

To our surprise, they wanted to talk
of armistice and we agreed.
They dispatched a team of thirty-eight men,
who came with arrogance and ease.
While they were resting in the square
our soldiers sprang at them like
eagles falling on chicks,
trussed them up, and carted them
to Peking under cover of night.

We displayed them in a market
where people spat on them, pulled
their noses, twisted their ears.
A young French devil asked for food,
but we fed him with dung and dirt.
As for their Chinese coolies,
we buried them up to their necks,
let dogs eat their heads.

Within a week twenty devils died.
Our princes were so pleased
they gave each soldier a silver dollar
and the fearless captain a wife.

The barbarian generals accused us
of breaking our word of honor,
so their army smashed our cavalry
(their artillery was more accurate).
They marched into our capital
and entered the Summer Palace.

After all its treasures were plundered
Lord Elgin sent our Emperor a word
by torching his favorite park
—the smoke flying north
choked the Son of Heaven to death
three hundred miles away.

The Rebel Leaders

In a godless land every hero may become a god.
When Hong failed the examination again—
his dream of being an official shattered,
he was carried home and for days remained
in bed, delirious, sweating, prattling.
He saw himself join God in heaven,
where God's wife treated him as a son.
When he couldn't answer a seraph's question
a lady gave him a clue. He recognized her
as his sister-in-law, the wife of Jesus.
What a blissful place heaven was,
full of angels and buxom maidens.

As he returned to this world
he realized he belonged to God's family
—he was the youngest son sent down
to replace Christ, to cleanse earth
and redeem it for their Father.

He began to baptize people in the manner
prescribed in the pamphlet given him
by an old Protestant missionary.
After he gathered enough God worshipers
he went to attack cities and towns,
his troops invincible and well disciplined,
men and women kept in separate camps,
sex prohibited, even among married couples,
because the genuine union of men and women
could happen only after the final victory.

Within a year they took Nanking
which he turned into the Celestial Capital.
He set up a new calendar,
ordered his subjects to call him
the Sovereign, the ruler of the
Heavenly Kingdom of Great Peace.

They prepared to march north to Peking
to topple the Manchu Court.

But one of his generals, who used
to be a charcoal burner,
began to have trances and claimed
to be the Holy Ghost, speaking
in the very voice of the Father.
He ordered the Sovereign to kneel
in a square for kicking a concubine
and spoiling his baby son.
The Sovereign obeyed the holy orders
and was flogged publicly.

A month later, another general
began to get into his trances
calling himself Jesus Christ.
The Sovereign had no choice but to
admit him into the divine household—
appointed him the West King,
allowed him to have a territory,
a staff, a harem, a band.

So they never crossed the Yellow River.
Even after the Kingdom collapsed
and the rebel leaders were wiped out by
each other and by the government troops,
people wouldn't bring them down
from heaven, their names still
invoked in thousands of prayers.

Starting Off

The bell was tolling as fire
was crackling in the pottery braziers.
Three hundred men gathered before the shrine
holding halberds, swords, shovels, forks.
A few knelt before the statue of
a local god, who had been a man
three generations ago and led people
to drive the Japanese pirates
back into the Pacific Ocean.
Above their shaved heads
white banners slanted in the breeze
which was full of chestnuts and beef.

An old man, the village head, fired a blank
at the naked chest of a young man,
then declared they were all divine soldiers
whose skin could block any foreign bullet.
Indeed the young man, unscratched,
only had a smudge on his nipple.
A Taoist priest went to the front
announcing that eleven million troops
would soon descend from heaven.
It was time to wipe out the foreign devils,
to reclaim China's sovereign land.

And so they set out, chanting:
"Give back our rivers and mountains.
Give back our silver and gold.
We dare to tread on knives and flames.
Even though the Emperor has surrendered
to foreigners, we won't stop,
not until we kill them off."

They were heading toward the nearby
church to decapitate
Christians like red poppies.

Help

At long last the Boxers were crushed,
but the foreign troops began looting.
The cities of Peking smelled of death
trembling with bugles and screams.
Abandoned by the Manchu Court,
all we could do was wait for our doom.
Rich men had fled to the countryside
with their wives and concubines,
their homes littered with bodies of
their servants and poor relatives
hanged or drowned in wells.
Like most people, I stayed in town
praying the Lord of Heaven would rain mercy.

A friend of mine said the Americans were
better than the other barbarians.
(The French, the British, the Russians
knew nothing but metals and stones;
they smashed and burned the treasures
that they couldn't turn into cash.)
So when an American marine came
I gave him ten tins of oolong tea
and begged him to write a notice
that might help protect my grocery.

His olive eyes winked at me
as his hairy fingers pushed his nose.
On a piece of rice paper he wrote:
"USA Boys—plenty of tobacco
and whiskey in this shop."

I posted the notice on the front door,
but it didn't stop any troops.
A group of Frenchmen burst in
ordering me to give them whiskey,
which I had no idea was booze

and didn't know where to get.
They knocked me to the ground,
kicked my face, caught our hens
and took my daughter away.

An Execution

The criminals to be executed
had killed two German missionaries.
The German soldiers in helmets
didn't know how to use our sword,
or maybe they were afraid of
being stained by pagan blood.
They stood in rows, rifle in hand,
their boots shiny in the sun,
their flag flapping noisily.

Three Chinamen wearing black aprons
worked as a team, one pulling
the kneeling man's pigtail, another
holding his bound hands from behind,
the third raising a crescent sword
still steaming with blood.
The criminal prayed to his ancestors,
then cried, "In thirty years
I'll be back as a warrior to kill
the foreign devils and all of you,
their shameless flunkies!"
Beside him lay his cousin, whose head
was twenty yards away before
a British officer's feet.

In silence hundreds of Chinese watched
—a boy sitting on his father's neck,
a toothless man sucking a pipe,
ladies waving fans under the parasols
raised by their servants.
None of them looked at the falling
sword, all their eyes
focused on the colossal camera.

The Victory

When Prince Chun was sent to Germany
to apologize for the assassination
of Baron von Ketteler, the Germans
wanted him to kowtow at the Kaiser's feet
in addition to offering them
Shandong province, an indemnity
of one hundred million taels of gold
and railroad concessions.

Adamantly our prince refused to
prostrate himself before Wilhelm.
He said to his entourage,
"Our Empire cannot demean her honor."
To his surprise, the Germans,
so pleased with what they got,
had forgotten his knees.

On his return, a victory banquet
was held at court for
the national face he had saved.
Later his three-year-old son
was chosen to be our last emperor.

A Ghost's Argument

I am a criminal in our history books,
which condemn me for not fortifying Canton
when the British ships gathered on the sea.
Nor did I ever try to pacify the enemy,
refusing their demands again and again.
In their eyes I was also a joke
and a monster, as all European newspapers
called me the Barbarian Governor.

When they came to attack the city
I didn't fight, so they prevailed easily.
They waited on the highland for me to
capitulate, but I never showed up.
Out of patience, they scoured streets,
districts, sampans, monasteries,
finally dragged me out from a local
law office and took me to their flagship.

I thought they'd execute me on the spot,
but they said it wouldn't be so easy.
They shipped me to Calcutta,
where I died of dropsy
and homesickness in a cell.
Thank heaven, they didn't take me
farther west to Europe.

Children of future, remember me as a wronged ghost.
It's true I was a passive man.
But what else could I have done to save
the city from being sacked?
Was there any way to stop their warships?
Better just bluff them, so that
our court wouldn't blame me for
not resisting the enemy force
and annihilate my clan when I was gone.

It's true I was a coward, to whom
honor and bravery were merely phantoms.
But children of future, remember
I died alone—unlike those
heroes and generals, I didn't bring
underground another soul.

Departure

Having put away their baggage in the cabin
they gathered at the prow, where
wine and roasted ducks were waiting.

Thirty-two students were about to cross
the oceans for the first time
in our Empire. Among them
were would-be experts in
weaponry, metallurgy, politics,
law, architecture, philosophy.

The air smelled of coal,
purple clouds hanging on the coast,
seagulls flitting,
a few petrels twittering in the smoke.

Together they emptied their cups
and swore they'd study hard to master
all the knowledge in the West
so that their Motherland would not
send youths abroad again.

Their tears were shed only for the wind.
None of them knew
this was just a beginning—
their children would travel
the same seas.

Verona

William Donoghue

Ah, but if it wasn't a Verona kind of day from top to bottom! thought Teddy Mulvaney as he strode down Parnell. He filled his lungs with air and clutched the box of diapers closer to his chest. Webs of early-morning fog still hung about in the gullies and yards, nuzzling the curbs and gutters and lying in patches in the empty street. It was damp and overcast. A fine day for an anniversary, he thought. Verona would be pleased. They'd been together for three years now. A personal best, he thought proudly. A long-term commitment was what it was. And wasn't that just the right thing? Wasn't that just what they recommended? Was it not something to be proud of? It was.

He glanced up a little nervously at the sky. Pendulous banks of clouds were scuttling in from the west, beetling about the spires of St. Mary's and clogging the rooftops. The paving stones were damp and glistening. Bullets, he thought, fired on such a day would hit their targets with a wet dull thud. A limp, persistent dripping pattered out at him from the side streets as he walked, as if the city were squeezing out its last nocturnal juices, dribbling its fecund luminous drops into the main artery in a last-gasp attempt to inseminate the intransigent morning. Limerick was milky and still in the gray light, an autopsy of mucous and veins. A miasma of waste and rotting vegetables was oozing out at him from behind all the clapboard fences. The city was pulsing, organs and secretions, wounds and aching joints. Even the metal pin in his hip was sweating.

He shivered and quickened his pace. Clearly, he thought, you had to feel good about yourself. That's what the book said. Be your own best friend. Be proud of what you were, without worrying about what you might have been, whatever that might have been, or be, whatever you might be now, as it were, to cut a long story short, or so it went, at least as far as he'd read, for he hadn't yet finished the book.

The basic problem, of course, remained unsolved. But now, given the odd new configuration of events that had, as it were, pursued them, overtaken them, surrounded them, the question was simply how to feel good about yourself and be all that you could be. His gaze ran off dizzyingly along the cracks that dissected the cobblestone street. The grid moved under him like the moist brown back of a cockroach. He shifted the box and focused his gaze up the street. Indeed, you had to feel good about yourself. He took a deep gulp of air and swallowed happily.

Verona would be pleased. She was wetting herself again, the darling. Leaving mysterious midnight puddles on the floor like a malfunctioning refrigerator. The result, he knew too well, of his clumsy repotting. She had soil problems, the little dear, couldn't adjust to the new lighter mix of perlite, couldn't hold her drink, in a manner of speaking. A tipsy *Nephrolepis exaltata* was what she was. A fern of extended dimensions. Winner of Best Boston two years running at the County Clare Botanical. And she was getting better with age. Her foliage. Now there was a subject for rumination. His fingers spread on the front of the box and pressed it tighter to his chest. A sultry shamrock green, she was. Laced to the teeth with shadows and lights, shimmering and whiskery. An outright slap in the face to the bony Roosevelts and Ruffles of Chaps Ahern and the Murphy boys, that was a dead-certain fact.

A low sports car wheeled round the corner off Mallow and stalled in front of the pharmacy. An old Jaguar, he saw, with the driver's half of the front windshield blacked out. He slowed his steps, came to a stop.

A woman got out of the passenger's side of the car. She was laughing. Her pumps were wet, as if the car held water. Her face was wet as well, as if she had been weeping. Teddy felt his teeth aching. The car's radiator was hissing out jets of steam through its chrome grill. The driver was invisible. Gassed, thought Teddy. Gas to pull teeth. He winced as the woman's laugh pierced the heavy air.

She swung back down into the car. For a moment her white knuckles hung gripping the roof. Then she was sheathed inside, sunk in leather. The Jaguar lunged ahead and was gone.

Teddy stood thinking. Where had he seen her before? Nowhere, he thought, would be ideal. To be exact. But then he would be left without an explanation for the feeling that he knew her. And that, precisely, was the question: where had he known her? He knit his brows. He was in error. True, he may have known her elsewhere; and that was precisely the question. But, he grinned wryly, was he not this very second a victim of a misunderstanding? He was. If the answer was nowhere, then he must seek elsewhere for an explanation of the feeling that he knew her. That settled, he continued his journey. "Attaway to go, kid," he murmured.

His feet, he noticed, were moving rather hesitantly. His spats were beaded with moisture. He glanced down at them nervously. Once they had been a brilliant white, the white of a healthy woman's incisors, Botticelli white, luxurious and threatening, stabbing into the future. Now, he noted, they were the color of a dead man's forehead, clammy with sweat.

I was once, he thought, Botticelli white myself. Threatening as well, if I am not mistaken. And most certainly stabbing into the future. Before, that is, the rads came down. Before the typhoons came up and the holes opened. And why, he pondered, all the mystery, McDuff? Why all the missing doors and windows? A student at Trinity, he thought. I was a married man like anyone else, after all. I had my corpuscles, my ligaments, my rights. I had a wife! he shouted out. I had a daughter! Was that not clear from the photographs? It was. He looked around. No one was listening.

He walked on. Facts. There was a shortage, it seemed. A dearth of the things. But why was he also unable to recall his feelings? There was the car. He had only to close his eyes to smell the wet wool of their clothes, feel the shuddering of the Volks as it skittered along past Dublin Castle over the wet cobblestones. They were all wrapped up in their mufflers in the winter air, the street wet, shiny, slippery. Before that there had been a car shed and tea on a stove and someone had been reading Bukowski and left behind and had been smoking and rapt and uncommunicative.

Had they left without knowing where they were going? He gave a disdainful harrumph. Not bloody likely! But they had been innocent after all! Innocent! The word made him feel guilty. He glanced nervously to the side. His feet were making too much noise. Had he given cause for complaint? No. He had been true to himself, if not to others. Beside him in the Volks she had been laughing. The little girl had been holding on between the seats to see out . . . their breath all foggy and groggy and their stubby woolen gloves wiping at the windows as they'd come up and stopped at the light. And there you were, my friend, there you were. That much was clear. Who would dispute it? No one.

They had been removed. A battle, if he recalled, the doctor had said. It will be a battle. Apparently it had not been a long one. Soon the survivor was driven away, removed to a place of refuge and healing, as they said. In the wrong place at the wrong time, they said. But how had that been possible? How, metaphysically speaking, of course, could anyone, let alone he and his family, be anywhere wrong at any time? The idea lodged like a recalcitrant, last-drink patron in the back of his brain. Anywhere at all wrong, let alone at the wrong time. The doubleness of the sin, in their view, had been paid off in bullets.

He had pretended at the time not to understand it any better than the priest. Together they were on the short end of the stick, as they said . . . on the outs, as it were, when it came to facts . . . to pure empirical explanations. God, he knew perfectly well, had had nothing to do with it. And did that not carry some promise? Whatever "it" was. Surely it had to. He shook himself. Life! Was life not what you made it? It was. It was up to the individual, as the book said. Was he an individual? No matter. Things were improving. He was showing initiative, taking the bull by the horns. For was there anything more absorbent than a diaper? There was not.

Diapers! he thought exultantly, crossing in front of the station. Quite astonishing that he'd never thought of it before. It had been on television, the baby wetting itself, that had given him the idea. Great notions, he thought, were like that. Obvious to everyone once they had been pointed out, once one original sly mind had cut through the foliage and undergrowth of ignorance and discovered them. Until then they were invisible, unconsidered as potential elements in a larger structure.

He hopped through traffic, attentive to the clots of black taxis pulling away with their passengers. The nine-twenty had thrown up its city-seekers, in for a bit of clubbing. They would be out later in bangles, knocking their ticks of pleasure to the floor like flies from the walls of the city's pubs and gobbling up the bits. The thought made him chuckle. He chuckled noiselessly, gleefully, snobbishly, rubbing the tip of his tongue back and forth on the tip of his left canine as he bumped along. While in the distance, rocking patiently in the gray winter light, lay the dark mutinous waves of the Shannon . . . Ah, but it was the rhythm of the thing that mattered! The right-thinking outlook, as the book said.

He made his way down to the river and turned onto the quay. It was already bristling with activity, the market stalls and kiosks were black and unkempt, laid out in an irregular line, their humped backs to the river. Why could they not seem to straighten up? They had only to follow the line of the wharf. So simple if you just put your mind to it. Laziness was what it was. Pure and simple. A result of faulty early training, as the book said.

He stopped, bought a glass of milk and stood drinking it in the crowd. The odor of new bacon, fish, cheese and burning potatoes stung his nostrils. Community, the book said. Indeed. You had to feel part of a community. He did. He had Verona. And he had the book.

Milk done, he struck off once more, clutching the box of diapers, and made for Sarsfield Bridge. A promising day. All the signs were there. A day for feeling good about yourself. And he was feeling particularly good about himself. That much was clear. Things were going well. Or at least, they were showing signs of picking up. Of really blasting off, as they'd said on the news last night, about Africa. His restless days were over. He'd come of age. Like the country itself. The configuration of events had changed since the rads had come down, and new vistas had opened up. Opened for them both. They had only to step forward with the right attitude and they would go far.

He pushed through the crowd, made the corner at Bedford, turned and ran head-on into a large, bagged plant moving in the opposite direction. The fast-traveling foliage gave him a bump and knocked off his hat. He watched it roll into the gutter, looked up and saw a square, military face glaring at him over burlap. Wisps of spidery green trickled over the man's hairy wrists. "Terribly sorry," Teddy apologized. He realized of course that he was not particularly at fault in the accident. But without his hat he knew that he cut too foolish a figure to stand on protocol. He must subsume, imbricate himself, as it were, in the discursive moment. He did so.

His gaze went to the whispering tentacles. "You appear," he went on, "if I am not mistaken, to be transporting a Verona fern." He bowed slightly. "My compliments. I have one myself."

The man's eyes narrowed nervously, but he did not offer the violence of a reply. Nor even the hint of an accusative sentence. Instead, he appeared to be worried by some other, some quite unforeseen circumstance, one that had possibly arisen in his absence, with which he was clearly preoccupied, or at the very least formerly occupied, and so perhaps unable to be presently tense, to think well of himself in the moment and be all that he could be.

Teddy blinked, and as he did fern and man hurried away. He watched them weave in and out of sight along the quay, diminishing jerkily. He stretched on tiptoe to follow their progress. For a moment he lost them, then they reappeared, fell on a low-slung sports car parked at the curb and plummeted inside. Fern and man vanished behind black glass.

Teddy bent over and retrieved his hat. It was stained with vegetable juice. He rubbed it on his sleeve, feeling vaguely irritated. What had he been thinking? What had been his thoughts in those days? They had been taken away along with the rest.

Looking up, he saw her coming along the sidewalk toward him. She had the sandwiches for the clinic. Her apron was stained with blood, her auburn hair in pieces. Watching her approach, he had the distinct impression that if she would only try a little harder she would recall their courtship. Stationary, hat in hand, clutching the box of diapers, he was aware that perhaps he gave the impression of a somewhat optimistic suitor. A position, of course, he had once held, indeed still held, with regard to the potential, unrealized affections of the young lady. His appearance now, however, appeared to give her neither pleasure nor pause. She hurried past, keeping as far away from him on the sidewalk as she could manage. He smiled after her brightly. "Juice of some sort!" he called out gaily. She disappeared in the crowd.

Teddy carefully resettled his hat. I appear, he thought, to be a series of interlocking events. He turned the corner at Henry and walked up to the clinic, took the walk at a brisk one-two and let himself in the side door. Dr. McNaughton was waiting for him.

"Good morning, Mr. Mulvaney." Her voice purred out of smooth, oiled tubes. "Been out for a bit of early shopping then, have we?"

He watched her gaze drop with an almost audible plunk to the box of diapers.

"For Verona."

Her eyes came slowly back up to his face and flickered over him like a pair of weak searchlights. She turned away and disappeared through a door.

He carried on up the corridor and rounded the corner into the lounge. A few people were sitting around the television. He walked through unhurriedly, went up the hall and opened the door to his room. As always, his eyes went automatically to Verona.

His eyes . . . as always. Without fail. Faithful as a turtle. And yet now, suddenly, this. She was not there. She was not waiting for him. Teddy stared at the small puddle of water on the floor where she'd stood. He looked up. He had erred. An errant thought. He looked round. Had he mistaken the room? The door? The street? He looked up at the refrigerator, at the clock, at the curtains, at the walls. He looked back at where Verona was supposed to be. She was gone. He blinked. His lids came down slowly . . . like the walls of mud in those old slow-motion newsreels . . . like the skyful of bituminous briquettes that fell on Pompei. They hit and bounced and he refocused. Facts. He had ordered facts. He had paid for facts. And all he had been given were more questions! He had been cheated . . . he had been innocent and he had been cheated. He looked up at the walls, the curtains, the clock. Answers were not forthcoming.

He turned, closed the door, went and sat down at the table. He held the box of diapers on his lap. The book was open on the oilcloth. The red letters of its title shouted up at him: "Be All That You Can Be!" Yes, indeed. How could that be bad . . . as nurse said. Unless of course, he thought, but then who, he countered, would try, who would make the knowing effort at all, as it were, if they knew? If they knew already, so to speak. No, it was a game for the blind, a risk. But in his case, was it not a risk that had to be taken? It was. One had to progress. One had to stab out confidently into the future, as they said.

He set the box of diapers on the floor at his feet. The motion appeared to go on for some time, as he slowly straightened up. As he did, he hoped briefly, for a brief fleeting second, as they said in the books, for a change. But everything was the same. And yet, he thought slyly, despite that . . . a pattern was developing. He was being duped, lied to. Love, they said, blinded a man. It did. That was a dead-certain truth.

He got up and went to the window. A particular configuration of events was being forced upon him. It was familiar, suffocating. He stared out across the rugby pitch. In the distance the Ard na Crusha commuter train came bolting down Connaught Hill and plunged into the black throat of the Shannonplex tunnel. As its last car disappeared from sight, a stain oozed back out of the mouth of the tunnel and hung in the air.

The train's sudden absence was upsetting. He continued staring fixedly at the black empty mouth of the tunnel, the black empty mouth with the stain hanging in the air. Nothing was moving. How dare it! he thought. How dare it all be like this, all just hanging in the air! Am I not a human being?

He looked at his hands. They were innocent and yet they were trembling. Had the priest not begged him to leave it alone? He had. But then neither Father nor wife nor child had known the hidden truth, the hidden purpose of the whole thing. That they never, ever, ever let you go . . . that they never forgave and never forgot. He pressed his trembling palms up against the window and brought his face up close to it. His breath instantly began to fog the glass. He smelled the wet and leaned his forehead against the coolness. The rain had begun again. He squeezed his eyes shut. There, he thought, it was forthcoming . . .

But no. It was only a haze. He stretched his eyes wide open. A small girl in a yellow raincoat had appeared on the pitch. She was cutting across, hurrying off for Coopers' Lane, her school satchel jumping and jiggling on her back. She was snaking away obliquely across the wet brown turf toward the tunnel. She was leaving him.

He felt his ribs pressing in on his heart, cutting off his breath. He pressed his chest painfully against the glass. "Wait!" he shrieked. She was steadily disappearing, getting smaller. She was gone.

He turned, walked back and sat down at the table. He looked at the walls, the refrigerator, the curtains. Verona was gone. The puddle of water was still on the floor. He looked down at the box of diapers at his feet, reached down, opened the box and took out a diaper. He got up, went over and laid it carefully on the wet. Then he went back and sat down at the table. The white diaper lay foolishly on the tile. Teddy felt himself blushing as he looked at it. He was waiting. Waiting, he realized. And yet, he thought, what was there to wait for now? What indeed. Nothing. That much, at least, he thought with a sigh . . . that much was clear.

One Small Stone

Mabelle Hsueh

Suling could feel the Hong Kong–China Express slow as it approached the train station. She pressed her face closer to the window for the first glimpse of Guangzhou, the "Gateway to Communist China," as the U.S. media liked to call it.

She noticed that the brilliant colors of the countryside had disappeared; the sky was no longer as luminous as a blue glass bead but stuffed with lumps of dark clouds from smoke stacks. Nearby, scattered around the wooden shacks were rusty pipes, wires, rolled metal sheets, bricks and garbage.

"Ugly, isn't it?" said the Singapore woman sharing her seat.

Suling pretended she had not heard her. Ugly or not, this was China, her motherland, or was it fatherland, which she had not seen for over two decades. In her mind's eye, she saw herself stepping off the train and kissing the ground. Wasn't that what people in novels did when they returned to their native soil after a long absence?

But this romantic picture disappeared as soon as she got on the platform and found herself in an ocean of people, pushing, shouting and hanging on to each other. In a panic, she swung both suitcases in front of her body, using them as ballast, and jostled her way toward one of the wooden columns lining both sides of the platform, and took refuge behind it.

Perspiration dripped down her forehead and stung her eyes. She lifted a corner of her T-shirt and wiped her face, wondering how she could ever locate the male guide from the Guangzhou Foreign Affairs Office.

As soon as the crowd thinned down a bit, she found him: a tall, untidy-looking young man standing near the platform entrance, one hand dangling a placard with her name printed on it and the other holding a fan in perpetual motion.

Suling jumped up on her toes, raised both arms and waved furiously.

"*Zhe-li, zhe-li*, over here," she shouted. "I am Suling Yang."

The man stared at her for a moment and motioned to her to follow him. He led her through an empty waiting room with a huge portrait of Chairman Mao on the wall and out to a car on the curb, a snub-nosed vehicle with a set of running boards. He plopped down beside the driver and continued to fan himself without missing a beat. Suling could feel the men's eyes on her as she climbed awkwardly into the back seat with the luggage.

You goddamned lazy sons of turtles, Suling thought, as she slammed the door with all her strength. Way in the beginning, she had told the Chinese Consulate that she didn't need, or want, a guide in China, even though the service was free of charge. But they had insisted. When she complained about the matter to her husband, he said, "Has it ever occurred to you that these guides are not there for your benefit?"

"You mean to watch me?"

"China's a police state." Then, seeing her stricken face, he had hugged her and added, "I'm not trying to frighten you. Just be careful and come home safe to us."

Within ten minutes they were at the People's Hotel, a gray, five-story concrete structure covered with dark stains as if someone had planned to wash the building, changed his mind halfway, and poured the rest of the dirty water all over it. There was another huge portrait of Chairman Mao rising from the fifth floor: hatless, with a blue uniform and a red background.

Again she struggled with the luggage. This time the guide reached behind him and snatched up her carry-on, the lightest of the three.

"Thank *you*," Suling said.

As soon as they entered the lobby, he plopped down again on the nearest chair, fanning away furiously. "Very hot outside," he said.

She felt sweat dripping from every pore. Her skin itched unbearably. "*Hai-hou*, not so bad," she lied.

"At least close to 40."

"That's over 100 Fahrenheit! I guess you don't have air in this hotel."

"Maybe next year. Chairman Mao always provides."

She looked around the room. There were a few visitors milling around, looking lost. Against one wall was a long counter with no one behind it. "Don't I need to check in?" she asked.

"You give me your passport and the health certificate and I will take them to the hotel manager."

"No," she replied instinctively. She knew that without the passport she would have no identity in China. Anybody could do anything to her and not be held accountable.

As if reading her mind, he said with a snicker, "Have no fear, I will give you a receipt for the documents. Tomorrow, when you leave, I will return them to you."

Oh sure, you just don't want me to leave this hotel at all, she thought. Out loud she said, "I'd like to go to my room."

He pointed at her with his fan. "You speak real good Chinese. Just like one of us."

"Why not? I was brought up in Fuzhou."

"But you have been living away from China, in the United States, for thirty years." He sounded accusatory.

"Twenty-six. I left China when I was eighteen."

"During the most glorious years of the Communist—"

"I was unable to come back because of the Cold War," Suling interrupted loudly. In a calmer tone she asked, "Where is my room?"

"On the third floor, number 317." He slapped his thigh with the fan, stood up and sauntered over to the elevator. "The Cold War is over now," he continued. "China and the United States are friends because of *Ni-ke-song*'s visit last year."

"Who is *Ni-ke-song*?"

"You live in the United States, do you not? He is the American President."

"You mean Nixon," Suling said.

"Yes, *Ni-ke-song*. He came to Beijing last year to talk to Chairman Mao. We saw the visit on TV. Have you ever talked to *Ni-ke-song*?"

"No."

"But the United States is a democratic country!"

Was he being sarcastic? Malicious? Now they were on the third floor. The hallway was so dimly lit that she could hardly see the numbers.

"Democracy has nothing to do with the availability of the president," she snapped.

They found number 317: a small room with one window and no balcony. The air stank of stale cigarettes, damp wood and sour bamboo matting. Suling pushed the window open in spite of the hot and humid air.

The young man had stopped talking since he entered the room. He stood in one corner tense and waiting. Then he clasped his hands in front of him and began to recite in a loud and mechanical voice, "Tomorrow morning at five I will conduct you back to the train station. You will take a train to Ingtan. From Ingtan you will take a different train to Fuzhou."

"How long before I get to Fuzhou?"

"Four days. I wish you a pleasant reunion with your parents." He bowed and backed out of the room.

She caught her breath. Of course he knows why I've come to China, Suling thought, but what else? She reached into her pocket and touched the stone she often carried with her. It was the size of a pigeon egg, with a coral fossil embedded in it, that she had found one day walking along Lake Michigan. Whenever she looked at it, she reminded herself that life was enduring, even for a fossil, and any hardship temporary.

She rattled the doorknob several times and locked the door. She went into the bathroom and saw a toilet, a sink, but no bathtub. However, there was a large basin and she filled it with water and carried it to the room.

Quickly she peeled off her clothes, sat down on the edge of the bed and soaked her feet in the tepid water. She opened the drawer of the night table and looked for a copy of Mao's *Little Red Book*. She had heard that all Chinese had to carry the book with them and that to be without it was to invite severe criticism from peers.

The drawer was empty. Somewhat disappointed, she leaned against the bed post and closed her eyes. She thought about the guide and wondered how much more he knew about her parents. Was he aware that her father had written her (granted, only half a dozen times) during these Cold War years and that he had secretly sent these letters through a friend, a Mr. Nam Sing, in Singapore?

Suling had asked the Singapore woman on the train if she was acquainted with this man. The woman had said she knew of him, a wealthy businessman with a huge house on Tanglin Street.

She thought of her own ancestral home by the canal with its courtyards, gardens and numerous rooms and realized she might not be able to see it this time. It had been, her father had written her, ransacked by the Red Guards so many times that when the city government asked them to move elsewhere, they had hardly anything to take with them.

In one of the last letters her father sent at the end of the sixties, he told her he had been in prison, "rehabilitated" by the Party over the course of three years. Therefore, he belonged, with all other re-educated intellectuals, to one of the lowest class of citizenry who, according to the Party, had contributed next to nothing to the glories of Communism. Below his signature he had added, "I am a nobody now. I belong to myself."

Not once had he mentioned Little Brother.

Early the next morning Suling boarded the train to Ingtan. She had a Pullman in a first-class compartment reserved for party officials and special foreigners. All the bunks were permanently pulled down and the curtains around them discarded. The decoration was exactly like what she had seen in old European continental trains in late-night TV movies: velvet upholstery, lampshades with fringes, and wall-to-wall carpeting. Looking closer, she was dismayed to find the rug matted with dirt and the velvet material full of bald spots.

The ticket assigned her to a lower bunk, opposite a man from Hong Kong, who was accompanied by a wife and four daughters. Suling wondered how the women were going to share the two upper bunks among them.

"My husband has a tumor in his lungs," the wife told Suling as soon as she had settled her husband in his bunk. "We do not want him to be cut open again by a Western doctor. We are taking him to Fuzhou to see a famous herbal doctor. Have you ever heard of Dr. C. S. Chen in . . . eh, where you are from?"

"The United States."

One of the girls said, "We're all overseas Chinese, but you Chinese from the States always get special treatment here."

"We'd tried so hard just to get these three first-class tickets," another chimed in.

"I suppose you didn't even have to ask, much less beg, for your ticket," the third one said.

Suling shifted uncomfortably in her bunk and remained silent.

The sick man coughed incessantly with his eyes closed and his hands clutching and unclutching the coverlet. Suling could hear mucus bubbling and swirling inside his throat after each spasm. At times the mucus dribbled out of his mouth; other times it burst through a hole in his trachea. The family gathered around him, cleaning his face and neck and murmuring soft comforting words.

The ceiling fan with a rusty motor squeaked on night and day. But the air remained locked inside the room and reeked of vomit and sweat. The only window was kept shut "because," the wife insisted to Suling, "dust and soot irritate his lungs."

She tried to detach herself from the surroundings: breathing through her mouth to eliminate the vile smells and stuffing tissues into her ears to tune out the sounds, all without much success.

When the day ended, she ate supper in the dining car, removed her lenses and tried to sleep. She was about to doze off when the youngest girl crawled into her bunk.

"Don't you have a seat somewhere else?" Suling tried not to raise her voice.

"Yes, in the third-class," the girl hissed at her.

"Well then, only three of you . . . "

"Can't you understand that we all want to be near our father? He is very sick. I am borrowing a little space in your bed to take a short nap."

When the young girl seemed ready to share Suling's bunk again the next day, Suling left the compartment altogether. It was not only the crowded condition and the wretched atmosphere that drove her out, but also the resentment, however imperceptible, of the girls toward her privileged status. Furthermore, the man's illness had started her worrying about her parents' health.

She spent most of the second day and night and the third morning standing barefoot in the aisle, staring out the window and flattening herself against the wall every time someone walked by. When the dining car opened for meals, she would rush in, grab a seat and order bowl after bowl of noodles in order to remain there as long as possible.

Once she asked for a bowl of soy milk with sugar and a pinch of *kuei-pi*, cinnamon bark. Looking at her severely, the waitress said, "*Kuei-pi* is used in cooking, never in a drink," as if the spice were something rare and expensive.

Around noon on the third day, Suling got off at Ingtan with her luggage. At first she was surprised to find no guide at the station to meet her. Then she remembered the consulate had not mentioned Ingtan to her. Perhaps they had forgotten about this little stop. Instead of being tired, she felt elated and carefree. She talked to the stationmaster, who agreed to keep her luggage there while she went in search of a hotel room to sleep for a few hours.

"Do not let them know you are from the United States," he whispered with one finger on his lips. "These people are frightened of foreigners. They do not believe the Cold War is over."

"How did you know I'm from . . . "

"I read your luggage tags," he said proudly. "I have not forgotten the English the missionaries taught me many years ago."

Suling found a hotel a mile down the road. As she approached it, she saw a small tree with delicate gray branches and small dark green leaves. It stood there by the doorway like a young girl, eyes down, hands folded in front of her and feet close together. She knew this was a sweet olive tree, exactly like the one her father had planted in front of her bedroom in Fuzhou. Suddenly she wanted to put her arms around it, smooth down the ruffled leaves, tell it to sit down and relax so that it could bloom beautifully when summer turned into fall, sending its fragrance across the ocean.

The hotel owner gave her a nice clean room. Suling stretched out on the bed and slept soundly for the first time since she entered China. Just before she left for the train station she asked for a bowl of soy milk with sugar and *kuei-pi*.

"We never put *kuei-pi* in soy milk!" the owner said. "Where you come from?" She told him she would drink it plain.

She boarded the Fuzhou train and, since it was evening, continued to sleep. She did not see the family from Hong Kong again.

As soon as Suling stepped off the train, on the fourth morning, she was greeted by a woman who appeared at first to be young, dressed in blue shirt and pants. But after a closer look at the woman's face, the deep lines between her brows and the eyes hidden under heavy lids, Suling guessed she was much older, closer to her own age of forty-four.

"Mrs. Yang, I recognized you right away because of your hair style. We are not allowed to curl our hair," the woman said, touching her two thin braids. "I am Hung Lan, your guide during your stay in our city."

"Are my parents well? Did they come with you?"

"They are in excellent health," the woman replied. "They are waiting for you in their apartment. There are many, many friends with them, Mrs. Yang. Will you . . . "

Suling did not hear her. She was staring at a young boy, less than two yards away. It was twenty-six years earlier when Little Brother had stood at the dock, along with their parents, to see her go off to college in America. He had cried and she had patted his hand, assuring him that she would be back in two years. Had she known that this was her last time with him, she would have reached out and held on to him tighter and tighter so that her arms, too, would remember him.

"Do you know that person?" Hung Lan now asked, following the line of her gaze.

Suling shook her head. "Are you sure my parents are all right? I mean, do they know I'm arriving today?"

"Naturally. We have informed them of everything ever since the first day you applied . . . "

"That was more than a year ago," Suling said flatly. "That's how long it took me." In a lighter tone she continued, "How should I address you? As Miss Hung or Hung Lan? Maybe Comrade Hung, even though I'm not a comrade?"

A smile appeared on the woman's face. "Call me Hung. But Comrade Hung is all right, too," she said. "You are my first visitor from America."

The driver took Suling's luggage and Comrade Hung took her arm and led her out to the street, noisy with bicycles, trucks and buses and their tinny horns.

Suling thought she would recognize Fuzhou as soon as she saw it, the way coming across a line of poetry and seeing the right words in the right places would trigger the brain into remembering the rest of the poem. Now, sitting in the car, another snub-nosed vehicle with a high roof, running boards and curtains over the rear window, she was in despair. She could not find any old landmarks: the huge banyan tree with branches that shaded old men playing chess and children skipping ropes; the shoe-repair store where customers stood on one leg, like so many herons in repose, waiting for their shoes to be fixed.

"We're going toward East Gate, aren't we?" Suling asked at last. "Where is that restaurant that has the best sweet rice balls with ground meat inside?"

"I did not know there were restaurants along here," Comrade Hung answered. "I came to Fuzhou only two years ago."

Then you have no memory of this city, Suling thought with sadness. She reached into her pocket and touched the stone.

Now the car was turning into a spacious driveway lined with pots of hibiscus exploding with flaming red blooms. In the middle of the lawn on the left was a statue of Chairman Mao with one arm stretched out. The hotel at the end of the driveway was seven stories high but brand new.

"This is the tallest building in Fuzhou," Comrade Hung said proudly, "and that is the biggest statue in Fuzhou."

They entered the lobby filled with people checking in or inspecting the crafts and herbal medicine in the display cases. Suling wondered why the hotel in Guangzhou had so few visitors.

"Your room number is 317," Comrade Hung said as they stepped into the elevator.

"That was the number of my room in Guangzhou," Suling exclaimed. "What a coincidence!"

When she entered the room and saw that the space, the layout and the furniture, although much newer, were exactly the same as those in the room in Guangzhou, she knew she had been too quick with her tongue. This was a special room and she had been assigned here for a special reason. Maybe the Communists thought she was a spy for *Ni-ke-song* and needed close surveillance. She recalled the look of discomfort on the other guide's face when he stepped into her room in Guangzhou. She would search this place later on.

While Comrade Hung waited, Suling went into the bathroom and washed her face and changed her clothes. Then she announced she was ready to see her parents.

"Have you prepared yourself to see your parents after so many years?" Comrade Hung began.

"Prepare?" Suling repeated the word like a child. She thought of the little notebook in which she had jotted down things she wanted to tell her parents: her student days at Denton College, her marriage to a Chinese physician, their rebellious son, and her decision to find a job after years of staying home and following the Confucian precept of being a "virtuous wife and devoted mother."

She had also jotted down things she wanted to ask about: the cocker spaniel, the piano, and the jewelry box her grandmother left her.

She did not write down one question because she dared not ask it, and because Mr. Nam Sing had warned her again and again not to do so. When she first received the news from him of Little Brother's death during the first part of the Cultural Revolution, she had run to the closet in the guest room and locked herself in. Only darkness and stale air in an unused space could contain her anguish.

She realized Comrade Hung was still talking. " . . . you must understand that, ah, that the place they are living now is nothing like your old home by the canal. Because of the housing shortage, many families have to live, ah, live under one roof. But this house is very big."

Suling gripped the stone in her pocket until she thought it was becoming part of her flesh. How did Comrade Hung know what their old house looked like? Was she one of the Red Guards who had informed on her parents, pillaged their house and robbed them of their belongings?

The house that Comrade Hung described was indeed a big house, if not a mansion, built on a gentle slope with the courtyard in front, the ancestral hall and living quarters behind that.

"Mr. Chu, the owner, was wealthy beyond imagination, but he is now in prison," Comrade Hung said and laughed loudly as she stepped through the small door on one side of the iron gate.

Suling stared at the courtyard. It resembled a city dump. Everywhere, in every nook and cranny, were piles of debris covered with rags. Looking again, Suling realized the piles were rocks of every shape and size, decorated with tiny clay pavilions and houses—an elegant rock garden presently used as a gigantic apparatus for drying laundry.

They walked on to the second area, the ancestral hall, an enormous room that, in her house by the canal, had contained the ancestral tablets and many sets of highly polished mahogany furniture. Now this was just a huge refugee campsite: beds with torn bamboo mats, broken chairs, benches, tables, pots and pans, cracked plastic sheets and old shoes without soles. Some families had erected partitions by stacking boxes on top of one another or draping sheets on ropes strung between the enormous columns. The noise made by the two dozen people was deafening: children crying and adults scolding. Fowl cackled when approached. The stench of rancid oil and decaying food penetrated everywhere.

"Your parents are living at the other end," Comrade Hung said as she steered Suling among people and their belongings.

"Not in the passageway!" Suling exclaimed. She knew what these passageways were like: narrow as aisles on a train, drafty as open chimneys, with corrugated plastic roofs and earthen flooring that was damp and slippery during the rainy season. Such passageways were provided for servants to move unobtrusively from the kitchen at the back of the house to the great hall, bringing food and drink to the guests on ceremonial occasions.

"But the Office of Housing has enclosed the passageway. It is now like an apartment with two fine rooms," Comrade Hung replied with enthusiasm. "There is a door between the bedroom and the sitting room and a front door that locks!"

Suling blinked several times to keep back the tears.

Months before the trip, Suling had tried to visualize the first meeting between her parents and herself, hoping and praying that the occasion would be free from pain and hysterics. Now, standing half in and half out of her parents' long and narrow sitting room jammed with strangers who wanted to see the reunion, Suling felt empty inside, hollow as the watermelon-seed shells that some were eating and spitting on the floor.

She had little trouble identifying her parents; only surprised that they looked so ordinary, like any old couple seated side by side in rickety bamboo chairs waiting patiently for a meeting to begin or a picture to be taken. The old man had a luxurious thatch of white hair and one good eye. The other eye was closed, sinking into his face as if there were no eyeball. She could not see the old woman's face, only her gray, wispy hair braided into a tiny tail that disappeared down her back, for she sat hunched over, her eyes glued to the earthen floor.

Observing the crowd of people more closely, she decided that they were not her parents' friends, as Comrade Hung had so warmly referred to them, but curious neighbors and onlookers who had turned up, hoping to see a good show. A pity, thought Suling, that she and her parents are such dull actors.

As if sensing the lack of drama around her, Comrade Hung, acting like the mistress of ceremonies, waved her arm in front of her and said in a piercing voice, "Comrade Xu, here is your daughter come all the way from America to see you."

Obediently the old man stretched out his palm. Suling leaned forward to grasp it. It was limp.

Then Comrade Hung turned to the old woman and said with another wave of her arm, "Here is your daughter, Mother Xu. Look at her." Comrade Hung stepped closer and jerked the old woman's face up with her hand. "Just look at her. Are you not happy to see your daughter?"

The old woman peered at Comrade Hung and asked in a cracked voice, "Did you say she is your daughter or my daughter? I do not remember ever seeing her."

Someone behind Suling said, "You've lost your mind, Mother Xu," and laughed. The old woman put her hand on her head and scratched around it as if looking for the lost item. Then she opened her mouth with its few teeth and laughed, too. Suling wondered whether she should join in. If she started, she imagined that the strength of her laughter could bring the roof crashing down on them, like Samson and the temple.

Suddenly, she felt cold fingers on her arm, clawing her flesh and throwing her off balance. She tried to extricate herself until she realized the old man had stood up and was dragging her and the old woman into the adjoining room, stuffing them into another long and narrow space that contained a bench and two beds.

Like a crab, the old woman moved sideways and climbed up on the bed further from the door. She said loudly to Suling, "Why are you following us?"

Suling could not bear to look at the old woman. She had once dreamed of not recognizing her parents. She was in a park, alone and lost. Suddenly a statue, looking exactly like the Commodore in *Don Giovanni*, came alive and tried to give her directions. Then another statue also began to talk. Terrified, she woke and realized too late that the statues were really her parents. She had tried to will herself back into the dream again but without success.

"I was not following you," Suling answered, but the woman had already turned away and forgotten her. Suling sat down beside the old man and watched him trying to shut the door with his foot. Her head throbbed as he kicked and kicked at the flimsy piece of wood. At last she got up and closed the door with her hand.

"Are you sure it is tight?" The old man stood up and gave the door another shove. Then he veered around and thrust his face up against Suling's. "Now then," he said, "who are you? Why are you here? What is this all about?"

She focused her eyes on his head, noticing for the first time that his hair was not completely white but flecked with gray. His skin was rough and pale but his lean cheeks glowed feverishly red. "I've come back to see you," she whispered.

"What is your real name, your Chinese name? Your husband's name if you are married and your son's name if you have a son. I want to know all the names in English and in Chinese. Do you hear me?" Questions poured out of his mouth like a water tank turned upside down.

"I am Suling. Don't you recognize me?" Instinctively she put her hand up to her hair. Twenty-six years earlier, she had long thick hair growing below her waist, glasses over her eyes and a gap between her front teeth that made her whistle whenever she talked fast.

She realized the old man was getting angry. "Answer my questions!" He stamped his foot to mark every word; his body shook and he had to grab onto the bed post to steady himself.

Suling tried to pronounce the names but the sounds were strange: neither Chinese nor English. All at once she thought of standing up and walking straight out of here. The bedroom door had no lock and the sitting room door was wide open.

"Young woman," he began to shout, "if you are here to intimidate me and make me confess that I was a spy for my daughter in the United States, I will . . ."

"That is not true." Suling cried. "You are trying to intimidate me. With your loud voice, you will have Comrade Hung running in here soon."

His gasped and sat down without another word.

Now that she had him under control she could not bear his silence. "All these years you were the one who wrote me," she began softly. "You didn't let her do it because you were afraid that if the letters were discovered by the authorities, the blame would be . . . "

"How many letters did I write?"

"Six or seven, depending how you count them. I've kept them all, all these years."

He nodded. "I have another question," he said. "Do you remember, in 1940, when the Japanese invaded this city? What happened the night before the invasion?"

Suling looked up, confused. She became more so as his good eye burned into hers. "What happened? What do you mean what happened?"

"I know," the old woman spoke up cheerfully. "That night we moved our piano down the canal to the temple. We hid the piano inside the Buddha, right in the hollow of his belly."

"Mother?" Suling got up and ran to the other bed. For a moment she could see a flicker of recognition in the old woman's eyes, but as soon as she moved closer, the old woman shrank into herself.

"Mother," Suling continued, "I did not go along with you that night. I was too young to help. I stood at the bedroom window with Little Brother . . . "

The name wobbled and exploded in the air. The old woman flung one arm over her face as if to protect herself from the flying shards. Suling remained where she was. Then she saw two lines of tears running down the old man's cheeks. Even the bad eye could weep.

"I didn't mean to mention him," Suling whispered.

"When the Red Guards dragged him away, your mother screamed so hard that she became ill. It was then that her mind . . . "

"Don't, don't, Papa," Suling cried. Her arms, which had hung so stiffly by her sides, reached out and enclosed him. She felt his delicate and vulnerable body and at last could not keep back her tears.

"I must tell you how he . . ." he began and stopped suddenly.

Following his eyes, Suling saw that the old woman crouched in the corner of the bed was yanking at her hair as if it were some kind of terrible outgrowth.

In a second the old man was beside his wife, locking her hands in his. "There is nothing to fear, my dear," he said. He glanced at Suling, "She is upset because she heard his name."

Suling took out the stone and placed it in her mother's hand. The mother moved her fingers and the stone rolled in her palm. "Is this for me to hold?" she asked no one in particular.

"Ah yes, Suling has given you a present." Her husband nodded. "Now would you like something to drink, my dear?"

"I'll get it," Suling said and reached for the thermos on the bench. She pulled out the stopper and quickly poured the soy milk in a cup and handed it to him. A few drops had gotten on her thumb. She licked her thumb and tasted the sweetness of sugar and *kuei-pi*.

Holding the Fort

Becky Hagenston

Alone in her parents' house for the first time since her separation, Alice feels a weird, exhilarating freedom she doesn't recognize from any part of her childhood—a sense that there is nothing at all preventing her from doing whatever she wants, if she could just figure out what that is. She stands at the kitchen window, watching the backyard roll out into the woods. She's slightly drunk. Earlier, she sat at the kitchen table in her bathrobe and drank two vodka tonics, which she'd never liked before and still doesn't. She feels as if she's rooting around for some trapdoor into the life she's supposed to be living now: single, footloose and fancy-free, that sort of thing.

Alice's parents take a European tour every August. Usually Mrs. Parrott from next door watches the house while they're away, but this year Alice volunteered. She told Glen he could clear his things out of their house while she was gone. "On vacation," she said, trying to sound mysterious. Glen told her he'd be moved out by the following Wednesday. "It's no hurry," she told him. "I'll be gone for two weeks." Her parents' house is a half-hour away. She was going to tell Glen she was off to someplace sunny, but he didn't ask.

When she told her parents that she and Glen were splitting up, her father had said sometimes people are better off living apart, and her mother had gone very quiet and vanished into the bedroom, as if this were something Alice was doing to her deliberately. Alice didn't mention the part about Glen deciding he was in love with someone else. That was too humiliating.

"Marriage is hard work," Alice's mother is fond of saying. "It's like a recipe you have to throw everything into, but in the right amounts. And you have to watch it so it doesn't boil over or freeze or turn goopy." She has another saying, about sex being like scrambled eggs one night, filet mignon another. "And both are fine," her mother says. "There's nothing wrong with scrambled eggs." Alice's mother never said what happens when your husband, after four years of perfectly good eggs and filet mignon, suddenly decides he wants nothing but pork chops, every night.

* * *

Alice drives to the grocery store, still feeling fuzzy from the vodka. While she's standing in the checkout line she realizes there's a possibility of seeing Glen here: the store is on his way home from work, and it's already past five. Alice herself would be coming home from her editing job at the university press—where she would like to believe she's indispensable, but suspects it isn't true. "I can take some manuscripts with me," she'd offered, but her boss Marjorie told her not to worry, to just go have a wonderful time with her hunky husband. Alice hasn't gotten around to telling anyone at work about her and Glen yet. "I will," Alice told Marjorie, with what she hoped was convincing enthusiasm.

Her plan was to simply lounge around her parents' house for two weeks—read, rent movies, think about things and come to terms with them—but after two days of this she's just restless and slightly miserable. She thinks there's something else she should be doing.

Her cart is full of things she doesn't even know if she likes—cayenne-flavored linguini, strange-looking canned sauces, water chestnuts, kiwi, toffee-flavored coffee. The man ahead of her is tall and handsome in a red-haired, ruddy way. He plunks a gallon of whole milk on the moving belt, then a box of sprinkle-covered cookies. That's all he's buying. Dessert for him and the wife? Or maybe a late-night snack while he watches a movie all by himself. At what degree of loneliness does one strike up conversations with strangers in the checkout line? Handsome male strangers. The cashier, she realizes with some alarm, is also handsome and male, and she feels suddenly conspicuous—a woman who has been dumped—and wonders if there is anything at all about her to signify that she is different from the person who has been coming here for years and years, the happily married person who didn't even consider the possibility of a Patsy.

She had seen Patsy before, at Glen's office Christmas parties. "Patsy in purchasing," he called her, as if there were lots of other Patsies who worked there. Alice hadn't suspected, not once, not ever. When Glen was trying to tell her about the two of them, she'd said, "People get crushes even when they're married, it doesn't mean anything, it goes away." Alice had had crushes, too. And they did, they went away.

"It's not a crush," he said, and only then did she understand that her husband was having sex with this woman, was kissing her and frolicking naked with her and falling in love with her. "Ah, Alice." He sighed, and looked at her as if she were dying and there was nothing anyone could do. "I know you're mad, I know you must hate me." He said other things, about never wanting to hurt her, about wanting to be friends—or stay friends, he wanted them to stay friends.

"I don't think," Alice said slowly, "that's such a hot idea." Was she mad? She must be, but all she could feel was something that was almost fear, a slow freezing. She took an inventory of herself, to determine if some piece of her was suddenly missing, to see if she could locate the place it had been. She couldn't tell.

She wanted to ask Glen: How do you find the time in a day for things like this? When you're supposed to be working, or at the grocery store, or home eating dinner with the person you married? But she couldn't bear to know the ways these things worked, as if knowing would somehow make her an accomplice to her own deception. She decided there must be a sort of balloon of time floating around, just for affairs. It contains them and keeps them safe and the wife never knows a thing.

Alice considers having a crush on the cashier, coming back here every week and standing in his line and finally making conversation, going out, sleeping with him. This could happen. Glen used to flirt with her when she was working at Barnes & Noble, standing around her register and asking questions and being charming, and look what happened to them.

The cashier looks young, maybe twenty-five. Not too young. Patsy is older than Glen, but not much—late thirties, Alice guesses, though she could be as old as forty-five. She's one of those women who used to be eternally tan and has the thick, leathery skin to show for it. She's not what anyone would call beautiful—short, slightly stocky, shoulder-length hair that's trying to be red.

Alice imagines that sex with the cashier would be pleasant and that he would be kind, but by the time he asks her if she found everything O.K. she has already decided it would never work. She smiles, a little regretful. Nothing at all is at risk. "Yes," she says, and asks for plastic, please.

* * *

At midnight, she calls their house. If Glen answers she'll hang up immediately, but the machine picks up. "Hi, nobody's home. Leave a message." Alice frowns, annoyed. He's changed the message. It used to be her voice: "Hi, *we're* not home." She imagines he's with Patsy somewhere, wherever it is that she lives.

It takes twenty-five minutes to get to the house, and she parks across the street and turns off her lights. The house is dark, the driveway empty. She sinks down in the seat as if there's somebody who might see her. A dog barks somewhere down the street. She rolls down her window a little and closes her eyes, and when she opens them, her neck is sore and the sky is beginning to bloom a dusty yellow. The driveway is still empty. From here, the house looks friendly, beautiful in its red-brick ordinariness. The roof, which Glen repaired last year, slants at an alarming angle (all those times he was up there, cleaning out the drainpipes!) toward the driveway.

Glen had volunteered to move out. "You keep the house," he said, and she had thought of saying: No. I don't want it. But she did want it. She had found it, and she wanted it. She wanted the red-brick ordinariness and the windows with their curtains that match the carpets, and the careless shrubbery in the front yard. She wanted the blue mailbox with the red flag—which is sticking straight up, she notices now, like a salute.

She feels suddenly sad at the thought of him tending to such small things, with her gone. Remembering to put up the flag.

The windows are beginning to lighten. She can see the blue curtains in the living room. She wants to stay right there and watch the house—her house—until she has seen it at every hour of the day, until she has memorized it from the outside the way she knows it on the inside.

But there are other things she should be doing. She drives back to her parents' house, and when she sees Glen's black Jeep she feels an odd thrill as he goes past without noticing her, as if she is suddenly invisible, or disguised.

* * *

There's a message on her parents' answering machine.

"Sweden calling!" says her father. "I was worried we might wake you, but I guess you're already out and about."

Then her mother's voice: "Hi, honey! Hope everything's well. It's raining here. Had a choppy time on the ferry last night, but we're fine."

Alice can't imagine what her parents do for two weeks alone together every year. She seems to remember, from when she lived at home, the three of them just sitting around in separate rooms, watching television or reading or talking on the phone. While her friends' parents were getting divorced, Alice's maintained a sort of detached camaraderie, like people in a boardinghouse who are civil when they pass on the stairs, but don't really go out of their way to get to know one another.

The trips were her mother's idea. Alice was fifteen the first time they went away, leaving her with their neighbor, Mrs. Parrott. They came back bubbling with stories of lochs and castles; laden with shortbread, tam-o'-shanters, woolly sweaters. Since then, the trips had been a ritual; the planning for the next one began almost as soon as they got off the plane. Stacks of brochures arrived in the mail and they pored over them, her father tapping at his calculator, her mother wondering aloud if such-and-such a place would be too expensive that time of year, or too crowded.

There was never a question of taking Alice along.

"You'll have your chance," her mother said. "You'll have your romantic European getaways."

Glen wanted to go to Hawaii for their honeymoon, which Alice thought was a cliché but she agreed. She'd been imagining someplace gray, with castles, someplace with canals and moats, where women wore scarves on their heads and you bought things from markets. Instead, they took walks on the beach under a metallic-blue sky and drank fruity coconut drinks. It was all very romantic in a predictable, unsatisfying way—like something out of a movie you've already seen. After that, there hadn't been the time or money to go anywhere.

If she had been able to pack Glen off to Scandinavia or the Mediterranean every summer, would everything have been different? They could be having a choppy time on a ferry right now, and Patsy in purchasing would be out of luck.

* * *

It's hard to know what to do during the day. She sleeps late, wanders through shopping malls, goes to movies. She calls Glen's and her house for messages and is relieved and disappointed when there aren't any. Part of her wants to hear a gooey, dirty message from Patsy; most of her doesn't.

At night, she drives to the house and parks across the street. She tells herself there's nothing strange about this—it is, after all, her house, and she has a right to know what goes on there. Or what doesn't go on—Glen hasn't been home at night. She wonders if he's already packed up and moved. In which case, he should at least leave the porch light on. He should at least make it look like somebody's home.

There had been a burglar once. He came in through the basement while they were sleeping, and in the morning the TV and the VCR were gone, and the dresser drawers were open and rifled through. Alice felt sick, thinking of the burglar right there, in the bedroom while they were asleep.

"He could have killed us," she said to Glen.

"But he didn't."

"He was watching us!"

"He wasn't watching us. He was too busy stealing. Relax," he told her. "All he got was replaceable things. And it's not like we watch TV that much anyway—we'll hardly miss it."

But that same day he went out and bought a new one, with a VCR built right in. "For convenient, one-trip stealing," said Alice bitterly. "I think we should get a dog."

"We don't need a dog," Glen said. "I'll protect you!"

But she was the one who suddenly couldn't sleep at night. She was the one so tired and distracted, worrying about a stranger taking their television, that she didn't even notice her husband was falling in love with somebody else.

* * *

The fourth night, his Jeep is there, parked at a sloppy angle in the driveway. She can see him sitting inside, in front of the flickering blue light of the television, and she feels literally heartbroken—as though something has cracked open and is rattling around inside her chest, loose. She wills him to stand up and come outside, to stand on the front porch and look across the street—would he recognize her parents' car?—but of course he doesn't. He just sits there on the sofa, with the curtains wide open.

"I don't want one of those fishbowl houses," Alice had told him one night after the burglary. She pulled the draperies shut. "I don't like the idea of people staring at us when we can't see them."

"But that," said Glen kindly, "would make it even *less* likely for someone to break in, wouldn't it? If they could tell somebody's home?"

"I don't think I'm being unreasonable," she said.

"I didn't say you were."

It had always seemed to her that their personalities complemented each other, that her sensible down-to-earthness served as a ballast for his occasional recklessness. She loved that he did things she never would—like skydive, or quit his job before he had another one. She thought it indicated optimism. Now, for the first time, she considers the possibility that it was nothing more than stupidity.

Glen is holding the remote up, pointing it toward the set. She's glad he left the draperies open, glad she can watch him—oblivious and alone and unprotected.

* * *

The next night there's a red car parked behind the Jeep and she knows it's Patsy's. It's the sort of car a woman like that would drive—flashy, shiny, expensive but nothing special. The curtains are open but the living room's dark. She thinks of Patsy moving through her house, using the coffee maker and watching the television, opening the medicine cabinet and seeing her Anacin and tampons and pink Mary Kay containers.

She feels, for the first time, that there's something she could do, but she can't think of what it is. At two the car is still there, and Alice drives home.

* * *

"Are you holding the fort?" says Alice's father.

"The fort's still here." Alice is in the living room; there's a pile of laundry on the floor where she dropped it to answer the phone. From the window she can see Mrs. Parrott, tiny and pink-haired, waving a green hose over her lawn.

"We were thinking," says her father, "that maybe next year, maybe you might want to join us. We were thinking it might be nice."

"Oh," says Alice, slightly stunned. She wonders if this means her parents have given up on the possibility of her ever having a romantic European getaway of her own. "Did Mom come up with that idea?"

"She did, actually. But I agree completely. It would be a good . . . family experience, we think."

Then her mother: "We'll pay for it, of course, don't you worry about that. We'd just love to have you along. We were thinking maybe Scotland."

"But you've already been to Scotland."

"But you haven't."

"No," says Alice. "I've just been to Hawaii. Maybe Scotland would be fun, we'll see."

Her father gets back on the phone, tells her the temperature is a refreshing fifty-four degrees and that tomorrow they're off to Copenhagen.

"Copen*hah*gen," he says. Before they hang up he recites their itinerary and reminds her to pick them up at the airport on Saturday.

Alice regards her laundry on the floor and decides to leave it there. Across the street, Mrs. Parrott has become slightly tangled in the hose; it's wrapped around her ankles and she turns in a bewildered circle before managing to untangle it. Mr. Parrott was dead before Alice was born; Mrs. Parrott used to tell her highly romantic stories about how they met, one of those love-at-first-sight-on-a-crowded-train things. Alice feels suddenly sad, and she's not sure if it's for Mrs. Parrott or herself. She wanders through the house, checking the locks, the windows, holding the fort.

* * *

Patsy stays for the weekend. Alice wonders if they'll go out for bagels on Sunday morning like she and Glen used to, if Patsy knows yet that the only kind he'll eat is onion. She wonders if Patsy has parents he can adopt.

Sometimes, on Sunday afternoons, Alice and Glen would go to Alice's parents' house for lunch. Her mother would pad around in her after-church clothes—mismatched sweats, footie socks—and her father would sit in the living room watching whatever sporting event was on television. Alice had expected Glen and her father to hit it off—they both liked Jack Benny, they both played chess—and they did, but her mother adored him with an intensity that Alice found almost embarrassing. "My gorgeous son-in-law," she called him proudly, as if he were something she had invented and could take credit for. Glen, Alice noted with amusement, would blush and duck his head like a child. He loved it.

Glen's father lived in San Francisco and had visited once; he was busy with his second wife, a surly real-estate agent named Michelle, who was very young and tan and had teetered around Glen and Alice's house in white heels, smirking at their décor.

"He's found himself another nut," Glen said when they'd left. Glen's mother was off in Canada somewhere, being, as he called it, an aging hippie freak.

Glen liked to help Alice's mother in the kitchen while Alice and her father sat in the living room, watching television and reading the paper, raising their eyebrows at each other when the laughter in the kitchen got raucous. "They're like puppies," Alice's father remarked one time, when dish suds came flying out the swinging doors onto the carpet.

And then, suddenly, Glen stopped going to the Sunday lunches. After his onion bagel he'd go off on some alleged errand, or hunker down in front of the TV, or just go into the bathroom for a long time, until Alice left.

"Where's Glen?" her mother would say. "Is he all right? Is he working?"

"He's all right," Alice told her. "I don't know what he's doing."

She could feel her mother's disappointment in her, for letting the delicate soufflé of her marriage collapse.

"My mother didn't even like you at first," she told Glen, after he confessed about Patsy. "She told me to stay away from you!"

What she had actually said was, "Why move in with somebody you've only known three months? You should get your own place, live alone for a while."

Alice was living with her parents after college to save money. She'd had every intention of getting a place by herself, but why should she, when she was in love and it was all inevitable anyway? She moved into Glen's apartment. And then one day on her way home from work she'd seen their house—her house, where she will soon live by herself, just like her mother wanted.

* * *

On Wednesday, Glen is still there. She knows he's still there because she can see him inside, moving around, watching television. Patsy hasn't been over the past two nights, and Alice wonders if there's trouble in paradise, if someone has given someone the old heave-ho. What if she comes back on Saturday and Glen is still there, as if nothing ever happened? What if he says he's sorry, he's so sorry, he loves only her, can he stay?

She's still wondering this when the lights go off in the living room. But the curtains are wide open so anybody can look right in, can step around the shrubbery and put their face to the window and see the corn chip bag on the coffee table, and the socks on the floor, and the two empty beer bottles—drinking alone!—and tell that whoever lives there isn't very careful or aware, that he's one of those people who just assumes he's always safe.

* * *

She enters through the basement, using her key.

When she pulls the metal chain above her head the room fills with dusty, orange light, and everything looks like it always did—olive-green washer and dryer, clothesline, Glen's metal shelf of tools. She takes off her shoes and can feel the cement floor, cold and hard, through her socks. Upstairs, the house is silent.

She isn't sure what she wants to do, but certain vicious, TV-movie scenarios occur to her: suffocating him in his sleep, tying him up and leaving him helpless. Or seducing him, seeing how long it takes for him to realize who she is. She goes up the creakless stairs, holding her shoes by the heels, and flicks off the light at the top. Their burglar had left the basement light on. Alice had found this strangely insulting, as if he wasn't even making an effort to be sneaky.

The basement door opens into the kitchen. Alice locates the flashlight in the junk drawer next to the stove, and when she switches it on the room fills with drippy-looking shadows. There are two crusty bowls in the sink. The dishwasher (she opens it) is full of clean dishes. The shadow of the microwave fills an entire wall. It hadn't occurred to her to wonder yet who would get what—the microwave, the matching ceramic dish set, the curtains over the kitchen window—but now she does. Moving through the living room, she waves her flashlight over the accumulation of their four years together, and she sees objects to be divvied up. He will take the sofa his mother gave them, she will take the bookcase. He will take the credenza, which she never liked anyway. He will take the television. She will take the rocking chair and the big mirror in the hall, a wedding gift from her parents.

It occurs to her, suddenly, that she will never live here again. She will take what's hers and go someplace else, where she doesn't have to find a way to fill the empty spaces Glen leaves behind. It's a joyful knowledge, and she wants to wake Glen up and tell him, the way she'd told him she had found the perfect house for them, the perfect place to live.

There's some evidence of Glen's packing—a cardboard box with his overcoat and a pair of his boots in it, sitting in the hallway next to the closet. She stands just outside the half-closed bedroom door and can make out the sound of his breathing. The window over the bed must be open— she can smell the oleander bush outside, hear the twittering of crickets. She turns off the flashlight and pushes the door open.

In the moony light it looks like there might be two people in the bed, but when she moves closer she sees that it's only Glen, with the covers thrown off him. He's scrunched up on his side of the bed, not sprawled across it as she would have thought, and she feels a sudden twinge of fear for his helplessness—and for her own—as if they have failed to protect one another from innumerable, nameless dangers. She wants to crawl into bed with him, and in the morning everything will be normal again, like in those movies where at the end you find out it was all a dream. She moves closer to the bed. Glen's face is pale as marble in the watery moonlight, like something foreign and breakable. She thinks of all those nights she stayed awake, vigilant, while he slept peacefully beside her— tired, she knows now, from sneaking around and falling in love, too tired to care about burglars.

His duffel bag he takes to the gym is on the floor and she picks it up. She takes out his shorts and T-shirt and running shoes, then changes her mind and puts one of the shoes back. The closet door is open and their clothes are hanging like limp ghosts. Certain things are missing—his blue suit is gone, and his gray one. She takes one of his black work shoes and puts that in the bag, too. She takes the alarm clock, and his watch from the nightstand. She takes his glasses and leaves the case.

While he sleeps, she moves silently through the house, shining her flashlight, taking objects and putting them in the bag—coffee filters, the batteries from his Walkman, the light bulb from the bathroom. She takes the toilet paper, the can opener, the remote control. Small things. Replaceable things that he will notice missing, that he will miss.

Three Poems

Moira Linehan

Memento Mori

Near the end he would not stop
stroking my cheekbones, my jaw.
Bedridden, he would not tire

of outlining my lips. Then again,
as if this time he'd get it right.
Those fingers, so weak but holding on

to what he would take with him.
Never had I held so still
as I held out, the world came down

to this man memorizing
my face. There was a time
the grieving had their dead

photographed. Not so bad, perhaps,
to have somewhere to go—
mantel, drawer, locket—

when I longed for, if I forgot
his face. Not his face, death's
door slammed again in my face.

Another Waking

How do I start over? Love again
the light amidst the shimmering
tree shadows? How, when each waking

is so confounding: What's dream? What's
not? Each waking, whipsawing you
at once here, and not, light, no shade,

fugitive shivers, moth wings
dusting the lawn, my arms, and then,
another dawn. Again I'm turning

toward your side of the bed, at once
knowing grief the way there's sun, a tree,
and off to one side, shadow,

that quiver of a dance, here, no
there, the tree rooted and I, tangled
in the turning toward you gone

and still here, I in bed more
and more of each day. The space
you hold slips between everything,

everything slips through my hands,
moth wings, opening, closing. Moth
that goes nowhere, nowhere to land.

In the Keep of Death

My dead have never come back
in dreams. Not mother. Not father.
Not husband. The dead do this:
Come back. Stay away. Frank says

his father was wearing long johns
though he'd never owned a pair.
But Frank gets what he wants, his father
answers, "I'm okay now." Frank's done

nothing more than I ever have.
Not so his dead. How they match
his longing. As if they'd dreamed it
so they'd have a way to return.

My unsummonable dead.
Who'll say if it's I or they
do not dream? Even in dreams
Death keeps me and my dead
each from the other, out of our minds.

Four Poems

Sharon Olds

Take the I Out

But I love the I, steel I beam
that my father sold. They poured the pig iron
into the mold, and it fed out slowly,
a bending jelly in the bath, and it hardened,
Bessemer, blister, crucible, alloy, and he
sold it, and bought bourbon, and Cream
of Wheat, its curl of butter right
in the middle of its forehead, he paid for our dresses
with his metal sweat, sweet in the morning
and sour in the evening. I love the I,
frail between its flitches, its hard earth
and hard sky, it soars between them
like the soul that rushes back and forth
between the mother and father. What if they had loved each other,
how would it have felt to be the strut
joining the floor and roof of the truss?
I have seen, on his shirt-cardboard, years
in her desk, the night they made me, the penciled
slope of her temperature rising, and on
the peak of the hill, first soldier to reach
the crest, the Roman numeral I—
I, I, I, I,
girders of identity, head on,
embedded in the poem. I love the I
for its premise of existence, for your sake
too, the I of the beholder—when I was
born, part gelid, I lay with you
on the cooling table, we were all there,

a forest of felled iron. The I is a pine—
resinous, flammable root to crown—
which throws its cones as far as it can in a fire.

The Untangling

Detritus, in uncorrected ·
nature, in streambeds or on woods floors,
I have wanted to untangle, soft talon
of moss from twig, rabbit hair
from thorn from down. Often they come
in patches, little mattednesses,
I want to part their parts, trillium-
spadix, mouse-fur, chokecherry-needle,
granite-chip, I want to unbind them and
restore them to their living forms—I am
a housewife of conifer tide pools, a parent
who would lift parents up off children, lissome
serpent of my mother's hair discoiled
from within my ear, wall of her tear withdrawn Red-brown Sea from my hair—she to be
she; I, I. I love
to not know
what is my beloved
and what is I, I love for my I
to die, leaving the slack one, bliss-
pacified, to sleep with him
and wake, and sleep, rageless. Limb
by limb by lip by lip by sex by
sparkle of salt we part, hour by
hour we disentangle and dry,
and then, I love to reach down
to that living nest that love has woven
bits of feather, and kiss-fleck, and
vitreous floater, and mica-glint, and no
snakeskin into, nectar-caulk and the
solder of sperm and semen dried
to delicate frog-clasps, which I break, gently,
groaning, and the world of the sole one unfastens
up, a lip folded back on itself
unfurls, murmurs, the postilion hairs
crackle, and the thin glaze overall—

goldish as the pressed brooch
of mucous which quivered upright on my father's
tongue at death—crazes and shatters,
the garden tendrils out in its rows
and furrows, quaint, dented, archaic,
sweet of all perfume, pansy, peony,
dusk, starry, inviolate.

The Seeker

Suddenly, at night, in a strange town,
in somebody's borrowed car, VW
smelling of a man I have not met,
suede, cords, smoke, emotion,
I remember the thrill of the strangeness of a man,
of the newness of a new mouth, of not
knowing the arc of the teeth, wild
model on the dentist's shelf, not
recognizing the satin of the gum,
necking too soon with a man in his car,
setting the curves of my sweater to his palms,
not knowing him well enough
to guess if he is dangerous,
putting the tasting first, the unknown
tongue, scoring cheek, pattern
of the bristles like a toy bed of nails,
a test of faith, its intricate fire
drawn across my skin—the *other*,
the one who seemed to come from almost outside the human, as in my dream
of conception my father had come up to me,
outside, I was not a creature, just salt
and oil, and he moved close, and with something like
a deep kiss brought me into existence.
Sometimes, when I necked with a stranger, I
went close to that, pheromone, sweat,
ash, kiss of life, as if tasting in him
some male, unmothered world, and through him
a male world tasted me.
Every time, I was playing, without knowing,
with the concept of a man as good—that I could
lay my clothed body like a soul in his hands
and he would not take it. But he might. But he would not.

White Anglo Saxon Protestant

> My twin brother swears that at age thirteen
> I'd take on anyone who called me kike. . . .
> I remember putting myself to sleep . . . dreaming of Hitler,
> of firing a single shot from a foot away, one
> that would tear his face into a caricature of mine,
> tear stained, bloodied, begging for a moment's peace.
>   —Philip Levine, "The Old Testament"

When Philip Levine kills Hitler, a man
of his species, a man he says is not
absolutely unlike himself,
nor, absolutely, unlike
the WASPs of Detroit, who looked down on the Jews
and the Blacks of Detroit, and on everyone else,
I kneel down, there in the kitchen,
bending over till my forehead is touching
the floor, my hands holding each other,
I am praying, for the first time since our son
was hours late, and I threw off the disguise
of not believing in a god, and I begged,
abjectly, for our boy to come home. The linoleum is
smooth, under my brow a blunt bulge
of the pattern, like a harrow-bank in soil.
I do not think I will get up again.
I think I have found my posture for life.
What I'm seeing about myself and my people
will not be seen and stood upright with,
but I am not upright, I am bowing to the power
of other hearts. I am begging forgiveness
for the gentiles, I am begging forgiveness for myself,
I had not realized I had thought that the WASP
was the regular, the norm, everyone
else a variation on the norm,
and I had not seen that as a child of my parents
I had privately, as if luxuriously, suffered,
I am bowing to achieve some comfort, making

a human letter in Hebrew or Arabic that
says I love who knows more than I know,
the saltier smarter heart. I came
from people who thought they were better than anybody,
no one else was quite real to them,
and among themselves they brooded over
the oldest white blood, the bluest white eye. O I was
theirs, they had me. Until today
I had not seen that I had shared their vanity,
wanting to hold my head higher
than anyone, to praise myself
at the expense of any person, or group,
and shine. Low down to the floor there is a small
wind like the one through a vineyard, down
where the root becomes the stem, and the smell
is of zinc, and slate, and tallow earth.
This is where I will live my life,
on the floor of love's vineyard, in the furrow.

Hotel

Richard Burgin

The second I looked at him I knew what he was doing. Extraordinary! I'd never recognized anything like that so quickly, never realized so much about someone in a single glance. I simply looked out at him two tables away from me in the restaurant and knew. But what was I doing? I was in the hotel alone waiting for the movers from Philadelphia to arrive so I could move into my new apartment. Like a lot of people I was nervous without my belongings. Without my possessions I felt somewhat disoriented.

It had been a long flight to St. Louis, made longer because I changed planes in Detroit to save money. I'd arrived at the hotel—one of those drably monolithic mid-level hotels (this done to save money because I was starting to exhaust what my company was allowing me)—tired and hungry and with the vague beginnings of a stomachache. I looked at the carpet on my floor, a labyrinth of dim maroon and dull brown and my head spun a little. Then I left for the buffet-style cafeteria, filled my tray with some kind of pot pie and a few other forlorn-looking dishes and sat down at a table that faced the pool (all St. Louis hotels of this kind have swimming pools). Right after my first bite of the too-salty stew I looked up, saw him and knew.

He was about my age (fortyish), with thin yellow hair and a balding head, and he had sharp blue eyes turned toward the pool where he was ogling a little brunette girl in a pink bathing suit who was no more than eight years old. I smiled disgustedly at him, but he didn't notice. I muttered a couple of curses, but his eyes stayed focused directly on the girl in the kidney-shaped pool. She was jumping into the water, running beside the pool, then jumping in and swimming a little, then repeating the routine. When I met my ex, her daughter, Sarah, was about the same age and size as this little girl, though perhaps a little heavier. Of course I never even stared at Sarah the wrong way for a second. She was very attached to her father and didn't want to be physically close to me, even during the years when we got along well. The truth is I never even had a single kiss from her in all the years I knew her. But this balding blond man—he couldn't keep his eyes off the little girl in front of him, and he didn't care who knew it either. He was transfixed!

With human weakness, especially sexual weakness, I'm generally pretty laissez-faire, but I've never looked kindly at men who do the kind of thing he was doing and this time it particularly infuriated me. I thought seriously about going over and talking to him, but what could I say? It's not against the law to look out the window. He'd claim he was just staring at the flower pots, symmetrically arranged behind each corner of the pool, or at the abstract sculpture that was dribbling a pathetically halfhearted, piss-like arc of water near the center of the pool. It wouldn't do any good to confront him, and could possibly turn into a catastrophe, so I concentrated on eating my food quickly instead.

When I got back to my room I tried to watch TV, but my stomach was getting worse. I took some Mylanta, waited until the cramps got unbearable, then sat on the toilet hoping for relief. I thought it was odd how throughout the years we were together my relationship with Sarah mirrored my relationship with her mother, Louise. I mean, when I was closest with Louise I also got along best with Sarah, and vice versa. Then, when things broke down completely shortly before our divorce, Sarah barely talked to me. Of course she sided with her mother in all our arguments, I expected that, but I didn't expect this mirror principle to continue the way it did throughout our relationship. I was also hurt when Sarah didn't answer my cards or letters after the divorce and returned the check I sent her on her birthday.

I began to think some more about that, but my cramps got worse, perspiration broke out all over me, and it soon became too painful to think about anything.

. . . An hour later the diarrhea ended. I turned on the TV and lay in bed, hoping to fall asleep soon. The usual shows were on and I wound up flipping between a political talk show and an inane but vaguely titillating movie about an island where people lived out their sex fantasies. Within minutes I started to hear a door slamming at fairly regular intervals. Ten minutes later it was still happening. I thought it was some sick lover's quarrel at first, but when the door kept slamming I thought no adults could possibly act like that, or could they? After fifteen or twenty minutes more of it, I got out of bed, opened my door, and peered out. I didn't see anyone, but a few seconds later the door to my right opened, and I saw a little girl smaller and probably younger than the one in the pool, smiling just before she was about to slam the door.

"What are you doing? It's one in the morning," I said, exaggerating a little. "Will you stop slamming the door? Why are you doing it? Why are you slamming the door?"

She didn't answer me, but the smile went off her face. I went back to my room, and, after a couple more times, the slamming stopped. I watched TV another thirty minutes until the movie ended, then finally fell asleep.

That night I had a strange and disturbing dream. I met a tall, muscular man with a thick beard—he may even have been a giant—and began walking with him in the woods. Apparently we'd met before. We walked down a path until we reached a small deserted barn. We were talking about how to kill someone, about just what it would take. The giant handed me an extraordinarily thick wad of paper and said, "You've got to will it and squeeze the life out of it and then kill it." I was afraid to do it and handed the paper back to the giant, who was reluctant, too. I noticed that he'd begun to perspire, but finally he grasped the paper tightly in his hands and squeezed so hard the veins stood out darkly on his forehead. The broken paper fell to the floor and seemed to whimper softly for a second. I was shocked at what the giant had done and knew he was, too. He looked tortured, as if he were about to cry. I began patting his head to comfort him, and he turned and said "Oh, Allen," which is my name. Then he started to sob, and I woke up perspiring.

For a moment I didn't know where I was. When I did realize, I felt sorry for myself. I thought, I've moved too much in my line of work, way too much. I was thirsty and walked out to the hallway to fill my paper cup with ice from the ice machine. A long stretch of carpet was in front of me. Every ten feet a light hung from the center of the stucco ceiling, yet the hallway was dim, as if it had eaten the light. In the far distance a bright red exit sign hung in front of a window that reflected the ceiling lights to infinity. The ice machine was under this exit sign. I looked at the walls while I walked. They were a very pale green. By the time I reached the ice machine, I knew I wouldn't get back to sleep.

Late the next morning I called the movers' home company in Philadelphia. They were vague, they were evasive. It would be at least one more day before they'd arrive with my things, maybe two. I got off the phone without any confidence that they'd arrive soon. Once they had their purchase order they weren't in any hurry. They did things wholly to please themselves. It didn't bother them if you were in hotel hell. They lived for their purchase order, that's all.

It was hot out again. I don't think it had been less than ninety-three degrees since I arrived. I went to the hotel cafeteria and wasn't surprised to see the pool full of people. My nemesis was at his table again when I sat down at mine (close to and perhaps at the same table I'd sat at before). I saw that the little girl in the pink suit was in the pool, too.

He was still watching her. His head was turned completely away from anything else in the cafeteria, his attention wholly on his little pink bathing beauty. I watched him watching her for a couple of minutes, then I stood up with my tray and walked toward him, stopping just in front of his table.

"Mind some company?" I said. I'd taken him so much by surprise that he didn't know what to say. I'd also irritated him, and the combination of the two seemed to paralyze him. He might have mumbled "sure," but probably didn't say anything. I sat down, and he forced himself to turn away from the window and look at me. His eyes looked nervous.

"I noticed you looking at the pool," I said. He still looked confused and vaguely agitated and didn't say anything.

"Those kids sure know how to enjoy themselves."

"Yuh, they do," he said softly, his blue eyes intense like spears pointed at me.

"Kids are great, don't you think? Kids are really beautiful."

I stared back at him. I wasn't going to say anything more until he made some kind of response. He nodded.

"They're so innocent and spontaneous. But they can break your heart, too, because they can be selfish, let's face it. Yup. I know all about kids. You know what I mean? But what do you think? You seem to be very interested in kids."

I thought I saw his chin quiver a little.

"What is it that you want to say to me? I don't understand. What is it that you want to talk about?"

"Nothing," I said, tapping myself on my chest with my index finger. "I notice that you seem unusually interested in the kids here, that's all, that you couldn't seem to take your eyes off them, off one little girl in particular."

His eyes tightened, and I stopped.

"I don't understand what you're getting at, but I'd like to sit alone, if you don't mind."

"Sure, sure. I'll leave you alone. I think one of the key things people need is to be left alone so, of course, we have to know when to make space for people. Just like that little girl out there. She wants to be alone too. She doesn't want her world disturbed either, by the likes of you or me, wouldn't you say?"

His face flushed with color,

"I don't know what you're getting at, bud, but you're way off base here, way off base."

"Maybe, maybe not," I said, as I stood up. "Anyway, I'll be watching her just to be sure, you can count on that."

I turned and opened the sliding glass door that led to the pool, and soon I was sitting in a straight-back folding chair not too far from the pissing sculpture and about fifteen feet from the little pink girl who had just jumped into the water.

To spite me, and/or to show he was guiltless, my nemesis stayed right where he was, head turned toward or rotating toward wherever his little girl roamed. After ten more minutes, when he figured he'd made his point, he got up and left the table. I barely noticed his leaving, incidentally. When he did make the decision to leave, he disappeared as quickly as a bug.

After he left, I thought I'd stay for a while, get a little sun and rest, maybe move to a chaise lounge when one of them became vacant, but something happened. Just before I was about to close my eyes for a nap, they connected with the dark eyes of a little girl coming out of the pool, whose face immediately contorted in fear. Then she started running in the opposite direction toward the exit sign as fast as she could. There's something terrifying about seeing a little girl run that fast. I used to feel that when I'd see Sarah run that way. I always felt she was like a machine then that had gone out of control. It took me a moment before I realized the terrified swimmer was the girl I'd caught slamming the door last night. Apparently I'd scared her that night more than I realized. A minute later I left the pool myself.

I can't be entirely sure what I did with the rest of the afternoon, though I've tried to reconstruct it several times. Since I arrived at the hotel I'd been misplacing whole pools of time. I know at one point I set off for Walgreens to buy a watch and a new briefcase for my job (the old one having split apart) as well as a number of things for my new apartment, so that must have meant I went back to my hotel room to change. I'd been told the Walgreens was only a half mile away, but I must have made a wrong turn somewhere because it took me a long time to get there. Also, it was so hot out I couldn't walk very fast.

When I did get to Walgreens I was disappointed in their stock. They didn't sell briefcases or any of the other things I needed for my apartment. Also, it was in a shabby part of town, and I wound up giving my change to a homeless man who hit on me as soon as I got out of the store. The only thing I bought in Walgreens was a watch. That's how I knew it was 4:45 when I got back to the hotel.

When I saw the lobby, gloomy thoughts filled my head, and I wondered if I could really make it through a month here (I was a lifelong East Coaster), much less live here permanently. But, of course, when you sign on with a company you have to go where they tell you to, you're so afraid of getting downsized out of existence. They could say to you, "We want you to pack up and report to Hell tomorrow and start working there as soon as your things arrive," and you'd say, "Yes sir," and probably salute them, too, because being unemployed is worse than hell.

I got off the elevator, looked at my watch and started walking down the long corridor of repeating lights. Suddenly I had a memory—just a picture, really, of walking with Louise and Sarah along a beach in Cape Cod. Then I began toying with the idea of calling Louise or someone else more recent and trying to arrange a visit. I was getting sick of watching sex movies on TV every night, which was what I'd do again tonight, no doubt. I opened my door with my card key, then took a few steps into my room and stopped straight in my tracks. Above my bed someone had written an obscene message with a red Magic Marker in big capital letters on the wall.

I turned away and felt myself reel, as if I'd stared too directly at the sun. When I got my bearings I walked up closer to the writing as if I might get a clue about who wrote it if I studied it long enough. But there was no author's signature to this poem and a minute later I began packing my things—moving as fast as a St. Louis cockroach myself now—so that no more than ten minutes later I was checking out (no matter that I'd already paid for that day), and started heading for a Best Western Hotel I'd noticed two blocks away.

I managed to rid myself of thoughts until I got to the Best Western. I have no memories of any thoughts at all until I was being checked in. I decided to pay in cash, so my company would have no record of my staying in two different hotels in a day. That would seem weird, at best, and I didn't want to get off on the wrong foot that way.

When I got to my new room, which looked a lot like my room in the hotel I'd left, I was still breathing heavily, almost hyperventilating. I was upset and lay on the bed to try to calm down. I began thinking about who wrote the message on the wall. My nemesis was the mostly likely suspect, but how did he find out what room I lived in? The other suspect would be the little door-slamming girl, or perhaps her enraged father. But how did he or she get in my room unless I somehow left the door unlocked? I began to pace my new room, thinking these thoughts, and then finally forced myself to lie down again. Soon I started reassuring myself the way a parent talks to his child. "You saw something scary and sickening, something that was at the ultimate level of hostility and all aimed at you, so of course you're upset. You have the right to be upset. It has blackened your day, it would blacken anyone's day, but you'll get over it. It will stop feeling so bad soon. It will get better eventually, it always does. Who knows, the movers may even come tomorrow, and you can get out of these hotels and move into your own place and feel like yourself again."

I went on in this vein for a while, but it didn't make me feel as good as I wanted, so I tried another approach on myself. I tried to review my happiest memories. I actually turned it into a kind of game and tried to remember my ten happiest memories and was very encouraged to find that I had at least ten such memories before I was even a teenager that were still clear and vivid to me. Memories of playing different sports with my friends on the playground, or Halloween and Christmas, or days spent at the beach. Then I decided to focus on my ten happiest memories of my more recent life as an adult. Again they came relatively easily. There was a clear memory of swimming with Louise on an island in Greece. In fact our whole trip to Greece, done in the first year of our relationship, was happy, and my memory of it was something I reviewed and protected as if it were a great work of art. But there were also many other less exotic times with her that were just as happy. I could remember a week I spent with Louise and Sarah at Atlantic City that was among my happiest times—playing Frisbee with Sarah and laughing at her jokes and imitations (she was a wonderful mimic even then), and I could remember as well a trip to the Poconos with Louise and Sarah when Sarah was quite young. How much fun I had in the pool that day with Sarah. And there were many other happy days, of course, just normal nonvacation days from the time I lived with them. So I had known happiness after all, I had been happy once. The mere memory of it, the mere realization that this had happened to me once seemed to calm me down, and I soon fell asleep on my back.

A few hours of sleep later, a nightmare came. I don't remember much of it, I tried to, but it was mostly a scramble in the dark. I was running after Sarah by the water feeling a terrible fright. I was running as fast as I could, but I couldn't catch up to her.

I woke up perspiring again and realized something clearly. What I realized, of course, was that I was the author of those awful words on the wall of my last hotel. I don't know who I wrote it to. I wrote it to myself, among others, I suppose, I wrote it to the life I was living, but beyond that I couldn't really say.

I felt myself shiver and held onto myself in the dark as if I were a mere chip of wood or piece of paper caught in a riptide. I needed to calm down and tried talking to myself. Tomorrow the movers will probably come, I said to myself over and over, tomorrow the movers may come.

The First Woman

Stephen Dixon

After his wife left him, what? First woman he had anything to do with was much younger than he. Thirty-five years younger, more. Didn't intend to. Sure, saw her numerous times walking on the street and entering or leaving what he assumed was her apartment building and admired her looks, body and face, intelligent expression, way she walked, her bounce, height, hair. Sometimes would turn around to look at her walking the opposite way and once slowed down so she could catch up and get ahead of him and he could look at her from behind. But she was so young, around the age of his oldest daughter: young body, young face, rest of it, her clothes. So he would never think of stopping her, saying something, doing anything to initiate a conversation and see where it would lead: even saw her in the market a block from their buildings and could have started something there. "We must live pretty near each other; seen you so often in the neighborhood and on my block and a couple of times here." (Wouldn't want to give away that he knew what building she lived in; that might seem a bit peculiar to her: Knows what building I'm in? Does he also know what apartment? Does he look through his window into mine? What else has he seen?) Wouldn't think of doing that to any woman stranger on the street or in a market and probably not in an elevator or waiting for one even if he knew they lived in the same building or he was in hers visiting a friend. Dinner parties perhaps but he's only been to two the last six months and both had people mostly his age to around ten years younger. At work at a lunch table might be all right if he happened to sit next to a woman and then found himself attracted to her or walked into the lunchroom and saw a woman he'd been attracted to and sat at her table with the intention of starting a conversation— "Excuse me, but pass the pepper, please? The chicken salad good? I've never had it here, if that is chicken salad"—which might lead to meeting her for a coffee or drink sometime. Possibly in the same lunchroom—"So, nice talking, and see you again, maybe; tomorrow, here at one?"—or to going out with her, even: movie, play, museum or just for a long walk. But she stopped him. That's how it happened. He was walking up the hill on his side of the street, she was walking down—her building's almost directly across the street from his—when she smiled at him, he smiled back, they were about ten feet from each other and he immediately turned away, thinking that was a nice smile; if he didn't know better he'd say she was interested in him a little; no, that's going too far. But this is the street and New York and even if he were thirty years younger he wouldn't try to capitalize on a smile to make a pass. Should he look around to see if she's looking back at him? If she is it'd embarrass him that she caught him looking and would make her uncomfortable and then when he saw her next he'd have to make a point of not looking at her when she passed or she'd think he was some kind of street letch and after that would avoid looking at him every time she came within a certain distance of him: thirty or forty feet, let's say. It could be she's just beginning to recognize him, having seen him so much; figures he lives on this block or around it on Riverside Drive so she's just being friendly. She could even be from out of town; so many residents around here seem to be, and still has that out-of-town hi-neighbor behavior and that's all it is. It's true he's fantasized about her, but he's living alone now and hasn't been close to a woman since his wife so he fantasizes about lots of women, ten a day maybe, especially good-looking ones he sees on the street, and because of all the colleges in the area, and one just for women, there are loads of them to fantasize about, when she said "Excuse me. Excuse me there, sir, you up the hill," and he turned around and she was about forty feet away and he pointed to himself and she nodded and started up the street to him and he walked down and said "Yes?" and she said "I'm sorry, I didn't mean to stop you and then take you out of your way like this, and I should have thought of it sooner," and he said "No harm done, a few feet, and I'm not really in a rush to anything, what is it?" and she said "You see . . . oh this sounds silly—will sound, saying it . . . I'm embarrassed, almost, and really will be if it isn't so, but I believe we're acquainted. It's why I did that smiley greeting before. You're a friend of my father's, knew him a few years ago—as colleagues—and came over to our house with your wife once or twice, or once or twice when I was there. I recognize you, in other words—wow, I don't know why that took so long and was so arduous to get out. I forget your name, but your face is the same. You both taught together, Dad and you," and gave the name of the school. "Well that's

right, I did. I no longer do there, but you are . . . or your father is . . . ?"
She told him, he said "Oh, how is he?" She told him, he said "And how's
your mother?—excuse me, I forget her name." Told him and asked about
his wife and children—"Two daughters. I don't think I ever met them but
I remember my father waxing on ecstatically about them . . . wanted me
to meet them, even be like them, I think. No, why wouldn't they have
come to the house with you if I was there, unless they had sleepovers that
night, or I did and—" and he said "I don't recall that ever happening,
double sleepovers. Maybe my wife and I only came by for drinks," and she
said "Could be, so it was just the adults and a quick introduction to me.
But they were supposed to be very smart, artistic and literary—reading,
writing, way beyond their years—acting too, I think," and he said "Your
memory, whew." "I always had—I still do—an extensive memory for
insignificant details—not insignificant to you, naturally, but to my own
life," and he said "That can't be true," and she said "Why do you say that?"
and he said "I don't know. But I'm like that myself in ways, but with
significant details—forgetting to take my pajamas off and put my shoes on
before I go out—only kidding," and she smiled, obviously didn't think it
funny, said "Wait a second. Are your daughters even my age? That could
be why they didn't come over," and he said "One's twenty-three, other's
twenty," and she said "So I was right. Your oldest and I are the same," and
he said "Really. And as for my wife—you asked about her—well, she left
me. It all happened pretty quickly. I'm sure your folks know. You can say
I'm still shuddering from the shock of it and moving back here
permanently, or maybe I'm melodramatizing it a bit there. Anyway, it's
very nice that you stopped me. You probably have someplace to go now,
too." Then he just looked at her, had nothing to say, she didn't seem to
either, or he couldn't think of anything to say—wanted to but nothing
came and he'd save the regards-to-your-folks for when they said
goodbye—she smiled, then almost laughed into her hand, he said "What's
wrong?" and she said "Why?" and he said "So where do you live, around
here? I've seen you on this street a couple of times, on Broadway too and
I think once in the market up the block. Of course you understand why I
didn't recognize you," and she said "Of course." "So. Regards home, and
I'll be seeing you," and was about to put out his hand to shake and she said
"You didn't ask where I live. I mean, you didn't wait for an answer. In that
corner building. Moved in a few months ago," and he said "It's a
Columbia-owned building. So I assume, and I should have asked this
before . . . grad student, same field as your father's. Or maybe your
mother's—I forget what she did. Anyway, we're neighbors and both

newcomers, though I'm an old newcomer, meaning I used to live here years ago but have recently come back. And that's a funny thing to say, at least to my ears, 'neighbors,'" and she said "No, it's all right, and we are. And I know you have to go now—you have your right foot pointed up the hill already, but—" and he said "Do I? It was unconscious, believe me," and straightened his feet so they were both facing her. "But maybe one afternoon, if you're free, you'd like to get together for coffee . . . you're probably always busy," and he said "No, that'd be nice," and asked her first name and said he'd pass by her building on his way back and get the number of it and would call Information for her phone number, "if it's in," and she said "It's in," though he doesn't get the point. He's certainly attracted to her, what man his age wouldn't be?—any age, if he likes women; she's practically a beauty—so he's flattered, but why would she want to have coffee with him? Entering her intellectual phase or something? No, that's condescending. And he should have asked what field she's in in grad school; it may be the same as his. Wants to talk to an older man, an academic, have her mind stimulated? Well, he'll stimulate her all right, but fat chance, and why's he thinking like that? She's a kid, has a sweet smile, she must be a lovely girl, parents were very nice people, intelligent, decent, so she must be, and he's got forty years on her, so he doesn't know. Doesn't know what? Doesn't know. "But maybe it's a good idea I take your name and phone number down now—the old mind ain't what it used to be, and never was much, when it comes to remembering," and wrote them down in his memo book. "Or I can call you, you know," she said. "That's what I originally intended with this open invitation. But to be honest, I forget your name," and he gave it and his phone number and said "You don't want to write the number down?" and she said "I can remember, it's an easy one. So," smiling, "see ya," and he said "See ya," and they parted and he thought he meant to shake her hand but was glad he didn't. Kids don't appreciate it, may even wonder about it, mostly because they're not used to it, or maybe he's wrong. Anyway, looking back—picturing it—it would have seemed funny to do.

She didn't call and he thought about calling her for a week. Then always thought no, why should he? She can't be too interesting. Or let's say she is, in a little way, but what would they talk about? Well, he'd have to know what she's interested in. But after a while he'd make as big a fool of himself as he's ever done in his life. That an exaggeration? No, because what could be more foolish than an old guy making a pass to what's really a girl. Being rejected, maybe, or accepted—he didn't know which. For that's what it'd probably lead to if it went on, since if they did have coffee he'd say at the end of it why not let's do this again, "that is, if you want to and have the time—it's been enjoyable"—politics, they could have talked about, literature, writers, painting, teaching, learning, living in the city—and if she agreed, fine, and if not, well that'd be O.K. too, but if they did meet again for coffee, or a couple of times after that—"We got a regular coffee klatch going," he could call it—he'd say "What about we go out for dinner one time, for a change of pace, or just lunch? My treat, someplace fairly simple around here—actually, I'm not much for lunch—if I eat a carrot it's a lot—but I'll go and have something," and suppose she said yes or "If you don't eat lunch, then let's have dinner." He'd pick her up at her door? Probably lives with a roommate. University housing off-campus can be very expensive. All this is to say if she doesn't have a lover or serious boyfriend, and with them is there a difference? And then what? When you have dinner or even lunch you talk about things you don't when you're just having a coffee—he thinks that's right, at least about dinner. And different too than when you're just having a drink. A drink—a bar—picturing it: all those college kids in the bars around here; it'd look absurd. And what would they drink: beer, wine, and the first time, clink glasses and make a toast? What would they even talk about that second time for coffee, and the third? Her father, mother. Siblings if she has any. Growing up in an academic household. What she's taking in school. They probably would have gone over that already. Well, what she learned that day or week in classes or read for them. A paper she might be writing: maybe he could help. But would he be interested in any of it? How does he know. And he hated writing papers in school. Movies, that's what young people like most today, and music, but not his kind of movies and music, he's sure. And no going to her apartment building if it's only occupied by young college students and no married couples and some with kids, nor going there either if she has a roommate, female or non-lover male. Maybe they could skip lunch or dinner and just go to a movie—he could meet her at a corner—and discuss it over—or in front of her building or the theater—and discuss it over coffee after, no matter how bad it is. Actually, the worse it is the more he could pinpoint what he thinks is good in a movie from old ones he saw. And while they were talking he would probably look covertly at her body and no doubt fantasize having sex with her, which would be wrong—sex with her would. She's too young. Besides, she'd be put off by the suggestion. How would he even make it? He wouldn't have the words, and if he found them, he'd feel too silly saying them. But say she was open and relaxed about it and said something like "Your look; what is it, Mr. Bookbinder?" and he'd say

"Gould, please call me Gould; what is it with you?" and she could say "It's still hard for me to, but O.K. Gould, even though my folks"—"Oh, your folks," he'd think, just at the right time—"weren't the type, when I was small, to insist I call all adults by mister and missus and their last names," and he could say "But you were saying?" and she could say "About what was on your mind. The look you had. I'd never seen it on you but recognized it from other men," and he'd say "Then I guess I'm caught and will have to come clean," and would apologize while saying it: "I know it's wrong, stupid, our respective ages, all of that . . . " and she could say "I don't know. It's true I haven't done it with a man more than five years older than me, maybe because there was never one who interested me. But it's not like I have anything terrible against it. And isn't it every young woman's fantasy—" and he'd say "Don't talk about girls and their fathers," and she wouldn't have; she could just say "I don't mind the idea" or "The suggestion's not the worst one, so what do we do next?" or not even that—none of it. He'd just come out with it, find the words—"I've been thinking"—say them clearly, wouldn't give any kind of look and she'd go along with it and they'd go to his apartment—well, where else, unless she was living alone in a building which didn't only have other young students in it and wanted to go there, and they'd do it—have a drink, sit down and kiss, whatever they'd do first—and it wouldn't work. Sure, it'd be pleasurable for him, though you never know what can happen when you get too excited, and maybe in a way for her too: the pleasure, as he knows what to do and still has plenty of energy for it and would just hope that he could go slow, because once is usually it for him till the next morning. But she'd see his body and even if it's in pretty good shape for a sixty-four-year-old, it's nothing like the bodies of the boys she's used to and she might be turned off by it, even repulsed. The gray pubic hair, or most of it gray; chest hair that's totally gray and in fact mostly white. Wrinkles everywhere, way the body sags in places no matter what strenuous exercises and long running and swimming he does. This, that, from top to bottom—the elbows; especially around the eyes—it's a ridiculous notion, sex with her, so what's he even thinking of it for? And it won't happen. He shouldn't call. It's probably why she didn't call: she somehow saw it in his face that time they spoke: that this is what he was interested in, not talk. And even if they had sex once—her experiment with a much older man, let's say—that'd be it, because she wouldn't want to do it again. Why would she? He's an old fart, far as she's concerned, and if she doesn't see it at first, or blocks it out for some reason, she'll see it after: older than her father by more than ten years, he figures, as he had his children late. So: nice to talk to perhaps but not to make love with, and then they'd see each other on the street once every other week, which is about how often he saw her before, and what then? What would he say, she? And suppose she let on to her folks about it? "I met this old colleague of yours—you'll probably remember him too, Mom—or former colleague, rather, though he's also quite old but still in some ways considerably attractive for his age"—not intending to tell them what happened, but her father's a smart guy and was a very good college teacher so knows how to ask questions and extract answers from students, and kids can't hide things well the way adults do, and maybe it's also not how they act today: the compulsion to tell the truth, lay it all out, no matter how much it hurts or shocks someone else, as if that's a virtue, or is he thinking of a time ten or more years ago?—and then her father could call or write him and say something like "How could you? Not just that you knew she was my daughter. She's thirty-five years younger than you, possibly forty. What are you, some sort of predator, ravener, plunderer, vulture, hyena, monster, perverse addled dirty old dotty fool? Women even twenty years older than she, which a man your age of any decency and brains would still think far too young for him, aren't good enough as pickings? Why are you trying to screw up her life? What's in it for you but a slap on the back you give yourself for fucking a child? If it weren't that I didn't want to embarrass her and that she's five years past the legal age of consent, I'd report you and probably try to prosecute you and if there were some academic court of law I'd work to get you fired from your teaching post." Or he wouldn't write or call but he'd think it or it could be he'd think "Lucky stiff. Shacking up with a girl so beautiful and young. Wish it could be me, though naturally not with my daughter."

So he didn't call but she did. "Hello, is this Mr. Bookbinder?" and after he knew for sure who it was he said "Damn, I had a premonition you'd use that if you called—the 'mister' or 'professor' or 'doctor,' which I'm not: I barely got through grade college—instead of just my name Gould," and she said "I didn't want to, honestly, nor thought beforehand how to address you. It simply came out, whatever that latency means. My subconscious should probably keep that a secret," and he quickly tried to think what she'd just meant but said "O.K. by me. So, what's doing with you?" and she said "My goodness, plenty of things, but we'd mentioned something about meeting for coffee one day—do you still want to?" and they met. She was interesting—wide range of interests, knowledgeable about a lot, quick mind, some wit, articulate delivery, funny at times, charming, her parents send him their regards—the "life of the mind" came up twice in her conversation and she seemed earnest about it—and she seemed to find him interesting: laughed at his jokes, said several times "What you say makes a lot of sense," looked into his eyes as if he were her equal: someone she could be interested in or even involved with is what he wants to say. He wanted to say to her right away "Listen"—or after they got a coffee refill and second pine-nut macaroon horn they shared between them—"Listen, what are you doing tonight?" He gave advice, after he asked about her graduate-school work, on some courses she was thinking of taking and eventual career moves. "But the truth is, if I had to take those same courses I'd no doubt fail and be mustered out of the program, especially the long novels of Melville and that one you said on Puritan literature," and she said "Oh please," and he said "No, I haven't the mind for that stuff. *Bartleby* and maybe *Billy Budd*, though I can't stand the grandiloquent language of the latter, if I remember the book correctly and have the word right, but those two are about it. I don't know: the brain; who knows where the hell it goes, or with me, ever was, but I couldn't keep up in your class, and write papers on the long ones? Forget it. It's a fluke that I'm teaching. But if you notice, I only do short things and very clear and modern and interpretable . . . so it's a good thing I'm retiring in two years. My youngest daughter will be out of college then and that'll be it for half-tuition remission from my university, and I bring down the entire profession. Now your father . . . I don't know how many years he's been professing or has left in it, but there's a teacher, a scholar, a learned man, with eclectic interests and the ability to compress and express them, just like you. I used to feel a little stupid sometimes talking to him, not that he was ever high-hat or pooh-pooh or self-important. He just knew what the hell he was talking about and had good ideas. Me, I'm a fake," and she said "No you're not," and he said "Oy-oy-oy, now you'll think I brought it up to get sympathy or lower my level or show I'm vulnerable or some other ulterior reason, but just ask him. I'm talking about teaching and understanding the subtleties and particulars of literature and making the connections and seeing its big reach. He'll tell you. But let's change the subject; it's too much about me." Politics: some things about the coming presidential election they both read in the *Times* and a couple of liberal weeklies. Then they analyzed the mind of the lit. professor turned U.S. senator who killed his wife and her lover a month ago: ran over them when he saw them walking hand in hand across a street. What could have induced him, so much to live for and all that, and they had three young kids? The story goes he was having an affair of his own with a young staff worker and had had several before with all kinds of women and wasn't living with his wife—they were getting a divorce, had amicably worked out a settlement and this was her first man since they broke up—so why, why? She said "Male honor—that another penis had superseded his?" and he said "Are you speaking metaphorically? . . . hey, how about that word?" and she didn't smile and said "Both," and he said "Anyway, no, I don't think so, or just a little, and what do I care about that vile jerk? I'm only interested in what happened to his wife and kids, and to a smaller extent, the poor schmo he killed. I'm sorry, I don't always mean to direct us, but the conversation's gotten too morbid, so can we change the subject again?" "Do you like movies?" and he said "Sure, some, who doesn't? though I prefer the older foreign ones in black and white—late fifties, early sixties, long before you were born—but I bet you like the new ones a lot," and she said only if they're good. Has he seen . . . ? and he said no, but does she think it's worth going to? If she does he'll make a point of it and she said if he's serious about that she'll go with him, since she wouldn't mind seeing it again: it was probably among the best five or six movies she's seen in her life and he said "Oh, it was that good?" and she said "Are you playing with me, because I don't like it," and he said "No, why, something I said, or the way I said it? Oh, I won't lie; I was playing—patronizing—and I'll try not to do it again. It could be I just don't know how to express myself well in social matters also, or have degenerated to that the last few years, no fault of anyone's but my own, so please excuse me," and she said "And stop flattering yourself too," and he said "What? O.K., if you say so, I won't. So what's our next topic?" and she said "That's not how I engage in conversation," and he said "Of course not, I was only saying," and she said "And the truth now: you weren't being a touch sardonic to me then?" and he said "No, why would I, I wasn't, though if you don't mind I think that should be my last apology for the time being. All right, that said, so when do you want to meet for that movie, if you still do? And it'll be Dutch treat, O.K.? because I know you'd object to my paying," and she said "I wouldn't—I'm just a grad student—but fine with me," and after he left her he thought they almost blew it then but that could be because they're both a bit unsure and maybe even nervous about meeting again because they think it's the wrong thing. Is it? No, it's simple, it's nothing.

They went to the movie two nights later. Met her at it, got there fifteen minutes early to buy the tickets and have the excuse "Got here early so thought I'd save some time in line by buying the tickets beforehand—not to save time so much but just to make sure we got some seats—I hope you don't mind," and she said "No, I told you, if you mean about buying both tickets. Do you want to be reimbursed?" and he said "It's not necessary," and she said "Excuse me, I shouldn't have put it like that," and took out her wallet and he said "Please, put that away. So, where do you want to sit?" as they entered the seating area and she said "Anyplace you do but not too near," and he said "Should we have stopped off at the candy counter?" and she said "I don't eat those things in theaters—distracts from what I'm seeing besides being too much noise," and he said "Same here: the snacky stuff and not sitting too near. In fact, because of my eyes I like to be pretty far in back. So maybe, if that's not what you want, we should sit separately and meet after," and she said "The back's good." They sat, movie started, she took his hand a few minutes into it. He couldn't believe it. He'd already decided—when he walked to the theater—that this would be the last time he'd see her except for chance meetings. He'd gotten too anxious about this movie date; it would lead to nothing and he could see himself falling for her a little, but not making a fool of himself—keeping it a secret from everyone—and it would be upsetting. He'd think of her a lot, want to call her, but wouldn't. He'd planned to say nothing about it after the movie and when he accompanied her back to her building or however they'd leave each other and if she said anything like "Want to meet again?" he'd say "It's probably not a good idea and I'd rather not go into why, though believe me it has nothing to do with you. Meaning nothing you did or said, since for you I've nothing but admiration and respect," or not quite go that far as it might come out sounding like a line to inveigle her into a relationship, and he was sure she'd say "O.K., if that's what you want," and shake his hand goodnight and that'd be the end of it. So, they were watching the movie, right at the start of it after the opening credits, his hands on his lap, when suddenly she was holding one. He didn't see or feel her hand crawl to it or anything. His right, her left, she just took it and squeezed, about thirty seconds after she started holding it, and he thought, still facing the screen, she's squeezing his hand, what does that mean? and then she squeezed it harder and he thought it's probably a signal for him to look at her, the second one harder because he didn't look at her after the first, and he looked at her and she was smiling at him and looking as if she wanted to be kissed and he thought he can't do that, it's enough she's holding his hand and squeezing it. It was a dark scene on the screen so the theater was fairly dark, and her head turned just so toward him and lips parted a bit and that smile that said "Kiss me, we could do it now, just once if that's all you want, but come on while we've time and the theater's dark and people around us can't see and if you do kiss me I'll kiss you right back if you don't pull away right after," and he thought not here, probably not anywhere, there are some things you don't understand, at least have to be talked about, and how would it look?—people will see and think look at the old fart and the young beauty, first I thought she was his daughter or even his granddaughter, then they're kissing on the lips, maybe doing worse things below, how could he, and even uglier to think of, how could she? He smiled at her, faced front, didn't squeeze her hand once but continued to let her hold his. Occasionally glanced at her and she was always watching the movie. She gently squeezed his hand a few times and then so hard his knuckles hurt and it wasn't during an especially tense movie scene as the other squeezes since the first one had been so it seemed she wanted him to look at her again and he did and her head was like it was an hour before: turned and with the mouth open and smile just so and he mouthed "What?" and she squeezed his hand and tugged it a little toward her and he pulled it back but left it in hers and said "What? What?" and she said "Oh, what?" and someone behind them said "Shh," and he mouthed "Something wrong?" and her expression said "With this look and smile and my neck arched and head turned so and mouth parted in a preparation-for-kiss position, you say you don't know what it is and that something could be wrong? What's wrong with you? What was wrong before? Or maybe I should ask what do you see or sense wrong in me? You embarrassed? Or you don't like? Our ages? Me? My looks, mind? People all around? That I made a move on you? That I'm stopping you from watching the movie? Listen, it's going to happen, mister, you better believe it, here or somewhere else, now or later, this kissing. And probably tonight or another night this week, unless you confess beforehand to being gay, impotent, perverted or having a sexually transmittable disease, we'll be in bed also, so you better get ready for that too," and turned to the screen and he thought suppose she was thinking some of that, he hasn't yet told her about his wife and why they separated. And there's her father, mother, all the other things. What else is she expecting him to do besides kiss her here: later kiss her on the street, at a bar, a big long one in an elevator? Dance with her at some preppy club? Double-date with her friends? Hold hands with her the entire way while they walk to wherever they walk to after the movie? Last time his oldest daughter was in she took his hand on the street and held it at her side and they walked that way for about a minute till he raised their hands to his mouth, kissed hers and took his out of it and said "This'll sound awful to you. But as much as I loved holding hands with you when you were a girl, probably as much as I loved anything, some people will get the wrong idea now. They don't know you're my daughter so they'll think what they think and half of it won't be nice things, and I don't want them to," and she said "What of it?

We know how we're related and that there's never been anything like that, so why let the petty small minds run you?" and he said "You could be right. Ideally, you are. But there's a certain public decorum I have to hold to. I get uncomfortable easily, for both you and me, even if I know I'll never see these people again, or if we do there's very little chance we'll recognize each other, so what else can I say except that I hate it to be this way. Maybe if we wore signs: 'his daughter'; 'her father,' and arrows on the signs pointing to the other person, which'd mean we'd always have to walk in the same position to each other. No, that's silly and nothing will work. Anyway, you're all grown up, and I've been wanting to say something about this since you were around twelve, so walk with me normally from now on and save the handholding for when you're with one of your beaus," and she said "'Beaus.' Oh boy, that's a word," and he said "You mad over this?" and she said "It's a bit sudden but no."

So he looked front, she pulled her hand away from his—a sign she was angry or disappointed, maybe—and he whispered close to her ear "Really, did I do something? Anything I said I should be thinking about apologizing for?" and she whispered, looking serious, "Why, because I removed my hand from your sweaty palm? It was getting physically unpleasant, just as mine must have been getting to yours, and I thought I might be annoying you with it and distracting you from the movie." "Shh," the person behind them said, or another one: "please, the movie. You want to talk, do it outside." He mouthed "Later," and smiled and she nodded but didn't smile and he thought "Jesus, I'm such a creep, I can't believe it," and they watched the movie and discussed it on the way to a pub, she called it, she knew around here and wanted to go to for a drink before heading home and standing at the bar in it he felt funny, all the young people standing around them, just as he thought he would a week ago. He'd suggested when they came in they get a table—his main reason: not to stand at the bar with all the young people, though what he told her was "We can relax and talk better"—but she said "A table's too formal for just a piddly beer. And I've been sitting all day at my desk at home, and then at the movie, so I'd like to stretch my legs." Some men around her age at the bar or walking past them seemed to want to make a pass at her. Anyway, were definitely interested. Kept looking over, tried to catch her eye directly or through the long bar mirror above the liquor bottles. One handsome young guy sitting at the bar stared at her through the mirror now. When they came in she looked around briefly, seemed to nod hello to someone in a standing group but he didn't see who, and then only looked at him—"Chins," she said, clicking her beer stein against his glass of wine, and drank from it and said "We done discussing the movie?" and he said "Unless you want to talk some more as to why they make these things so noisy, fast and uncomplex," and she said "I don't. Now tell me what happened in the theater. And don't say 'What do you mean?' I won't allow you to give yourself extra time to think up an evasive answer, though of course my going on about it now has given you that time. How come, to put it bluntly—oh I hate phrases like that when it's obvious I'm being blunt—you didn't kiss me? Was I, and I don't like babbling people either but feel I have to finish this, so forgive me—asking for so much? Or you simply didn't want to, or thought it the wrong place to, or the shusher behind us stifled you, or what? There, you've had lots of time to think up a clever evasion and meanwhile I've exposed myself as an unattractive babbler, but say something," and he said "I have to talk here? How do you know we're not being monitored? This looks like the kind of joint that might do that—state-of-the-art slick and insipid singles bar with its newest gimmick being to entertain its masses through hidden recorders. One of the drinkers nearby could have one under his shirt or up her armpit and then management lowers the deafening music a few dozen decibels and plays our conversation back over the same sound system and everyone laughs himself silly," and she said "You're not talking then," and he said "O.K., I talk. 'Didn't want to kiss'? You said that, lady? Well, let me think about it, not with any excuse-making goal but to see my reluctance then as clearly as I can," and he looked at his glass and thought. This is the approach. He can have it both ways and also appear thoughtful. He can protest his unresponsiveness yet give all the arguments for not getting involved further: the age difference, her family, he has a daughter also twenty-three and maybe a few months older than her, that she's just a student, she should be going out with much younger men, same frame—frames?—of reference, and "just a student" meaning he's a teacher, she's a grad student, it just wouldn't look right or seem good. Other things he'll come up with: what could it lead to? That it'd embarrass him being affectionate to her in front of people, and kissing? Out of the question. Meaning in front of people, not that he wouldn't like to. Mention the handholding incident with his daughter. That he'd think himself a hypocrite he could only be kissy-poo alone with her—no "kissy-poo" reference. Besides it sounding awful, he doesn't want to ridicule the act of kissing her, because then he'd be ridiculing her: she was the one who practically put her lips to his. Anyway, something like that, and if she accepts his reasons and respects his reactions but says it still doesn't make any difference to her: she'll go along with however he wants to conduct himself in public, within reason (she's not going to be passed off as his daughter, for instance)—then what? Then, well, he doesn't know. Does he want to see her again? Yes, he thinks so. Yes or no? Yes. Sleep with her eventually? Yes, surely. Sleep with her tonight if she lets on that's what she wants and actually does all the asking or prompting? All depends: his place or hers, roommate, type of building she lives in. But his building. People in it have begun to know him. If one's waiting for the elevator with them or the next morning is already in the car when they get on it to ride down? They could walk down—it's only the seventh floor and he could say it's good exercise and how he almost always goes downstairs—that's the truth—but someone could see them going through the lobby to the street and what if a floor-neighbor's waiting for the elevator when they leave his apartment? So? Means nothing in the morning: student of his who dropped by early to deliver a late paper and they just happen to be leaving at the same time. Doorman? Why would he care? He'd see them come in at night and think hey, what a doll, lucky old fuck, or maybe that's another one of his daughters. But he's way off track: first the negative arguments. "I've thought about it," he said, "even if the music's hardly conducive to thinking—that bang bang screech bong," and she said "It's not anything like that and don't digress; tell me what you thought," and he said "For one thing, I'm still married," and she said "This is what you sunk into deep contemplation for? Because I thought you were separated, the two of you marching lockstep to an amiable divorce," and he said "Where'd you hear that? I never told you. Maybe your folks did, but I never told them either, though it's true," and she said "I've only spoken to them briefly since we met, and not about you—I forgot to," and he said "Ah, best you not, right now—what would they think? Anyway, you're right about the divorce—you must have just assumed it, or something I said—but you don't know the reasons for the amiability. My wife's quite sick. She wanted to divorce because of that. Sort of sacrificing herself. Thought she was being a drain on me. I took care of her as much as I could but couldn't anymore. She was that sick—still is, but even worse—and—she's eight years younger than me—moved back with her elderly parents and they're taking care of her now with a nurse, the kids coming around often but not to help, and she doesn't want to see me anymore when she's so sick, because—" and she said "I didn't know; that's terrible," and he said "It's awful, yes, except it isn't true," and she said "What isn't?" and he said "What I said, all of it except the separation and amiable divorce procedure. I don't know what came over me to do that— I'm sorry," and she said "Wait, what you just—" and he said "Yeah, made up. As I said, I don't know what—" and she said "But why? Something wrong with you, a screw loose, to play with my emotions like that?" and he said "Listen, I can understand why you'd be mad, but maybe we should tone it down here," and she said "O.K., but answer," and he said "No screw loose. Oh, I'm normal, so like everyone else who is, minimum of a little. But I'm nervous with you, so maybe my nervousness makes me feel a tiny bit extra screw-loose, giddy, say dumb things, even turned me into a liar," and she said "O.K., O.K. Not entirely satisfactory and I'm not sure what to say, but O.K., O.K. What's the real situation between you and your wife?" and he said "Separation and eventually a divorce, all quite amiable and compatible. Thirty years, which includes the five we lived together before marriage, and she got tired of it, felt we had little to say to each other, et cetera. No common interests left, now that the kids were grown, though the youngest is still in college, so we should separate for a while and if it's what we continue to want . . . I'm sorry about that bizarre story. As I said, where it comes from, who knows, since she's healthy as all hell, and that excuse about my nervousness around you can't be all of it. I think, maybe, and this is just speculation, and I don't want to go into another long solitary thought session to try and figure it out," and she said "What were you saying?" and he said "I didn't want to talk about a separation, one we're trying out, because then you might think Sally and I could go back together," and she said "So, fine, if you did, but what's it got to do with our silly kissing?" and he said "I suppose little, that what you're saying?" and she said "Well, does it? Just for curiosity's sake, where's the separation stand now?" and he said "Oh, that's another thing. She met a man, is very happy with him, lots in common, so we'll probably end up getting divorced and she remarried. I don't know what could stop the divorce—certainly I wouldn't, if it's what she wants—thus the amiability," and she said "Fine, and you don't seem too torn up by it," and he said "I'm not, but you know . . . " and she said "Which means what, the long stretch with her is enough to stop you from stepping out some too?" and he said "You mean with you?" and she said "Not only, but for argument's sake, yes," and he said "No, but our respective ages, you bet. Every time I think I knew your parents twenty years ago—" and she said "Fifteen, probably less," and he said "And now you're all grown but still forty years younger—forty-two; that's a chunk," and she said "I'm not looking for anything long-term. I'm just interested in you, would like to see where it goes. We stop when we want to, even at this pub's door. We for certain don't have to get serious. We have fun, talk a lot, do what comes naturally if that's what develops, see movies, read, stay away from my parents, go to the beach if you like beaches—" and he said "I don't. I like mountains. Beaches are too bare and hot." "Then I could never go out with you." "Good, you shouldn't. And I look ludicrous in a bathing suit and with my shirt off." "What are you saying? You've a nice build." "How would you know?" "I can see through your shirt, the way you fill it out, and your big arms." "Maybe the arms are the last to go. But I'm gray. I've gray hair on my chest and, if you want to get personal and frank—can I say it?" and she said "Say anything you want," and he said "Around my pubes, on them, but there, and in some spots, white." "What of it? Maybe I do too." "You couldn't." "I could be prematurely gray, coloring the gray away in my head hair, maybe everywhere else too, or the places where I don't shave it off. You never know." "Listen, let's walk and talk, and if it rains, run for cover." "It's not supposed to rain, but were you speaking metaphorically?" and he said "No, I thought I read it in a weather report."

They walked and talked. She took his hand, he let her for a minute and then pulled it away, patted the hand that had held his and said "I might meet someone—this is home territory, the whole Upper West Side is—or you might. They won't know what to think. That concerns me, what can I tell you? They'll maybe think you're with your grandfather. And if they see us crossing the street, that you're helping him across, and if they do think that, we'll be lucky," and she said "Don't be maudlin. And how can anyone think I'm helping you across if I'm not holding on to you?" "I see you, I see my daughter, what can I tell you?" and she said "And I see you and I don't see my father." "You have to." "Don't tell me what I have to see. And you don't see your daughter in me either. Besides, you need as much help getting across the street, and look it, as I do. Please, don't be such a schmuck. You're too old for it; it's unbecoming and to me unattractive," and he said "Listen, I can't take a girl forty-plus years younger than I—a young woman—a woman, all right, a woman—calling me a schmuck. 'Unattractive,' fine. When I was your age or ten years older that might have hit me, but not now." "I meant in an ugly way, that 'unattractive,'" and he said "Still, I don't care. But you don't know what that 'schmuck' does to me." "Then what should I call you, 'my darling'?" "Of course not; it wouldn't be true." "I know. That's why I said it," and he said "Good, then you also know now I'm slow." "Really, Gould, we should talk some more about this and your perspective on it, but not while we're walking. Would you care to go in someplace quieter and less crowded this time for another wine and beer?" "Coffee," and she said "I could make us coffee at my place." "Oh jeez, I don't know. Haven't I turned you off sufficiently where you'd rather have seen the last of me?" "You're doing your darndest but it hasn't reached the point where I see anything too difficult to overcome." "Nicely and graciously put, but I don't deserve it. O.K., your place, so long as you know there'll be no commitment from me to go further. 'Urgency . . . push.' I'm not saying it right—I'm doddering—but you must know what I'm getting at." "Just coffee. If it only comes to that. Because I don't like any prearranged restriction if there really seems no call for one." "Listen. Suppose it went further—I'm definitely not saying for today—and you hated it, were even repulsed by it because you suddenly saw how old and doddery I was and then we'd have to walk around each other on the street after that when we met, not wanting to say anything to the other or even approach him—" and she said "So? First of all, we wouldn't stalk around, or what you said. What does it mean anyway? You make it look like two snarling panthers—lions, cheetahs, one of the feral cat families—because one's in the other's territory, by gosh—or maybe cheetahs and panthers only go roaming—but the other doesn't want him there." "That's not what I meant. I was talking about potential embarrassment, uncomfortableness." "So I got it wrong. My turn to be incoherent. Sorry. But we'd just—and my 'sorry' was for insinuating you were being incoherent; you weren't, or not much. But if I now have it right, we'd just say hello, talk politely a little, ask after the other's family—I feel I know enough about yours to do that, or would by then, and I also know how much you love talking about them—and then go our two ways, something that shouldn't be new in relationships to either of us. We all come across people we don't particularly want to meet, but we deal with them civilly, don't we?—no inclination to hurt or take revenge? But tell me why we're talking like this. It's ridiculously premature. For now, let's just have coffee. Or if you want—I feel I'm pushing you too much on this, as you said, or did I get that wrong too?—maybe we should go home, you to yours, me to mine, so long till the next time, if we meet on the street or in the market or one of us wants to call and the other doesn't object to receiving." "No, coffee and dessert, on me and at a coffee bar, please." "You paid for the movie tickets and drinks." "I like to pay; I do it without argument or for reward," and she said "If we've settled on coffee and dessert—I have some Mondel's chocolate lace cookies in a tin, just a few days old . . . well, I've given myself away: but at my apartment? I also have a new espresso machine never used—cappuccino, espresso—the works. And brandy, which I use for cooking, but it's good stuff, if you want to cap the night," and he said "Do you have a roommate? Only because I don't want to converse with anyone else tonight under forty," and she shook her head. "I live alone. I thought I told you that," and he said "Not that I remember, but we're both pretty aware by now of my deficiency that way," and she said "Well I do, my big luxury; the espresso machine was a housewarming gift from my folks, along with a Bokhara rug."

They cabbed to her place. He looked at his building as he went into hers. He forgot to ask if it's a student building, lots of young students around, and if there's a Columbia University security guard at the door, but there wasn't and nobody in the lobby or at the elevator, and what would he have done if there was one of those things? He'd have gone in with her. She was the one who wanted to cab. "But it's only ten blocks," he'd said, "and I like walking and it's a nice night," and she said "I'm tired; my feet; I haven't been on them all day but they hurt. I'm older than you think, physically; I also have a waitress job three days a week," and he said "Oh, you didn't say," and wondered where it was and what would happen if he went into it by accident in the next few days and saw her there, or let's say if they said later tonight it isn't a good idea to see each other again and then sometime in the next few days he went into the restaurant, sat at a table alone, or at the counter—he prefers counters to tables when he eats alone: it's quicker and also easier to read a book there—and she turned out to be his server. In the cab she'd asked if he had any siblings and he said "One, a year younger, but he died when I was a boy," and she said "So did mine, an older sister by two years, but she was killed by a hit-and-run when she was nineteen," and he said "I didn't know; I'm very sorry. I only remember one girl from my dinner at your house, and I'm almost sure it was only once, so maybe it wasn't even you I saw then," and she said "You forget it was I who first recognized you. It could be Sue was sick that night and had to stay in her room, or was on a sleepover. Anyway, we have something very deep in common," and he said "But my loss was almost sixty years ago. It was in Central Park. We were standing by the bridle path, I was supposed to be looking after him—I was actually eighteen months older—and a horse went nuts, tossed its rider off and kicked my brother." He thought, riding up the elevator and staring at the gash in the ceiling panel and the cable moving above it, what's going to happen? He's not prepared for it. What does he do with a young woman? Not prepared with a bag either, though she probably has a packet of them in her night table or another kind of protection. If it comes to that, as she said, if that's what she meant. It's been so long, with any woman. But a young one with such a young body, everything flat and firm it seems. And he hasn't made love with anyone but his wife since he met her thirty years ago—has kissed a few but hasn't even touched one on the breast and he thinks every kiss he did was when he was a little high and standing in someone's kitchen. All his hand and finger movements will be the ones he did with his wife thousands of times. He knew what she liked, way she wanted it done, and if he didn't, she told him, so he thinks he'll probably do things to this girl's body as if it were his wife's. If he ends up inside her, he'll come in a few seconds. No, he knows how to hold it back if he wants, or for a few minutes after it seems he's going to come soon, but that was with his wife and after many years with her. It's going to happen, though, sex, if not tonight then soon with her. If there's a chance for it tonight will he do it? Yes, because when she decides to do it—his age and looks again—that might be the only time she does. She'll give him the smile, he'll kiss her this time, it could even start right after they close the door and hang up their jackets: she'll start rubbing his back, he'll rub hers, they'll be standing and embracing at the time—best it starts up after their jackets are off and maybe even their sweaters: more maneuverability, fewer layers to tug up and go under—then the legs, sides, behinds, they'll feel around and this piece of clothing will be off and that one and soon all of them, and it'll be many kisses later and he'll be worrying if his breath stinks to her, if she's imagining it stinks because he's old, if she isn't already turned off by him, his skin, wrinkles and flab. But she'll still be kissing—lips and tongue don't change, he doesn't think—and maybe thinking she'll do it with him this once, what's the harm? a different kind of experience, et cetera, and she's already a little excited, see him on the street after that, say it just wasn't going to work, that's why she didn't call or answer his answering-machine messages, but no regrets—and they'll go to the bedroom and so on and then he'll have done it, first time with someone since his wife, if it, please God, comes to that.

So they went to her apartment. She asked for his jacket, hung it in the closet alongside hers and went into the kitchen to make coffee; he stayed in the living room, flipping through some of the books on her end tables, cocktail and dining tables and a few on the couch. "Would you like some of that brandy in your coffee?" she yelled out. "I see it's Spanish," and he said "On the side, why not, sure, thanks, if you'll join me, but even if you don't," and she said "Yeah, I could." They both had brandy in a small glass that looked like half a shot glass with a stem. They had another. "Two of these is just one," she said, "so don't think you're going to get sick by the morning." She sipped from her espresso coffee—she wasn't able to figure out how to operate the steamed milk part of the machine and didn't want to disturb him to try and help her; he didn't touch his coffee and she never referred to it till it was cold. "Want me to heat it up or, better yet, make a fresh one for you?" and he said "The brandy's all I need," and then "May

I?" and poured himself another. They talked about a lot of things quickly. Does her waitressing job cover her rent and other expenses? No, not in this city, so her parents contribute about half. Does she get in some reading at work? A little, during customer lulls or when she escapes to the toilet, but there's this dismal recorded restaurant music that never stops and the readings she has to do are often unnecessarily complex or unpardonably impenetrable, so it's hard to concentrate. Next year she's supposed to be a teaching assistant, which will mean full tuition waiver and a stipend, so she can give up the waitressing job. "You're a teacher, so give me advice as to what to do when you know a student isn't doing the assignment. I've always wanted to know and I think now I'll have to." "You whip him or her," and she said "Be serious, this is important." He told her his tricks how to make sure the students read everything he assigns them. She said "I should get this down on paper, but I'll remember," and he said "Or you can ask me at the time, if you run into the problem," and she said "You may be too busy with your own work then," and he said "No, I'm always accessible, and to my friends, even more so." She asked if he liked teaching; he said "Not especially." She said "Maybe because you've been doing it so long." He said "No, I've never liked it, and if your next question is why do I do it"—"It would've been"—"Well, to support myself and the things I like doing." She asked what they were and he said "Too few to enumerate," and she said "Come on, don't get highbrow and fussy; it's the one thing I've disliked most about academics," and he said "You're right. Reading, long-walking, my daughters, of course; my typewriter diddling most times, and for more than twenty years of our marriage, my marriage and wife, who is still quite nice." "What made you break up?" and he said "I thought we talked about that. If we did, I shouldn't have, as I don't like discussing it, I'm sorry," and she said "Please, no excuses or apologies required. Have you seen any women since you separated?" and he said "Dated?" and she said "I guess you could use that term," and he said "No, what about you? When was the last time you were involved, or maybe you are even now with someone special," and she said "That's a funny question, and if you don't mind I'd rather not answer it, and not to get even with you, you understand." "Why, did I say something inappropriate again? If so, I'm sorry, but I've been out of circulation for many years and in ways I'm like a rustic," and she said "You were married, though," and he said "Yeah, but my wife acted as my social intermediary. I, for the most part, reclused myself except in school, though I'd flee from there the minute my work was finished, and could barely endure answering the phone at home. I've come out of that somewhat since I've been living alone; I mean, you gotta if you have a phone but no answering machine," and she said "Good, I'm glad, it's better for you not to be that way. As for me, let me just explain that I don't like talking about someone I was involved with, at least not to someone I only recently met," and he said "You mean me?" and she said "Who else? I don't even have a pet here," and he said "I see, and that was dumb of me to say 'You mean me?' Of course me. As you said, who else?" Then they were silent. Something about her face: he was saying the wrong things, and that she was looking away. It wasn't going well. It had become strained. She wanted him out of here, he was sure of it, and well she should. It's not that it's late. What time is it? He'd look at his watch but that might annoy her even more: "He's that bored with me?" she could think. "Well who the hell does he think he is?" Or give her the impetus to say "It's getting a little late, isn't it? and I'm also feeling tired, so perhaps we should call it a night." He looked at his empty glass, wanted to pour another but thought she might think he drank too much or had to drink to be with her and have things to say. "Would you mind if I have just one more of this?" tapping the brandy bottle. "It's very good stuff. I always thought Spain, brandy, it'd be harsh, but it's not. I was once there but I don't remember having brandy. I only drank beer then—lots of it; I had a terrible pot—and some wine: white, which wasn't produced much in Spain, while I now mainly drink red and hardly touch beer. So, I missed my big chance, with the brandy and red wine. Port I remember in Portugal—I was even in Oporto, where they made it, or you took a tour of the porteries—what would they be called?" and she said "I wouldn't know." "Maybe just distilleries. And these glasses are pretty small, as you said, and I'm not used to drinking this much, so I'm curious—you're curious, I'm curious—the effect it'll have on me. What an awful thought, you taking care of me—awful for you—if I got really pissed. Only kidding about all that except the beer, red and pot," and she said "Please, I'll join you in one more." She seemed back in the mood from before and asked when was he in Spain. He said "Several years before I met my wife. I went with a woman and her kid—I'd been living with them—and we mostly hitchhiked. The boy had blond hair, so it was easy," and she said "You know, the truth is—as you'll see, all this time you've been talking, I've been listening some but mostly thinking—why not talk about that subject from before?" and he said "What do you mean?" and she said "Why am I reluctant to talk about it: my last two involvements. And I couple them up like that because they were practically back to back—a mistake; I don't think I had a week's break between them—and equally intense and both men seemed so young for their age and they even looked alike. Very tall, gaunt, lots of shocks of dark head hair; even the bony noses and enormous feet and hands and same-shaped eyes. I know it wasn't unintentional on my part, choosing the second with the looks of the first. I mean, with the second one—but you know what I mean. And the hair matter—that's no reflection on you, you understand. Younger men just have more hair. You must have had it too," and he said "I actually began going bald when I was thirteen, I think, or started worrying about it. That I still have some hair on top and so high on the sides surprises me; I thought I'd be a billiard ball. But these two young men; you liked them both, equally, what?" and she said "I loved them, one no more than the other and both a lot, but knew it wouldn't last with either for more than a few months, if that. Still, I fell for them because they were so attractive and congenial, and it quickly worked out well. The conversation wasn't that good, though did it have to be, right at the beginning? but the sex was, and that's something. So there," and he said "How long ago, the last?" and she said "Not long, but maybe I've spoken enough about it; not so much confessed but gone on almost nonstop," and he said "And sex, now there's a subject," and she said "Why, do you have something to say regarding what I told you? It could be you found my quick activities with successive men repugnant, or something less severe, or my cavalier attitude to the whole thing," and he said "Not in the least, we're just talking. I only meant *sex*, the universal subject for adults, the Esperanto in body language of a different kind, we could say, or not only for adults. Kids are good at picking up languages easily, right? so whenever it starts. So much to talk about there, in so many aspects," and she said "I'm not sure I understand what you're saying," and he said "I wasn't being clear?" and she said "Not really. What is it you're sort of circulating around, something again about those two men I mentioned?" and he said "Well, if you've no objections talking about it, yes, you and these two guys, back to back, front to front, but instead we can start at the start, since I assume the first wasn't the first and so the second not the second, were they?" and she said "Oh you're funny; of course not. I'm twenty-three," and he said "So how old were you when you had your first involvement?" and she said "Do you mean sex or just liking a guy?" and he said "I guess so, sex, involvement, one and the same I suppose today or for about the last twenty years—I'm not sure. But let me know if this is the wrong question—out of line—if I'm being that, and I'll immediately change the subject or shut up," and she said "Real sex? Being penetrated? losing the locket? Fifteen. You?" and he said. "Closer to fifteen or to sixteen?" and she said "I forget; what's the difference?" and he said "For me, things were a lot different when I was a kid," and she said "So you were much older when you first did it?" and he said "No, fourteen. I remember it was December, right after Christmas— I was on school vacation—but with a whore. Most girls I went out with didn't do anything but kiss and if you were lucky, on the fourth or fifth date, would let you touch a breast through the blouse, and after a dozen dates, through the brassiere. For more, you had to go steady with them for half a year to a year, and I'm not saying 'too much more,' or go out with a particularly wild usually homely girl you didn't want to be seen on the street with, and with her on the first date you could sometimes get 'bare tit,' as we called it—it really sounds stupid now, and the way we regarded these girls, repulsive," and she said "But a professional whore. What a depressing introduction, though I suppose how most adolescent boys lost their virginity then," and he said "That's right. Most of my friends first went to prostitutes. I don't like the idea of it now, but didn't think it depressing then. In fact, I have to admit I found it very exciting—the prospect of going to one and seeing a woman for the first time totally naked. I was practically heady at the thought of it, though it wasn't a great experience when I actually did it: she was crude and smelly and smoked a cigarette during a little of it and her apartment was ugly. And it isn't, as I said, that I didn't want it to be with one of the girls I liked and dated," and she said "And you continued going to prostitutes after that?" and he said "With my friends, when I was a teenager, yes, sometimes five or six of us to the same one in the afternoon. She'd take us one at a time and the others would wait on the street telling infantile dirty jokes to one another or in a small waiting room she had, all of us crammed into one couch. But not for forty years, I want you to know. Which means as a man—twenty, twenty-one—a very young man, my first two times in Europe? . . . yes, there more than anywhere else. The women in the Amsterdam windows, a London prostitute or two right out on a quiet side street, against a car fender—that's where and how you did it, standing up. I'd never seen anything like it in New York and it was much cheaper there too. And Paris, *rue du* or *de* something, or other—it was famous as a hooker street, but all gone now, I hear . . . near Les Halles, which has been torn down too. But I didn't do much whoring here, maybe none at all, or only once or twice when a friend set something up and maybe—this is, I'm still in my early twenties, you realize—because he had the dough and didn't want to go alone—was afraid he'd get beaten up and robbed; I was a big guy, he was a rich little guy . . . anyway, where he paid for me." "As far as my first, it wasn't that great either. I didn't want to, but wasn't forced; I did it mostly because all the other girls my age did, or said they were doing it—wouldn't that be something if they were all liars? But why are we talking about this, or focusing on it rather, after all the other subjects we started to discuss?" and he said "We just got into it; who knows why," and she said "No, I bet there's a more deliberate reason," and he said "What?" thinking he knew what she was going to say and she said "Simply to get ourselves excited. What do you think?" and he didn't want to say "I knew you'd say something like that," but said "What do I think? Well, truthfully, I am a little excited, genitally—so you think I started the conversation for that reason, both for you and me, or intentionally turned it around to it at a time when we really didn't know each other or much about the other?" and she said "I'm not accusing you. I feel I'm just as much responsible for the conversation's sudden turn and focus and am a little excited by it myself and enjoying the feeling. Because what's wrong in it? Is there any danger, do you think?" and he said "Why should there be? Or maybe I'm missing your meaning," and she said "I'll put it this way: what do we do next? What about that? What do you think we should pursue next?" and he said "You mean, do something?" and she said "Only if you want to; it has to be consensual; I'm not about to spring on you," and he said "Of course, I know, and I'm delighted, but where?" and she said "So let's go to the bedroom. We don't have to do, unless you insist on it, the preliminaries out here, do we? We've done most of it with chatter, so we can skip the couch stuff and save the rest for inside after we've taken off our clothes," and he said "You don't like being undressed?" and she said "Not especially; I can undress myself," and he said "My wife did, even long into our marriage, and rebuked me for not doing it more often with her, undressing," and she said "If you're asking me to undress you, I'll do it if you want, but in the bedroom. I think this room we should keep as is," and he said "Nah, it'd be silly; I can undress myself too," and she said "Fine," and stood up, put her glass down and said "One more thing before we go in. I'd prefer you not mentioning your wife again tonight or till much later and only if necessary or involuntary, like if you're talking in your sleep about her. It can be disconcerting," and he said "Sure, though you can talk about your gaunt hairy men all you want," and she said "Why would I want to? That's so stupid," and he said "Hey, maybe it was—no, I'll concede it was and that I don't know where it came from—but I wish you wouldn't tell me that something I say is stupid, at least not till much later," and she said "O.K., I can see that's important to you, and I was wrong. So we won't talk about anything like that—your age, your wife, my youth or any of my former boyfriends or lovers and nothing about either of our intellectual and social deficiencies," and he stood up, finished his drink and said "Can we at least, while we're here, and without messing up the room and because I think the moment can use it and that it's also important we do, kiss?" and she said "I want us to," and they moved to each other, he said "My mouth has brandy on it but so will yours, but if mine's stinkier with it it's probably because I drank more, so excuse me," and she said "Really, it's not an offensive smell. I even kind of like it: that and cognac and a French pear brandy, have you ever had it?—I forget what it's called in French," and he said "I don't think so, what's it look like?" and she said "Clear, like vodka," and he said no, and they kissed.

They went into the bedroom. They'd kissed a few times standing up in the living room and he felt woozy from it, lightheaded, at one moment he thought his legs might give way, but that's all he needed: "Screwy old guy," she could think; "next thing I know I'll have to hold him up, sit him in a chair." Such soft lips, he thought. His, in comparison, he was sure, were a bit cracked and stiff. She knew how to kiss, her hand on his neck and squeezing it a little and then fingers climbing up the back of his head almost in a spiderlike way, but only in the way the spider moves, nothing about being trapped or any of the other bad spider associations. Doing it almost as if she was thinking this is how she's supposed to hold a man and move her hand when she kissed, but he liked it. Her hand was warm and soft and it made him shiver a few times. The brandy was a good idea; it had relaxed him, maybe made him say a couple of things he shouldn't have, but because both of them drank it it sort of neutralized any smell he might have on his breath. He didn't sense brandy on hers; it just smelled fresh. Kept his tongue in place because she didn't use hers, but he was thinking as he kissed her that if she started to use it he would too. She undressed, unbuttoning her blouse and taking it off, sitting on the bed and removing her jeans, unhooking her bra, but her breasts didn't plop out as he expected when the bra came off; they just stayed there, sticking straight out and almost pointing up. Maybe only the breasts of girls fourteen or eighteen or so did that. He's only seen them in photos, never even saw his daughters' once they started to develop, and when he was young and felt girls up and once got a shirt and bra off one, or maybe just the bra, the shirt she kept on but open in front, it was always in the dark. She slipped off her panties and then her socks—he tried not to watch, or just made quick looks, and she sometimes caught him but didn't say anything with her expression—and threw them under the bed. Light hair down there, he thought he saw, while her head and underarm hair were almost black. She color it to make it lighter? Wouldn't think so—doesn't see the purpose; shaving, yes, or whatever depilatory process if you're self-conscious of having what you think's a lot of hair—but he won't bring it up. "Aren't you going to disrobe?" she said, and took off her watch and shoved aside two little heart-shaped wooden boxes at the edge of the night table to put it down. That's probably the side she'll sleep on, he thought, since there's a night table on the other side. What could be in the boxes? Maybe one day, if they're still there and the relationship goes on that long and when she's not in the room, he'll look inside. "I'm sorry," he said, "but I've been dillying. I have to admit I became a bit fascinated, almost like a voyeur, or voyeur minus one, watching you undress. Excuse me," and she said "Why? It's got to be natural. Which might seem as if I'm admitting to the unnatural in that the peeper instinct has never been in me," and he said "That's hardly unnatural; neither is, wouldn't you say?" and she said "I suppose," and he took off his shirt and watch, put the watch in his pants pocket, and undid his belt. His penis was erect and sticking through the fly of his boxer shorts as he pulled the pants down. She looked at it, made no expression, and looked away; but it had to look comical sticking out that way, maybe even obscene, and he pushed it back in, folded his clothes up and put them on a chair. She shut her eyes, twisted her arm around her back to scratch the middle of it, gritted her teeth as if the scratching or something else back there hurt, yawned, said without opening her eyes "Sorry if you heard that," and he had but said "Heard what?" and she said "I yawned, but nothing to do with you. Just I'm tired . . . long day," and got up to get something from the top dresser drawer. We're like an old couple already, he thought; ah, maybe that's good: we'll be relaxed, no poses. And a diaphragm, probably, from the drawer, but he can hardly believe the whole thing. Stepped out of his shorts; he was still erect but so what? Just that he was going to make love with her, this beautiful body and face, that's what he found so unbelievable. Because she was so young, maybe she was more beautiful to him than she actually was, but again so what? Firm, lean, strong, no fat or bumps, impressions or pocks in her thighs and buttocks, ass so high, nice-sized breasts and the shape they're in—she's in perfect shape all around. Slim legs, body like one in a bathing suit or Caribbean beach ad. No tan, divisions of dark and light on her skin, whatever they're called. She's evenly white as if she's intentionally stayed out of the sun and in fact had rarely been in it or never without covering or chair or beach umbrella or wide-brimmed hat. But the light pubic hair, dark head and underarm hair; something there he didn't understand. Important? No, but why was she letting him go through with it? Look at the differences, lady, compare; for one thing, his neck. He saw it as john-whore, but only because she had a body and face a guy his age usually had to pay for. And smart too, going for a degree he'd never have the brains to get. Any advanced degree: never wanted one, but that's another thing. Not that he would pay to lay her. What's he saying? Sure he would, once: a hundred, maybe even two hundred, once, but if it was in a normal apartment, not a whorehouse, and she said something like "I don't ever do this but I suddenly need the money," and she was absolutely clean. Clean? Hadn't thought of it but sure she's clean and she must know he is after no woman but his wife for more than thirty years. But he's not going to tell her what he thought. Unless, let's say, they were lying around on the bed after lovemaking one night or any other time, tonight, for instance, tomorrow morning, but lying around casually, maybe her head on his chest, his arm around her shoulder and that hand resting on or holding her breast, and he said "For curiosity purposes only, and you don't have to say if you don't want, but what did you think when you first saw my body with no clothes on, and I'm not talking about my penis, but if you want, even that—the testicles, the works. And don't worry about offending me about this. I know what I look like—the neck, for instance. I don't want to call any more attention to it than would seem necessary or normal, because then it'll seem like self-pity's motivating me, but there it is, the neck, getting a little scrawny just like everyone's eventually does. So believe me, say what you thought about my body at that time, even what you think of it now, even the neck, what it does to you, if it in any way repulses you—that's not a good way of putting it—but I'd really like to hear."

She turned around, had what looked like a miniature athletic bag in her hand, bright red with electric blue straps and some words inside a circle on it—a basketball he now saw—and said "I'm going to wash up," and he said "I should too," and she said "Why, what do you have to do—you mean the toilet; you want to go first?" and he said "No, my body—you know, wash my penis; I mean, it's O.K., but just to wash it anew—and also all around the anus and inside, sort of like that, if you want me to be honest," and she said "With what? Not with one of my washrags, I hope," and he said "Why? You just throw it in the wash after. But if it bothers you . . . anyhow, I wasn't thinking of using a washrag, actually. My hands— lathered up—one hand, and if you have tissues in there, or toilet paper will do, which I'd dry myself with. And I won't throw the tissues into the toilet bowl, so I'd need a wastebasket too," and she said "Good, my bathroom's fully set up for all of that," and he said "Then good, we're set. Now, before you go, and you should go first—my activity isn't crucial—

may I also hold you little and maybe a kiss before? I suddenly want to," and she said "That'd be nice, I'd like it," and smiled, stepped toward him, they kissed, he pressed his body into hers, ran his hand up and down her side, rubbed her back, on her rear end, clutched it, leaned over and stretched his arm down till he got his hand under her buttocks and between her legs and she said "Please, Gould, not so fast," and he said "Oh, my name," and she said "What about it?"—his hand was away by now—and he said "Nothing; that you used it; a first, I think. It sounded nice, and I'm sorry but I didn't think I was going so fast," and she said "It was, for me, and I also want to wash up, as I said, and do some other things in there," her head nodding to the bathroom, and he said "O.K., all right, but so many rules here; whew. Don't do this, do that; or not so many do's, just don't do this or that," and she said "I'm only telling you what I have to do first and what I don't like done too fast—that's so bad? Standing up and fooling around here, for instance. It's nice for a minute, but maybe you even had in mind doing it right here," and he said "I didn't," and she said "Well I'm glad, because we don't have to, isn't that true? The bed's a much better place. And I'm tired; I already told you. So standing up and feeling each other after a while can be an effort when I'm this way," and he said "Come on, will you? Stop telling me—please, I mean—how to make love and how not to. I've done it before, I do have some experience. O.K., you do too, but understand that everything I'm doing here with you—if there's any action that isn't, I'd be surprised—is coming from some need or urgency of mine or something to touch and feel and paw you and the rest of it, now and later, so what the hell's so goddamn wrong with that—tell me," and she said "You don't have to get vulgar and I think angry there, all of a sudden. And the truth is, too much talk too, O.K.?" and he said "Listen, don't now tell me not to talk or how to and then when to talk and more of the not-to-do-this stuff unless something I'm doing is physically hurting you—that I can respect," and she said "Right now your talking is hurting me, is that coming through?" and broke them apart and pushed him away a few inches. He said "Hey, maybe this isn't a good idea—this whole thing—how about that?" and she said "I think you're right," and he said "So maybe then I should get dressed," and she said "I think that would be the best thing to do, yes," and he said "Boy, that was one fast coming together and breakup," and she said "It was, though I wouldn't exactly use either of those terms for it. Let's just say something is definitely wrong, or had become that, and whatever was materializing between us tonight isn't such a good idea now," and he said "O.K., everything's wrong, even the goddamn terms and words," and she said "Please, don't get angrier and make it into a big clamorous embroilment. And I'm really not trying to escape from this conversation—I just have to go badly, excuse me," and went into the bathroom and shut the door.

He started putting his clothes on. Should I? he thought when he had his shorts on. Or should I stay naked and when she comes out say "I thought maybe you had a change of mind. I know I have, but if you don't, fine, I'll get dressed," but then thought no, just go, they're never going to end up in bed and if she sees him sitting here naked . . . well, he could say something quickly why he is, that business about her possibly changing her mind and he didn't want to get dressed when he'd only have to undress again—he'd say it jokingly—but she could get annoyed that he hadn't started dressing and say something like "It's no laughing matter and your delirium about my changing my mind is in fact a bit depressing," and he got his shirt and pants on and was sweating heavily and his stomach hurt and chest felt empty because he had so much wanted to do it with her and had even seen something good and happy and long-term from it for a while and he knows he's going to kick himself to kingdom come once he leaves her place, a chance like this will never happen again, never, and was putting on a sock, thinking maybe he can come up with something to say to change things around, an artful apology, blaming it on his newness to this kind of male-female situation and which he swears—"I'm a quick learner"—will never be repeated, when she came out wearing a bathrobe tied tight at the waist. "As you can see, I'm almost dressed and would have been completely but I couldn't find the mate to this," pulling at the sock on his foot. "No, that's not true; I just didn't want to be entirely dressed and out of here by the time you came out, don't ask me why," and she said "I see; it's all right, take your time. And look, I want you to know—I don't want you to think I was being a tease before. I meant to do what we were both heading for but it was something you said, and the bad feelings I felt coming from you . . . a certain crossness—" and he said "All right, all right; can it; Jesus!" and she said "You don't have to become insulting," and he said "How was I?" and she said "Just now, in what you said; another example of what I meant about the bad feelings coming from you," and he said "I'm sorry then. I'm feeling particularly lousy and frustrated about this evening—mortified too, in a way . . . morbid, even. I feel just terrible, to tell you the truth, but I'll get over it, though the whole thing should have been avoided because it was stupid from the start," and she said "No it wasn't," and he said "No?" and she said "I never would have asked you up or even wanted to see you a second time if I had thought it was," and he said "Well, you don't feel any different about it now, do you? because I think I do," and she said "I'm sorry, no," and he said "Then it was stupid, and now even stupider than when I said it was. It's got to be our vast age difference," putting a shoe on and she said "You certainly do struggle with that theme, and so sedulously," and he thought "'Sedulously,' what's it mean?—oh yes," and said "Listen, I'm trying to be nice about this, polite, civil, because I feel so goddamn rotten about everything and I don't want to feel even worse, but will you stop telling me about myself—will you just please stop?" and she said "You're angry again; I'm sorry," and he said "Angry? You're sorry? Oh, I don't know," and had his other shoe tied now and said "So long," and left.

Saw her a week later. It was late afternoon and they were going opposite ways again on the same sidewalk and he said "Hi," and she smiled and said "Hi, how are you?" and he said "Fine thanks, and you?" and she said "I'm in a rush to something very important now so I really can't stop, excuse me," and he said "Don't worry, I understand," and walked on. He turned around a few seconds later and looked at her hurrying up the hill. God, what a shape, and so fucking beautiful. If only he had gone along with what she was saying that night, stopped talking or only spoke softly, not got angry or vulgar, touched her where and when she wanted to, pretended to have more dignity, just held back, let her make the moves, call the shots, the rest of it, because it should have been obvious that was what she wanted, something he only realized after he left her place, then it would have happened. She was a little scared, or wary, had reservations, that much he knew when he was there—meaning, she had to, it would only be natural; you don't want to just jump in with an old guy—no matter how forward and out-front she was in the apartment, bar, movie theater, et cetera, but he didn't deal with it intelligently. And again, with someone so young and lovely. Ah, you've gone over it plenty, too much already, so don't start killing yourself some more over it. That it didn't happen, wasn't successful, but got so close: no clothes, their bodies pressed together, kissing, his hand on her ass . . . forget it, and you don't ever want to try it again with someone her age, not, as he's also told himself too many times, he'll ever have another chance. They really don't want to be doing it with you, that's what it comes down to. They think they have the body and face and youth and spirit and who knows what else—the time; they got just about everything, far as they're concerned, and instant oblivion also—and can dictate the terms because of that, if they do, for whatever fluky reasons they have, want to go through with it, and that can take care of the scariness and wariness and so on. So what's he saying?

He's saying nothing. Or he's saying little. But he just should have shut up. But also done what he did in the theater and that's pull his hand away from hers—in other words, something like that—or is that what he did? No, he just didn't, when she wanted him to, kiss, but anyway, done what she wanted but with some reservations and reluctance or wariness himself till he got her in a position where she couldn't call things anymore, where he had her pinned or locked but was inside her and nothing was going to stop it till he was done, and after that told her to screw off with her demands if she made any from then on or made them excessively. Because just to have done it once with her. To be walking down this street, after having just stared after her from behind, and thinking "I laid that gorgeous girl," and then to be able to go over it all in his head. But he didn't think of that then.

Saw her a few more times after that and they waved or smiled at each other or both or said hi or hello and went on. Then he saw her when he was with his youngest daughter. They were going the same way, she was at the corner waiting for the light to say "Walk" and he was a little behind her and got alongside her and said "Hi," and she said "Oh, hi, hello," and smiled, "how are things going?" and he said "Couldn't be better, and you?" and she said "Same here, thanks. Well, I'll see you," when the light said "Walk" and she crossed the street and he and his daughter crossed it a little more slowly. Then he yelled out "Lorna, by the way . . . " and she turned around and he said "This is one of my daughters, Josephine," and she waved and said "Hi, Josephine, nice to meet you," and continued on and Josephine said "Who's that? One of your students?" and he said "No, just someone I know from the block," and she said "I didn't know you were so popular," and he said "I'm not."

Honeysuckle

Michael McFee

for Marie and Seamus Heaney

Sweetest of weeds, it threads the margins
of early May's illuminated manuscript
with a flourish of flowers that we'll pick
once they deepen to buttery yellow,
pinching the bottoms off and gently pulling
the pistils out until a single drop
of honey gleams at the base of each bloom
and we suckle from that little nipple,
drunk on the updrafts of aromatic air
and nectar blooming on our once-mortal tongues.

Contributors

David Baker is the author of four books of poems, including most recently *After the Reunion* (University of Arkansas Press, 1994). He is the editor of *Meter in English: A Critical Engagement* (University of Arkansas Press, 1996) and poetry editor of the *Kenyon Review*. His latest book, *The Truth About Small Towns*, is being published by the University of Arkansas Press in 1998. Baker's poems appeared in *TQ* #84 ★★★ **John Barth**'s most recent books are *On With the Story: Stories* (1996), and a collection of essays, *Further Fridays: Essays, Lectures and Other Nonfiction 1984–1994* (1995), both published by Little, Brown. An essay of Barth's appeared in *TQ* #17, and his stories appeared in *TQ* #41 and *TQ* #95. ★★★ **Richard Burgin**'s latest book of stories, *Fear of Blue Skies*, was published by Johns Hopkins University Press in 1997. He is the author of four other books, including two collections of stories, *Private Fame* (1991) and *Man Without Memory* (1989), both published by the University of Illinois Press; and two books of interviews, *Conversations with Isaac Bashevis Singer* (Doubleday, 1985; Farrar Straus & Giroux paperback, 1986) and *Conversations with Jorge Luis Borges* (Holt Rinehart, 1968; Avon, 1970). He teaches in the English Department at St. Louis University and is the editor of *Boulevard*. His fiction appeared in *TQ* #81, #89 and #96. ★★★ **Daniela Crăsnaru** has published ten books of poems and two collections of short stories. "The Grand Prize" is part of a projected book of fiction that she translated with Adam J. Sorkin during a residency at the Rockefeller Foundation Center, in Bellagio, Italy. Her poems have appeared in *Poetry*, *Prairie Schooner*, the *Michigan Quarterly Review* and several other journals. ★★★ **William Donoghue** is a teaching fellow in the English Department at Stanford University. His fiction has appeared in *Grain*, *Trois* and *Passager*. ★★★ **Stephen Dixon**'s most recent books of fiction are *Gould: a Novel in Two Worlds* (Henry

Holt, 1997) and a story-play collection, *Man on Stage: Playstories* (Hi Jinx Press, 1997). A sequel to *Gould,* entitled *Thirty* will be published by Henry Holt in 1999. His new book of stories, entitled *Two Collections,* is being published by Coffee House Press in 1999. "The First Woman" is part of a long, interconnected work of fiction, which is still in progress. Dixon's fiction has appeared frequently in *TQ.* ★★★ **Sandra M. Gilbert**'s most recent book of poems is *Ghost Volcano* (W. W. Norton, 1995), which comprises the poems she wrote about her husband's unexpected death. She is also the co-editor, with Susan Gubar, of *The Norton Anthology of Literature by Women: The Tradition in English* (W. W. Norton, 1985; second edition, 1996); *No Man's Land: The Place of the Woman Writer in the Twentieth Century,* 3 volumes (Yale University Press, 1989, 1991, 1994); and *The Madwoman in the Attic: A Study of Women & Literary Imagination in the Nineteenth Century* (Yale University Press, 1979). She teaches at the University of California, Davis. ★★★ **Linda Gregg** is presently completing her fifth book of poems. Her most recent book is *Chosen by the Lion* (Graywolf, 1994). She lives in Northern California. A poem of Gregg's appeared in *TQ* #95. ★★★ **Marilyn Hacker** is the author of eight books of poems, including *Winter Numbers,* which received the Lenore Marshall Prize of the Academy of American Poets; and *Selected Poems 1965–1990,* which won the Poets' Prize in 1995. Both books were published by W. W. Norton in 1994. Poems of Hacker's appeared in *TQ* #89. ★★★ **Becky Hagenston**'s stories have appeared in *Prize Stories 1996: The O. Henry Awards* (Doubleday) and several journals, including the *Crescent Review, Shenandoah,* and the *Antietam Review.* "Holding the Fort" will appear in her book of short stories, *A Gram of Mars,* which received the Mary McCarthy Prize in Short Fiction and will be published in 1998 by Sarabande Books. ★★★ A previous story by **Mabelle Hsueh** was published in *Into the Fire: Asian American Prose,* edited by Sylvia Watanabe and Carol Bruchac (Greenfield Review Press, 1995). ★★★ **Ha Jin** is the author of four books, including two volumes of poems, *Between Silences* (University of Chicago Press, 1990) and *Facing Shadows* (Hanging Loose Press, 1996); and two books of stories, *Ocean of Words* (Zoland Books, 1996) and *Under the Red Flag* (University of Georgia Press, 1997). He teaches at Emory University. A poem of Jin's appeared in *TQ* #86, and a story of his appeared in *TQ* #92. ★★★ **Karl Kirchwey**'s latest book of poems, *The Engrafted Word,* will be published by Henry Holt in 1998. He is the author of two other collections, *A Wandering Island* (Princeton University Press, 1990) and *Those I Guard* (Harvest Books, 1993). He has received several honors, including the Norma Faber First Book Award of the Poetry Society of America and the Rome Prize in Literature. He is the director of the Unterberg Poetry Center of the 92nd Street Y, in New York City. ★★★ **Gini Kondziolka** became design director of *TriQuarterly* in 1981 with #52. The cover of this issue is her fiftieth *TQ* cover. Besides being a designer in business with her husband, Bill Takatsuki, for the past sixteen years, she is also a watercolorist. One of her paintings was featured on the cover of *TQ* #88. She is a member of NOMAD*Central*, a nomadic cooperative gallery. ★★★ **Claire Malroux** is the author of five collections of poems published in France by Rougerie. A selection from them, entitled *Edge*, has been translated by Marilyn Hacker (Wake Forest University Press, 1996). The recipient of the Grand Prix National de la Traduction in 1995, Malroux has translated into French poems written by Emily Dickinson, Elizabeth Bishop, Charles Simic, C. K. Williams and Derek Wolcott. Her poems, translated by C. K. Williams, appeared in *TQ* #94. ★★★ **Moira Linehan**'s poems have appeared in *Poetry*, *Kansas Quarterly*, the *Nebraska Review* and other journals. She lives in Winchester, Massachusetts. ★★★ **Michael McFee** is the author of five books of poems, including most recently *Colander* (Carnegie Mellon University Press, 1996). He has also edited the anthology *The Language They Speak Is Things To Eat: Poems by Fifteen Contemporary North Carolina Poets* (University of North Carolina Press, 1994). He teaches poetry writing and English literature at the University of North Carolina at Chapel Hill and is the assistant poetry editor of *DoubleTake*. ★★★ **Sharon Olds** has published five books of poems, including *The Wellspring* (Knopf, 1996). She teaches in the Graduate Creative Writing Program at New York University and helps lead a writing workshop at the Sigismund Goldwater Memorial Hospital, a public facility for the severely physically disabled. Her poems appear in *TQ* #84 and #95. ★★★ **Jacqueline Osherow**'s latest book of poems is *With a Moon in Transit* (Grove Press Poetry Series, 1997). She is the author of two other collections, *Conversations with Survivors* (1994) and *Looking for Angels in New York* (1988), both published by the University of Georgia Press. She has received several honors, including the Lucille Medwick Memorial Award, the John Masefield Memorial Award of the Poetry Society of America, and the Witter Bynner Prize from the American Academy and Institute of Arts and Letters. Her poems have appeared in the *New Yorker*, the *New Republic*, *Partisan Review*, the *Paris Review* and *Best American Poetry 1995*, edited by Richard Howard (Simon & Schuster/Touchstone Books). A poem of hers appeared in *TQ* #95. ★★★ **Alan Michael Parker** is the author of a book of poems, *Days Like Prose* (Alef Books, 1997) and the co-editor of *The Routledge Anthology of Cross-Gendered Verse* (Routledge Books, 1996). He teaches at Pennsylvania State University, Behrend College. An essay of Parker's appeared in *TQ* #95, and his poems appeared in *TQ* #89 and #95. ★★★ **Carl Phillips**'s most recent book of poems is *From the Devotions* (Graywolf, 1997). His other books are *In the Blood* (Northeastern University Press, 1992), which received the Samuel French Morse Poetry Prize; and *Cortège* (Graywolf, 1997), a finalist for the National Book Critics Circle Award. He is an associate professor of English, African, and Afro-American Studies at Washington University, where he also directs the Creative Writing Program. His poems also appeared in *TQ* #95 and #98. ★★★ **Chaim Potok**'s distinguished career began in 1967 with the publication of the novel, *The Chosen* (Simon & Schuster), which received the Edward Lewis Wallant Award and was nominated for the National Book Award. He is the author of six other novels, all published by Knopf, including *The Promise* (1969), which received the Athenaeum Prize; and *The Gift of Asher Lev* (1990), which won the Jewish Book Award for fiction. He has also written a book of nonfiction, *Wanderings: Chaim Potok's History of the Jews* (Knopf, 1978), and two plays, *Out of the Depths* and *Sins of the Father*. His most recent book is *Gates of November: Chronicles of the Slepak Family* (Knopf,1996; Fawcett Books paperback, 1997). An essay of his appeared in *TQ* #84. ★★★ **Adam J. Sorkin**'s translations have appeared in the *New Yorker*, *American Poetry Review, Prism International* and other journals. *The Sky Behind the Forest*, his translation of Liliana Ursu's poems, prepared in collaboration with Ursu and Tess Gallagher (Bloodaxe Books, 1997), was a British Poetry Book Society Recommended Translation. ★★★ **Mark Strand**'s new book of poems, *Blizzard of One*, will be published by Knopf in 1998. He has recently returned to painting, drawing, and collage-making.

TriQuarterly is pleased to announce that William Meredith's *Effort at Speech: New and Selected Poems* (TriQuarterly Books/Northwestern University Press) received the 1997 National Book Award for Poetry. Meredith, born in 1919, is of the generation of Elizabeth Bishop, John Berryman, Theodore Weiss, Robert Lowell and others who changed the face of American poetry after World War II. His first volume, *Love Letter from an Impossible Land*, won the Yale Series of Younger Poets Competition in 1943. His subsequent books have received many honors and awards, including the Pulitzer Prize in 1988. This is the second National Book Award nomination in six years for TriQuarterly Books. In 1991, Linda McCarriston was a finalist for her poetry collection, *Eva-Mary*.

Sharon Solwitz was awarded the 1997 Carl Sandburg Award for Fiction from the Friends of the Chicago Public Library for her collection of short stories, *Blood and Milk* (Sarabande Books). A story from the book appeared in *TQ #92*.

Leon Forrest died at age sixty on November 6, 1997. Forrest was the author of five novels, including *Divine Days* (W. W. Norton), which Henry Louis Gates referred to as "the *War and Peace* of African-American literature." A story by Forrest appeared in *TQ #60*, a special Chicago-related issue; and an excerpt from his forthcoming novel appeared in *TQ #100*. For twenty-four years he was a professor of African-American Studies and English at Northwestern University. He will be greatly missed.

SPRING 1998 BOOKS

1997
NATIONAL
BOOK AWARD
WINNER

WILLIAM MEREDITH

Effort at Speech
New and Selected Poems

A contemporary of Berryman, Bishop
and Lowell, William Meredith is a
poet whose unadorned verse marked him from the beginning of
his career as a singular voice. This is the definitive collection of
Meredith's lifework.

This trove of old and new Meredith is a medic's kit for the tired at
heart. . . . So easily digestible in their precise meter and perfectly
tuned end-rhyme, their power goes virtually unnoticed until the reader
lifts his eyes from the page to find himself moved, affected."
—PUBLISHERS WEEKLY

For the past 45 years [Meredith] has looked generously and hard at
our common human world. . . . William Meredith's work suggests that
we can recognize the hardest truths about ourselves and still live in
the world. —NEW YORK TIMES BOOK REVIEW

256 pages
$39.95, cloth / $17.95, paper

STEVE FAY
what nature

Steve Fay brings a naturalist's attentiveness to poetry. As responsive to nature as Gary Snyder or Mary Oliver, Fay combines a command of the poetic craft with rich, exact descriptions of physical and psychological landscapes, particularly of his native Midwest.

With startling range—from political satire to portraits of loneliness and regret to humor—these poems form a multi-dimensional meditation on the relationship of man to nature, and a unique contribution to the canon of contemporary poetry.

96 pages
$35, cloth / $14.95, paper

PAMELA WHITE HADAS
Self-Evidence: New and Selected Poems

Pamela White Hadas won enthusiastic recognition for her early books of poetry, *Designing Women* and *Beside Herself*. A decade later, *Self-Evidence* gathers together the best of that published work and poems never before collected. Brimming with legendary, mythic, historical and imaginary characters—Lilith, Pocahontas, Simone Weil, the wives of Watergate, a circus performer and others—these poems weave tapestries of women's loves and labors. Perhaps uniquely in our time, Hadas contrasts a spareness of autobiographical detail with an unusual intimacy of tone. Howard Nemerov describes her work as "odd, quirky, humorous and exact."

154 pages
$35, cloth / $14.95, paper

ANGELA JACKSON

And All These Roads Be Luminous: Selected Poems

Drawing from earlier works contained in the chapbooks *VooDoo/Love Magic, The Greenville Club, Solo in the Boxcar Third Floor E* and *The Man With the White Liver*, this selection of Angela Jackson's poetry is filled with an impressive variety of characters engaged in compelling explorations of identity, creativity, spiritual experience, and the rites and rituals of race and sexuality.

Jackson's ear is keen; her memory of traditions is crystal clear.
—**FEMINIST BOOKSTORE NEWS**

The craft and quality of poetry has been enhanced by Angela Jackson.
—**CHICAGO SUN-TIMES**

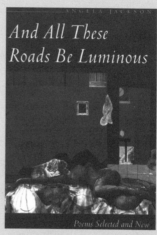

152 pages
$39.95, cloth / $14.95, paper

ALANE ROLLINGS

The Logic of Opposites

In her fourth collection of poetry, Alane Rollings grapples with the power and potency of philosophical and psychological opposites.

Written by a poet who has suffered from bipolar illness, these paired poems represent oppositions of stasis and action, depression and activity, sorrow and joy. They are confessional without being autobiographical in detail; intimate and accessible while maintaining a curious detachment; utterly serious, yet often seductively casual in tone. Rollings explores the nature of contradiction through the darkness and light that shapes both individual life and society as a whole.

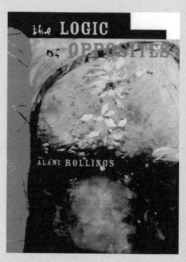

96 pages
$35, cloth / $14.95, paper

CYRUS COLTER
City of Light

Paul Kessey is caught between two worlds. Handsome and well-connected, from a privileged Chicago community of successful blacks, Kessey is uncertain of his place in the African diaspora, partly because of his own light skin. Throughout a sojourn in Paris, he is attracted and repelled by the contradictory possibilities of life in a white society. Intertwining race, class, and politics with the intense struggles of one man's heart, *City of Light* presents a vivid portrait of the personal effects of prejudice and its hypocrisies.

This powerful writer should win the attention of every reader of serious fiction. —SATURDAY REVIEW

432 pages / $17.95, paper

Order Form

Order from your bookseller or from:
Northwestern University Press
Chicago Distribution Center
11030 South Langley Avenue
Chicago, IL 60628
TEL. 773/568-1550
FAX 773/660-2235

Name _____

Address _____

City_____ State _____Zip _____

Author/Title	Cloth/Paper	Quantity	Unit Price	Total

❑ Check or money order enclosed
❑ Mastercard/Visa number:
_____

Expiration Date_____
Signature: _____

Subtotal _____
Shipping and handling* _____
TOTAL _____

*Domestic—$3.50 first book, $.75 each additional book
*Foreign—$4.50 first book, $1.00 each additional book

The 1998
Summer Writing Program
at the University of *Vermont*

FACULTY

David Bradley
Joyce Johnson
David Long
Philip Baruth
Stephen Dunn
Gary Margolis
Jennifer Armstrong

VISITING FACULTY

Galway Kinnell
Bill Roorbach
Ellen Bryant Voigt
Lori Haskins

Workshops and seminars in Poetry, Nonfiction, Fiction and Children's Books

Program Dates: *July 6 - 24*

FOR MORE INFORMATION CALL:

The Summer Writing Program Coordinator at:
800-639-3210 or 802-656-5796

THE UNIVERSITY OF
VERMONT

http://uvmce.uvm.edu:443/sumwrite.htm

TriQuarterly thanks the following past donors and
life subscribers:

David C. Abercrombie
Mr. and Mrs. Walter L. Adams
Amin Alimard
Lois Ames
Richard H. Anderson
Roger K. Anderson
Sandy Anderson
I. N. C. Aniebo
Anonymous
University of Arizona Poetry Center
Gayle Arnzen
Michael Attas
Asa Baber
Hadassah Baskin
Tom G. Bell
Sandra Berris
Simon J. Blattner, Jr.
Mr. and Mrs. Andrew K. Block
Louise Blosten
Carol Bly
Susan DeWitt Bodemer
Kay Bonetti
Robert Boruch
Mr. and Mrs. Richard S. Brennan
Van K. Brock
Gwendolyn Brooks
Timothy Browne
Paul Bundy
Eric O. Cahn
David Cassak
Stephen Chapman
Anthony Chase
Michael Chwe
Willard Cook
Mr. and Mrs. William Cottle
Robert A. Creamer
Andrew Cyr
Doreen Davie
Kenneth Day
Mark W. DeBree
Elizabeth Des Pres
Anstiss Drake
J. A. Dufresne
Mr. and Mrs. Donald Egan
John B. Elliott
Christopher English
Carol Erickson
Steven Finch
David R. Fine
Mr. and Mrs. H. Bernard Firestone

Melvin P. Firestone, M.D.
Mr. and Mrs. Solway Firestone
Paul Fjelstad
Torrence Fossland
C. Dwight Foster
Jeffrey Franklin
Peter S. Fritz
Mrs. Angela M. Gannon
Kathy M. Garness
Robert Gislason
Mr. and Mrs. Stanford J. Goldblatt
Lawrence J. Gorman
Maxine Groffsky
Jack Hagstrom
Mrs. Donald Haider
Mrs. Heidi Hall-Jones
Mrs. James E. Hayes
Joanna Hearne
Ross B. Heath
Charles Hedde
Gene Helton
Donald Hey
Donald A. Hillel
Mr. and Mrs. David C. Hilliard
Mr. and Mrs. Thomas D. Hodgkins
Craig V. Hodson
Irwin L. Hoffman
Irwin T. Holtzman
P. Hosier
Mary Gray Hughes
Charles Huss
Curtis Imrie
Helen Jacob
Del Ivan Janik
Fran Katz
Gary Michael Katz
Dr. Alfred D. Klinger
Loy E. Knapp
Sydney Knowlton
Mr. and Mrs. Martin Koldyke
Mr. and Mrs. Carl A. Kroch
Greg Kunz
Judy Kunz
Conrad A. Langenberg
John Larroquette
Isaac Lassiter
Dorothy Latiak
Elizabeth Leibik
Patrick A. Lezark
Patricia W. Linton